The Bridemaker

The Bridemaker

REXANNE BECNEL

St. Martin's

For Dion, Jim, and Betsey,
Guardian angels in the truest sense.

CHAPTER 1

This was the part Hester liked best, the part that made all the other less pleasant aspects of her job worthwhile. She fastened the Ainsley family emeralds around Dulcie's neck, then tugged at the tissue-light silk that draped with such deceptive grace across the girl's shoulders and neckline.

"There." She smiled down at her student who, despite her past two months of hard work, looked panic-stricken at the thought of attending tonight's ball. "Are you ready to view yourself now?"

Dulcie heaved a great, woeful sigh, then stared down at her new apple-green gown. "It's a very pretty dress," she admitted. "That Madame Henri you suggested is indeed a most talented dressmaker. But . . ." Her voice wobbled a bit. "But," she continued in little more than a whisper, "I hate balls. I hated them last year, and I shall hate them even more this year."

"Now, now. What have we discussed in the past about the importance of attitude?" Hester gave her young charge an encouraging smile. Dulcie Bennett was too plain, too plump, and too shy to make much of a splash in this, her second season. The first season had apparently been dreadful: social gaffes, humiliating disappointments, storms of tears, and a vow by the girl never to attend a party again. Ever.

From what Hester could tell, that had been the first act of self-will the girl had ever evinced. And more than overdue, Hester had decided when she'd heard about it. Fortunately Dulcie's mother, Lady Ainsley, had done as one of her old aunts had advised: she'd engaged Mrs. Hester Poitevant of the Mayfair Academy to properly prepare Dulcie for her next round on the marriage mart.

Hester knew what they said of her, and she took great satisfaction in it. Gossip had it that every girl Mrs. Poitevant coached inevitably became a bride. And more importantly to the harried mamas, the matches were accomplished with a minimum of bother to them.

Some called her the Bridemaker. Others referred to her as a miracle worker, given the raw material she often had to work with. Word was that Mrs. Poitevant could make a stout young lady appear slender, turn a wallflower witty, groom a plain girl into handsomeness, and make a graceless creature endearing. In short, her girls learned how to charm men. The *right* men.

So long as your daughter had a reasonable dowry attached to her hand, the wags said, Hester Poitevant could get her married with a minimum of fuss and investment. Considering the expense of a second, third, or even fourth season, the fees charged by the Mayfair Academy were actually a great bargain. Hester often made that point when the subject of her fees came up, and it always silenced the protesting papas.

But Hester was not thinking of fees right now. She was thinking, rather, of Dulcie who, despite her outward limitations, was as sweet and loving as a young person could be. Truly amazing, considering that thoughtlessly blustering brother of hers, and her shallow, self-important mother.

Under Hester's steady stare Dulcie bashfully lowered her eyes. "I know. I know. I mustn't allow myself to speak so negatively about myself."

"Nor *think* negatively," Hester added. "You have focused so long on your perceived shortcomings, Dulcie, that you quite overlook your lovelier aspects. And in the process you convince others to overlook them as well. Now, turn around. Take a good, long look in that mirror and tell me what you think."

Slowly—reluctantly—the girl complied. Hester caught her breath in anticipation.

As usual Madame Henri had worked wonders with the pattern adjustments Hester had requested. Into the most current pattern of pinch-waisted dresses, Hester had instructed her to add a wider and lower corsage with drapery folds which did not descend completely to the waist. The bodice beneath it and also the skirt were fashioned with several gores piped at the seams with a slightly darker shade of apple-green silk.

As she'd expected, it created an amazingly slimming illusion. Higher heels than normal added to that illusion.

Dulcie's eyes grew huge as she caught sight of herself in the tailor's mirror. Her mouth formed a small, shocked O, and for a long moment she could not speak. Finally she said in a reverential whisper, "It's . . . it's lovely."

Hester's eyes danced with glee. "No. It's *you* who are lovely." Indeed, the dress was even more becoming than Hester had imagined when she'd selected the fabric and patterns. Cream and soft apple green complemented the girl's coloring far better than white and mint. Dulcie's hazel eyes glowed as green as the gown, and her delicate coloring fairly bloomed.

"With your hair styled this way—and that little touch

of makeup we applied—" Hester added that last in a whisper. "You have become beautiful. Absolutely beautiful."

"Oh." That was all the stunned girl could say as she turned back and forth before the tall mirror. "Oh."

To Hester's satisfaction, a smile began to curve Dulcie's lips. First hesitant, then happy, and finally ecstatic. At the same time the girl's posture straightened, and she relaxed her shoulders as Hester so often reminded her to do.

Dulcie had a beautiful complexion, not a spot or a freckle in sight. She had a lovely bosom and delicate, expressive hands. Plus a beautifully shaped mouth. A longish nose, shortish chin, and a too high brow prevented her being considered pretty. But Hester had had girls with far greater flaws. In truth, she'd rather work with a sweet, plain girl than with a pretty petulant one.

Hester folded her hands neatly at her waist. "I take it you like the dress?"

When their eyes met in the reflection of the mirror, Hester saw the glitter of tears in her young student's eyes. Dulcie nodded, for she seemed unable to speak. But that was all right with Hester. Though she endeavored never to reveal any sign of favoritism, Dulcie was without a doubt the favorite of her students this year. To see her so happy gave Hester a thrill of her own.

But enough of all this sentiment. It was time for the ball.

"All right then." Hester pushed up the spectacles that were always sliding down her nose. "Here's your reticule. And your fan. Now, let's go show you off to your mother and brother, shall we?"

George Bennett, Viscount Ainsley, clearly was struck speechless by his sister's appearance. He'd been impatient to depart for tonight's entertainments so that he could sample Lord Soames's renowned selection of cigars and brandies. When Hester and Dulcie reached the head of the stairs he was pacing the foyer, slapping his gloves against his thigh and complaining to his mother about tardy females and their endless vanities.

But when he spied Dulcie, his expression mirrored that of his dumbstruck parent: eyes wide and staring; mouth hanging open in stunned appreciation.

As well they ought to be, Hester thought with no small amount of pride. In addition to the handsome gown, Dulcie's hair had been arranged to disguise her high brow. Plus Hester had added a few touches of shadowing—dark to shorten her nose, and light to bring her chin forward. And of course the striking green gown and slippers made her look taller and slimmer.

But more than the illusions applied to her person, it was Dulcie's bearing that most altered her appearance. The girl's family might not recognize that fact, but Hester did. The changes to her clothing were all well and good. But it was the confidence they lent the girl, the belief in herself, that made the greatest difference.

Dulcie Bennett had never thought herself beautiful, nor even passably pretty. But tonight she believed it, and so tonight she *was* beautiful. There was a proud tilt to her head, an excited light in her eyes, and a pleased curve to her lips.

As was her custom with her clients, Hester was attending tonight's event to lend the girl support. But even if she hadn't been planning to be there, Hester knew Dulcie would succeed as she never before had.

Hester paused three steps up and let Dulcie proceed without her. Her family hurried forward, twin smiles on their faces.

"My dear, you look wonderful," her mother gushed.

"Indeed," young Lord Ainsley admitted, recovering his more normal arrogant tones. "You actually look pre-

sentable, Dulls. P'rhaps now I can convince Westham to
dance with you."

Hester shot him a quelling look. It had only taken two
weeks for her to learn to hate George Bennett. He might
be handsome and considered by some to be quite a
match, but she thought him a selfish boor.

"The dress is lovely," Lady Ainsley said, circling her
daughter with an examining eye. "I would not have
picked that color, nor such a plain style. But it suits her.
Yes. It suits her."

The woman turned toward Hester, and for a moment
their gazes held. Then Mrs. Bennett nodded, a concession to Hester's greater skill and knowledge. "Perhaps
you and I should take tea tomorrow," she said to Hester.
"Just you and I. Why don't you come at four."

Not a request of course, but a demand. Hester gave
the woman an aloof smile. "I'm afraid not, Lady Ainsley I've a previous engagement in Portman Square." No
need to reveal who her other clients were, only that their
address was very good. "Perhaps Friday. Around ten?"

Viscountess Ainsley hated being dictated to, especially by a woman she employed, a woman she looked
upon as little better than a tradeswoman. But she agreed
to Friday, and Hester knew why. This wasn't the first
time a society matron was so amazed at Hester's im-
provement of her daughter that she sought Hester's serv-
ices for herself.

Perhaps it was time to elevate her fees, Hester thought
as she donned her cloak and gloves. People like Lady
Ainsley could certainly afford it.

They took two coaches. One would not accommodate
three women's full skirts as well as Lord Ainsley. Hester
was only too glad to ride independent of the puffed-up
viscount. He and his widowed mother were two of a
kind. Self-involved and greedy, with only one view of

sweet Dulcie and her three younger sisters: pawns to be bartered with; potential brides to men who could fatten the Ainsleys' pockets and increase their standing in society.

An earl or his heir for Dulcie. That's what the mother had specified. The brother wanted money and connections.

Neither of them cared in the least what Dulcie might want.

Across from her Dulcie sat, running her small hands along the elegantly piped skirt, fingering her fan, and all the while smiling.

"I see you no longer dread this evening," Hester remarked.

Dulcie averted her eyes, but her smile only deepened. "I suppose not. Though I remain just as nervous."

"You shall do wonderfully well."

"Yes, but . . ." Her hands knotted together around the fan.

"But what?"

After a long pause, when all they heard was the metal-clad wheels rattling against the pavement and the busy city sounds as they passed along High Street, Oxford Street, and Regent Street, Dulcie cleared her throat. "There is this particular gentleman, you see."

Aha. Hester idly fiddled with the cuff of her own plain gloves. The first phase of her work with Dulcie, preparing her for the season, was done. The second phase, making her into someone's bride, had begun. "A particular gentleman?"

"Oh, yes." The words were said with such breathless reverence Hester had to suppress a smile. "He is a paragon among men," the girl rhapsodized.

Even by the light of the carriage lantern Hester could see the pink glow that flared in Dulcie's cheeks, making the girl almost pretty. Hester had yet to see Dulcie so infatuated. She hoped the man was someone suitable.

"So. Who is this paragon of manliness?"

Again came a great, heartfelt sigh. Really, it was like something out of a lurid novel, Hester thought, amused. But her amusement swiftly faded. Hadn't she sighed just that way when she was Dulcie's age?

"His name is Adrian Hawke."

Hester nodded. She'd heard that name several times now. Every year society seemed to fix upon a new darling. Mr. Hawke seemed well on his way to capturing this season's title. "Adrian Hawke," she repeated. "Have you been introduced?"

"Well, no. Not yet. But . . . But I'm hoping we will be. Perhaps tonight," she added in a lower voice, as if speaking of some exalted personage and not simply another attractive, unmarried young gentleman.

"Tell me about him," Hester said. She considered it an important part of her work to keep up to date on the most eligible men in society.

Dulcie's round face turned serious. "Well. He's very handsome. Very. And I've heard that he's terribly rich."

Hester pursed her lips. He would not have become society's latest darling if he were not.

"There's only one thing," Dulcie added more hesitantly.

"Yes?"

"He's from America." She gave a dejected sigh. "You know how Mother feels about Americans."

Indeed Hester did. The phrases "radical upstarts," "crude provincials," and "untitled *nouveaux riches*" came to mind. Dulcie's mother was nothing if not a snob.

"But he's not really an American," Dulcie went on. "He was born in Scotland, you see. Southern Scotland. He's certainly not one of those wild men from the north. But he's lived in America for years and years. They say he has only come over for his cousin Catherine's wedding."

"If you haven't even met the man, how do you know all this?" But Hester knew how. Gossip during the season had legs of its own, galloping through the *ton* like a town crier might. Anything new or curious or, best of all, scandalous, was pounced upon, dissected, digested, and inevitably passed on considerably modified from the original truth.

She of all people knew that.

So a rich, handsome American was fair game for the gossipmongers. Hester wondered if the man had any idea what he was in for.

"I don't know. I've just heard about him. That's all. But I've also seen him. He was riding down High Street last week with his uncle, the baron," Dulcie explained. "The family resemblance was much in evidence, though of course he is much younger. And handsomer."

Lord Hawke of Scotland. Of course. His uncle was Baron Neville Hawke, the war hero who was also much respected for the stable he kept and the quality of horses it produced. His daughter's betrothal and upcoming marriage to Lord Findlan's son was considered quite the event of the next several weeks.

Still, an untitled cousin to a baron would never be acceptable to Dulcie's family—especially her mother. Hester supposed it would be her unhappy duty to discourage any ill-advised infatuation.

The girl went on. "He is extraordinarily handsome, Mrs. Poitevant. I'm certain even you would be affected by his manly bearing."

I doubt that. But Hester kept that ungenerous opinion to herself. She'd learned many years ago that handsome men, or terribly rich ones, or those otherwise gifted with power or influence, were the ones most prone to misuse their gifts. Power had the tendency to corrupt, especially the male of the species whom she did not generally hold in very high esteem. That's why she'd never married, nor accepted any of the insulting offers and disgusting propositions made to her. That's why she'd left London in the middle of her second season.

She'd only come back to London several years later when her mother had suddenly died. It was her friend Mrs. DeLisle who'd convinced her to come to work at the Mayfair Academy. But Hester had only agreed after hitting upon the idea of disguising herself as a recent widow.

Respectability and independence, that's all she wanted, and she worked hard to maintain it. Through the academy she took special pleasure in helping other young girls recognize and develop a power of their own.

It troubled her that her young students' powers must be obtained through the judicious use of their personal charms, for she knew beauty was a double-edged sword, as capable of destroying a woman as saving her. Wasn't she proof of that?

But for girls who were protected by their families' names and social standing—girls like Dulcie and the rest of Hester's wealthy clients—beauty was an invaluable tool. With beauty and charm on her side a woman could negotiate a far more advantageous marriage contract. And an advantageous contract was the only way a woman could gain access to her own money and the attendant power it provided. Women without that benefit too often lived at the whim of the men in their lives, whether father, brother, or husband.

Hester never took for granted that she'd been lucky enough to create her own independence without the necessity of deferring to any man.

"Well," she said as they drew up before the extravagantly lit house on Berkeley Square. "I look forward to meeting this paragon of an American fellow. Meanwhile, we are arrived. Here, pinch your cheeks. And remember to employ your fan gently."

The evening progressed relatively well. Though Hester made it a rule never to dance at these sort of affairs, she nonetheless remained very busy. Another of the girls from her academy was here tonight, Anabelle Finch. So she was doubly vigilant to shepherd them through this, the first of their many social outings of the season. An awkward beginning could spell doom for any of her overly sensitive students. She was determined that that not happen.

But thus far both Dulcie and Anabelle seemed to be managing handsomely. To her satisfaction they both had nearly filled their dance cards. Each of them had invitations to dine with perfectly acceptable gentlemen, though Dulcie's dinner partner was second in line for an earldom, not first. But as Lady Ainsley had so crassly pointed out, since his elder brother was the pale and sickly sort, the young brother might yet inherit.

Hester stood now among a cluster of matrons. Though not truly of their ilk, she was widely accepted among them. After all, they needed her.

She pushed her slippery spectacles up her nose, then frowned down at her dull gray gown. Yes, they accepted her because she was useful, because she did not outshine them in any way.

It hadn't been like that ten years ago. Then she'd been the focus of so many men's attentions that she'd inadvertently alienated most of the other girls and their mothers. They needn't have feared, however. For the men of the *ton* weren't interested in marrying a girl like Hester, no matter how beautiful she was. With no family connections, no dowry, and a mother of suspect morals, Hester had been the recipient of only one sort of proposal: the lewd sort. Which was why she'd fled London.

She glanced around, noting several matrons who'd

known her back then. Yes, they remembered her. But her "status" as a widow, still grieving her long-dead husband, gave her a sort of respectability she'd never had before. Now that she wore spectacles and a hideous wardrobe to disguise her appearance, their envy had turned to pity. So far as they knew she was a poor widow and no longer a threat to them.

There were times when she chortled over the deception she had so successfully played on them all, another ploy she'd learned from her mother. But there were other times when her dowdy clothes and her carefully woven web of lies chafed.

Tonight they chafed.

It was because the season had just begun, she told herself as she pretended to follow someone's story of the "most marvelous" new shoemaker who'd set up shop on High Street. Absolutely marvelous!

She had three long months of just this sort of conversation to look forward to. Three endless months of propping her girls through every sort of social situation, of directing them toward the sort of men their families would approve, and of dressing herself like a dried-up old woman.

She joined in when the three matrons laughed, though she hadn't heard whatever *bon mot* fueled their amusement. Perhaps she'd better excuse herself before they noticed her inattention.

But as she meandered toward the refreshment area, her thoughts remained gloomy. The fact was, she practically *was* a dried-up old woman. Well, maybe not yet old. But dried up? Yes.

She was twenty-eight, pretending to be older and a widow. And all for the sake of her blasted independence. Though she was proud of all she'd accomplished, it had come with one unanticipated cost: loneliness.

She took a cup of punch, determined to throw off that

last self-pitying thought. Better to be lonely some of the time, than miserable all of the time, under the thumb of some selfish society sot.

A stir near the entrance of the ballroom drew her attention, and she looked up with interest, grateful for the distraction.

Part of her success with her students was due to her attention to the details of society: who was eligible, what their needs were, and how to place her well-prepared girls in the paths of the right men. A new face on the scene made her doubly diligent.

So Hester's every sense went on the alert when she spied a tall, dark-haired man she'd never before seen.

In truth, she did not simply spy him, which implied a casual glance turned a trifle curious. Instead the glance turned into a wide-eyed stare. Forgetting every tenet of her well-honed sense of good manners, she stood there and gaped at the man.

Who *was* he?

Though he was dressed much the same as every other man in the room, he still managed to stand out. She forced herself to assess why.

His hair was very dark, black even. But then, other men had black hair, thick and wavy.

He carried himself well, straight and confident. Confidence was always an attractive trait for both men and women. It was why she emphasized posture and movement so much at her academy.

His shoulders were wide enough to suggest a blatant sort of masculinity. And his face . . . She tilted her head down to peer over the slightly wavy glass of her spectacles. His face was striking. Lean with straight black brows, a bold nose, deep-set eyes, and a wide mouth.

Then he smiled down at their hostess, Lady Soames, displaying a flash of straight white teeth. A wide mouth with a seductive slant to it.

An unsettling little spiral of heat began to curl down low in Hester's stomach. She couldn't look away. A seductive slant and the most sensuous-looking lips she'd ever seen on a man.

The spiral became an alarming buzz.

Oh, no. Not one of that sort. That was the last thing she needed this season. A new man to start all her girls' hearts fluttering. Who *was* he?

Then suddenly, without being told, she knew. This must be Adrian Hawke, the so-called paragon Dulcie had been mooning over.

Hester watched him press a kiss to some frivolously garbed woman's hand, conscious the entire time of her own increased heartbeat.

This would never do. She of all people knew the inherent danger of men with that sort of virile magnetism. No matter how visceral her response to him, she would not succumb to so base a reaction. Under no circumstances would she allow herself to become affected by him.

But what of Dulcie? And perhaps Anabelle and Charlotte as well. What if they got it into their heads to desire a man like that? Dulcie already seemed half in love with him.

She set her punch cup aside, then knotted her hands together at her waist. It didn't matter who her girls might wish to wed. In the end their parents would make the final decision.

Usually Hester resented that fact; it seemed so unfair. But she accepted it because she had no other choice. When it came to men like this Adrian Hawke, however—for that's surely who he must be—well, she was glad her girls must defer to their parents' wishes.

Men like this Adrian Hawke, and a hundred more of his ilk, made terrible, terrible husbands.

With an effort she tore her gaze from Mr. Hawke's

elegantly rugged profile. She'd hoped that the most difficult part of her work was done with, now that all three
of her students were officially launched. But she could
see that she was wrong.

Her only solace was the knowledge that men who
looked like Adrian Hawke tended not to waste time on
the sort of girls who needed help from the Mayfair Academy.

CHAPTER 2

Within minutes Dulcie had a death grip on Hester's arm.

"That's him! That's him, Adrian Hawke. The one I told you about." She gave one of the huge sighs Hester was beginning to associate with Dulcie and the magnetic Mr. Hawke. "Oh, my. He looks even handsomer in his formal evening coat, doesn't he?"

It was a rhetorical question, of course. Hester had never seen him before and so had no other image to compare him to. But she perversely could imagine him in more casual garb—and imagine him looking even more masculine. Even more appealing.

Goodness sake! She gave herself a mental pinch. She'd only just laid eyes on the man. She was not going to think about him in that way. Bad enough that Dulcie already did.

"Yes, Dulcie. He is quite the handsome fellow."

"Can you . . . Can you introduce us?"

Hester retrieved her wrist from Dulcie's convulsive hold. "I cannot introduce you to someone I have not previously met myself. You know that."

"Oh. Yes." Another sigh. Then the girl brightened. "Catherine can introduce us, can't she?"

"It would seem so. She is, after all, his cousin."

In a flash Dulcie was off, homing in on Catherine Hawke like a fledgling kestrel after its very first hare. Awkward but enthusiastic.

Hester watched her go. The girl was not likely to succeed in her ultimate goal: to capture the attention of the striking Mr. Hawke.

But that was all right. The Dulcie who had come to Mayfair Academy two months ago would never have had the confidence to finagle an introduction to any man, let alone a man like this Mr. Hawke. Hester decided to count it another measure of her success with the girl that she could be so determined at this, her first test of the season.

She just hoped Dulcie did not humiliate herself in the process.

Hester observed covertly as Dulcie approached Catherine Hawke. The young woman graciously drew Dulcie into her circle of chattering friends. Meanwhile Mr. Hawke made his way toward his cousin, stopping to greet several men along the way.

Hester had heard he was quite the businessman, another strike against him with Dulcie's family. A businessman of no family title was considered a tradesman, no matter his success or wealth. It would not matter how many society men flocked to him for investment advice, nor how many of them made money as a result. Hester knew he could never truly be one of them. He would be tolerated for his usefulness, just as she was.

The difference was that she knew precisely how she fit into this society. But did he?

Undeniably curious about the man, Hester drifted nearer the point of eventual intersection of him and his cousin's merry group. It was for Dulcie's sake, she told herself. So she could assess her student's performance and help her overcome any shortcomings in her behavior. Nothing more.

But before Hester could get close enough to overhear anything, a hand caught her at the elbow.

"I say, Mrs. Poitevant," Dulcie's mother hissed in a half-whisper. "Who is that fellow? The tall one?"

Hester swallowed her instinctive dislike of Lady Ainsley. "A Mr. Adrian Hawke, I believe. Of the Scottish Hawkes—"

"Oh, yes." Lady Ainsley nodded, her feathered headpiece bobbing above her brow. How many roosters had given their lives for that feathered monstrosity? "I've heard talk of him. Humph. I can't believe Lady Soames invites men like that to her parties."

"Men like *that*?" Hester could not resist saying, though she understood precisely what the woman implied. An American tradesman had no place in Lady Ainsley's world.

"I was told," the woman answered in a voice lower still, "that he is merely a by-blow offspring of some minor Scottish baron. You know, that Lord Hawke's deceased brother."

A by-blow. It was such an archaic and insulting term, though no more than Hester should expect from the toplofty Lady Ainsley. But how unpleasant for Mr. Hawke, she thought, to have his unfortunate heritage discussed so. If anything, Lady Ainsley's disdain of the man's circumstances elevated him in Hester's esteem, though only a very little.

She was relieved when Lady Ainsley departed for the company of several of her equally unpleasant cronies. But that relief was short-lived, for within minutes, her son, the viscount, took her place.

Hester had to force herself not to step back from Lord

Ainsley, her distaste for the man was that immediate. George Bennett was a big man, tall and overbearing. In just a few brief meetings Hester had categorized him as a man of unhealthy appetites, whether in drink, food, or choice of companions. He'd not come into society until after her season, but she knew the type: born to privilege with never a thought for anyone but himself. An unpleasant young man, now grown to be positively detestable.

But he was her employer, at least until Dulcie was betrothed. So Hester gave him her reserved "proprietress of Mayfair Academy" smile, and waited for him to speak.

"Well, well. I'm gratified to see I did not waste my money when I hired you to help my sister."

"Thank you." *I'm so pleased not to be a waste of your precious money.*

"Yes. Indeed." He held on to his lapels and rocked back on his heels. "Dulls actually looks presentable. P'rhaps this year she'll land herself a husband."

He glanced at Hester, a quick, sliding glance that started and ended at her bosom. "I've got three more sisters, y'know."

Hester pushed her spectacles up her nose and pursed her lips into the primmest, most prudish expression she could manage. Most men were lascivious pigs. But George Bennett was worse than most if he was ogling an employee, especially one as deliberately unattractive as she worked at being.

"I certainly hope that Dulcie has a productive season, Lord Ainsley. And of course, I would be pleased to assist your younger sisters should they require my aid."

Hoping he would go away, she focused across the dance floor, watching Dulcie watch Adrian Hawke. *Subtlety, Dulcie. Subtlety and grace.*

Lord Ainsley rattled on about something or other, and

she nodded and gave him her polite-but-disinterested smile. All the while, however, she spied on the little tableau unfolding not thirty feet away.

Catherine drew her cousin into the group of young people, hooking her arm in his. She introduced him around, and though the din of music, laughter, and multiple conversations prevented Hester from hearing what was said, what she saw looked perfectly acceptable. He bowed over each woman's hand, Dulcie's included. For her part, Dulcie curtsied and smiled, her face positively beaming.

They were chatting. Everything appeared nicely done, and Hester felt a glow of satisfaction. Dulcie was doing very well. As for the focus of her infatuation . . .

Hester shifted her gaze to Adrian Hawke. For an outsider he handled himself more than equitably. It helped, of course, to be handsome, successful, and rich. But that would only take him so far in London's inbred society.

"Bloody hell!"

Hester stiffened at George Bennett's sudden obscenity. She shot him a reproving look. "I beg your pardon, Lord Ainsley—"

"D'you know who that is?" A scowl drew his heavy brow down as he stared at the man conversing with his sister.

"Why, yes. I believe he is—"

"It's Hawke. It's that skinny bastard from Eton!"

"Really, Lord Ainsley. I must protest your use of such profanity in front of a lady."

He glanced at her but didn't apologize. If anything his expression grew uglier still. "That wasn't a curse. It was a fact. He *is* a bastard. Born one."

"I'm certain he did not plan it that way," Hester snapped.

He gave a snort of laughter. Then he clamped a hand on her elbow and started them both toward his sister's little group. "Come along, Mrs. Poitevant. This should be entertaining."

A knot of dread formed in Hester's stomach. Bad enough to be thrust into George Bennett's unwelcome company. Now the man planned some entertainment—some unpleasant entertainment, she feared—that included Mr. Hawke.

How had she gotten caught up in this mess?

For some urgent reason that she didn't understand, Hester did not want to meet Adrian Hawke. Not now. Not here. Not with Lord Ainsley holding on to her arm, and her looking like a dried-up old widow.

Lord Ainsley kept a tight grasp on her, however, and steered them right into his sister's group. She braced herself, reminding herself it didn't matter how she looked. She was glad she looked like a dried-up old widow tonight. That's what she *wanted* to look like. That's why she wore dark clothes and strict coiffures, and these eternally annoying spectacles.

Dulcie shot Hester an excited smile when she and Lord Ainsley joined their circle. Truth to tell, the girl actually glowed. Then she turned her shining face back to Mr. Hawke and the glow, impossibly enough, seemed to increase.

It was like watching a lamplighter at his task, seeing that tiny yellow glow become a golden halo. And all on account of one man.

"Well, well. If it isn't my old school chum," Lord Ainsley boomed, interrupting the ongoing conversation with his false heartiness. "Hawke. Am I right? Hawke from up north, eh?"

Hester saw when Mr. Hawke recognized George Bennett. His face was already carefully composed: the right smile; the correct manners; the perfect words. He knew how to behave in society and had obviously prepared for his visit to London.

But as he stared at Lord Ainsley, something changed in his expression. Or perhaps it was only in his eyes. One light faded away; another kindled and began to burn. A harder light. A more dangerous one.

The men might have been schoolmates, but it was obvious they had not been chums.

"I don't believe we've been introduced," Mr. Hawke said to Lord Ainsley. "You are?"

Beneath her trapped hand Hester felt Lord Ainsley stiffen. Round one to Mr. Hawke, she decided, suppressing a smile. He'd delivered the first slight by pretending to forget the self-important George Bennett. She wasn't sure, however, that she wanted to stay to witness Lord Ainsley's response.

That's when Dulcie stepped unwittingly into the fray. "Oh, Mr. Hawke. This is my brother, George Bennett, Viscount Ainsley. George, may I present Mr. Adrian Hawke."

The unsuspecting girl accomplished the introduction with such hopefulness in her manner that Hester winced. Dulcie was not astute enough to sense the animosity between the men, but Hester was. It rolled off them, like steam off horse droppings on a frigid winter day.

Not until George released Hester's arm and extended his hand did Mr. Hawke respond. "George Bennett. Of course." His eyes were like flint. "How could I have forgotten?"

Exactly like steam off horse droppings, Hester thought. Foul and to be avoided at all costs.

But Lord Ainsley was not to be outdone. "Did I hear some tale about you? That you'd gone off to America to make your fortune, or some such nonsense," he finished with a derisive chuckle.

"Yes." Then the man's gaze moved from Lord Ainsley to Hester, with no particular casing of that hard, burning light. For a moment there was an awkward pause, and then Catherine Hawke filled it.

"Mrs. Poitevant, may I present my cousin, Adrian Hawke."

They exchanged pleasantries; afterward Hester couldn't say exactly what. She was more conscious of his burning gaze on her, disapproving, it seemed. But was it due to her dull appearance or to the company he must assume she kept? Namely Lord Ainsley.

"So, what brings you back to England, Hawke? Homesick, are you?"

Mr. Hawke's gaze returned to Lord Ainsley. "My cousin's upcoming nuptials is the impetus. However, there are other matters I am involved with."

"Indeed. Indeed." Lord Ainsley rocked back on his heels as he had before, a pompous, annoying habit, Hester decided. "And how's that mother of yours?"

Hester stiffened at the insult implicit in George's inquiry. If Mr. Hawke was natural born, that meant his mother was . . . Well, she was *not* a lady.

A hasty glance told her that Dulcie and the other two girls didn't understand what Lord Ainsley was up to. Obviously they hadn't heard the particulars of Mr. Hawke's birth. But Catherine's face had gone pale. She understood full well the insult implied. After all, she was Mr. Hawke's cousin.

To his credit, Adrian Hawke did not respond with anything other than cold civility. He stared at George Bennett, then shifted his stance just enough to dismiss the man. The sort of set-down any snobbish lord would be proud to deliver. Only this time it was the snob who was on the receiving end. A part of Hester wanted to cheer.

Unfortunately, Mr. Hawke's shift in stance brought Dulcie directly into his line of vision. When he smiled down at the girl, hot color flooded her cheeks, until she looked as if she might melt from the heat. "I hope, Miss Bennett, that you have a dance free for me on your dance card."

This was not good, Hester worried as their small circle moved aside to accommodate a group of dancers for the next cotillion. Dulcie went off with her next dance partner, as did Catherine. With a curt nod Adrian Hawke departed to join his aunt and uncle. That left Hester standing with Lord Ainsley. A very angry Lord Ainsley.

With only a murmured excuse, Hester escaped into the milling crowd. Not that Lord Ainsley would notice. He was too enraged, too busy glaring at Adrian Hawke's broad, unconcerned back.

No, this was not good at all, Hester fretted from her spot in the shadows of an archway. If she was correct in her assessment of the situation—and she was certain she was—Mr. Hawke and Lord Ainsley had just resumed an adversarial relationship they'd developed as boys in school.

On the surface she did not care. They could spar verbally; they could come to fisticuffs; they could engage in a duel, for all it mattered to her. The two of them were none of her concern.

But Dulcie was. Hester had no doubt at all that Mr. Hawke had only asked Dulcie to dance as a way to tweak her brother's nose. And it had worked.

Hester did not even mind that part so much. The problem was Dulcie's infatuation with Mr. Hawke. Hester could not, in good conscience, allow the two men to use Dulcie as a pawn in their stupid battle.

But how was she to prevent it?

Adrian ignored George Bennett, at least outwardly. But inside he seethed. George Bennett was the nastiest of a trio of bullies at Eton who had made Adrian's time there a living hell. And now he was a viscount, and therefore a member of the House of Lords. Was it any wonder Adrian preferred America to England? You couldn't vote a man like George Bennett out of Parliament. With that title to protect him, you couldn't undermine him in any way at all.

Except, of course, by toying with his sister.

Adrian scanned the enthusiastic line of dancers and found the girl there. What was her name? Dulcie. Miss Dulcie Bennett.

Asking her to dance had been an impulse. Not a particularly kind one, he acknowledged. But it had accomplished his purpose. George Bennett had nearly choked when his sister said yes so quickly.

Normally Adrian avoided girls such as Miss Bennett like the plague. He dismissed them as marriage-minded misses with no thoughts in their heads beyond dresses and jewels and dancing. And they all giggled, that annoying, virginal, high-pitched giggle.

Well, he had no interest in marriage, but he would endure Miss Bennett's giggling if only to aggravate her brother. Let the man worry what a barbarian bastard like Adrian was doing with his sister.

The barbarian bastard. The bonnie by-blow. The poor plaid lad. All the old insults came back to Adrian with a vengeance, and he clenched his teeth in fury. He'd hated Bennett back then; if it was possible, he hated him even more now.

But he was no fourteen-year-old lad to be intimidated like he once was. He was a man now, fully capable of making George Bennett's life miserable if he wanted to.

Maybe Bennett would go so far as to challenge him to a duel if he incited him sufficiently. Wouldn't that be satisfying, to put a bullet clean through the man's nonexistent heart? "For you, Mother," he muttered, lifting a glass of scotch to his lips and tossing it back.

"Adrian?"

With a start he looked up to see his cousin Catherine beside him, a concerned expression clouding her pretty face. Banishing his violent musings, he smiled. "I hope you haven't come to complain that you've no partner for the next dance, for I'm already committed."

"Yes, I know. Dulcie Bennett." The furrows between her brows deepened. "I hope you know that her brother is—"

"Don't mention him," Adrian broke in. "I know who he is and also what sort of man he is."

"I'm not trying to defend him."

"I didn't think you were." Adrian shook his head, even more furious with Ainsley for worrying Catherine. "I can handle George Bennett. You needn't worry on that score."

"Of course. It's just that, well, he has a somewhat unpleasant reputation."

"Does he?"

Catherine lowered her voice. "Papa said he keeps a terrible stable. Grandmama once told me he has a vile temper should he lose at cards. *And* he didn't mourn his first wife but three months. Three months!"

Given the man's viciousness as a boy, Adrian suspected Viscount Ainsley of far worse crimes than that. But that was a subject he did not need to discuss with his fair cousin. "So, does the woman who was on his arm know of his unpleasant disposition?"

"Who, Mrs. Poitevant? I don't know."

"Frankly, she doesn't look like his type—unless, of course, she's well connected or filthy rich. Or both."

Catherine laughed. "Oh, no, Adrian. You have the wrong idea entirely. Mrs. Poitevant is not Lord Ainsley's lady friend. I mean, she is a widow, so she *could* pursue an acquaintance with him. If you know what I mean," she added with a knowing glint in her eyes.

"Catherine Hawke. What do you know about things like that?"

"Oh, nothing," she answered, laughing again. "But as for Mrs. Poitevant, I understand that she is employed this year to oversee Dulcie's season."

"What do you mean?"

"I mean Mrs. Poitevant has a business, the Mayfair Academy. She helps those families whose daughters are, shall we say, ill at ease on the marriage mart." At his look of confusion she added, "She helps them find suitable husbands."

"What do you mean? Like a marriage broker?" Adrian let out a bark of laughter. "They actually have such people?"

"No. Not a broker in the way you mean. Her role is to help the girls learn how to present themselves better. You know, in a more appealing manner. They say she can make a silk purse out of a sow's ear and a bride out of a wallflower."

Somewhat amused, Adrian searched out the woman in question. She stood not far from them, in the shadow of an archway, as if she were trying to hide from the frenetic pace of the ballroom.

For someone who supposedly could make a silk purse out of a sow's ear, she certainly didn't apply her skills to herself. He'd seen women twice her age dressed more appealingly. She was buttoned down tighter than a Puritan schoolmistress, her coiffure did not allow for a curl or tendril to escape the taut twist and pins that restrained her hair, and those awkward looking spectacles rendered her eyes practically invisible.

She certainly must not suffer from vanity, he decided, else she would loosen that mass of hair, reveal a little more of that creamy flesh, and remove that regrettable bit of wire and magnifying glass.

"She actually makes a living doing that?"

"What?" It was his Uncle Neville approaching to circle his daughter's waist with one arm. "Has some woman caught his eye, Catherine?"

"Mrs. Poitevant," she replied. "Adrian is intrigued by the idea of a woman hired to help other young women get married."

"My Catherine needed no such help," Neville said with a proud smile down at his radiant daughter.

"That's because Catherine has her lovely mother and grandmother to guide her. And also, she was born beautiful," Adrian added.

"Thank you," Catherine said. "But there's more to love than how a person looks."

"Oh, we're speaking now of love?" Adrian teased.

"Of course!"

"Then I would assume you disapprove of Mrs. Poitevant's businesslike approach to helping her plain-faced clients marry."

"Not at all. It depends on how you look at it," Catherine explained. "Dulcie Bennett is a perfect example. She has never looked so handsome, nor comported herself so well as she did today. She is painfully shy, you see, and so easily overwhelmed by that family of hers." She gave a delicate shudder. "I think Hester Poitevant has worked wonders with Dulcie. She may call her little business the Mayfair Academy. But we call her 'the Bridemaker.' And rightfully so. I know of at least a dozen marriages credited directly to her."

"The Bridemaker," Adrian scoffed. "To look at her I wonder she ever managed to trap a man into marriage."

"That is so cruel!" Catherine exclaimed, even as her father stifled a chuckle behind his hand. "It's just that she's widowed. She must have loved her husband very much. That's why she still wears mourning for him. I'm certain she dressed more becomingly while her husband was alive." When they both looked unconvinced she jutted her chin forward. "I think she's someone to admire, someone who has made the best of her unfortunate circumstances. Certainly we should not judge her by her appearance."

And what of the company she keeps? Adrian wanted to ask. Was he not to judge her on that either? But he wisely kept silent.

Satisfied that she'd successfully made her point, Catherine said, "If you'll excuse me, I must speak with Lady Farnsworth before she takes her leave."

The two men watched her walk away. Then the music started up and they shared a look. "Duty calls," Uncle Neville said, starting toward his wife.

"Yes," Adrian agreed. Duty called. The duty to annoy the hell out of a man who'd made torturing him an art form. Though he meant Dulcie Bennett no harm, he planned to enjoy every step of the dance to come, for he knew Ainsley would be watching—and steaming— the whole time.

As he made his way through the crowd, however, he passed near the odd Mrs. Poitevant. She was speaking now with another woman, and in passing he caught her low, husky laugh. Not the giggle of a silly girl, but the husky, musical laughter of a woman.

He slowed, seeking her out with his eyes, and this time he studied her more carefully. Beneath her drab appearance lay a woman of some potential. Neither too fat nor too thin. Delicately colored complexion. Perfectly even features. In truth, no dreadful flaws that he could see. He suspected that with the least amount of effort she could be quite beautiful.

But she chose not to be. Very curious.

Then she laughed again and his gaze sharpened.

For all her prickly, standoffish appearance, there was something interesting about her voice, something not so easily hidden as her hair and her bosom and that slender waist.

As if she felt his scrutiny, she tilted her face toward him, and for a long moment their gazes held.

It was only a moment, one that ended in alarm on her part. She looked away, shifting her stance so that her back was to him.

In that haughty gesture, she reminded him how she and the rest of her kind thought. She might only be connected to George Bennett through business. But she might as well be his twin when it came to preserving the almighty English traditions of intermarriage among the elite.

If George Bennett did not want him paying court to his sister, most assuredly Mrs. Poitevant would not either. After all, what would become of her fee should the girl run off with a bounder like him?

He grinned at Mrs. Poitevant's stiff, gray-clad back. What better reason to pay court to Dulcie Bennett?

CHAPTER 3

Hester had a massive headache.

It had begun when Adrian Hawke first asked Dulcie to dance. It had increased throughout the lengthy dance, every time she spied Dulcie's glowing face.

To be fair, the two of them made a handsome couple. She suspected, however, that any woman's appearance would be enhanced by having a man like him attached to her arm. His height and dark appeal were the perfect foil for Dulcie's softly rounded femininity. And they danced very well together.

She'd never seen Dulcie so animated and so lovely.

A pity her newly found joy was based on pure sham. Pure vindictiveness.

All through the endless hours of the ball Hester had watched George Bennett and Adrian Hawke. She saw Lord Ainsley's black glares and Mr. Hawke's far more subtle mocking ones. Poor Dulcie had no inkling of the storm circling her. She danced on a cloud, infatuated with the suave Mr. Hawke, believing his attentions to her were honestly motivated. But Hester knew all the while that it was revenge driving him. She also knew she must not let it go any further. But she hadn't the faintest idea how to prevent it.

Then things had gotten even worse and her headache had become a red pounding thing centered at the top of her head. George Bennett had become so inebriated, so loud and coarse, that Lady Soames had sent her three burliest footmen to put him out and deliver him home.

Lady Ainsley had been furious at her son for embarrassing her in front of so many people. She had been equally furious with her hostess for presuming to criticize her humiliating excuse for a son. Of course, she was not so foolish as to confront a woman of such consequence as Lady Soames. So she'd settled for venting her fury on the first person she could lay her clutches on in private.

Unfortunately that person had been Hester.

"This is all your fault!" she hissed, her fingers tight around Hester's arm like vulture claws. She dragged Hester into a niche in one corner of a deserted chamber. "If you hadn't let her dance with that man, George wouldn't have become so upset and none of this would have happened. And now she's out there on the floor with him again!" The woman's nostrils flared with outrage and she shook with fury. "I'll not have some bastard upstart paying court to my girl! Do you understand me? I mean it. You get her away from him and send her to me at once. We are going home!"

Hester did not normally allow her clientele to speak to her so rudely, and she was sorely tempted to instruct Lady Ainsley about what she could do with her ugly, high-handed manner. But Hester didn't want Dulcie to fall under Mr. Hawke's spell any more than Lady Ainsley did, albeit for different reasons. So she bit her tongue.

She did register her displeasure by jerking her arm free of the older woman's hold. "I assure you, Lady

Ainsley, that I will do everything I can to discourage his attentions to Dulcie—and hers to him."

"Don't you worry about Dulcie. I'll see to her. Indeed I will. But that man—" She jerked furiously at her cuffs. "You see how his very presence upsets George. I will not have it. Do you hear? I will not have it!" And with that she had stormed off.

Hester stood now, waiting for the dance to end so that she could collect Dulcie and depart.

"Ah. It is Mrs. Poitevant," Mr. Hawke said when he saw her approaching. "Come to rescue Miss Bennett, have you?"

"Hardly that," she said, lying through her stiffly smiling lips. "Lady Ainsley is preparing to depart, however." She switched her gaze to Dulcie, whose cheeks still glowed with color. "She's waiting for you now."

"So soon?" Dulcie exclaimed. "But what of the breakfast?"

"Perhaps you should discuss that with your mother," Hester said, arching her brows and praying Dulcie would not argue the matter in front of Mr. Hawke.

Fortunately Dulcie sensed her silent reproval. With a guilty tuck of her chin, the girl nodded. "Very well."

One of the knots in Hester's neck unkinked. At least there was one person she could still intimidate.

After Mr. Hawke bade them both a good evening, Dulcie let loose with one of her enormous, heartfelt sighs. "This has been the most wonderful, enchanting, marvelous evening of my entire life!"

Hester bit back the words of warning she'd intended to issue. If she scolded Dulcie, then sent her to her mother for an even more severe scolding, the girl would be crushed. She might also see Hester as being entirely on her mother's side, and perhaps become less prone to confide in her. Hester did not want that. Better to prop her up, Hester decided. Lady Ainsley certainly meant to tear her down.

Hester steered Dulcie toward a sheltered area just outside the ballroom. "I'm glad you enjoyed yourself, dear. It only goes to show how all your hard work has paid off."

"And yours," the girl said, turning to her with gratitude shining in her eyes. "You were right, Mrs. Poitevant, about everything. Good posture." She straightened. "A confident attitude." She thrust her chin out. "And this dress. My hair." She snatched up Hester's hands. "I feel like Cinderella, and you are my fairy godmother. I can never, never thank you enough. Never!"

"Yes. Well." Hester gnawed her lower lip. She hated the situation she'd been put in. "You should know that your mother is very upset about Mr. Hawke's attentions to you. He . . . His circumstances do not fall within the parameters she is prepared to approve in a potential son-in-law."

Another huge sigh. "I know, I know. But if Mother were to meet him I'm certain she would change her mind. I'm convinced of it. He is so handsome. And so kind."

And devious and willing to use an innocent girl to annoy that girl's horrible brother. But Hester swallowed any further remarks on that subject. Dulcie would never believe her. Besides, she would find out soon enough how wrong she was when it came to convincing her mother to accept him. "We'll talk more about this tomorrow," she said. "For now, however, I believe your mother is waiting for you in the foyer."

"But aren't you coming with us?"

"No. You're going home with your mother. The second carriage will carry me home."

"What of George?"

Hester resisted rolling her eyes. "Your brother went home some time ago."

"Oh. I wondered if he might have. I saw him glaring at me. He is always so exacting. But then he was gone."

Yes, gone, as in three sheets to the wind.

But Hester only patted Dulcie's hand. "Run along, dear. We'll talk tomorrow."

"I suppose I must. But I shan't be discouraged, no matter what Mother says. Or George." She squared her shoulders and again lifted her chin, showing Hester her very best form. "It shall all work out in the end. You'll see."

After Dulcie left, Hester remained in the hall niche collecting herself, considering her next move. It appeared she'd opened up a Pandora's box with the heretofore repressed Dulcie. One little taste of success at a ball and the girl had become a whole new person. What would happen if her family crushed that newly blossomed spirit? Or if Adrian Hawke did?

What a stew she found herself in.

She mulled over her choices. She would have no influence with Lady Ainsley or her son, that was plain. George Bennett hated Adrian Hawke for particular reasons known only to him. Mrs. Bennett hated the man for general reasons: he simply was not good enough to suit her.

Likewise Hester doubted she would have any impact on the starry-eyed Dulcie.

That left Adrian Hawke.

A little thrill of fear shivered its way up her spine. Did she dare approach him and ask him to leave Dulcie out of his battle with Lord Ainsley?

She frowned at her own perversity. What sort of an attitude was that? Did she *dare* approach him? She was well within her rights to approach him on the subject. She was not afraid to speak to him on *any* subject—or to anyone else, for that matter—so long as her convictions were strong.

And in this case her convictions were strong indeed. Any association with Mr. Hawke spelled disaster for Dulcie. His attentions to her were insincere and therefore cruel. Since Dulcie's welfare in society was Hester's concern, it was plain that she must speak to the man.

And there was no time like the present.

Bucking up her courage, Hester started for the ballroom. People had begun to make their way into the breakfast, and she was delayed several times by acquaintances inviting her to dine with them. But aside from pausing to smile approvingly at Anabelle and her perfectly acceptable escort, Hester made her apologies and moved on.

She must find Mr. Hawke before he sat down to eat. She wanted to get this over with tonight, before she lost her nerve.

She found him in the nearly empty ballroom, speaking with a pair of men well known in society. She heard him say, "With a constant supply of raw wool my textile cooperative can maintain a consistent level of work for the carders, sorters, washers, spinners, and weavers."

"And you think you can keep employment steady year round?" Lord Thigpen asked. He was one of the richest, most tightfisted men in London.

"That's our intention. Good for the workers; good for the textile market; therefore good for us."

"Harumph. Well. It makes a certain sort of sense."

"I thought you might agree."

Hester frowned. Adrian Hawke certainly was persuasive in his manner. If he could sway the thinking of a pinchpenny like Lord Thigpen, what chance did a starry-eyed innocent like Dulcie Bennett have should he turn those powers of persuasion on her?

Finally the men parted amid much backslapping and

a promise from Mr. Hawke to meet with Lord Thigpen tomorrow for cigars. This was her chance.

Once the two men left she stepped into the now empty ballroom. As soon as he saw her he stopped.

"Mrs. Poitevant." He stared at her in such a searching manner Hester felt herself begin to color. "Are you lost?"

Was that a smirk on his face? A surge of anger renewed her strength of purpose. If he thought good looks and a teasing manner carried any weight with her, he was sadly mistaken.

"I'm quite familiar with the arrangements of the Soameses' townhouse, Mr. Hawke."

"I see. Then I can only assume you have come looking for me. Could that be true?"

Ooh, but she wanted to slap the amusement off his face! If pure cheek were a virtue, the man would qualify for sainthood. But Hester was used to men who thought too highly of themselves. She gave him an utterly false smile. "Yes. I would like a private word with you. If that's convenient?"

"But of course." He gestured toward a gilded lyre-back settee with striped cushions. "Shall we?"

"Thank you, but no. This will not take long."

"Very well." He crossed his arms and waited, his legs splayed in an aggressively masculine stance. Intimidating. At least *meant* to be intimidating.

With an effort she repressed her outrage, or as much of it as she could manage. "I am concerned about a friend of mine. Dulcie Bennett is—"

"Dulcie Bennett is your *friend*? And here I thought you merely in her employ. Or perhaps in her brother's employ?"

She met him stare for stare. "You are partially right. I am hired to help her make a better season than she did last year. But I am also her friend, and I don't want to see her hurt."

"I'm sure no one does. So why come to me? I only met the girl tonight. We danced. Surely you cannot construe that as any sort of threat."

She tried not to glare at him as she considered her words. Best to be completely candid. "You asked her to dance just to annoy her brother."

"Did I?" At some point his eyes had turned from dark and hard to a brilliant, taunting blue.

It flustered her. "You know you did. I watched you do it, and I watched you watch him grow more and more furious over it."

"What? Good old Georgie furious with his old Eton chum? Surely, Mrs. Poitevant, you misread the situation."

"I did not misread it!" she exclaimed, stamping her foot. A mistake, she realized. For losing her temper only increased his amusement.

"Perhaps old George—or should I call him Lord Ainsley now? No, I'll call him old George. Perhaps old George harbors some ill will toward me. But I assure you, he has no cause to. You may also rest assured that I do not hold Miss Bennett in anything but the highest regard."

Hester blew out a breath. "While I am most relieved to hear that, Mr. Hawke, as long as you encourage the girl in any way I believe you *will* end up hurting her. Even now she is very likely being harangued for having paid you so much attention."

Their gazes held in an awkward sort of competition. She would not back down.

But he would not give in. "It seems then that we have reached an impasse. For I intend to pay my compliments to whomsoever I please. Your Miss Bennett is likewise free to accept or decline any invitation extended to her. As are you and any other lady of the *ton*. By the way, do you dance? I didn't notice you on the floor tonight."

Hester shoved her spectacles back up her nose. "That is neither here nor there. Perhaps I should be plainer, Mr. Hawke. Dulcie Bennett has developed a partiality for you, as I'm sure you have detected. But we both know that men like you are not interested in girls like her. I am asking you not to lead her on and not to use her as a tool to strike out at Lord Ainsley. She does not deserve to be treated so."

"It may come as a surprise to you, Mrs. Poitevant, but whatever it is you've taught Dulcie, it has taken. No matter how you choose to categorize me, I am no different from any other gentleman. I find her a pleasant and charming young woman, an excellent dancer as well, very quick on her feet. Rather than berate me for using her, perhaps you should credit her—and yourself— for a job well done. Now, is there anything else?"

If blood could boil, Hester's would have done so. She couldn't believe he refused to admit he was using Dulcie against George. And now the ingrate somehow had turned his less than honorable behavior into a reflection on *her*. A flattering reflection, no less.

Except that they both knew it was a lie.

She drew herself up, glaring daggers at him. "You leave me no choice but to reveal your cruel plan to Miss Bennett and—"

"Why don't you admit what's really bothering you, Mrs. Poitevant? I know what you do for a living. You match up the spoiled daughters of the arrogant nobility to appropriate men of even more arrogance. What happens if one of your girls marries down? Horrors!" He pretended to shudder. "Dancing with a no-name tradesman, and from America, no less."

He advanced on her, one slow step at a time. "Despite your protestations, you don't give a damn about her getting hurt. All you care about is the match she makes,

about keeping people like me out of your exalted society—"

"That's not true!"

"About your reputation if you fail," he continued,
forcing her to step back as he advanced. "And the fee
you're likely to lose." He stopped mere inches from her.
Hester tried to back away. But she came up against the
settee and sat down hard.

He leaned forward, placing a hand atop the wooden
settee back on each side of her shoulders. "Did I leave
anything out?"

Hester could not reply. Outrage warred with terror.
How dared he treat her so?

But a long-ago memory intruded as well, the memory
of being stalked just so by a man she had *wanted* to be
stalked by. A bittersweet memory of being happily
trapped in a chair very like this. A handsome young man
with fire in his eyes had leaned nearer and nearer. Only
when she had been breathless and about to burst from
anticipation had he dipped his head and kissed her. He
had kissed her, and for those few moments it had been
glorious.

Was Adrian Hawke going to kiss her now?

Did she want him to?

She licked her lips and his gaze flicked down to them.
In her ears her blood roared ferociously, heating her
through and through. The answer was yes. She wanted
him to kiss her. Now.

She licked her lips again. His face lowered.

Then abruptly he pushed upright and stepped back.

Hester sucked in a greedy breath of air, as if she had
forgotten to breathe. Why had he stopped?

Then she blinked and was assaulted at once by reality.
Thank goodness he *had* stopped. Good gracious! What
had she been thinking? From arguing with the man to
wanting him to kiss her—

No. She straightened up on the settee, clenching her jaws in rigid denial. She had not wanted him to kiss her. Not at all. It had just been an aberrant memory, probably fueled by the lateness of the hour.

But she could swear he'd been considering kissing her. She could swear it! Thank heaven he had not.

Adrian stared down at the woman pressed back into the settee, and backed up another step. Behind her spectacles her eyes were round with shock—shock and fear which he had put there.

Already she thought him a crude upstart, an unsuitable addition to her social sphere. So what had he done? He'd gone ahead and acted like a coarse brute, intimidating her and in the process proving her right.

He suppressed a groan at his perversity. Why had he gotten so worked up by her accusation? He didn't care about her opinion, even if it was damned close to the truth. Nor had he been considering kissing her, even though she must think he'd been going to.

Even though she probably needed kissing very badly.

He raked a hand through his hair even as his eyes raked over her. Kiss *her*? Not likely. Hester Poitevant wasn't his type, not in looks, nor in attitude.

Gritting his teeth, he gave her a curt bow. "I apologize for my temper, Mrs. Poitevant. I have overstepped my bounds. I assure you, it will not happen again."

Then he quit the room, and quit the grandiose house as well. He called for a hack, forgoing the Hawke family carriage. He needed to be alone, to think out what had happened tonight—especially his furious reaction to George Bennett and Mrs. Poitevant.

God help him, he had almost kissed the haughty little prude! No use denying it when he knew it was true. He'd been furious at her, both who she was and her perceptiveness. He'd only meant to tell her off, though, not to kiss her.

But everything had changed when she licked her lips.

This time he didn't hold his groan in. What was wrong with him? He must be in desperate need of a woman. More desperate than he'd guessed. "Driver!" he called, deciding to nip this problem in the bud. What he needed was to make a discreet stop on the way home. That would solve his problem.

Anything to banish the image of Hoity-toity Poitevant's pink, bow-shaped lips.

Hester shook the whole way home from the Soameses' ball. Not trembled, not shivered, but actually shook; hard tremors she could not get under control. It was worse than those terrible times ten years ago when she'd been one of the eligible misses, not one of the matrons.

Then, as now, the delayed reaction of her tightly strung nerves was due solely to a man. Always a man.

She had thought herself past such behavior.

But she wasn't. She sat now jammed into the corner of the Ainsleys' smaller carriage, keeping a death grip on the door post, staring at the flickering carriage lamp, but seeing a man's face instead. Tonight it had been Adrian Hawke, handsome, sure of himself, then angry and at the end, lusting.

But that couldn't be right.

That part about lusting . . . that part she must be confusing with her memories of other men and other times.

She groaned and closed her eyes. *Don't think about them.* She was almost home. Once there she could escape to the solitude of her own bedchamber, remove this hideous ensemble, let loose her hair, and blot anything of the *ton* or the season—or Adrian Hawke—right out of her head.

And she could start now by removing her wretched spectacles.

With an angry swipe she ripped them off, then

frowned and checked to see if she'd broken one of the delicate arms. She hadn't. She stuffed them in her reticule, then flung wide the door curtain and stared out into the London night. The streets were quiet but not entirely vacant. During the season people were always out and about. Going to parties, leaving parties. Late breakfasts. Cards until dawn.

Oh, Lord. Could she possibly endure another long season of this?

You have no choice.

With another groan she slumped down into the squabs. Only yesterday she'd had everything under control. After all, three Mayfair Academy students were embarking on the season better turned out than they'd ever been. Her girls were never garbed like every other girl, in pale pink and blue frills and froufrous. Instead she fitted them out in the colors and styles that best flattered them. Even within the limitations of the accepted mode she knew all the ways to accentuate an individual's best features while disguising her worst. Dulcie's transformation was proof of that.

Beyond appearances, however, her girls had exhaustive lessons in dancing, cards, and parlor games. They knew at least three piano pieces, had memorized a poem or two should they be asked to recite, and they practiced conversing on their favorite subjects. For Dulcie it was horses. The girl loved to ride and was an excellent horsewoman. The Honorable Anabelle Finch loved to read and had a considerable understanding of English history and all the poets. As for Charlotte Clotworthy, she could talk anyone's head off about her needlework: embroidery, tatting, needlepoint, smocking, beading, knitting.

Yes, Phoebe had prepared them well and she should now be anticipating their success. Instead she was huddled in the Ainsley carriage falling to pieces because some arrogant man whom she'd confronted had dared *not* to be intimidated by her.

What had she been thinking?

Worse, how was she to deal with his presence when next she encountered him? For she knew she would, if not tomorrow, then surely the next day, or the next.

As the coach clattered down Bond Street toward Mayfair and her little cottage on the edge of that fashionable district, Hester resolved not to think about tomorrow, nor about him. Not tonight. There was nothing she could do about it now. And even remembering her reaction to him, how she'd actually wanted him to kiss her—

"Ooh," she groaned again and rubbed her aching temples.

All she wanted was to get home and have Mrs. Dobbs prepare something for her pounding head. She would pet Fifi and Peg. Then she would seek the solace of her bed.

Your solitary bed, a spiteful little voice rose up to haunt her.

She refused to listen. If her bed was solitary, it was by her own choice. She did everything she could to discourage men, to appear invisible to the toffs who circulated at the parties she had to attend. It was easy to overlook a plainly garbed widow of limited means who displayed no interest in men, which was what she had been ever since she'd adopted her disguise. People saw only what they wanted to see, especially the shallow, self-involved sorts she dealt with. They never looked at her twice.

But Adrian Hawke had.

Why?

She grimaced. Because she'd stupidly drawn attention to herself. She'd challenged him and he'd called her bluff. She'd counted on him feeling guilty about how he was using poor Dulcie, on his having some sort of conscience.

Only he had none. She'd tried to protect Dulcie and she'd failed.

When the carriage turned into her street, Hester let the curtain fall. Almost home.

Rather than fret over tonight's disaster, she'd be better served counting her blessings. She had her independence, her work at the academy, and a pleasant little house in a respectable neighborhood. She had Mr. and Mrs. Dobbs to keep life comfortable, and the respect of the people she relied on to provide her a living. She even had a modest sum invested in the four percents.

Quite a feat for a girl with a background as notorious as hers. She shuddered to think what would have become of her had Verna DeLisle not taken her under her wing.

At the thought of Mrs. DeLisle, the frown lines between Hester's brows began to ease. That's what she needed, a visit with Mrs. DeLisle. She would lay out her problems, and her wise old friend would put it all into perspective.

Besides, she remembered as the coach stopped before her front door, Mr. Hawke was only in town temporarily, for his cousin's wedding. She had only a few more weeks of his presence to endure.

Once he was gone, life would go back to normal.

CHAPTER 4

Hester arrived at the Ainsley townhouse at half past two. She and Dulcie had an appointment at the milliner's at three. She was no sooner ushered into the foyer than the butler bade her follow him. "Lady Ainsley requests your presence."

"Oh, wonderful," Hester muttered under her breath. After yesterday evening's debacle and the sleepless night that had followed, the last thing she needed was to spar with Dulcie's overbearing mother.

For one brief moment, last night's shakiness returned. But with ruthless self-will she banished it. She had to. Mrs. Bennett was undoubtedly not done blaming her for Dulcie's dances with Adrian Hawke—Adrian Hawke whom she did not want to think about, let alone discuss.

But Hester had no intention of being Beatrice Bennett's whipping boy.

In the back sitting room which functioned also as her office, Lady Ainsley sat at her elaborately inlaid Chinese desk. Dulcie's mother did not trust either her housekeeper or the butler to be competent at their jobs. As a result thc desktop was a series of stacked papers, one for each of the service areas she oversaw: housekeeping, kitchens, grounds, tradesmen.

She also kept a calendar with every social obligation marked on it. Events not to be missed were underlined, with the most important, the most elegant, written out in large capital letters as well. Lady Ainsley's social life and how she could benefit from it were her sole concern. She was an utter incompetent when it came to her children, and she possessed not a smidgen of maternal instinct. Of course she was completely unaware of her failing.

With three more daughters to marry off in the next decade, Lady Ainsley was destined to have a long relationship with Hester and the Mayfair Academy—assuming, of course, that Hester could stomach dealing with her that long.

Lady Ainsley looked up and her eyes narrowed. "Good. You're here." She made a notation on the next day's menu and handed it to the housekeeper, who bobbed and let herself out.

It was now or never. Hester chose to go on the offensive. "Lady Ainsley," she began. "My time is short, so if you wish to complain about last night, we will have to discuss it another day. What I wanted to discuss with you now will only take a minute or two."

"Now see here, Mrs. Poitevant." The woman shoved her pen down into its silver and crystal inkwell. "I will have my say. I have *not* raised my child for some . . . some by-blow tradesman to ruin. I will *not* have another night like last night. That—"

"Nor will I," Hester interrupted through gritted teeth. "That's why I have some specific suggestions for your family outing this evening."

Somewhat mollified, the woman tugged at the lace drapery at her chest. "Well, that's more like it. That daughter of mine does better with specific suggestions. The more specific the better."

"My instructions are for you."

"For me?" Lady Ainsley's stiffly coiffed head swiveled on her neck and she stared at Hester. Her eyes were as small and pale as the aquamarines that glinted at her throat, her ears, and on her fingers. "Instructions for me?"

"Indeed. It is essential that Dulcie be allowed to answer for herself tonight—and to not be corrected by you or anyone else."

"Now see here—"

"You harangued her sufficiently last night. You must not do so again today. My work with Dulcie will be pointless if you cannot cooperate." Resolved not to be intimidated by the self-important viscountess, Hester fixed the woman with a steady, expectant stare. She'd dealt with people like Mrs. Bennett in the past; she could do it again.

For one moment only the woman appeared inclined to argue. Her haughty brows lowered, her autocratic mouth opened. But when Hester arched her own brows and lifted her chin—just a fraction—the woman backed down. Her mouth closed. Her lips pursed. But she said nothing, only nodded.

Hester allowed herself a faint smile. *So there.* "Last night was a ball," she continued on, as nonchalantly as if she hadn't just trumped the woman. "Tonight is a more intimate gathering. It's an opportunity for Dulcie to put into practice all we've been working on. She has two piano compositions prepared, no more. And she will be wearing another of her new gowns. You are not to remark on her in any way save with approval. But not so effusively as to make her self-conscious."

"Are you saying I should not extol her virtues? My word, Mrs. Poitevant, it's not as if she has that many."

Hester's mild expression turned instantly to steel. "Your daughter's virtues are quite extensive, Lady Ainsley, and remarks such as that can only undermine her confidence. If you cannot manage even one evening allowing her to shine . . ." Again she arched her brows.

"No, no. I can manage," the woman hastily replied. "You are perfectly correct."

"Very good." Though Hester did not by nature enjoy intimidating people, sometimes it was the only way she could bring herself to work for prigs like Lady Ainsley. By the time people like her made their way to the Mayfair Academy with their unmarriageable daughters, they needed Hester so badly they actually would pay to suffer her sometimes superior attitude.

But this was about Dulcie, Hester reminded herself. She might dislike the girl's family, but she meant to complete the job she'd been hired to do, and well. So she tucked her true emotions away, and forced herself to be pleasant. Cool, but pleasant.

"If I might make a suggestion, Lady Ainsley. You will find it easier to abide by my instructions if you seat yourself on the same side of the table as Dulcie, as far down from her as the arrangement allows. That way you will not be tempted to cast any speaking looks her way, and she will not be so likely to defer to you."

Lady Ainsley knotted her hands at her waist. "Yes. I see. You are . . . You are quite clever. I will do what I can about that."

Hester gave an approving nod. "Very well then. We are off and I shall return her to you by four-thirty. If I do not see you then, I hope you have a lovely evening."

Lady Ainsley managed a nod, obviously the nearest she could come to a civil response. But Hester didn't care. As she made her way to the marble-floored foyer of the Ainsleys' townhouse, with its marble niches everywhere holding marble-carved statuary, she decided the house was just as cold and rigid as the lady who presided over it.

At least she would not have to suffer the woman's presence tonight, nor her unpleasant son's.

Nor Adrian Hawke's.

The same persistent shiver crawled up her spine, just as it did every time she thought of him. All morning she'd sternly suppressed those thoughts. She'd deal with him when the time came. Not before.

But for a moment now she let herself remember him, and how he'd made her feel. Amid all the other emotions he'd provoked in her, the most memorable was that he'd made her feel desirable.

Desirable!

For one split second it had lasted, only to be overset by fear, then outrage. But that one split second had tortured her ever since.

He'd done the same for Dulcie, she reminded herself, and probably every other woman he met. She could put no more stock in those foolish feelings of hers than they should. The fact was, Adrian Hawke was trouble. He'd spawned a storm with Dulcie, with Lady Bennett and George, and also with her.

But she wasn't going to think about him any longer. Tonight Dulcie would be safe from him, and that was good enough for her. Though Dulcie was certain to suffer paralyzing bouts of self-doubt, once she had her piano piece out of the way the girl should be all right. And maybe next time she could be convinced to sing as well.

Two evenings later Hester ducked behind a palm tree at Lady Dresden's annual ball. She'd been jumpy all night, expecting at any moment to be accosted by the notorious Mr. Hawke.

It was utterly ridiculous, of course. But tell that to her overwrought nerves. She'd just begun to relax, assuming he must not be coming. That's when she'd spied Horace Vasterling. That's why she'd ducked behind the lush, potted palm.

Chiding herself for such foolishness, Hester edged back into the open. *He doesn't know who you are,* she told herself. He might be her brother, but the man has never even laid eyes on her. Yet still she raised her cup of punch to her lips, half-hiding her face behind the overly sweetened, claret-hued drink she held.

Horace Vasterling did not know her face. For all she knew, he had no inkling she even existed. But she knew him very well. From his first venture from the far reaches of Cumbria into London society five years ago, she'd watched his every move with morbid curiosity.

She'd wondered if he would come to town this year. She had her answer now. From behind her cup she observed his progress across the crowded room.

She hated him. At least that's what she'd been telling herself for the last twenty years. The truth, however, was that she *wanted* to hate him. She didn't always succeed.

But she *definitely* hated the father who had sired them both, then proceeded blithely to forget that his daughter and wife had ever existed.

She studied the Honorable Horace Vasterling over the rim of her irksome spectacles, noting every detail of his appearance. He had their mother's coloring, the sandy hair and blue eyes. Did that mean she had inherited her father's? Her mother had never said. Certainly Horace and she looked nothing alike.

Her eyes narrowed, raking over him. He was still too stout, perhaps even more so than last season. The real problem, however, was that he still wore last year's clothing. His waistcoat appeared a little shabby and it had begun to strain across his middle. One of the buttons looked about to pop loose. Didn't his valet attend to him at all? Or was his father—*their* father—so tightfisted as to restrict payment to his tailor?

Hester pursed her lips in disapproval. If Horace's intent was to make a good match, as surely it must be, since he was back in town yet again, then he ought to present a better appearance than he currently did. A baron's son was perfectly acceptable in most cases. But the Vasterling estate was small and its income limited. She knew it and so did the rest of society. Barring some other outstanding virtue, that meant Horace's prospects were limited as well.

She watched him shake hands with one fellow and share a joke with another. Had their father come to town with him this year?

"He's not here."

Caught up in her own thoughts, Hester blinked at the intrusion of that small, pouting voice. "What? How do you know?" Then as her wits returned, "Who?"

"Mr. Hawke," Dulcie said, her face the very picture of dejection.

"Mr. Hawke," Hester repeated, forcing herself into the present. Thank goodness he wasn't here. "Now, Dulcie, have you already forgotten your mother's instructions to you? It was just this morning. A viscount or higher, she said. Preferably an earl or his heir. That is the only sort of offer she will entertain for your hand." Hester paused to let that sink in, though how anyone could forget Beatrice Bennett's remark, she did not know. Lady Ainsley's tone had been exceedingly loud and exceedingly unpleasant.

Trying now to be kinder than the mother, Hester added, "Did you see that Lord Tonleigh's eldest son is here? Also, young Lord Aveshim. Have you spoken yet with either of them?"

Dulcie sighed, then answered as the dutiful young lady she'd been taught to be. "They have both approached me. I am to dance the quadrille with Lord Aveshim, and dine with Tonleigh's heir. But I cannot imagine *marrying* either of them," she finished in a burst of desperation. "Not *either* of them!"

Yes, and Hester understood why. Aveshim was the prissiest man in town while Tonleigh's heir was surely the coarsest. Not that either of those facts presented a problem for Lady Ainsley.

"It's not fair," Dulcie went on. "Mama blames him for being baseborn." She whispered that last. "But it could hardly be his fault. If you think about it, he should be Baron Hawke, not his uncle."

"Even so, your mother would still rebuff him, Dulcie. A viscount, she said. Remember?"

"She cannot force me to wed against my will."

No, Hester supposed she could not. Fortunately it was not likely to come to that. Soon enough Adrian Hawke would return to America. Then Dulcie would return to her normal sweet self. Hester had no doubt of that.

There were other gentlemen who would be acceptable to both mother and daughter. For now, however, with Dulcie fixated on Mr. Hawke, the girl was unlikely to notice them.

"Now, now, I'm sure you have other more acceptable dance partners."

Dulcie sighed. Her shoulders slumped, her chin sagged. "Yes. Lots and lots of dance partners. But what purpose is there to any of this if I cannot dance with the one man I most want to dance with?"

Hester frowned. Were those tears in the poor girl's eyes?

Witnessing Dulcie's utter dejection and the total collapse of her budding self-confidence set all of Hester's maternal urges in motion.

It was so unfair. Society had arranged its rules to protect and empower the great estates of England. But those unyielding rules left in the margins far too many unhappy lives.

Hester had managed to create a place for herself in society, not through marriage, but through her own hard work and ingenuity. She'd built on what she'd learned at her poor, misguided mother's knee: how to charm anyone; how to create the impression of beauty; how to coax money from the wealthy.

Her mother, of course, had used her knowledge only on herself, to gain the attention she craved and never could get enough of. Hester used that knowledge on other people, to make a living for herself, and hopefully to help her clients find more contentment than they otherwise might. As confused as Hester's emotions toward her mother were, at least Isabelle had left her some talent to fall back upon.

But what did Dulcie have to fall back on? Between her mother and brother, she would eventually be bullied into a terrible marriage, one arranged solely to consolidate wealth and breed yet another generation of bullies and victims. And so the cycle continued, season after season.

Hester fingered the line of buttons on her plain gray gloves. The truth was, she could hardly blame the girl for her emotional storm. After all, even she was not immune to Adrian Hawke's appeal. He was so . . .

She sighed. He was so manly. So virile. Obscenely so, she decided, pursing her lips in disapproval. Not her sort at all.

But she certainly understood Dulcie's infatuation. Just like herself, Dulcie chafed at the limitations society placed on her. She took Dulcie's hand in hers, patted it, and for a moment allowed her imagination free rein. Would it be so awful if a girl like Dulcie should marry for love? Would it destroy some great master plan if one awkward British miss should marry a baseborn American businessman?

The answer was a resounding no.

But no matter her own feelings on the subject, this particular baseborn American was not the right man for her Dulcie. She frowned, remembering that split second of awareness when he'd leaned over her in a towering rage and yet also . . . also . . .

She shook her head to erase the heart-stopping memory. The fact was, men like him were not the right sort for any woman. Too much charm. Too much money.

"Here now." She offered Dulcie a handkerchief. "You're bound to see Mr. Hawke again at some party or other. And I'm sure he'll ask you to dance." She could practically guarantee it.

"Oh, Mrs. Poitevant. Do you think so? Do you?"

"Yes, I do." For he was unlikely to pay any heed to Hester's request that he leave Dulcie alone. "Remember, though, that he is not here looking for a bride."

"How can you be certain of that?"

"Because he has come here for his cousin's wedding and to conduct what business he can. I'm told he's returning to America long before the season is done."

Again Dulcie's shoulders drooped. Hester stared at her. Which was worse, to have Dulcie moping around for the next three weeks, or to have her smiling and enjoying herself? Either way the girl would be crushed when the man finally left. "Now, now," Hester said, before she could prevent herself. "I have an idea."

When Dulcie looked up Hester smiled encouragingly. "Since he will not be here long, why don't you enjoy his company while you can?"

"You mean . . . go against Mama's orders?" The girl gaped at her.

Hester felt a little dumbfounded herself. What heresy was this? She was hired to help her girls make the most advantageous matches according to the parents' wishes. The parents, after all, were who paid Hester's fees. To encourage Dulcie or any of her girls to ignore her family's orders . . . well, that was courting disaster. That was risking everything she'd built for herself: her reputation; her business; her very livelihood.

"What are you saying, Mrs. Poitevant?"

I don't know. Foolishness. Idiocy. "I'm saying," Hester began slowly. Cautiously. "I'm saying that it is your future being planned. Your life and your happiness. Or perhaps, your unhappiness. If your only opposition to your family's plan is to weep, then you shall have only yourself to blame when you find yourself wed to some unpleasant but well-fixed lord of the realm."

There. That wasn't entirely radical.

Dulcie's gaze had not budged from Hester's face. "Are you suggesting that I pursue Mr. Hawke?"

"No. I told you, I don't believe he wants a wife. But . . . Well . . . I believe he may be an appropriate person for you to practice your social skills upon."

What had been the glint of tears turned now into the glitter of rising joy. It lent Dulcie's plain face a beauty Hester had never before seen there.

Hester smiled back. Happiness and hopefulness, like self-confidence, were inner qualities that provided a measure of beauty no amount of powder or rouge or artful coiffures could match.

"Oh, Mrs. Poitevant!"

"Now listen," Hester hurried on. "This is a chance for you to enjoy yourself. But I have one very important condition."

"Yes, yes. Anything."

"I am serious, Dulcie. Now, I believe my instructions so far have been of some use to you?"

"Oh, yes." Dulcie nodded so hard her chestnut-colored ringlets bounced. "I have never felt half so satisfied with myself as I have since you have come to my rescue."

"Good. So you concede that my advice is worth following?"

"Oh, yes." Again the ringlets bobbed alongside Dulcie's round cheeks.

"Then you must agree to mind my instructions now."

"I will. I promise." By now the curls were in full swing. "Whatever you say, I shall do."

"You already know the rules. No more than two dances per night with any man."

Dulcie sighed. "Very well."

"And since I intend to discuss this matter with your mother and bear the brunt of her disapproval, you must agree in return to put a full heart into your interaction with the other men you dance with."

When the girl hesitated Hester raised her brows. "Dulcie?"

"Oh, very well. I'll be charming and pleasant and laugh at everything they say. I'll even dance with Kermit Underwood—every night!—if you can appease Mother when it comes to Mr. Hawke. I shall take my courage from Juliet. Such a heroine as there never has been, before or since. She gave up everything for her Romeo, you know." She sighed and clasped her hands to her chest. "I can do no less for my Mr. Hawke."

Hester had to force herself not to roll her eyes. Really, but Shakespeare put so much foolishness in an impressionable young lady's mind. "Juliet is a fictional character, Dulcie. And I hardly think you shall have to die for Mr. Hawke. Or, for that matter, any other man you may fall in love with."

"Only him," Dulcie repeated, smiling that same smile that made her so lovely. "There shall be no other man for me. Only Mr. Hawke."

They would just see about that, Hester thought.

Hadn't she felt that way about more than one fellow whose names she now no longer recalled? Sad to say, but silly young girls sometimes had to learn the hard way.

No matter Dulcie's optimism, Hester knew Adrian Hawke was not the type presently interested in obtaining a wife. Though she could not put her finger on it, there was this reckless quality about him, this dangerous air guaranteed to attract any woman, no matter her age or marital status.

Heavens, even she found the man attractive, and she'd sworn off men years ago.

In any event, he was unlikely to be drawn to Dulcie, no matter the girl's efforts to entice him. It was revenge against her brother that Mr. Hawke sought. Though Dulcie's heart might become broken, in time it would heal.

Hadn't hers?

Dulcie's gait was light and animated as the two of them made their way back to the crowded ballroom. Her eyes sparkled and a smile hovered on her lips.

But Hester didn't smile, for she still had Lady Ainsley to deal with. Oh, well. There was no time for unpleasant tasks like the present.

Adrian had not made it through the Dresdens' overflowing foyer before he spied George Bennett.

The man was waiting for him, lying in wait just as he used to at Eton, in that narrow stairwell that had led up to the younger boys' rooms. Back then George had always kept two of his bully boys with him. Now in this brightly lit center of town society, it felt as if Bennett had a hundred bully boys with him.

But he didn't, Adrian reminded himself. Adrian had met most of these people and had already entered into serious financial negotiations with enough of them to feel secure here. George Bennett was no longer a threat to him.

In fact, *he* was the threat to Bennett. All he had to do to enrage the man was ask his sister to dance.

Unfortunately Adrian had already decided against using the poor girl that way. Not that he cared anything about that prissy Mrs. Poitevant's opinion. But fair was fair. Dulcie Bennett was an innocent and he couldn't deliberately hurt her.

But Bennett better not start any trouble.

As Adrian made his greetings to the host and hostess he lost sight of Bennett. But near the entrance to the ballroom they came face to face.

Just as at Eton, Adrian's hands knotted into fists, bracing for the worst. But George Bennett was smiling, a careful, assessing smile. Now what?

"So, Hawke. Good to see you again." The man thrust out his hand which, after a moment, Adrian shook.

"Bennett," he curtly replied, refusing to acknowledge him as Lord Ainsley.

At the deliberate slight, anger flared in the other man's eyes. But he swiftly tamped it down.

Yes, something definitely was afoot.

"I've been hearing good things about you," Bennett said.

"Have you?"

"Indeed. Seems you've beaten the odds, old man. Made a bloody fortune off those provincials in America."

Aha. George Bennett smelled money and he wanted some of it.

Adrian relaxed, sure of himself once more. Business was business no matter where you went. And where there was money to be made, smart men came out in droves. So did greedy ones. Adrian knew Bennett was greedy. But was he smart?

"I've done pretty well for myself, and for those provincials smart enough to invest with me."

They took each other's measure a long minute before Bennett said, "And so you're back in England, looking for new investors here, I'm told."

"That I am. And finding them, too. Could you excuse me? I see my cousin."

It shouldn't have felt so good to dismiss George Bennett and walk away, but it did. As Adrian strolled off, it felt damned good. Better even than dancing with the man's sister.

When he spied Bennett's battle-ax of a mother, he gave her a smile and a nod, and enjoyed her scowl all the more. How did such a nasty family produce a sweet girl like Dulcie Bennett? Then again, she probably wouldn't stay that sweet, not if the scheming Mrs. Poitevant had anything to do with it.

"What was that about?" Adrian's Uncle Neville asked, coming up beside him. "Are you considering including Ainsley in your venture?"

"When hell freezes over," Adrian said. "That horse's ass made my brief sojourn in Eton miserable. I plan to return the favor."

They were both silent a moment, remembering the angry young man Adrian once had been, a baron's bastard, Scottish at that, and totally ostracized by his upper-crust classmates.

"I should never have sent you there," Neville murmured.

Adrian shrugged. "If I hadn't gone to Eton, I would never have understood how impossible my situation was. I would never have been angry enough to make the decision to leave for America with Sarah and Marsh." He grinned at his uncle, the closest thing he'd had to a father during his early years. "I certainly wouldn't be in London now, wealthy in my own right, and sought out by every canny businessman in town. Don't bother yourself with regrets, Uncle. I don't. My life is going exactly as I want. By the time I depart London, my plans will have worked out just as I intended. It only sweetens the pot that I am courted now by the same greedy fool who once considered me not good enough to attend the same school as he."

Neville acknowledged his words with a nod. "Speaking of greedy, Henson and his cousin will be here later, and they've both expressed interest in this cooperative venture you've come up with. Between them they run nearly two thousand head of sheep. But enough of business. Olivia will have my hide if we don't put in an appearance in the ballroom."

Hester dreaded her confrontation with Mrs. Bennett. She'd hoped to put it off to another time, but as soon as she spied a certain tall, raven-haired man descending the stairs into the ballroom, she'd ducked her head, taken a deep breath, and headed straight for her unpleasant employer. What a hideous night this was turning out to be.

When she found Lady Ainsley she was being led away by her son, and none too happy about it. Hester hesitated, not certain this was a good time. Mrs. Bennett was bad enough. George Bennett was impossible.

But when George spotted Hester, he gave a short jerk of his chin, signaling her in his typically coarse manner to join them.

"Glad you're here, Mrs. Poitevant. Now I only have to say this once."

As soon as they stepped out onto the darkened terrace, Lady Ainsley jerked her elbow out of her son's grasp. "What is so important, I'd like to know? Why have you dragged me out here, away from Lady Lancaster? D'you have any idea how long I've been trying to get her ear?

She's got three young nephews in line for titles. Three—"

"Be quiet, Mother. This is more important than you know."

"What then? What?"

"Adrian Hawke is here."

"Oh!" Lady Ainsley craned her neck to see past her son into the ballroom. Then she swung to face Hester. "You'd better keep him well away from Dulcie tonight."

"No."

Hester stared at George. Had she heard him right? Wasn't that supposed to be her line?

Lady Ainsley gaped at her son. "Have you taken leave of your senses?"

He chuckled, an unpleasant sound. "Not at all. Quite the opposite, in fact. You see, I've been asking around about the newly wealthy Mr. Hawke. It seems the man has a knack for making money. Since I'm always amenable to making money, I've decided to do some business with him."

"But what about Dulcie?" The words spilled out before Hester could stop them.

George smiled, a smug, satisfied smile that lifted the hairs on the back of Hester's neck. "Dulcie does not seem to mind his attentions. Instead of warning her away from Hawke, I've decided I want you to encourage her."

"But George," his mother said. "He's a nobody."

"Yes, but he's a rich nobody, and we're in dire need of—" He broke off with a quick glance at Hester. "Go on, Mrs. Poitevant. Find my sister and give her the good news."

Though confused by his sudden change of attitude, Hester nodded and left. But she didn't go far. She paused just around the doorframe, and though she knew it was shameless to eavesdrop, she did it anyway.

"Now listen here, George," Lady Ainsley began.

"What's this all about?"

"Money, Mother. Money. D'you have any idea how much it costs to live these days? Season after season. And we've got Eliza, Penelope, and Mary still to make their come-outs."

"If this is about Mrs. Poitevant's fees, I don't think Eliza will need her."

"This isn't about her piddling fees."

Piddling? Hester frowned. He thought the amount she charged was piddling?

"We're in a bad way," he muttered, though so quietly Hester had to strain to hear.

"What do you mean?"

"I mean debt. Creditors. We need money, Mother. And from what I hear Hawke has got lots of it."

There was a silence and Hester could just imagine how stunned Lady Ainsley must be if she was shocked into silence.

"What of . . ." the woman said. "What of your sisters' dowries?"

He did not answer. However, a choked sound from Lady Ainsley was answer enough. Hester chewed the inside of her lower lip. Good Lord, what a mess. And poor Dulcie caught squarely in the middle of it.

Hester took a breath, then turned to the ballroom. Dulcie would be pleased with the news about encouraging Mr. Hawke. Certainly it solved Hester's immediate dilemma. But if George thought to marry Dulcie off to Adrian Hawke, he was deluding himself.

Hester considered it from another angle. Perhaps all George wanted was to appease Mr. Hawke sufficiently to involve himself in Mr. Hawke's apparently successful businesses.

But either way, the results would be the same. Mr. Hawke was not going to offer for Dulcie, nor was he likely to change his attitude toward George Bennett. It was only a gut feeling, but Hester was sure of it. She had the sinking suspicion that the Bennett family was not going to have a particularly satisfying season.

She found Dulcie right away in a small circle of girls. Though circumstances did not permit her to speak directly, it didn't matter. In answer to Dulcie's anxious look, Hester gave a brief smile and a subtle nod.

At once the girl's eyes lit up and a huge smile brightened her face.

What Dulcie took as approval to dance with Mr. Hawke, however, was far more complex and, Hester knew, far more dangerous. The poor girl was as caught as ever between the machinations of the two men.

It's none of your business, Hester told herself. She could no more control Dulcie's reaction to Mr. Hawke than she could control George Bennett's. Goodness, she could barely control her own reaction to the man, which fact was driven home the very next moment. For whom did she spy heading toward them but the notorious Adrian Hawke himself.

CHAPTER 5

Well, well. Mrs. Poitevant. Adrian halted when he spied her darkly garbed figure. So erect. So severe.

When she met his gaze, then looked swiftly away, his eyes narrowed. She might appear stiff and unyielding, but he'd seen something more in her eyes the night of their confrontation. Panic, shock. Yearning.

He straightened at the thought. Had he really seen yearning in her eyes? Damn him if he didn't want to torment her again, just to find out.

The fact that she stood with Dulcie Bennett made the decision easy. He strolled toward the little group, never removing his eyes from the dark figure who stood out so noticeably among the fluttering pastel girls around her.

"Good evening, ladies. Mrs. Poitevant."

"Mr. Hawke." Mrs. Poitevant gave him a stiff nod. But she maintained her manners. What else should he expect of her? "May I introduce Miss Charlotte Clotworthy. You will remember, of course, Miss Bennett."

He smiled at the girl. "Miss Bennett. I just spoke with your brother."

"Did you?" The girl stared up at him so expectantly he was momentarily nonplussed.

He had decided not to dance with her tonight. Mrs. Poitevant's accusations had managed to prick his conscience. But given the girl's enthusiastic response to him, it seemed rude not to ask her. "I know it is late, Miss Bennett, but have you any dances still available for me?"

"Oh, yes. Yes. The last dance of the night, as it happens."

Fortunately Dulcie's partner for the upcoming waltz appeared at just that moment. A faint smile stole onto Adrian's face when both she and Miss Clotworthy went off with their partners. Just as he'd hoped, he now had Mrs. Poitevant all to himself.

Laughter and excited chatter filled the air, but between them an icy silence fell. "What?" he said, succumbing to a perverse need to aggravate her. "No accusations? No admonishments?"

If it were possible, her posture grew stiffer still. "I'm sure I have no control over your actions or hers."

"No, you don't." He studied her profile as she watched the dancers queue up. "Actually, I had not intended to dance with Miss Bennett tonight."

"No? Then why did you ask her to dance?"

"Because she so obviously expected me to."

A muscle in her smooth jaw flexed once. Twice. But still she did not look at him. He took it as a personal challenge to make her do so. "Would you like to dance?"

Success. She gave him a startled glance, then immediately frowned and looked away. "Thank you, but no."

"Don't you like to dance?" he prodded her. "Or are you working tonight and so feel unable to join in the festivities?"

Her head tilted slightly and she looked at him again, eyeing him over her wire-rimmed spectacles. "Both."

He noticed two things: her eyes were green, and she didn't seem to need those spectacles.

But as if he'd held her gaze too long, she again looked away. "If you'll excuse me?"

"Wait, Mrs. Poitevant. Don't go." When she hesitated he smiled. "I believe I owe you an apology for the other night. I hope you'll accept it."

He saw the doubt in her eyes, the suspicion. Finally, however, she nodded. "Accepted."

"Thank you. So," he said, for some reason wanting to keep her there. "You're working tonight. I was told you're a bridemaker. That's a rather curious profession."

Once again she stiffened. She might have accepted his apology, but she was still prickly. "Curious? I suppose it might seem so to a man. Of course, it is not men who have to fear being labeled spinsters."

"You think men are immune to concerns of being alone, of becoming confirmed bachelors?"

He watched her mouth tighten into a pursed knot. He hoped she hadn't kissed her late husband with that pinched expression on her face. If she had, it might explain his early demise.

"I'm sure I need not point out to you, Mr. Hawke, that a spinster is generally looked upon with pity. Not so a confirmed bachelor."

He grinned at her response, but she turned her gaze fixedly upon the dancers. Damn, but for such a stiff-necked thing she had an awfully tart manner about her. It was enough to make him want to whisk her out on the floor and force her to loosen up. "Are you sure I can't convince you to dance?"

"Thank you, but no."

"Thank you, but no," he echoed, irked by her determined rebuff. "Is that how you put off everyone who tries to be nice to you?"

"I don't put off everyone."

"Ah. So it's just me you put off with that prissy 'Thank you, but no.' Now I understand."

Hester wanted to stamp her foot and shout, *No, you do not understand at all!* But of course, she could hardly explain such a thing to him.

From the first moment she'd seen Mr. Hawke, she'd recognized his appeal for what it was: pure animal magnetism. Virile male, exceedingly dangerous, and completely forbidden to most young ladies. Or he should be.

Dulcie's interest in him was understandable. But he was a mature man; Dulcie and all the eligible misses were still girls. Added to that, he did not strike her as the sort seriously searching for a wife.

Now she had to contend with this mess between him and George Bennett.

That was not the worst of it though. The worst part was the way he disturbed her. Normally she was not affected by men; she did not allow herself to be. Long ago she had learned to keep her emotions above it all and observe the men she came into contact with for what they were: insincere, greedy, and shallow. In short, most men did not affect her in the least.

But Adrian Hawke did.

The past three days she'd fought that annoying buzz of awareness he provoked in her. She'd fought it and had almost convinced herself that she'd won the battle. If she *did* feel anything for the man, it was only because he was a curiosity among the rest of society.

But now she knew differently. Though surrounded by the crush of people in the Dresdens' noisy ballroom, she felt completely alone with him. First their clash. Then his unexpected apology. Now this awkward conversation and their silent companionship. Somehow he'd created a distressing sort of intimacy between them which increased her unwonted awareness to an alarming degree.

This would never do. *He* would never do, not for

Dulcie or for herself. As Hester watched the dancers finish their set, she kept her gaze strictly away from Adrian Hawke. But the whole time she racked her brain for the date of Catherine Hawke's wedding. Two weeks from tomorrow? Or three? Whichever, God willing, Adrian Hawke would depart immediately after the ceremony. If he did not, there was no telling what havoc he might wreak.

Then, as if matters were not already awful enough, who should she see heading directly toward her but Horace Vasterling. At once her unsettled emotions turned to utter panic. First Adrian Hawke. Now her brother. Had Horace finally discovered who she was? Did he mean to confront her?

She licked her suddenly dry lips. "If you will excuse me?" she muttered to Mr. Hawke. Then with pounding heart and sweating palms, she turned and fled.

Adrian frowned at Hester Poitevant's departing backside. What in blazes was that all about? He'd been polite. He'd apologized for his previous behavior. He'd asked her to dance. Then he'd accepted her refusal with what he considered good grace. So why was she stalking away as if he'd just insulted her?

Damnation, but English women were an annoying lot!

"I say, Hawke," Catherine's beau said, coming up on Adrian's other side. "Thought you might like to meet an old school chum of mine. Horace Vasterling. Adrian Hawke. Been telling him about your new business venture, Hawke. He runs a goodly sized flock of his own, you know."

Adrian shook Vasterling's hand. A decent grip, he decided, firmer than the man's soft, somewhat slovenly appearance would indicate.

"Glad to meet you, Hawke," the man said. "Glad to meet you. The gossips say nothing but good about you. Nothing but good."

"I'm relieved to hear it," Adrian said, pushing any lingering thoughts about Mrs. Hoity-toity Poitevant to the back of his mind. English women might be incomprehensible, but the men were like men everywhere, at least in one regard: they all wanted to strike a better deal than the next fellow did. This Vasterling was no different. "So you raise sheep," Adrian said. "Where are your holdings?"

"Cumbria. We've got a flock of nearly four hundred. Though we could double that amount with the acreage we have."

"So why haven't you?"

A faint wash of color rose in Vasterling's face and it occurred to Adrian that he ought to introduce the man to the blushing Miss Bennett. Then the two of them could raise a brood of blushing little Vasterlings.

"My father is old-fashioned," the man responded. "Our weaving sheds can support only a certain amount of wool production, and he will not expand either the sheds or the flocks."

"But you wish to?"

"I do," Vasterling said with a firmness that matched his grip.

"I see," said Adrian. "Then perhaps we can do some business, for at present I'm more interested in raw wool than I am in finished cloth. That's the whole point of the textile venture I've designed."

They went off together to the smoking room, unaware of the avid gaze which followed them until they disappeared. Only then did Hester let loose the breath she'd not even known she was holding.

Horace Vasterling hadn't been coming to speak to her after all. He didn't know who she was. Relief came in a cool, hard rush, followed almost at once by an unreasoning spurt of anger. He did not know who she was, his own sister. His only sibling! How could he be so woefully ignorant of his own family history?

For a moment she allowed herself to fantasize. What if she made the four-day journey to her father's estate in Cumbria? What if she presented herself to her father as his long-missing child? Would he welcome her into the bosom of his family? Would he weep over her, so glad to have her returned to him after almost twenty-five years?

A painful feeling welled up, as she considered the sort of man her father was. Of course he wouldn't welcome her back. Nor did she want him to, unless of course it was so she could soundly reject him.

How satisfying it would be to arrive there in her own carriage with a finely matched pair, a driver, *and* a footman. To address her father in his own parlor, and then berate him for everything she'd suffered due to his indifference. For despite her mother's inconstancy, Hester had not been the one at fault. She'd been a mere child, caught between two parents whose differences her mother had regularly complained of.

Edgar Vasterling was too cold. Too disapproving. Parsimonious. Inflexible. A pinchpenny. Boring. Fixed in his thinking. And tightfisted with his money as well. That had been the crux of her mother's discontent, Hester now could see. Her mother had found her father stingy, and so had left him for a more generous fellow. It had been painful for Hester to accept that her beautiful mother's flight from her marriage had been utterly selfish. Utterly foolish. She should have found a way to do her duty as a wife and mother to both her children.

But that did not absolve Hester's father from his responsibility to his daughter.

If Hester had been a boy he would have pursued her. A man's heir, even the second or third in line, would never be given up without a fierce fight. But then, that's why her mother had chosen to leave when she did. She had delivered her husband his son and heir, and figured rightly that he wouldn't care about the older girl-child she took away with her.

But he should have cared.

Hester blinked at the sudden dampness in her eyes. Oh, no. She would not cry over her coldhearted father's perfidy. Nor over her mother's. She'd spent far too much of her childhood crying over them. She was not about to waste any of her adult years in so useless an activity.

So she drew herself up and tamped her emotions down. Horace Vasterling seemed a harmless sort. She doubted he knew anything about a sister gone missing or, probably, the true story of his mother's defection. Certainly he would not know the name Poitevant, his maternal grandmother's maiden name. Should she ever find herself face to face with her brother, Hester vowed to treat him no differently than she would any other innocuous gentleman. She would give him her cool, aloof smile, and refrain from any conversation but the mundane. She would do the same with Mr. Hawke as well, she decided when she spied Dulcie hurrying her way.

"Where is he?" the girl whispered, her face the perfect picture of youthful agony. "You let him get away?"

Hester just raised one brow. "Subtlety, Dulcie. Subtlety. It serves you ill to chase a man until he is ready to be caught. And Mr. Hawke is hardly ready for that. Besides, he's not likely to forget about your dance."

"You're certain? He didn't leave for the evening, did he?"

"Of course not."

From agony to joy to a fearful sort of hopelessness, the evolution of Dulcie's emotions showed in every aspect of her bearing. "He only asked me to dance because he's a gentleman, didn't he? Not to single me out. Oh, this isn't going to work at all. I'm far too silly and stupid for a man like him."

"You are not." It took all of Hester's efforts to bolster Dulcie's flagging self-confidence. But only for the duration of her dance with Mr. Hawke was the girl content. The next day when he did not attend the festive matinee Dulcie was invited to, she was once again in the doldrums. On the following evening at an elaborate dinner party it took every bit of Hester's encouragement to keep the heartsick girl's spirits up. So when Hester arrived home in the early hours of the following Friday, she was exhausted beyond telling.

She'd been sent home in the Ainsleys' smaller coach, an accommodation she insisted on when she knew the evening would be a long one. No need for Mr. Dobbs to wait around with her conveyance all night. As it was, Mrs. Dobbs, her housekeeper, often waited up for her, no matter the hour.

And so it was tonight. Mrs. Dobbs pushed up from her rocking chair beside the hearth in the spotless kitchen, straightening her faded nightcap and her high-necked wrapper. "Ooh, it's late you are, miss. Have you had a proper supper?"

Hester smiled at the stout little woman, then bent down to reassure her aging pets that she was indeed home. "There you go, Peg," she said, scratching her old three-legged hound. "There you go. And you, Fifi." She picked up the nervous little poodle. "Yes, Mrs. Dobbs. I've had my supper. You needn't wait for me every time I come in late."

"Pish, child. I'm a light sleeper and that's the whole of it. Not like Mr. Dobbs. That one could sleep straight through the fire of London, he could."

Again Hester smiled. They had this conversation almost every night. "So. How's our patient doing?" Hester combed her fingers gently through Fifi's shorn curls. "She looks a little better."

"She's not scratching so much. I noticed that. It appears that smelly concoction is working. Mind now, you might stain your gloves."

Hester set the little dog down. She was an ugly thing, with her back all blotchy due to great clumps of missing hair. But in spite of that she was the dearest creature, so grateful for her new home and regular meals that she had endured the shearing and subsequent application of the apothecary's recipe with trembling patience.

"And what of our nighttime visitors?"

Mrs. Dobbs frowned. "The food is gone—though why you insist on feeding those nasty street cats is beyond me."

Another familiar conversation.

Mrs. Dobbs went on, shaking her head. "You'll never be rid of them, you know. Then they'll all end up having litters in the woodshed."

"Not all of them." Hester smiled. "Not the toms, anyway."

"Huh. In my experience *all* cats is female. *All* of them. And they all have litters, one after the other. By feedin' even a few of them, you take the chance that we'll soon be swimmin' in cats. *Female* cats."

Hester smiled. "At least we won't have any vermin to contend with. You go on now. Go to bed. I can manage without you."

Mrs. Dobbs yawned and turned to comply. "Any proposals yet for our young ladies?"

"No. Not yet. But they're all three doing very well."

"They's nice girls," the woman said, trundling away. "They'll make good wives someday, thanks to you."

Hester sighed. Thanks to her? If only she could do as she truly wished and help her girls make lives for themselves independent of becoming anyone's wife. If only every well-born girl wasn't raised to think marriage and motherhood the only choices available to her.

Unfortunately, unless a girl was independently

wealthy, or else willing to live under her parents' or other relatives' rule, there really were no other options. Except for going into trade, of course. As she'd done.

She sighed once more, then started up the straight run of gleaming stairs. She supposed she was lucky. She earned a living as a tradeswoman might. But because her product was in essence the girls she worked with, she did not suffer the same taint of "being in trade" that a seamstress would, or a milliner or a cobbler. She retained the status of gentlewoman, for what that was worth. Widowed gentlewoman.

The dogs had come up the stairs behind her, Peg thumping up every step with her odd, off-centered gait. Now the two of them sat, watching with cocked heads as she shed gloves and shawl, then shoes and hose. The spruce-green dress came next, and her various petticoats and shift.

She put everything away, draping the dress and petticoats over the armoire door to air. Somber colors, simple patterns. Sometimes Hester hated the appearance she felt necessary to the success of her academy. Despite her ripe old age of twenty-eight, she knew she looked younger. That's why she wore the spectacles and such unbecoming hairstyles and clothes. Her dresses were all well made and of the finest fabrics, but unbecoming all the same. Still, since she functioned as a glorified sort of governess, and was supposedly a widow, she had to dress the part.

But only when she worked. The rest of the time—her time—she could dress as she pleased. So, smiling, she pulled a pale aqua-green night rail and wrapper from the armoire. She'd sewn them herself from nine yards of the most expensive India cloth Mr. Connair's dry goods store had ever carried. It was downy soft with a fluid hand, a luxury to be sure. But worth every penny, she thought each night when she put it on. After a long evening in somber green, a night spent in airy aqua with silk embroidered flowers, delicate pin tucks, and cunningly drawn threads seemed only fair.

She let down her hair and massaged her fingertips along the sore spots of her scalp where the pins had pulled too tightly. Ah, that felt good. She'd been working awfully long hours with three demanding families. But not tomorrow. Tomorrow was her day off, and she would dress as she pleased. She would visit the booksellers and the apothecary shop. And the sweet shop. Mr. Dobbs's birthday was next week and he had a weakness for chocolate and peppermints.

Fifi hopped up onto the bed. "Oh, no you don't," Hester said, and promptly lifted her down. The petite creature ignored her and hopped right back up. They repeated that scenario three more times before Hester gave up. Then, of course, she could not bear poor Peg's long face and had to heft her up onto the bed too.

She found a space between the two dogs and slipped beneath the cool sheets, perfectly content, she told herself. Between her sweet little house, her loyal servants, her adoring pets, and her work at her popular academy, she had everything an independent-minded woman could want.

But when she slept and when she dreamed, it was not of contentment or of young girls successfully shaped into suitable young brides. She dreamed instead of an aqua-green ball gown and dancing every dance with a succession of handsome, admiring men. And if all of them were tall with wide shoulders and thick black hair—and a broad American accent flavored faintly of the Scottish countryside—well, it was only a dream.

To his surprise, Adrian actually liked Horace Vasterling. They'd met twice now since their introduction, and he was impressed with the man's practical intelligence.

Though he looked a soft, muddle-headed sort of fellow, it was a false impression. It was only his aging father that Vasterling seemed unable to manage—a common problem for first sons waiting to inherit. Still, like him or not, if the man could not get his father to agree to Adrian's proposal, the Vasterlings would not be able to participate in Adrian's textile cooperative.

They exited Vasterling's club, an unpretentious place just off Aldersgate Street in Cheapside. "As the figures show, it could take three years to build your flocks if you decide not to purchase outside stock," Adrian said. "During that time you'll lose the profit on mutton. Once you have sufficient wool production to join our co-operative, you'll more than make up for the first few years' losses. But if you could purchase the additional breeding stock now, the amount of time till you turn a profit will be considerably reduced."

"Hmm. Yes, I see," Vasterling said. "Fortunately we had a very good lambing season. Well, I shall present these figures to Father next week."

"You're not staying in London for the duration of the season?"

The man coughed. "I have been honest with you about my financial picture, so you will understand why I am not presently on anyone's list of the most eligible bachelors. My father expects me to marry a girl with a generous dowry. My mother had very little, you see. But he is sadly out of touch with the realities of the marriage mart. Families with those sorts of fortunes want more impressive titles or more impressive estates for their investments. I've been firmly reminded more than once that when I marry it will have to be a younger daughter of a lesser lord, or else someone who loves me for other than the great fortune I do not possess." He gave a wry grin. "Of course, I could wait another three years until my profits come in. Perhaps then I could snag a well-fixed bride my father could approve of."

"When your profits come in you won't need a well-fixed bride with a big dowry." Adrian shook his head, not understanding this English system of strategic marriages. "Besides, would it be so bad to marry a woman for love, one who actually loves you as well? Not one of these fashion plates whose marriages are contracted with no more emotion than you and I conduct our business dealings."

"I suspect it would be wonderful," the man conceded. "And I should like nothing better. But as his heir, I have a duty to my father and to our estate. But enough of that. Tell me, are you also shopping for a bride?"

"Me? Oh, no, I'm in no rush to wed. And when I do take that step, it certainly won't be to an English woman—no offense meant."

"None taken. Actually, I am encouraged that you are holding out for love."

Holding out for love? That's not what Adrian had said, nor what he meant. While he'd seen one or two examples of wedded couples who loved one another, he suspected they were a rarity. American society was not unlike British society in that regard. When and if he wed it would probably be for lust, to a woman he could not possess any other way.

Then he scoffed at that ridiculous thought. If he could not have some particular woman he wanted, he would just find another he wanted more. When he did finally wed, it would most likely be for practical purposes. No one wanted to grow old alone. Even his own brazen mother had finally settled down.

"I guess every man wants an heir," he finally said.

"Yes," Horace agreed. "I certainly do."

They paused at a busy corner, waiting for a coal cart to rumble past. That's when Adrian spied an elegant figure exiting a bookshop, an elegant figure both familiar and strange.

At first he wasn't certain it was she. Her walking dress was ivory and salmon stripes with a dark salmon-colored jacket. She wore a nearly brimless bonnet, and her hair was loose and bouncy beneath it.

Bouncy and soft. Imagine that.

He didn't move when Vasterling started forward; he was too captivated by the image before him. The Widow Poitevant, looking more like one of the carefree young ladies she tutored than the severe companion she portrayed by night.

"I say, Hawke. Aren't you coming?"

"Perhaps not."

Horace Vasterling followed the direction of Adrian's gaze. "Oh, I see. Do you know her, then?"

"Yes." *And no.* "Have you never met Mrs. Poitevant? No? Well, you should. It's her business to make brides of awkward young girls. And to be a bride, a girl must find a groom. Come along," he added, when she merged into the flow along the sidewalk. *Was she alone?* "I'll introduce you."

Hester adjusted the ribbon ties of her bonnet as she waited to cross the street. She had returned her books to the lending library and now had to stop at the greengrocers and also at Murray's Sweet Shop. She never visited Mrs. DeLisle without bringing her some sort of sweet treat.

But when a voice hailed her and she looked up, her heart leaped in her chest, then started a terrible clamoring there. Not Adrian Hawke. Not here, in Cheapside where she shopped for the pure pleasure of not running into anyone of the *ton*. And not when she was dressed in her most stylish, carefree manner.

Then her frozen wits registered the man beside him, and her distress turned to outright panic. It could not be!

Of all the men in London, the two she should most like *not* to meet. But there was no avoiding them.

"Mrs. Poitevant." Adrian Hawke doffed his hat, grinning at her in that smug, satisfied way he had. Very wolfish, and she felt like a vulnerable little lamb. "What an unexpected pleasure. You are looking particularly fetching today." His eyes, full of devilment, swept over her, head to toe. Though brief, his gaze was alarmingly thorough, and felt entirely too intimate. But then, what else should she expect, given their previous two encounters and her very different appearance?

Worse than his cheeky American greeting, however, was the frankly admiring gaze of the man at his side. Horace Vasterling. So unanticipated was their meeting that she could not recall any of the admonitions she'd given herself regarding the possibility someday of an introduction to her own brother. When Mr. Hawke presented him to her, she blushed to the roots of her hair.

So did he. "I'm very pleased to make your acquaintanceship, Mrs. Poitevant," he murmured, doffing his hat to her.

Mr. Hawke's keen eyes darted from Hester to Horace Vasterling, then back again. "I'm amazed that you two have not already met. You seem to receive invitations to many of the same parties." He squinted at her. "Are you overly warm, Miss Poitevant?"

"No." She cleared her voice. "No, I'm not warm." *You just caught me unawares.*

"I . . . I believe I may have seen you at the Dresdens' ball earlier this week?" Horace said, his voice rising in question.

"Yes." She cleared her throat. "Yes, I was there. Were you?" *Oh, what a stupid thing to say. He already said he was there.*

"Yes."

Adrian watched their exchange with some bemusement. All was not as it appeared. Vasterling turning out to be sharp as a tack. Mrs. Poitevant looking prettier than the girls she shepherded through the season. And both of them blushing at each other. Was the bridemaker looking to become a bride?

If she dressed like this all the time, showing off her curving figure, that sweet cream complexion, and that staggering quantity of luscious, shining hair, he wagered she'd be wedded—and bedded—faster than any of her girls. And then there was that husky voice of hers. A bedroom voice.

Without warning desire pooled, hot and hard in his loins, and he shifted uncomfortably from one foot to the other. This was damned inconvenient. If poor Vasterling's reaction was anything like his own, no wonder the man was blushing. Truth be told, were he in the market for a wife himself, he'd certainly give the Widow Poitevant more than a passing glance.

He wasn't in the market for a bride though. But Vasterling was.

Adrian slanted a look at Horace. No doubt about it, the man was definitely smitten. He looked as though someone had just boxed his ears—and he'd liked it! But how did Mrs. Poitevant feel about him?

"And . . . and . . ." Poor Horace was stumbling over his words now. "And shall you be at the Murchisons' fete on Tuesday?"

"Um . . . I believe I may be there," she finally answered.

Vasterling blinked, then swallowed hard. "I hope . . . I hope you will save a dance for me?"

Instead of appearing flattered, however, Mrs. Poitevant's expression screwed up in a horrified expression. "Thank you . . . Thank you, but . . . but no. I'm afraid not." She spoke so stiffly it bordered on rudeness. Then, "Good day," and she turned and left.

Like poor Horace, Adrian could only stare at her stiff back as she hurried away. "What in bloody blazes was that all about?" he muttered.

"I was too forward," Horace berated himself. "I had only just met her and I acted like an idiot."

"You did nothing wrong," Adrian countered. But as for Miss Stiff-necked Poitevant, she had no cause to insult a man as good-natured as Horace Vasterling. Stunning as she looked in her pretty dress and softened appearance, she was still the severe bridemaker, judging men by their title and money, and dismissing fine fellows like Horace Vasterling as being unworthy of a simple dance.

Even before Hester disappeared around a corner, his resolve hardened. She didn't approve of Vasterling for herself, nor of Adrian for Dulcie Bennett. Like that fool George Bennett, she held staunchly to the rigid rules of her society, rules that kept the classes distinct and apart from one another.

But he didn't believe in those rules, and he'd be damned if he'd abide by them.

He turned to Vasterling, whose face had settled into lines of forlorn resignation. "The Murchisons' fete, you say? I believe I may also have received an invitation to that."

Horace brightened. "And shall you go then? They say the Murchisons' wine cellar is legendary."

"I'll be there," Adrian replied, glancing one last time in the direction Hester Poitevant had taken. "I wouldn't miss it for the world."

CHAPTER 6

By the time Hester arrived in Milton Street, she had herself under better control. But it was a struggle. Had she not sent word ahead to Mrs. DeLisle that she would call on her today, she would have cut her outing short.

Even now, nearly an hour later, she could not believe that terrible, terrible scene with her brother. And of all people, Adrian Hawke a witness to everything!

She pressed her embroidered handkerchief to her lips as the carriage swayed to a halt. Oh, but she'd behaved like a perfect fool. A graceless dolt. A stuttering idiot. To even remember the awkwardness, the embarrassment, made her want to cry.

How was she to behave when next she saw them? Either of them?

There was no way she could avoid them. While Horace might justifiably keep a safe distance from her after the awful set-down she'd given him, she knew with a sinking certainty that Adrian Hawke would not. Indeed, she feared he would do just the opposite.

She gave Mr. Dobbs a distracted look when he handed her down from the chaise. "I shall be an hour at least. If you go round to the kitchen, I'm sure they'll give you tea."

"A'right, miss. Just you have a good visit with Mrs. DeLisle."

The front door to the narrow little townhouse opened before she reached the front steps. "Hester!" came Verna DeLisle's happy cry. "Don't you look pretty as a picture."

Except for her cane, Mrs. DeLisle appeared very much the same as she had the first time Hester met her. A good twelve years had passed since that day, and certainly Hester had changed. But not Mrs. DeLisle. The only change to her was that she had retired from her Mayfair Academy, leaving it to Hester six years ago.

"So," the elegant old woman said, scrutinizing Hester from head to toe and back again. "It's salmon today. What a pretty color for you. I wonder though." Her eyes narrowed. "Is it the color of your dress or the heat of the day which has your cheeks glowing so?"

"Neither, I'm afraid." Hester advanced into the tiny but perfectly appointed parlor. She removed her bonnet and gloves, tossed them onto a pink damask slipper chair, then collapsed onto the ornately carved settee. "I have had the most dreadful, dreadful day."

Verna DeLisle had known Hester since she was a green girl. She'd known her frivolous mother as well, and she'd worried terribly at Isabelle's ill-advised plan to give her daughter a proper season.

Really, but the woman had been so insensitive to her situation. Had she actually believed that the child of a woman of suspect morals could ever enjoy a normal season? Had she honestly thought her daughter's stunning beauty enough to raise her above the back-stabbing and small-minded gossip that made up so much of what passed for good society? Why couldn't she have encouraged Hester to marry a soldier or a merchant or some other reasonably ambitious, hard-working fellow? Why must it only be a lord?

But Verna knew why. Isabelle had been a tradesman's daughter from the north of England, so of course she'd never had a season of her own. After running away from her husband with her first lover, then moving on to London with her second one, Isabelle had created an entirely new identity for herself. As Hester had grown up, Isabelle had become determined to give her daughter a proper season and to find herself a rich, well-connected son-in-law.

It had been the height of foolishness, but she'd been adamant. Of course, Hester had been the one to pay the price for her mother's single-minded determination. Not a single honorable offer, but there had been plenty of vulgar ones. Added to that Hester had been gossiped about, ostracized, and made to feel simply horrid.

Still, something good had come of that awful season and a half. For in her grief and humiliation, Hester had turned away from her self-absorbed mother and impulsively taken a teaching position in York. She'd returned to London only after her mother's sudden death. That's when she had sought out Verna's comfort, and that's when they'd hatched their plan to turn Hester into a bereaved widow.

In the years that followed, the relationship forged between Verna and Hester had benefited them both. Hester had come to work at the academy, then eventually taken over when Verna retired. As time went by Hester had altered the academy's purpose somewhat, placing as much emphasis on appearance and self-confidence as on the practical niceties of manners, and presentations and all the rules attendant to them. But Verna hadn't minded the changes. The girl had created a unique place for herself in society, and Verna was proud of her.

Were it not for Hester's continued disdain of all men,

and her suspicion of their motives, Verna might consider both their lives perfectly arranged.

But Hester was determined to be nothing like her mother. That's why she insisted on maintaining such a dour image in all her dealings with the *ton*. The fact remained, however, that Hester was not happy, and now something had upset her more than usual.

So Verna seated herself, then rang her little enamel bell for tea. "My goodness, child, it's been years since you've flung yourself into a chair like some great, ill-mannered country girl. Perhaps you'd better tell me just what has put you in such a tizzy."

Verna listened without comment. So at last brother and sister had met. She'd known eventually it must happen, and that Hester would not deal well with it. But it was Hester's constant reference to this other man, this Scotsman lately come from America, that most piqued Verna's curiosity.

"I am a little confused," she said once the girl had subsided. "I understand your aversion to Horace's unwitting interest in you. For that reason alone I believe you must tell him the truth. Wait," she said, holding up one hand when Hester would have interrupted. "Let me finish. Eventually you must reveal yourself to your brother," she repeated. "But presently I am more interested in this other fellow. I cannot determine from what you've said whether you approve of him or not." She stared at Hester's stubbornly frowning face. "So. Which is it?"

Hester sighed. Then she let her head fall against the settee back and closed her eyes. "I . . . I'm not certain. I mean . . . Well . . . It's complicated."

"Is it?" Verna smiled to herself. Well, well. A man who could put her serious young friend into a fluster. He must be quite an exceptional fellow. "You haven't touched your tea."

Hester opened her eyes, then straightened up. She sent Verna a quelling look. "I know what you're thinking, but you're wrong. It's just so . . . so complicated. One of my students has convinced herself she is in love with the man, only her mother finds him completely unsuitable. No title, you see."

"Oh, these women and their machinations. Don't they know there is life beyond the *ton*?"

Hester didn't even bother answering that question. She went on, "Added to that, Dulcie's brother, George, and this Mr. Hawke seem to have bad history between them. Schoolboy conflicts, that sort of thing. It's obvious to me that Mr. Hawke's attentions to Dulcie are motivated solely by revenge."

She paused and rubbed one of her temples. "The very worst part is that the Ainsley fortune is apparently hamstrung by debt. So naturally Dulcie's brother has decided to reverse himself. He now proposes throwing Dulcie at the man in hopes of gaining some sort of financial benefit."

Verna arched her brows. "This Adrian Hawke fellow must be awfully rich."

"Not just rich, he also has a knack for making money. He's come here to solicit investors for some new sort of venture. And George wants in."

"Do you think Lord Ainsley's scheme will succeed?"

Hester shook her head. "Not at all. Poor Dulcie is caught between two warring men, and as a result, so am I. My new instructions from her family are to promote her association with Mr. Hawke, when it's plain as day he's not the marrying sort."

"How can you know that?"

Hester bent forward to lift her teacup. She drank, grimacing at how tepid it had become, then set it down. "Mr. Hawke is one of those roguish fellows. You know the type. There's always one or two of them each season who sets all the girls' hearts aquiver. Handsome. Properly turned out, but with a rakish bent that cannot quite be disguised."

"Oho. The manly sort, no doubt."

Verna saw Hester sigh. "Very." She was silent a moment. "Naturally Dulcie is in a complete dither over him."

And perhaps someone else is as well. Again Verna smiled to herself. It was long past time for Hester to fall in love and marry. Verna did not normally hold love to be a prerequisite for a successful marriage. Common interests, compatible personalities, similar beliefs and morals—those were what made for a solid, reliable marriage.

But she also recognized that in some circumstances love was the only thing powerful enough to bring certain parties together.

In Hester's case, the girl had convinced herself long ago that men were never to be trusted. Not fathers. Not brothers. Certainly not potential husbands.

She had good reason for her fears, of course. But not all men were so untrustworthy. Logic, however, would never convince Hester of that. It would take something much stronger, much harder to resist. Hester was one of those women who must fall in love and receive love in return. For her it would be the only way.

Maybe this Scottish American was the answer.

"So," Verna said. "Dulcie Bennett wants this Adrian Hawke. Who do you think he wants?"

Hester straightened up, tugged her bodice down, and smoothed her skirts across her knees before replying. "I'm sure I don't know what is in his mind other than revenge against George Bennett. Did I tell you? He refuses to refer to him as Lord Ainsley. George didn't like that one bit." She smiled, but it faded away. "At least he won't be here for long. Once his cousin is wed I understand he's to return to America. Poor Dulcie. She and who knows how many others will be left with broken hearts."

"Tut, tut. I'm sure they'll recover."

"Yes, I suppose they'll have to." Hester was silent a moment. "Perhaps then I'll be able to find her a more suitable man, preferably someone halfway between her family's strict requirements and her own romantic ones."

"Perhaps so. It sounds as if you have everything perfectly under control."

"How can you say that? He is bound to quiz me about my appearance today."

Verna smiled, rather pleased with this turn of events. "I told you long ago to give up that somber black and gray business. Didn't I? It simply isn't necessary. Perhaps now you'll listen to me."

Hester scowled. "How can you still believe that after today? This just proves why I must maintain my straitlaced-widow image. When these self-indulgent men of the *ton* spy an attractive woman, especially one like me, without a husband or other protector, they become relentless in their pursuit."

Verna waved one of her hands. "You could acquire a protector easily enough."

Hester stiffened. "I am *not* like my mother."

"I meant your brother."

That took the wind out of Hester's sails, but only for a moment. "I can hardly do that. No. It's unthinkable."

Verna shook her head. "Hester, when will you come to see that instead of spying on the fellow, you ought to be truthful with him?"

If anything, Hester's expression grew even more mulish. "Be truthful with him?" She rolled her eyes, but then she sighed and in a muffled tone said, "I'll think about it." She reached for her bonnet. "For now, however, I will just have to discourage him."

Verna suppressed a smile. Finally, a crack in the walls

of Hester's self-imposed exile from her family. But all she said to the young woman was, "If poor Horace is as awkward and unsure of himself as you have described, I suspect he shall not come anywhere near you, not after the cold manner with which you treated him today."

No, he probably would not, Hester thought as she took her leave of Mrs. DeLisle. She'd probably frightened him off for good.

But as for Adrian Hawke, she already knew that nothing would frighten him off. And if the curious, assessing look in his eyes was any indication, she feared he would soon be seeking an explanation for today's fiasco—both for her rudeness, and also the striking alteration in her appearance.

The next day Hester was even more convinced of that fact.

She'd had a poor night's sleep. Peg had whimpered in canine dreams the entire night, exciting Fifi as well. Then a cat had yowled outside her window off and on. Come the dawn she'd arisen with a headache, which was not improving as she stared at the contents of her armoire.

What was she to wear to the Murchisons' fete tonight? No matter her selection, plain or pretty, Adrian Hawke was sure to confront her.

Dressing for her work had never been a problem in the past. She'd ascertained long ago that potential clients expected a certain air of sobriety and experience from her. A too pretty, too youthful woman was suspect to them, so she'd turned herself into a serious woman of indeterminate age. She'd acquired a series of dark dresses—spruce green, deep burgundy, charcoal gray— all made from simple patterns. Her only concession to style was the quality of the fabrics she used: the best wools, the softest muslins, and the richest silks.

She'd worn the green and the burgundy most recently. So tonight would be the gray, a simple enough decision. Yet she rebelled at the thought, and her gaze insisted on straying to the other side of the armoire where additional gowns and day dresses hung. The salmon outfit from yesterday was her current favorite, but there was also a gorgeous aqua ensemble and a striking cream and teal confection. They were old dresses, some from the days of her own season, and other reworked gowns that had been her mother's.

Her mother had worn only the best. Delicate Saracen cloth shot with gold, watered silk embroidered with doves and ivy leaves, silvery lace, and soft-as-butter velvet. Then there were also the braids and ribbons, buttons and other gewgaws.

Hester had inherited them all, four massive trunks stuffed with her mother's dearest possessions.

Sometimes she opened those trunks simply to smell the slowly fading scent of French perfumes and dusting powders. She would lean over the trunk and inhale, and remember the best parts of life with her mother: the pride of having the most beautiful mother in the world; the excitement when her mother was happy and in love.

But her mother's mercurial appeal had held a dark side too. The petulance. The selfishness. The angry outbursts and storms of tears.

So sometimes Hester hated the very sight of those trunks. Sometimes she wanted to tell Mr. Dobbs to load them into the coach and deliver them to the second-hand shops for whatever paltry amount they might choose to pay.

The only time she'd gone so far as to give Mr. Dobbs those instructions, however, Mrs. Dobbs had promptly countermanded them. Caught between his employer's orders and his wife's, Mr. Dobbs had retreated in confusion to the nearest public house, leaving Hester and Mrs. Dobbs to work things out.

Mrs. Dobbs, of course, had won.

So the trunks remained in the extra room. And Hester remained in a quandary before her own armoire, clutching the gray taffeta dress, but staring at the aqua muslin. She knew what Mrs. DeLisle would say.

Behind her a thump, thump, thump signaled poor Peg's awkward attempt at scratching her ear. "What do you say, Peg?" Hester bent over and scratched the itchy ear for the grateful dog. "Shall I shock the ton and abandon my severe garb for once?"

Peg did not answer, of course. She was too busy luxuriating at being scratched, her favorite pastime. Fifi, however, was more responsive. She waddled over to the open armoire, stared up at the clothes as if she truly were considering, then let out a plaintive whine.

"You're French," Hester said, "so I know you have an opinion."

But Fifi's opinion was impossible to interpret and with a smile Hester stooped down to stroke the tiny animal's slowly healing back. "I think you shall be quite pretty once your fur grows back," she murmured to the affectionate little dog. "Then I shall brush you and trim you into the prissy little thing you long to be. Shall I give you bows above your ears and paint your toenails red?"

Peg limped over to reclaim her share of Hester's attention. "Yes, yes. You are a beauty too," Hester cooed to the ungainly old mutt. "You have beautiful, loving eyes, and a beautiful spirit as well."

When Hester rose to face the armoire again, she reached reluctantly for the gray dress. To wear one of her pretty dresses would be too drastic a change. But like scruffy little Fifi, perhaps she might benefit from a different coiffure. Maybe she would even go so far as to abandon her spectacles.

Still and all, as she prepared herself to accompany Dulcie to the Murchisons' annual fete, she knew she would have to deal with Adrian Hawke tonight. One way or the other he was bound to challenge her behavior the other day. And her appearance.

But she was ready for him, she vowed.

She sighed, then collected her spectacles after all. She would avoid Adrian Hawke when she could and keep Dulcie or Anabelle or Charlotte near her the rest of the time.

And if pushed, she would plead a headache and retire to the ladies' room.

Adrian spied Hester Poitevant the moment she entered the Murchisons' vast ballroom. Amid the pastel fluttering of so many giddy girls and the dandies that fluttered around them, she appeared an island of calm, tall and serene and more enigmatic than ever.

He'd had a busy day, securing warehouses and drawing up contracts for several investors already committed to his venture. But business had not been enough to make him forget about his run-in with Hester. In fact, with every passing hour he'd become more and more keen to unravel the mystery of London's so-called Bridemaker.

Something was not right about her situation. The dreary widow and the sparkling woman he'd seen in Cheapside seemed impossible to reconcile—except that they were both, at their core, the same nose-in-the-air snob.

She did not look quite so dreary tonight, however. He peered more intently at her. What was it? Certainly not the dress, which appeared left over from her days of mourning. But something . . .

Her hair. It was not so severe, not scraped back into that painfully tight chignon. She did have on her spectacles, though.

What a cunning little deceiver.

He watched her come down the short run of steps. She moved like a queen, head up and back straight, but not stiff. She glided, almost as if her feet did not have to take steps like other women did.

He supposed she had to present a good example to the girls she advised. Certainly Miss Bennett moved in a graceful enough manner. The girl's gaze flitted frequently to her mentor, and as Adrian watched, Miss Bennett adjusted both her movements and her bearing to mirror Hester's.

Hester Poitevant. What game are you playing?

Her hair looked incredibly soft, not as loose and luxuriant as yesterday, but silky and gleaming in the lamplit ballroom. *Touchable,* the aberrant thought struck him.

"Look there, Hawke. There she is," Horace Vasterling said in a half-whisper. "D'you think I should approach her tonight? You know, apologize for my offensive behavior yesterday?"

"Apologize to her? Why in blazes should you owe *her* an apology? She was the rude one." Then spying the indecision on Horace's face, he relented. "Look. Let me approach her first. She and I have a longer acquaintance between us, so perhaps I can ascertain her mood." Besides, there was no need for Horace to be rejected again, for Adrian was sure that's what Mrs. Poitevant would do. He had a suspicion that if even the "Bridemaker" rejected him, and in so public a venue, Horace's reputation would be undermined even further.

It was a revelation to Adrian that a baron's son like Horace could be so ill at ease in town. Yet he was coming to see that even within the *ton*, some people just did not measure up.

He wouldn't normally care. But Horace was a decent fellow, not defined by arrogance and greed like most of his peers. Though it was illogical, Adrian didn't want to see the man humiliated again, especially not by the irksome Widow Poitevant.

"Enjoy yourself, but stay strictly away from her and her charges," Adrian told Horace. "I'll let you know how matters stand as soon as I figure them out."

He took his time approaching. He wanted her to know he was coming, to be flustered by his slow but relentless approach.

It worked. Wherever he went, her gaze followed, flitting away when he stared back at her, but always returning to him. She surrounded herself with people, at all times keeping someone nearby. But if she thought that could protect her from him, she was dead wrong.

When he decided finally to make his move, she was conversing with Miss Bennett, whose gaze also kept returning to him. The perfect invitation.

"Good evening, Miss Bennett." He bowed over the girl's hand. "Mrs. Poitevant," he added in a cooler tone. She did not extend her hand. He did not bow.

"Oh, Mr. Hawke. I was hoping to see you tonight," Miss Bennett gushed. Though her customary blush rose as fiery as ever, she seemed more self-assured than in the past. How it must gall Mrs. Poitevant to see all her efforts with Miss Bennett directed now on the wrong sort of man. It served her right for being such a snob.

He smiled down at Miss Bennett. "I may spend my days involved with matters of business, but I try to keep my evenings for more pleasant activities." He paused a moment, for effect. Then, "If your dance card is not already filled, it would be my pleasure to partner you in a dance."

Adrian thought the poor girl was going to pop. But after a few false starts she took a great gulp of air. "How

. . . How nice of you to offer. I have the third dance of the second set free," she said with almost painful correctness. "A polka."

"Thank you. I look forward to it."

When he turned to Mrs. Poitevant, however, he did not find the disapproving frown he expected. A little pucker creased her brow just above the line of her spectacles. But it looked more like confusion than anything else. Did she fear she might get called down by Miss Bennett's mother or by Georgie-boy if they saw Dulcie dancing with him? He hoped she did.

Without pausing to consider his words he said, "I wonder, Mrs. Poitevant, if you too would be gracious enough to grant me one dance."

Where Miss Bennett's blush was hot and fiery, Mrs. Poitevant's was subtle and restrained. Much like she was.

"Please," he added, when she did not immediately respond. From the corner of his eye he saw Miss Bennett poke her mentor. The student guiding the teacher?

"Thank you, but . . . but no."

"Do you not know how to dance?" He turned to Miss Bennett with a grin. "Doesn't she know how to dance?"

"She dances very well," the girl said, entering into the spirit of his banter. "I have only seen her dance the male part, though. That's how she helped me to improve my steps."

Mrs. Poitevant pursed her lips. "Dulcie!"

"Is that so? Well, then, she must surely need a refresher in how to dance the female part."

"I agree." Miss Bennett smiled, revealing a sparkle he'd not previously seen. "If she starts to lead, just whisper at her to stop."

"What do you say, Mrs. Poitevant? Do not disappoint me when I am so eager."

Like a fox cornered by a persistent hound, Hester felt

a sudden spurt of panic. He was trying to unsettle her, and he was succeeding awfully well. Were it up to her, she would turn the man down, and none too nicely either. But that would require too many explanations to Dulcie.

And then, who knew what tales he might spread about their meeting in Cheapside yesterday?

She slanted him a look and saw the challenging light in his eyes. He was full of questions. Maybe she should simply get the interrogation over with.

"Very well," she said, before she could change her mind.

The slow grin of triumph that spread across his face forced Hester to acknowledge the other reason she was accepting his invitation, the dangerous, extremely unwise reason she was accepting: she wanted to see how it felt to dance with Adrian Hawke.

Such insanity! But the fact was that the man had an aura about him, a virility that was as enticing as it was terrifying. Though she had no intention of succumbing to his blatant appeal, she was conscious of an irrational need to prove herself impervious to it. To prove it to him as well as to herself.

He was the first real test she'd had since she'd sworn off men. If she could resist him, she figured she was safe forever.

"Very well," he echoed, his dark blue eyes locking with hers so that she could not quite look away.

Fortunately Tonleigh's heir appeared to retrieve Dulcie for the next dance. As the men were introduced, Hester looked away from Mr. Hawke with relief. Once alone with him, however, with the musicians warming up, the danger of her situation became clear.

He held out his arm to her. "Shall we?" he said, a wolfish gleam in his eyes.

She took a slow, shaky breath and lifted her chin to an arrogant angle. "Yes. Perhaps we should."

CHAPTER 7

Not once during their dance was Hester conscious of her movements. Not the steps, not the music, not the other dancers around them.

It *would* be a waltz, was her last coherent thought as they advanced to the floor and positioned themselves among the other couples. After that her thoughts revolved around another set of sensations entirely. Beneath the fine woven wool of his sleeve his arm was hard and warm. His grasp on her gloved hand was sure and even warmer.

He smelled faintly of tobacco and . . . and peppermint, she decided after a couple of surreptitious sniffs. Though he was a big man, he was utterly at ease with the graceful movements of the waltz. No doubt he had lots of experience with lots of other dance partners.

She peered up at his face, far too near her own. No man should possess such ridiculously long lashes, she thought. It wasn't fair when deserving girls like poor Anabelle possessed practically none.

"I like your hair," he remarked. "It's prettier than your

usual style, though not nearly so attractive as how you wore it yesterday."

Hester forced herself to focus not on his physical nearness but on his challenging tone. If he meant to intimidate her, he would soon find that she was not easily intimidated. Not by men of the *ton,* anyway.

"Hmm. I wonder, is it your intention to compliment me with such a remark or insult me?"

He grinned. "That's up to you. Running into you in Cheapside was a most enlightening experience. You appear to be a woman of some mystery."

Here it was, the beginning of his inquisition. "I assure you I am not."

"Come now, even putting aside the remarkable alteration in your appearance, there is the astounding fact of your actually setting foot in Cheapside. Considering your disdain of the lower classes, I could hardly believe it was you rubbing elbows with the folk in that part of town."

"I . . . I do not disdain anyone!"

He shook his head as if dismissing her protest. "I wonder if you encourage your students to follow your example. Somehow I can't see any of your girls strolling those teeming streets. High Street, yes. Oxford, certainly. But Aldersgate Street in Cheapside?" He lifted one dark brow as he spun her in a swift turn. "So, why was the arrogant Hester Poitevant in Cheapside, dressed in a manner so unlike her normal fashion?"

Hester could hardly keep her balance, let alone think how to answer him. That he thought her attractive in her pretty salmon ensemble was no great surprise. She knew what attracted men and he was, after all, a man. The fact that he thought her too arrogant to set foot in Cheapside, however, upset her. If he only knew the truth.

But he didn't, and he never could.

All the same, it bothered her that he thought her arrogant. It was enough to leave her utterly discombobulated. She couldn't let him rattle her, though. All she had to do was answer his questions. The best lie was no lie at all, only a variation on the truth. So she rallied her nerves as he spun her about, and stared straight into his unnerving blue eyes. "I was in Cheapside to shop and to visit an old family friend. I go there often."

"How very good of you," he said in a faintly mocking tone. "And what a fine example you set for your students. I wonder, though, do you have specific requirements? You know, two sick calls a month; one hospital visit; an afternoon spent folding bandages or packing food baskets or other such charitable works?" Again he spun her until she was breathless.

"You are too vigorous, Mr. Hawke. I will answer your inquiry, though I do not believe it sincere on your part. Charitable works are not a part of my responsibility to my students. Their parents are well able to cover that portion of their education. I strive only to give them confidence and poise—"

"While indoctrinating them in the importance of class distinction." He pulled her closer than he ought. "You, Mrs. Poitevant, are a snob."

"I am not!" She tried to pull away, to no avail. *First arrogant; now a snob?*

"You were inexcusably rude to Horace Vasterling. What was that if not snobbery?"

Hester had no reply, at least none she was willing to share with Adrian Hawke. "I am sorry if my behavior seemed rude. I assure you, I did not intend to insult him."

"Really?" His hand shifted at the small of her back, his fingers splaying out in a most disturbing manner. More heat. If this dance did not soon end, she would begin to perspire in a most improper fashion. Already she felt a suspicious trickle between her breasts.

She had to take control of the conversation. So she steeled herself and assumed her haughtiest tone. "If you have such a poor opinion of me, I wonder that you seek out my company now."

Again his hand shifted. He did that on purpose!

"The woman I seek is the woman I met in Cheapside. The pretty one dressed all in salmon with her hair soft and delicious looking."

Delicious looking!

Those two words should not have made Hester shiver, but they did. They were just the deliberately chosen words of a practiced seducer, she told herself. No more blatant than a hundred other compliments she'd received from men of the *ton*. But those other compliments had come nearly ten years ago. If Adrian Hawke's words affected her now, it must be that she was out of practice. She hadn't been subject to such compliments in a very long time.

"It has always been my routine to dress in a fashion appropriate to my activities."

He nodded. "I see. So yesterday you were dressed to please, not your students and their families, but someone else. Your old family friend." He arched one dark brow in that aggravating manner he had. "A man, perhaps?"

"No!" She stopped so abruptly another couple nearly collided with them. But though they no longer danced, he held her still in a dancer's embrace.

"It seems, Mrs. Poitevant, that I have touched upon a sensitive subject."

Her heart raced with anger and frustration—and also panic. Though why she should feel panicked she did not know. The music continued endlessly. The dancers swept past them on either side, like a river parting and rushing past a boulder stuck in midstream.

"I am done with dancing," she hissed, conscious of

the curious looks cast their way. Dowdy Hester Poitevant and the charismatic Mr. Hawke. Good heavens, but
the talk would be awful. "Release my hand," she ordered.

But he did not. "It would be extremely rude of me to
abandon you in the middle of the ballroom floor. I shudder to think what people like you say about any man
who could be so crude and ill-mannered. I'll be happy
to escort you off the floor, however. Perhaps to the refreshment tables. I wouldn't want anyone to gossip about
your abrupt departure from my company. Would you?"

The devil lurked in his eyes, dark and laughing at her.
Had she not so many responsibilities to Dulcie, Anabelle, and Charlotte, and a reputation to maintain for the
academy's sake, Hester would have left him flat. Maybe
she would even have slapped him. After all, the cad had
implied that her visit to Cheapside was for some unsa-
vory purpose.

But she couldn't take that risk. "Very well," she muttered. She regretted it when, still laughing, he took her
arm and steered her to the side. The way he held her
arm had a disturbing intimacy to it. She'd strolled arm
in arm with dozens of men in the past. But even the
boldest had not unsettled her by just the feel of his arm
next to hers. The distressing thought occurred that if he
was like this around every woman he danced with, it
was no wonder half the unattached women in town
mooned over him.

She tried once more, out of stubbornness, to disengage her arm from his. But he clamped his hand over
hers.

"You needn't run off so fast, Hester. Mrs. Poitevant,"
he amended when she glared at him. "I saw a mutual
acquaintance of ours, someone I know you will wish to
greet in your friendliest, kindest manner."

Hester's heart leapt into her throat, and her gaze

darted frantically about. She knew precisely to whom he referred. Yet still she hoped she was mistaken.

Of course, she was not. For there stood Horace Vasterling, just a little distance away. His expression as he stared at her was doubtful until Mr. Hawke waved him over.

"Be polite," her nemesis whispered, so close his breath tickled her ear. Again she shivered.

She leaned away from him. "I'm always polite."

But she hadn't been polite to Horace yesterday. He seemed such a harmless sort. No wonder Adrian Hawke thought her an arrogant, class-conscious snob.

She swallowed hard and watched her brother's wary approach. She must be pleasant to him. But no matter what Adrian Hawke thought, she couldn't allow Horace Vasterling to harbor any unseemly feelings for her. None.

Should he exhibit the least sign of leaning in that direction, she must squelch it at once. But gently.

"Good . . . Good evening, Mrs. Poitevant," Horace said with a jerky little bow. "You look very nice tonight."

"Good evening, Mr. Vasterling," she replied, repressing the urge to roll her eyes at his banal remark. She did not look very well at all, not compared to how she'd looked yesterday when they were introduced.

"I'm very pleased to meet you again," he went on, his expression sincere and pathetically hopeful.

She nodded. "As am I."

Horace glanced from her to Mr. Hawke and back again. He was so ill at ease, she realized, so unsure of himself. Just like most of her students when first they arrived at the academy: shy, awkward, and out of their element in social situations.

She'd not previously considered the plight of men who suffered those afflictions. From her lowly position in the world it seemed as if society men had all the power. They held all the cards. No matter their appearance, their vices, or their failings, the men with titles and money were always the ones in control, not the women they chose to wed.

But there were some, she realized now, some with little money and less grace, who were no better off than one of her girls. There were men like Horace Vasterling.

Before she could prevent it she asked, "Are you enjoying yourself in town, Mr. Vasterling?"

He brightened at once. "Oh, yes. Though it's not my first time here."

It was his fifth season in town. She knew because she'd followed his progress with the dedication of a French spy in the royal court. Though she should not, she had to ask, "Do you have family in town with you?"

"Not at present. I'm from the north, you know. Few connections in town. But this year my father intends to join me for a while."

His father! *Their* father.

Hester had never laid eyes on her sire, at least not that she could remember. She'd been only four years old when her mother had fled her husband. But he was coming to town. Soon.

"Vasterling and I may do some business together," Mr. Hawke remarked when the silence grew awkward. "He's got quite the head for business."

Horace blushed, then glanced shyly at Hester. "I'm sure Mrs. Poitevant does not care about business. But perhaps . . ." He stuttered to a halt. Hester braced herself for what was to come. "Perhaps you would prefer to dance?"

She felt both pairs of male eyes on her: Horace's hopeful, Mr. Hawke's expectant. She did not want to dance with her brother. But she also did not want to be labeled a snob, not by him or by Adrian Hawke.

"I believe the next dance is a country cotillion," Mr. Hawke prompted, his voice so innocent as to be suspect.

Drat the man! But she had to respond. "That . . . That sounds lovely."

In a matter of minutes she was back on the dance floor queuing up for the cotillion, facing her brother across a distance of only a few feet. Beyond him she could see Adrian Hawke, a smug smile on his lips.

What was he up to? Why did he care whether or not she danced with his friend? Did he consider himself some sort of matchmaker, pairing his awkward comrade with the awkward Widow Poitevant?

Or was he simply trying to aggravate her? She knew she'd roused his curiosity with her role in society, her change in appearance, and her perceived rudeness to his friend. Was this just his way of nettling her? If so, he certainly had succeeded.

She curtsied when the music began, then lifted her chin to a pugnacious angle, reminding herself that Adrian Hawke could only annoy her if she allowed him to. Handsome, arrogant men of his sort were the worst. The only way to best him was to become impervious to his appeal, impervious to his manipulations.

Yes, she was dancing with Horace Vasterling, just as Adrian Hawke intended. What she must do now, was turn that concession to her advantage.

So she smiled as she circled around her brother and returned to her position. She put her best foot forward, both literally and figuratively as they executed the steps of the cotillion.

Horace was a reasonably decent dancer. He'd improved with his every season in town. He was also a harmless, gentle-natured fellow, she was coming to see. If she could spar with the likes of Adrian Hawke, surely she could deal with the likes of Horace Vasterling.

Not to hurt him, of course. But there were things

about her father and her original home that she wanted to know.

"How nice for you that your father will soon join you," she said as they promenaded.

"Yes." But he looked doubtful.

"Does your father come often to town?"

"No. He . . . he hates London."

"Really?"

"He's a countryman at heart. As am I," he confessed with reddening cheeks.

"I am a confirmed city dweller myself," Hester said. *Pay attention, dear brother.* "I can't think of the last time I was out in the countryside."

His face fell a little.

"So," she went on. "Why has he decided to join you this year?"

"I'm not certain. But it is most fortunate, for I have business to conduct which involves him as well."

She took a steadying breath. "And shall your mother join him as well?"

"Oh, no. You see, my father is a widower."

Yes, as she well knew, he'd been a widower for the past six years. But how much did Horace know about his mother? Hester forced herself to continue. "I'm so sorry. How sad for you."

"Thank you. You are very kind. But then, I suppose you of all people would understand."

Hester's heart did a sudden leap, for she thought he also referred to the loss of their mother. Then she recovered. He meant her late husband, of course, the fictional man she'd created shortly after her mother's death.

Meanwhile he went on. "I never knew my mother. She died shortly after I was born."

It was a blessing he handed her off to the gentleman across from him, for Hester might otherwise have stumbled to a halt. As it was, had she not practiced these steps just last week with Anabelle, Charlotte, and Dulcie, she would never have made it through that set.

He believed his mother had died in childbirth? The unfairness of it made her want to scream!

Yet what else should she expect? What else was a stiff-necked man like Edgar Vasterling likely to say to his motherless son? "Your mother fled from her humorless, pinchpenny husband with a new man and a new name; she chose the society of town over the boredom of the countryside"? Of course Edgar Vasterling had said his absent wife was dead.

Hester avoided Horace's eyes when they came back together and she responded only vaguely to his further attempts at conversation. Yes, the party was lovely. No, she did not often attend the races. Yes, she had already seen the latest incarnation of Marlowe's play.

But the whole time she struggled not to release her anger at the father upon the son.

Horace did not know. He did not know so he could not be held accountable. Still, she was enormously relieved when the dance ended. Before he could escort her back to where Adrian Hawke awaited them, she excused herself. "Thank you, Mr. Vasterling, but you will understand that I must tend to my charges." Then she left him, walking stiff and straight, and not relaxing until she'd turned a corner out of his sight.

Adrian watched as Mrs. Poitevant disappeared, and his noncommittal expression turned into a frown. Now what? Bad enough that he'd been unable to tear his gaze from her lithe figure, dancing so easily in Vasterling's arms. Now he had to rely on Horace to interpret their interchange. He put down his glass and started toward Horace, only to be intercepted by George Bennett.

Like an animal confronted with a threat, Adrian tensed and the hairs rose up on the back of his neck.

But George was smiling. Friendly. "We meet again,

Hawke. Good to see you. Hope you're enjoying yourself
in town."

"I am. If you'll excuse me?"

"Wait a minute. Wait." He grabbed Adrian's arm.
When Adrian jerked it free, the man stepped back. "No
offense meant. I only—"

"What?" Adrian glared at him. "What do you want
from me, Bennett?"

As before Adrian watched the man tamp down his
anger and replace it with a conciliatory expression. "I
. . . ah . . . I was hoping we could let bygones be bygones. Y'know, all that business at Eton. We were just
a bunch of rough-and-tumble lads back then. A gang of
rowdies full of high spirits and hijinks. No need for that
to be a problem now."

Adrian didn't buy a word of it. Men like George Bennett didn't change so drastically. One day insulting
Adrian's mother and seething when Adrian dared dance
with his sister; less than a week later saying he wanted
to forget the past.

No. The man had an ulterior motive and it didn't take
a genius to figure out what. He decided to be blunt. "So
you've heard about the business venture I'm assem-
bling."

The man didn't even have the grace to look embarrassed by his transparency. "Indeed I have. Appears
you've got a good head on your shoulders, Hawke. A
good head."

"Listen, Bennett. I don't have time for this."

"Of course. I didn't mean now." He jammed his hands
in his pockets and rocked back on his heels. "So, when
do you have time?"

Adrian wanted to laugh, the look on Bennett's face
was that desperate. The man must be in a real financial
bind if he was reduced to courting the Bonnie By-blow
of Eton. Perhaps he should hear him out, if only for the

entertainment. Nonchalantly he straightened one cuff. "I'll check my calendar and see what I can do."

"Good. Good." Again the man rocked back on his heels, grinning as if he'd just made a brilliant deal. "I look forward to it."

With a nod Adrian turned away. He'd come to this party to force Hester Poitevant to be nice to Horace Vasterling. And he'd succeeded. But now he'd been offered more, the satisfaction of seeing George Bennett dance attendance on him.

It occurred to him that between them Hester Poitevant and George Bennett symbolized everything that was wrong with British society. Elitist. Greedy. The measuring stick they used on people was flat-out wrong.

As a boy he'd been sadly misjudged with that stick. Now his money and reputation in business had begun to alter that judgment. But even that was a skewed measurement. Many a good man existed who had more energy and ideas than money and family name.

Then he spied Horace standing apart from the chattering masses, with his shoulders slumped and his face turned down, and Adrian's resolve hardened further. George Bennett was not nearly the man Horace Vasterling was. Moreover, the Widow Poitevant was in no position to feel superior to a man like Horace. Did she really think she could do better in this vermin-infested jungle that they called good society?

Despite the honorific in front of Vasterling's name, it occurred to Adrian that the man was a lot like him: not good enough for the upper crust of society. He might be smart and well intentioned, but that wasn't sufficient.

In that moment he decided to help Horace, both with his finances and with his romantic endeavors. For some reason Horace liked the difficult widow. Of course, Adrian knew why: that form-fitting dress she'd had on the other day, and that silky mass of hair. Both dress and hair made a man's hand itch to touch them. Even his.

He wasn't the one interested in her though. Horace liked the woman, and if Adrian had anything to do with it, Hoity-toity Poitevant would learn to like Horace in return.

Between that and seeing George Bennett grovel, what more could he ask of this trip to his "homeland"?

He strode up to Horace and clasped him on the shoulder. "What a handsome couple you and Mrs. Poitevant make. Did you ask her for another dance later?"

Horace gave an unenthusiastic smile. "I forgot to ask. But . . . Well . . . I don't know. She doesn't seem to like me."

Damn her snooty little soul. "I find that hard to believe. What exactly did she say?"

"Well. That she had to tend her charges."

"As I'm sure she did. You can't take that as a rejection, Vasterling. I think she's just shy." *And a ferocious snob.*

"Shy? D'you really think so?"

"Of course. How many times have you seen her dance at one of these shindigs?"

"Hmm. I s'pose you've got a point."

"If you like her, you have to pursue her, man. Women like to be pursued."

"Yes. Well." Horace still looked doubtful.

"What?"

"Well, I don't think she's the type who would be content in the countryside. You know, we live rather remote, my father and I. Far north, and miles to any sort of decent society. It's no good to pursue a woman who couldn't be happy with that kind of life."

"True. But have you considered that Mrs. Poitevant works very hard to make ends meet? She might be long past ready to remarry and give up this academy of hers.

And don't forget, all women want children. They all want children. But she needs another husband first."

He could see the wheels spinning in Horace's head, and for a moment Adrian felt a twinge of guilt. As quick as the man was about matters of money, he was just the opposite with women. At the first hint of adversity he sounded retreat.

And Hester Poitevant was going to provide more than just a *little* adversity.

But if Horace persevered he might win her over, and Adrian was determined that he do so. A little self-confidence, that's all Vasterling needed. A little direction, a little polish, a little chance to shine. Horace Vasterling could have women flocking to him, even if Hester Poitevant wasn't able to see his good points.

Then like a bolt of lightning it came to Adrian, the answer to Horace's problems and the perfect solution to his own little project. What was it they called Hester Poitevant? London's premier bridemaker? Well, he was known as Boston's savviest deal maker.

Maybe it was time for *him* to make a deal with *her*.

CHAPTER 8

"He's *here*?" Hester stared up at Mrs. Dobbs, barely aware that she'd just jabbed her thumb with her embroidery needle. Without conscious thought she raised her thumb to her lips, sucking the sore spot. "Are you certain of the name?"

"Aye, miss. Mr. Adrian Hawke. Here's his card."

Hester stared at it, not wanting it to be true. But of course, it was. It said so right there on the stiffened stock in charcoal-gray ink. But why was Adrian Hawke here at her little cottage? Why was he seeking her out?

Wasn't it bad enough that he'd crept into her dreams last night, an unwelcome visitor waltzing her through the night until she was warm and perspiring, waking to a tangle of sheets and a tangle of emotions?

And now he was here. Oh, but this was turning into a nightmare.

With a jerky movement she set the card aside. "Tell him . . . Tell him I am out."

Mrs. Dobbs grimaced. "I'm afraid I've already given him the impression you're t'home."

Hester shook her head. "All right then. Tell him I am

presently indisposed. Tell him," she repeated when the little housekeeper only stared doubtfully at her.

"Pardon me, miss, but he says it's very important. Very important."

Hester rolled her eyes. "I assure you, it is not."

Again Mrs. Dobbs hesitated. "He seems a very proper sort of gentleman. Whyn't you just see what he wants?"

"I believe *I'm* the one who pays *your* salary, aren't I?" Then regretting her sharp words as soon as they were out, Hester set her needlework aside. "I'm sorry. I'm being rude, aren't I? To you and to him. Very well, then." She heaved a resigned sigh. "Send him in."

The housekeeper bobbed her head and scurried away. But Hester saw the sparkle in her eyes and the faint grin on her aging face. Good Lord, had the man charmed her too? Half the women of the *ton* were talking about the tall, handsome American.

Frustrated, Hester stood and smoothed her skirts. If only she could put order to her emotions as easily as she put order to her appearance.

Her appearance!

She had on a plum-colored day dress, her favorite. And her hair was caught up at the crown but fell loose down her back in a style better suited to a young girl than an aging widow. She often wore it thus when she was at home, not expecting visitors. But now she did have a visitor.

"Wait," she called to Mrs. Dobbs. But the woman was gone, and in a matter of seconds Hester heard the heavy tread of a man approaching. She was trapped and there was no help for it.

Sucking in a breath she steeled herself.

Mrs. Dobbs entered first, her averted gaze not at all disguising the satisfied expression on her round face. But the housekeeper's meddling manner was of far lesser import than the man who followed her into the little sitting room. Once Adrian Hawke entered, Hester saw nothing but him.

He should not be here. That was her very first thought. He was too big, too masculine. Too . . . Too . . . She took a labored breath. Why, he seemed to suck the very air out of the room.

What was it about the man?

It was only that he *was* a man, she told herself. She'd never had a man in her sitting room before. For that matter, she'd never had any man in her house except, of course, for Mr. Dobbs.

When Mrs. Dobbs melted away, Hester forced herself to speak. "Good morning, Mr. Hawke. I gather you wish to see me."

His eyes, the most disturbing shade of blue she'd ever seen, flickered across her, top to bottom, observing everything in their path.

Right then she knew her shortness of breath was not because some man had breached her parlor walls. Nothing quite so simple. It wasn't that he was a man, it was that he was a *particular* man, a particularly difficult, arrogant, obscenely virile man. And for some reason he rattled her right down to the toes of her Spanish leather boots.

When his probing gaze lifted back to hers it took all her resolve not to avert her eyes. Especially when he smiled. "It's very good of you to see me on such short notice, Mrs. Poitevant. I apologize for interrupting you at your needlework," he said, gesturing to the embroidery hoop she'd laid aside. "Apparently your vision has improved sufficiently that you can now forgo wearing your spectacles?"

Hester clenched her jaw against a tart retort. Drat the man. He *would* notice.

His grin increased. "Why don't you just abandon

them, Mrs. Poitevant? No one really believes you need them."

Hester crossed her arms, refusing to be baited by him. "I believe you told my housekeeper that this unexpected visit was a matter of some importance?" She did not smile.

Though he tamped down his cheeky grin, his eyes nonetheless sparked with devilment. "Yes. I have a business proposition to make you."

"A business proposition?" Hester could not say what she expected from his unanticipated visit, but it certainly wasn't this.

"Yes." He cocked his head to one side. "May I sit?"

A business proposition? "I suppose," she muttered with less grace than she ought.

"Thank you. You know, I've heard a number of complimentary remarks about your academy."

Was he patronizing her now? The rich American businessman amused by a woman's attempt to do business on her own? Whatever his game—and she knew it was one—she needed to be wary. "How kind of you to say so."

He paused as if weighing how to continue. "I'll get right to the point. I'd like to hire you to help a friend of mine."

Shocked, Hester stared at him. He wanted to hire her to help a friend? Then her shock turned to a darker, murkier emotion. Who was she, this so-called friend?

He went on. "You come highly recommended. My aunt and cousin sing nothing but your praises. They tell me that not one of your clients during the past four seasons has failed to make a satisfactory marriage."

"Well, yes. That is true."

"How proud you must be," he said, smiling straight into her eyes.

Hester swallowed hard. That smile, so bold and blatantly masculine, could not be trusted. He was up to something. But what? "Yes. I'm pleased. Of course. Not proud, mind you. But pleased. Very pleased." *Good Lord, she was babbling like a ninny.*

She sat up straighter in her chair. He relaxed back on the settee and stretched an arm across the back. "So. With your obvious success in matters of this sort I believe you're the best person to assist my friend. The only person."

Something did not ring true about any of this. Hester's mind sifted through a list of every woman she'd seen him speak to or dance with. Surely it would not be any of them. She decided to play along. "I assume your friend is already out?"

"Out? You mean presented into society? Yes. I believe you might say that."

"I see. Without much success, I take it. No acceptable offers?"

He shook his head. "I'm afraid not."

"I see." Of course she didn't see at all and a part of her was afraid to find out. He was too dangerous a man to feint and parry with. On the other hand, she did not like being made sport of. "I'm rather committed to the clients I already have, Mr. Hawke." She gave him a regretful smile, completely insincere.

He smiled back, probably just as insincerely, though she couldn't tell. He was that good at it. "I thought you might say that. I'm prepared to more than meet your fee."

"I'm sorry, but the season is already well under way."

"What's your price for a full season?"

He was not going to give up, was he? And who *was* this woman he'd so befriended that he'd foot the bill to help her make a good match? If she was already presented, Hester must know her, at least by sight.

On impulse she named an amount fully double her

normal fee. "In advance," she added, a challenging glitter in her eyes.

"Done."

"Done?"

"Done. I'll have my banker write a note of transfer to your account this very afternoon."

He stood up, business concluded, she supposed. But she was slower to rise. Heavens, but that was an extraordinarily large amount of money.

"It's a pleasure doing business with you, Mrs. Poitevant. When shall I bring my friend around?"

When indeed? Hester was so nonplussed by the sudden turn of events, it took her a moment to respond. He *had* come here for legitimate business purposes, and as a result she'd just come into quite a windfall of money. A veritable fortune by her standards. "Perhaps . . . Perhaps you could come tomorrow? Early. Say, ten in the morning."

"We'll be here."

Then he did the oddest thing. He stuck out his hand, not as he might to a lady, but as one businessman to another. And not in the least patronizing. He stuck his bare hand out and waited until, with her first sincere smile, she stuck hers out too and took it.

There was something heady in it, two business people confirming a business transaction with a handshake. It was so seldom she was treated like an equal by the people who hired her. Hester hadn't realized how liberating it would feel.

But the feeling was short-lived. Because once his hand closed around hers, any thought of business flew right out of her head. His hand was large and warm— and strong. It enveloped her own slender hand with an unnatural sort of heat. She stared down at it, seeing the long fingers, the squared-off nails, the light dusting of dark hair, so masculine and unlike her own hands—and that unnatural heat became an unnerving tingle.

Oh, where were her gloves when she needed them?

But gloves would offer no protection from this man, she realized. The unnerving tingle raced up her arm to become a violent trembling that shook her all the way to her belly.

She snatched her hand back, her heart hammering from fear. This man was not a man to be careless with. This man was dangerous beyond all reason, the same sort of man who had almost ruined her so long ago.

She lurched back a step, wishing she could flee the debilitating weakness which had nearly caught her and which, she now realized, would continue to be a threat so long as this man remained anywhere near her.

But there was no place for her to flee. Her parlor—perfectly adequate to her needs—had turned unnaturally small today.

Then she reminded herself that this was her home, her place of business. She had no need to flee any man, especially the arrogant, overly confident sort like Adrian Hawke.

So she clasped her hands together at her waist, forbade any further trembling at all, and gave him her steadiest, most aloof stare. "I'll see you and your friend tomorrow at ten. Do try to be prompt."

He smiled, an odd, self-satisfied smile she noticed in one part of her mind. "I assure you, we'll be prompt, Mrs. Poitevant." A short bow, then he was almost out the door and she was almost able to breathe.

His hand lay on the doorknob and he had pulled the door open when something compelled her to make him linger. Something stupid and perverse. "Mr. Hawke, wait."

He paused in the doorway, filling it up with his wide shoulders and excessive height. "Yes?"

Her heart did a ridiculous flip-flop. His hair was as

black as midnight; his eyes were bluer than the sky. Dear Lord, he was turning her into a very bad poet. But it was patently unfair for a man to be so attractive.

Somehow she composed herself. "I . . . You didn't say . . . What is your friend's name and her situation?"

"*Her* situation?" Again that dangerous, mocking grin. Alarms began to sound in Hester's head. "I'm afraid you have misconstrued my words, Mrs. Poitevant. My friend is not a woman."

"What? Not a woman?"

"Of course not. I have no daughter or other such female relative who requires my aid in such matters, nor yours."

"But I thought she . . . you . . ." Hester drew herself up. She had known he was up to mischief. "I'm afraid my clientele is limited strictly to women."

"I'm certain your talents will be just as effective with a man."

"No. I don't believe—"

"We have a deal, Mrs. Poitevant." One of his dark, slashing brows arched in the most imperious manner. "We shook hands on it."

So they had. But Hester was not about to be manipulated this way. "You misrepresented yourself—and your friend."

"I never said he was female. You made that assumption. Besides, you misrepresented yourself."

"I most certainly did not."

"You charged me twice what you charge other clients."

As quickly as that her righteous indignation fizzled out. She could not deny his words.

"Plus, you demanded the entire amount in advance. No half now, half when a betrothal is announced, as you allow your other clientele."

He'd been checking on her. Oh, but the man was

infuriating. She crossed her arms scowling. "If you didn't like the terms, you needn't have agreed to them."

"My point exactly."

Staring into his laughing eyes, knowing she'd been had, stiffened Hester's resolve as nothing else could. Bother the man! If he wanted to spar with her, she'd meet him more than halfway. "Very well, Mr. Hawke. I'll see you and your friend tomorrow. But be sure to bring the entire payment with you."

"Of course." He made her an abbreviated bow and started to depart, then paused. Another of those slow, mocking grins lit his face. "I almost forgot. You asked my friend's name and situation."

With a sudden awful clarity Hester knew what he was about to say. She knew and she wanted to clap her hands over her ears to shut out the terrible truth. She didn't do any such thing, of course. The need to always appear composed and in control of every situation was too deeply ingrained in her to be abandoned, even now. So she just stood there, her hands knotted at her waist, trumped once by him and now trumped again.

"You know him," he went on, enjoying her discomfort, but oblivious to the *true* cause of her distress. "Horace Vasterling. A fine young man, as I'm sure you will agree. But he's a little rusty when it comes to the social niceties. I have every confidence, however, that you can improve his chances in the cutthroat business of making a suitable match."

Then he left, and Hester could do nothing but sit down on her chair with a jarring bump.

Horace Vasterling, here in her house. Her brother who already exhibited an unacceptable interest in her would be in her house, hoping to learn how to attract a bride. Were it not so utterly ludicrous a situation, she would put her head down and weep.

Weeping, however, was a complete waste of time, as

she well knew. What she needed to do was think, to figure a way out of this hideous mess.

She did not understand Adrian Hawke. Why should he take such an interest in Horace—and in her? What was any of this to him? Was it the man's goal in life to wreak havoc upon her? First Dulcie's ill-advised crush, then her own ridiculous reaction to him. And now he must throw Horace at her.

Good heavens, if Mr. Hawke ever learned about her true relationship to Horace, just think of the ruin he could effect upon her and her business.

That gave Hester pause, and for a moment she sat there, considering how dangerous her situation had just become. What to do? What to do?

In the end it was fairly simple. She must make Horace irresistible to other women while rebuffing him herself. Get her brother properly betrothed, collect her fee from Mr. Hawke, then take a well-deserved holiday away from London and society and especially Adrian Hawke.

Adrian felt pretty damned good—or well pleased with himself, as the Widow Poitevant might better term it. He'd shocked her, just as he'd intended. Those creamy cheeks of hers had heated with the softest shade of pink, and her green eyes had gone wide and dark, the clear color of bottle glass where normally they were more the shade of new sycamore leaves.

He'd been a little shocked himself when he'd first entered her parlor. Her house was so feminine, so unlike the austere persona she adopted in public. She'd not been that severe, judgmental woman today. Just as he'd hoped, he'd caught her unawares. She'd been relaxing in her pretty pink parlor wearing a pretty plum-colored dress, her unnecessary spectacles put aside, while her pretty hair tumbled freely around her shoulders.

God, that hair! It wouldn't surprise him if her late

husband had wed her just for the pleasure of touching that hair. It had taken all his willpower not to pick up one of those heavy, shining curls and wind it through his fingers. When she'd taken his proffered hand, he could have reached out with his other hand and lifted the wayward lock that had cascaded across her shoulder.

"Damnation!" he swore under his breath as unseemly desire surged through him. It was Horace who wanted the woman, he reminded himself. Not him. Horace who would have hours of her undivided attention to woo and win her, if that's what he desired.

But as Adrian mounted his waiting horse, his satisfaction with the beginnings of his little plot did not resonate so fully as he'd expected. It all had made sense when Hester Poitevant appeared the arrogant snob who needed to be taken down a peg. But when she was soft and womanly, and out of her element, that's when things got muddy and confused. That's when he got what Horace wanted mixed up with what *he* wanted.

What was it he wanted, anyway?

He guided his horse down New Bond Street, hardly aware of the afternoon throngs brought out by the day's fair weather. What he wanted was to pass this time in London with whatever entertainments he could find. What he wanted was to make a lot of money, have a little fun, attend his cousin's wedding, and then go home to Boston.

So why was he spending a small fortune on a woman he didn't like, helping a man he hardly knew circulate better in a society he'd always despised? What was the logic and, more importantly, the value to him in so harebrained and expensive a scheme?

He should forget about Horace Vasterling and his paltry investment, and instead focus on using town society to his advantage. And to getting Hester Poitevant into bed.

He shifted in the saddle, cursing the rise once more of desire. Hester Poitevant in his bed? What a joke. The good Widow Poitevant believed in marriage. She lived and breathed arranged marriages and was probably the least likely woman in London to land in a man's bed without benefit of a ten-page marriage contract clenched in her stubborn little fist.

He, meanwhile, was the master of uncomplicated sex. The erotic pleasures of the bedroom with women who understood the situation.

No, Hester Poitevant was the last woman he should be considering as a bedmate.

But Adrian was nothing if not a realist, and he accepted the truth when he saw it. The fact was, he wanted to get under Hester's skirts. He was desperate to do so. Just flip up those overstarched petticoats, unloosen that cascade of silky hair, and kiss that prissy mouth into breathless acquiescence.

It wasn't logical, but that's how he felt. Except that there was Horace to think of.

Horace Vasterling was taken with the troublesome woman, and he had just arranged for the two of them to spend hours and hours together.

"Find some other woman to lust after," Adrian muttered to himself.

When his horse's ears flicked back at the sound, he leaned forward, patting the gelding's well-muscled neck. "You don't know how lucky you are," Adrian said. "Women are nothing but trouble."

But they were worth it. Otherwise he would not be so eagerly looking forward to ten o'clock tomorrow morning.

CHAPTER 9

Hester was ready at nine-thirty, though it took her twice as long as usual to dress. This was turning into an unpleasant habit, not knowing what to wear when Adrian Hawke was around. He'd seen her buttoned up and scraped back, her public persona. But he'd also seen her in a vain moment, dressed in her prettiest, most feminine ensemble. Then yesterday he'd seen her looking practically like a girl with her hair down about her shoulders, all undisciplined.

And, of course, no spectacles.

She blew out a frustrated breath. She ought to just do as he suggested, abandon the annoying things once and for all. Except that she hated letting him best her at anything. Added to that, she didn't want to dress in any way that might encourage poor Horace.

Poor Horace?

She turned away from the parlor mirror where she'd been arranging and rearranging the snood she'd decided to catch her hair in. What was wrong with her? Poor Horace indeed. Horace Vasterling might not be the most eligible bachelor in town, but he had far more advantages than she'd ever had. If he couldn't snare the rich, beautiful wife his father wanted for him, that was not her problem. He should simply lower his sights.

So why all this worry about her clothing and hairstyle? She didn't care what Horace Vasterling or Adrian Hawke thought. It didn't matter if Mr. Hawke taunted her about the drastic differences between her public and private choices of apparel.

He and she had made a deal, and she, for one, meant to abide by it. The extra money would be a boon to her meager savings. She would also have the chance to get to know her brother.

Hester had tossed and turned through many sleepless hours last night considering how best to deal with Horace. She'd come to the simple and obvious conclusion that she must treat him as she would any other student. Determine his strengths and weaknesses, and go on from there.

He was a decent dancer, she knew that much. And though not the best conversationalist, he was not surly or coarse, nor did he stammer or lisp. His clothing, however, and his grooming habits—those might prove a bigger challenge.

He ought to visit Mr. Hawke's tailor, she mused. The cut of the American's suit . . . The way it hugged his wide shoulders, yet did not bind—

She broke off that thought with a little groan. The cut of Adrian Hawke's suit was hardly pertinent to her current dilemma. Anyway, his tailor was probably in Boston, so it was a moot point. But she did need to recommend Horace to someone. Perhaps Madame Henri could give her the name of a reasonably priced person.

They were prompt. Hester heard them outside handing their horses off to Mr. Dobbs. Mrs. Dobbs greeted them in the foyer, then they were in her second parlor, the room she used for most of her instructions.

"Mr. Hawke and Mr. Vasterling, here to call," Mrs. Dobbs announced with a curtsy and an undeniably curious look on her face. She'd been curious when Hester explained that her newest client was a man, and she obviously remained curious still.

"Good morning, Mr. Vasterling. Mr. Hawke."

"It's very nice to see you again, Mrs. Poitevant," Horace said.

"Indeed it is," Mr. Hawke echoed.

Hester nodded, her eyes flitting back and forth between them. Her brother was actually inside her house, an occasion she'd never anticipated. Added to that, a man who made her pulse race was also standing in her parlor. She could not have said which happenstance unsettled her more.

"Well. Perhaps we should begin. You will excuse us?" She directed that last at Mr. Hawke who was dressed today in a charcoal frock coat which turned his eyes an astounding shade of smoky blue. Not that the color of his eyes mattered in the least to her.

He grinned at her. "Don't mind me. I'll just sit down over there." He dragged a chair into a far corner. "You won't even know I am here."

She wanted to object, but for some reason, not in front of Horace. She gave Mr. Hawke a terse nod and turned to face Horace instead, consoling herself that Adrian Hawke was not the sort to sit silent and idle in someone's parlor for long. The best way to rid herself of him was to bore him to death. Soon enough he would be on his way, leaving her to draw out Horace.

Her plan with her brother was initially to practice the art of conversation, ensuring he had responses for every sort of dialogue, and genteel questions guaranteed to put even the shyest young lady at ease. She'd decided to groom him for the shy ones as opposed to the glittering butterflies of town society.

Leave the gadabout girls to Adrian Hawke and his ilk, the charming rogues. They were the heartbreakers, never satisfied with one woman. But men like Horace . . .

Though she hated to admit it, honesty bade her accept the truth. Her brother Horace, whom she so wanted to dislike, might actually have potential as a decent sort of husband. Unlike their father.

She didn't realize how long she'd been staring at him until he shifted from one foot to the other. She snapped back to the moment. "Well. Let's begin, shall we? Let's see. Why don't you tell me about yourself, what your life is like away from town? Please, sit."

"Thank you."

He started to sit, then stopped when she frowned and shook her head. "Always seat your female companion first, Mr. Vasterling."

"Of course. I knew that. But . . . but I forgot. S'pose I'm nervous," he added with a hesitant smile.

Once she sat, he did as well. But he looked more rattled than ever. "Tell me about yourself," Hester began. "You live in the north, I believe?" *In a cold, stone fortress of a place, according to her mother.* Their *mother.*

"Yes." He sat stiffly erect, tugging nervously at his too snug waistcoat.

This would never do. She must put him more at ease. "Tell me about your home, why don't you? Anything you want to talk about."

Horace glanced at Adrian, whom she was determined to ignore and wished would just go away. Then turning back to her, Horace cleared his throat and began. "The family estate is Winwood Manor, an ancient building of curious history. A portion of it includes an old Celtic wellhouse, you know. When Great-great-grandfather Vasterling added on to the house, he enclosed the well.

Mrs. McKeith and her kitchen help appreciate that, I can tell you. 'Specially in the winter. Right down the stairs they go, then up with fresh water."

"The house must be very large. Do you have an extensive staff?"

He waggled his head back and forth. "Most of the house is closed up. Too much to heat and keep up, you see."

"Yes. I do see." Her mother had called it the cave, cold and moldy with nothing to delight the eye or the spirit. "You understand, of course, that your wife—your bride-to-be—will be very interested in how the household presently is run, and also, what changes she will be free to make."

He nodded, but a faint frown appeared on his face. "Yes. Of course. That makes perfect sense."

"So. How many house servants are there? And how resistant will they be to a new mistress?"

Adrian listened to the conversation, hearing Horace's answers, but mainly observing Hester Poitevant in action.

She looked . . . interesting. That was the best word he could come up with. Her hair was drawn back, but softly. Rather than twisted into a repressive knot, the heavy length was folded into some sort of netlike contraption that hung heavy on the back of her neck. And what a graceful, slender neck it was. Unadorned, of course, and her dress was that gray outfit he'd seen her in before. Plain at the collar with only three buttons to relieve the bodice. The color was actually nice on her, but the cut did more to disguise her curves than accentuate them.

It was deliberate. He could see that now. She of all women understood exactly how to display her appearance to its best advantage. But she chose not to.

He supposed she did it to present herself in a sober

light to those who employed her. It would probably be bad form for a companion to outshine her young charge. It seemed to him, though, that she embraced that soberness to an excessive degree.

Why would she do that? She was young enough and certainly attractive enough to remarry if she so chose. And if she married again, she would not be forced to work on others' behalf as she did now. At least she seemed to have abandoned those silly spectacles of hers, revealing the rare green tint of her eyes. He wanted to stare deeply into those eyes and discover what went on in that devious mind of hers.

Even under his close scrutiny, though, she wouldn't look at him for long, just a quick glance and then away. But she'd done it several times now, and he had to admit it pleased him. So he rattled her, did he? Yet she always refocused on Horace, continuing in her line of questioning.

He shifted in the feminine side chair and crossed his arms. You'd think she was planning to marry Horace herself the way she quizzed him. Numbers of servants, size of the house, the distance to town and the proximity of the nearest neighbors. She asked also about the household allowance and pin money, both apparently minimal by town standards. But she didn't seem perturbed by that.

She also inquired in some detail about the elder Vasterling, the state of his health and his involvement in household affairs.

Adrian supposed a prospective wife might wish to know exactly what she was getting into. Entering into a marriage was, after all, like any other significant business deal. The more information you had, the better deal you could make.

But the Widow Poitevant's questions seemed excessive, not really geared toward shaping up Horace. Then again, perhaps the inquiries were for her own edification. Maybe she *was* interested in the man.

Again he shifted, frowning at the thought. He'd had a restless night. It had taken two tall glasses of whisky to settle him down. Even then his sleep had been fretful, and it was all due to Hester Poitevant. He'd plotted to throw her together with Horace Vasterling, to admit that her snobbishness toward him was without merit.

But now he found her focus on Vasterling annoying.

What was his problem? Why was he getting all worked up over some prissy female with her nose in the air?

Damnation! What he needed was an energetic afternoon in some talented woman's bed. That would put a quick end to this ridiculous fascination he'd developed for Hester Poitevant of the aristocratic manner and the seductive hair.

When he stood, both Hester and Horace turned to look at him. Hester and Horace. Even their names were well matched. He gritted his teeth. "I'll take my leave of you now. No doubt you two have much to accomplish today."

She stood to bid him farewell, and even in that simple movement her composure and grace were noticeable. Was she that composed in bed?

He coughed to cover the curse that rose to his lips. He wasn't going to think about that.

"I'll show you out," she said. "If you'll wait here?" she added to Horace.

In the narrow hall they were close enough that Adrian caught a whiff of flowers on her. Roses? No, lilies. He wanted to bend nearer and sniff. But she stepped back and folded her hands neatly at her waist.

"I believe you have something for me?"

For a moment he drew a blank. Then his mind clicked back into place. Of course. Her fee.

Without smiling he pulled a letter from his upper pocket. "I do. This bank draft should suffice. From time to time I will wish to discuss Vasterling's progress with you."

"As you wish." She took the paper but did not examine it. "I wonder—" She broke off.

"Yes?"

She hesitated. "I suppose I still wonder why you are doing this for him. Surely you and he have not been acquainted for so very long as to require such largesse on your part."

"I have my reasons." When she only arched her brows and waited, he added, "It benefits me if my business partners are presentable."

"I thought you hired me to help him find a wife."

"That will be an ancillary benefit. He is the one who wishes to wed."

"I see."

No, he didn't think she did. He wasn't sure he understood either what had propelled him to strike this deal with Hester—and the very fact that he'd begun to think of her as Hester only magnified his confusion.

He inhaled. There it was again, the scent of lilies, and all at once he realized the idiocy of what he'd done. He'd foisted marriage-minded Horace onto the very woman that he wanted to bed. Right here, right now, with an erection growing ever more painful in his breeches, he wanted to muss up that glorious hair of hers and bury his face in it. He wanted to breathe in her lily scent, to surround himself in it. Drown in it. And drown in her warm female flesh.

He straightened with a jerk and bit down on a foul oath. "Good day," he managed to mutter. Then he turned and exited with no further pleasantries. She already thought him a clod, a stupid, ill-mannered American boor. A crude Scottish bastard, all money and no class. What did it matter if he'd just proven her right?

Hester stood in the hallway a long while, listening as Adrian Hawke strode out, hearing Mrs. Dobbs scurry after him.

He'd left his hat behind.

She should count that a success. For she'd hoped to bore him into leaving and so it seemed she had. In her hand she held his bank draft, money enough to double her meager savings. All in all, a rather successful morning.

There was still Horace to deal with, of course. Horace, who happened to be a very nice man, though not a particularly forceful one. But then, given her abhorrence of those men who demanded that everything be done their way and on their time schedule, she could not fairly criticize him for that. Truth be told, he had much more potential as a husband than most of the men she came into contact with.

"Mrs. Poitevant?" Horace's hesitant voice drifted out from the parlor.

"I'll be right there." With a last lingering glance toward the front door, Hester turned back to her new student. She would go to the bank this very afternoon. She would deposit Mr. Hawke's fee, and that would be that. Short of seeing his hat returned to him, she meant not to interact with Adrian Hawke any further than absolutely necessary.

"Well," she said upon rejoining Horace. "Let's move along to personal appearance, shall we?"

She circled him slowly, examining every aspect of his bearing with a sharp, discerning gaze. "You must decide, Mr. Vasterling, whether you will purchase a new wardrobe, a tight corset, or embark upon a more restrictive diet than you have in the past."

His crestfallen features only increased her stern demeanor. If he'd harbored any *tendre* for her when he arrived here, she'd soon beat it into submission. Though she meant to earn her fee and make him eminently presentable, she would make certain also that any attraction he felt for her died a quick death.

She liked Horace as a brother, quite a surprise considering how many years she'd spent hating him. Eventually, once the current situation eased—namely, once Adrian Hawke departed London—she might actually consider revealing her true identity to Horace.

But not yet. Not just yet.

CHAPTER 10

Hester did not approve of Vauxhall Gardens for young ladies, at least not in the evening. Outdoors at night, with too much liquor in their bellies, so-called gentlemen seemed to revert to their basest forms: lechers, oglers, octopuses with multiple, groping hands.

Suffice it to say, she did not have good memories of the pleasure gardens at Vauxhall.

But Dulcie's family had been invited to an afternoon event there, the fortieth birthday celebration of Mr. Bennett's brother who was recently wed to a flighty young woman with a penchant for extravagant parties. Though Mrs. Bennett held a haughty disdain for "that silly goose my brother-in-law married," she was not one to miss a party that featured tigers, bears, jugglers, and fire-eaters.

The party was to conclude with a candlelit supper al fresco, and at Dulcie's insistence, Hester was to accompany them.

They'd both decided Horace would attend as well, as a sort of test for him. Unfortunately, he'd secured his invitation through Adrian Hawke, who seemed to be on everyone's guest list these days—Adrian Hawke to whom she'd not spoken during the past three days.

As was becoming altogether too common, her stomach turned into a twisty knot of confusing emotions at the thought of the man.

She faced her armoire frowning. What was she to wear? Nothing too dark, not for an outdoor afternoon event. She could wear the gray dress again, but she'd been wearing it so much lately. Perhaps a lace shawl to give it a different look. And white gloves for a change. A straw hat?

No. That would be too dramatic a change. After all, she was supposed to be a widow. Of course, after six years no one expected widows to continue even in half-mourning garb, not unless they had one foot in the grave themselves.

Holding the walnut doors wide, she scowled at the limited choices. Two weeks ago she would not have had this dilemma. Two weeks ago she would have pulled out whichever dress was next in rotation. Her hair would be twisted tight, her gloves dark, and with spectacles firmly in place her demeanor would be as serious and sober as ever.

But that was before Adrian Hawke had come on the scene, capturing Dulcie's heart and starting a war of wills with George; before he'd forced Hester to dance with him and started her behaving as foolishly as silly, smitten Dulcie. It was also before he'd hired her to polish her own brother into a dashing man about town.

In two short weeks Adrian Hawke had tilted her neat little world right off its axis. And so she stood here, uncertain what to wear, how to style her hair, and how to behave should he approach her.

He hadn't approached at the opera, though. He'd seen her, but when Horace came to greet her, he'd stayed to converse with Mrs. Eversham and that overendowed daughter of hers. Chesty Betsy, she was called behind her back, though she'd probably laugh if she knew. The way the girl thrust those huge things in everyone's face, she seemed awfully proud of them.

Hester sucked in a deep breath, then eyed her inflated profile in the tailor's mirror. Not so bad. Then she let it out in a loud whoosh and frowned at her more ordinary proportions. This was idiotic. She had no desire whatsoever to attract a man. That was why she'd assembled this selection of such severe dresses in the first place. Certainly she did not wish to attract the likes of Adrian Hawke.

Wasn't it just such vanity that had been the ruination of her own mother? Isabelle had been obsessive about her appearance. Dresses, shawls, and capes; jewelry, combs, and hats; gloves and shoes without number. Parties and men and constant, constant attention. But it still had not been enough for Isabelle.

Long ago Hester had vowed never to succumb to her mother's weaknesses. But wasn't that exactly what she was on the verge of doing, dressing in a manner to attract some man's attention?

An inappropriate man, at that.

So she snatched the burgundy dress from its hook and vowed never to suffer this indecision again. Her pretty frocks were for her own time and her own, private world. Today was about business and she would dress accordingly.

Adrian saw Hester before Horace did. She stood a little apart from Dulcie Bennett, in the afternoon shade of an avenue of pollarded elms. Unlit paper lanterns dangled from the branches around her, waiting for dusk and the lamplighters. Just like her, he thought, dangling there, waiting for the right time to light up and glow.

Adrian shook his head at such a fanciful thought. Hester Poitevant was not interested in glowing. If she was, she certainly wouldn't dress the way she did.

He hadn't spoken to her since the morning at her house when he'd departed with that unbelievably stupid erection. He'd barely made it home; the ride had been that painful. Worse, he'd had variations of the same problem off and on ever since. Off when he wanted it on, and on when he least wanted it there.

In frustration he'd visited a discreet house on Mortimer Street, an establishment quietly recommended to him by his uncle's butler. Unfortunately he'd seen no women appealing enough to take upstairs. The blatant ones were too blatant. The floozies repulsed him. The seductive ones were just too coy. Everything about the women there seemed false and contrived. The madam had even offered him a special treat, a very young girl, she'd said. Neither brazen nor coy.

He'd departed then, completely disgusted, both with the madam and himself. No fake virgins for him. No *women* of any sort, it seemed. Instead he'd lain in his lonely bed, servicing himself—and not very happily either.

He didn't understand it. This had never been a problem in Boston. He stared around him now, everywhere but at Hester Poitevant.

He lusted after her.

He'd finally come to accept that. He lusted after a rigid biddy of a woman who did everything she could to make herself unattractive to men.

Except when she was in Cheapside. There she dressed as the incredibly feminine, desirable woman that she was.

He gritted his teeth. She must have a lover there.

Last night while he was tossing and turning in his bed, he'd decided that was the only logical answer. Why else would she dress so beguilingly except for some man.

The thought of her indulging her passions with some faceless man had tormented him further, not even allowing him the meager pleasure of his pitiful release. He'd been in a temper when he finally slept, and in a temper when he'd awakened as well.

Seeing her now, scraped back and buttoned down, stoked that temper all the more. She looked less likely to have a secret lover than any other woman in the Gardens. Than any other woman he'd ever known. But on some level she was a fake, and he knew it.

And for some reason he wanted her to know that he knew.

"I say, Hawke," Horace said, coming up beside him, interrupting his sour thoughts. "What d'you think? Been to Vauxhall before? I'd wager there's nothing like this in that Boston of yours."

Welcoming the distraction, Adrian turned to the man. His brows went up at the sight that met his eyes, however. Horace Vasterling was barely recognizable.

Horace gave him a sheepish grin and looked down at himself. "Not so much the country squire, eh?" He took off his hat and smoothed a hand over his neatly shorn hair. "Mrs. P made me do it."

Mrs. P, was it?

"She had me cut my hair and reshape my whiskers. And then I purchased two new waistcoats. What do you think of this knot?" he asked, fiddling with his neatly tied stock. "It's called the Eagle's Nest. Very fashionable, she said. You ought to try it."

"Maybe I will," Adrian responded, still staring at his friend. It was more than a knot, a waistcoat, and a haircut that had changed Horace. The man seemed to stand taller today, and he was noticeably thinner.

Seeing the direction of Adrian's gaze, Horace leaned nearer. "A corset," he whispered. "A corset until I've shed a pound or two. Taken up fencing, you know. Good exercise, since I'm not a man for boxing."

"You look like a new man," Adrian said, impressed despite himself.

"I owe it all to Mrs. P," Horace reiterated. "And to you for convincing me to go to her." He glanced around, then spying Hester, straightened further. "There she is. I believe I'll go and make my address to her. Will you join me?"

It took forever to traverse the short distance between them and Hester. Several of Adrian's new investers greeted them, much to Adrian's impatience. It annoyed him all the more to realize how completely Hester had distracted him. He'd come to London to prove he was his own man, a success despite society's initial rejection of him. But here he was, dancing attendance on a woman who wanted nothing to do with him.

He'd shaken off the last of the investors when George Bennett tried to gain his attention. With a scowl, Adrian warned him off. But the man wouldn't take a hint. He reminded Adrian of a braying foxhound, determined to corner his prey no matter the obstacle. But unlike a fox, Adrian was not afraid of his pursuer.

"Hello, Bennett," he said when the man approached him. "Nice party. We'll talk later." All without pausing as he made his way toward Hester.

Fortunately Dulcie Bennett spied him and after she nudged Hester several times, the two of them began their approach as well, Miss Bennett in the lead, Hester trailing reluctantly behind.

Adrian braced himself. Given George Bennett's single-minded pursuit, Adrian suspected that the man was now encouraging his sister to chase after him—not that she needed much encouragement. It was plain the girl had formed some sort of infatuation for him. Meanwhile, he had developed a perverse interest in Hester. But Horace also harbored warm feelings for Hester.

The question was, who was Hester interested in?

And who was her mystery "friend" in Cheapside?

"Miss Bennett. Mrs. Poitevant." Horace gave them a crisp bow, then grinned at Hester, an eager puppy anxious to please his owner. "I was hoping to see you here."

After a fleeting glance at Adrian, Hester focused on Horace, smiling at him with such genuine pleasure Adrian had to resist the urge to scowl.

"Mr. Vasterling," she said in that husky tone, so much more feminine than the girlish trills around them. "It's a pleasure to see you again."

"I was hoping you might allow me to escort you on a stroll around the park. And you as well," he added to Dulcie.

"That would be lovely," Hester replied, hooking her arm in Horace's proffered one. Adrian could hardly believe the performance, though he witnessed it with his eyes. How had she banished the shy bumbler and turned Horace so smooth in such a short time?

Finally she turned her gaze on him, her smile fading. "Perhaps you will accompany us as well, Mr. Hawke?"

"My pleasure," he answered. He smiled at her, holding her eyes a long moment before deliberately dropping his gaze to her mouth with its full lower lip and enticingly curved upper bow. Damn, but he wanted to kiss her!

As if she sensed the wayward turn of his thoughts, her cheeks flared with faint color and she looked away. Then Dulcie sidled nearer and he knew the role he was supposed to play in this little farce. With Hester already arm in arm with Horace, he had no choice but to extend his arm to Dulcie, and to carry on the strained sort of conversation with her that silly young girls always engaged in.

It took a good half hour to meander the South Walk, passing beneath the three grand arches, then under the elms along the Grand Walk and back to the tents that marked the birthday celebrations. Ahead of them Hester and Horace carried on animated conversation punctuated by laughter and smiles and exclamations of glee.

Adrian told himself he should be satisfied that his plan was working. Hester was warming to the amiable Horace, just as he'd known she would.

But what he felt was a growing fury. It made no sense of course, but he didn't care. He'd changed his mind, and now he wanted Hester Poitevant for himself, not for Horace.

Three paces ahead of him Hester's skirts swayed with every step she took. He could envision the slender waist beneath the stiff fabric. He could picture that delicious hair spilling free from its confining net to bounce and coil down her back.

He wanted to push Horace aside and take his place, then drag the annoying woman into the nearest shelter where they could be alone—

"—I so wish to go riding." He caught the last of Dulcie Bennett's words.

He gave her a tight smile. "I'm sure you do." How was he to discourage her? Then an idea occurred to him. "You know, Horace is a great one for riding. Isn't that so, Vasterling?"

"What's that?" When Horace paused and turned back, Adrian took that opportunity to disengage his arm from Dulcie's grasp.

"Miss Bennett has been looking for a companion to go riding and I recalled that you enjoy a daily ride. What's your favorite route here in town?"

"I would have to say Hyde Park. The northern green is wonderful for a hard run." He glanced at Hester whose brows were raised in the barest arch. It had an effect on Horace, though, for he added to Miss Bennett, "Of course, you may prefer a more sedate ride."

Dulcie's eyes had widened and she addressed Horace, greatly animated. "I am not at all opposed to a smart gallop."

"Indeed?" Horace took a step closer to Dulcie.

"Oh, yes. At home what I like best, though, is a good, long ramble. You know, fields and forests. Along the Stour River." She clasped her hands fervently to her breast. "Riding is truly my greatest pleasure in life."

"I feel the same way," Horace said.

As Horace engaged Dulcie, Adrian sidled nearer Hester whose gaze remained fixed on Horace. "Do you ride?" he asked. *Look at me.*

Slowly she turned his way. "Not often, especially in recent years."

He drew nearer still. "Perhaps I could entice you to try it again."

"Thank you, but no."

"Then perhaps I could take you driving. I've yet to see the full extent of the park. Perhaps you could be my tour guide."

She averted her gaze. "Thank you, but—"

"But no. Tell me, Hester, what *would* you like to do?" *Look at me!*

She did, and there were sparks in her eyes, like the fire inside emeralds. "You do not have leave to address me so familiarly."

"That could be remedied."

She turned abruptly away, ostensibly to address Horace and Dulcie. But Adrian saw the pulse racing in her throat, the little throb in the hollow of her pale, elegant neck. He'd wager a small fortune that her pulse did not race like that for Horace.

He had to grit his teeth as she caught Horace's arm and prompted him on. Dulcie slipped her hand in the crook of Adrian's arm, and manners demanded he address his attentions back to her.

"I would be so pleased should you join us as well," she said to him. "Mr. Vasterling assures me that if one rides early enough, before the crowds are about, one could almost mistake the park for the countryside. After a month and a half in town, I anticipate the ride with great joy." She paused and looked up at him, thrusting her chest out and batting her eyes. "I do so wish you could join us."

If not for the embarrassed blush that accompanied her awkward attempts to attract him, Adrian would have thought her a brazen hussy. But that blush reminded him that she was only an awkward pawn in her brother's scheme. So he chose to be gentle.

"Thank you for the invitation, Miss Bennett, but I have business matters to attend. Perhaps another time."

He should not have added that last part, for the initial disappointment on her face turned instantly to hopefulness. Good God, how was a man to discourage a naive girl without insulting her?

By the time Adrian and Horace took their leave of the two women, his temper was in a worse state than ever.

"I am to circulate," Horace said. "Mrs. P instructed me to greet everyone I know, and attempt at least three new introductions. I must report my success to her on the morrow." His eyes scanned the shifting birthday crowd, the revelers and the entertainers. "Is there anyone new you can introduce me to?" he added hopefully.

"I'm sure there is." Adrian paused, then went on. "You are satisfied with Mrs. Poitevant's instruction, I take it."

"Oh, yes. She is quite astute, and she has a way of dispelling all your doubts. Or at least, most of them."

"I see." Another pause. "Ever since we saw her in Cheapside I've wondered why she chooses to dress so plainly in society."

Horace shrugged. "It is curious." Then he sighed and added, "She is quite marvelous, don't you think?"

Adrian didn't bother to answer. But there was such a wealth of admiration in Horace's eyes that Adrian felt guilty. In his determined effort to force Hester Poitevant to abandon her snobbish ways, he'd ignored Horace's feelings on the matter. Horace was sure to be hurt if Hester did not return his affection. Somewhat like his own predicament with Miss Bennett.

At the same time, Adrian had become equally determined to have Hester respond only to him. It was the damnedest, most inexplicable thing. He wanted Hester Poitevant and he was willing to fight both Horace and her mystery lover to have her—meanwhile, business could wait.

He shook his head at his own perversity. Then consoling himself that he was saving Horace a world of heartache, he said, "I hope you aren't foolish enough to form an attachment to Mrs. Poitevant."

"Well, I'm not certain I would call it an attachment of the sort you imply. But if it were, why would that be foolish? She is, after all, a lady."

Adrian gazed idly about, affecting a blasé attitude. "She's in trade. She has no resources to speak of. How likely is your father to approve of her?"

Horace's resigned frown was clear answer. Though Adrian felt like a louse, he went on. "Anyway, Mrs. Poitevant does not strike me as a woman currently considering remarriage. You saw her that day in Cheapside, how stunning she looked. If she wanted to attract men's attention, she would dress like that all the time."

A mulish expression came over Horace's face. "I don't care about how she dresses."

An admirable response. Adrian's esteem for Horace, already high, rose higher still. "Nor do I," he said. "But she must have her reasons for choosing so plain an image. To ignore her wishes would not be the gentlemanly thing to do."

Then wanting to lift the man's spirits, he slapped him on the back. "Come on, now. She's given you your instructions. You won't meet anybody standing here just talking with me."

Always amiable, Horace followed his lead. The subject of Hester Poitevant did not come up again.

But the thought of her did, at least to Adrian. With each meeting his fascination with her had increased, and it annoyed the hell out of him. Something about her made no sense. Something about her little masquerade had become an irritant under his skin. He needed to know her secrets, even though she should mean less than nothing to him.

Intellectually he understood a part of it. Like George Bennett, Hester Poitevant had come to symbolize for him all that was wrong with English society: if you weren't titled or rich, or preferably both, you didn't count. The pairing of husbands and wives was as unemotional as the merging of two business concerns. And as London's premier bridemaker, Hester Poitevant sat right in the middle of the whole sordid mess.

If he could put her in her place, make her fall in love with a fellow like Horace, then he would have proven his point. Their system was wrong and it could be changed.

But somehow everything had gotten confused, and now it was he who wanted the damned woman.

And he who seemed unable to get her.

Across the party grounds, Dulcie's conversation with Hester followed a track similar to Horace's, though the principals were different.

"He is the handsomest man in all creation!" Dulcie

gushed. She clasped her hands to her chest. "Isn't he, Mrs. Poitevant? Isn't he?"

Somehow Hester managed a smile. "Yes, I'm certain he must be." *And also the most perverse.*

In truth, however, it was she who was perverse. For when he'd invited her to ride, or to drive out with him, she'd wanted to say yes to those offers—and any *others* he might make as well.

How she'd managed her all-purpose "Thank you, but no," she wasn't at all sure. It must be the many years of practice, of repeating that phrase to so many men, that had guided her through this latest proposition. For it was a proposition. She knew it and so did he. Though she'd adopted the guise of a widow in order to give herself credibility in society, it did not entirely protect her. Widows, especially young, attractive ones, were prime targets for randy men of indiscriminate morals. What respect she gained from the women of society was offset by the leering assumptions of too many of their men.

But since it was the women—the mamas—who hired her, it was to them she must look most respectable. The men she had learned how to rebuff.

Rebuffing Adrian Hawke, however, had not been so easy. And now Dulcie must go on and on with her effusive admiration of the man. If she only knew how base he really was, she would swiftly change her tune.

Then again, Hester knew his true nature, and that did not seem to change *her* response to the man.

But that was physical, she told herself. It had been a very long time since she'd been so attracted to a man. She'd simply forgotten how powerful those emotions sometimes could be. Pounding heart, damp palms. And that distressing awareness in all her most private parts, as if the blood rushed through her body, warming and exciting every least bit of her.

On one level it was rather glorious, and the thought

of succumbing to those forbidden sensations made her almost giddy. But on another level—a sensible, self-protective level—she knew she could never do that. Adrian Hawke was no more the right man for her than he was for Dulcie.

If she, who understood what men like Mr. Hawke were really like still had a hard time accepting that fact, how much harder must it be for Dulcie? And how was she ever to convince her of that fact with her brother urging her to pursue him?

"You know, Dulcie," she began. "After Catherine Hawke's wedding next week, Adrian Hawke is very likely to be returning to America."

"I know. I know." The girl let out a huge sigh. "What am I possibly to do?"

Let him go and count yourself very lucky. "Well . . . Has he indicated any partiality toward you?"

"He's always looking at me. I've caught him several times. See?" She leaned over, hiding her face behind her fan. "He's staring at me right now."

He was staring at one of them all right, Hester thought. The one he figured most likely to do with him what a proper lady should never do.

"I'm afraid, dear, that if he wanted to pursue a deeper acquaintance with you he would. He does not strike me as a man lacking in self-confidence." *Anything but.*

They both watched as a couple approached him and introduced a pretty young blonde dressed in lavender and cream, wearing an enormous straw hat.

Hester pressed her lips together. The man was far too attractive to make a good husband to anyone. Not that fresh-faced blonde or Dulcie—or herself.

Not that *she* wanted a husband. Heaven forbid. But it worried Hester that Dulcie could not see him for what he was. Once he returned to America, would she prove just as foolish with the next handsome cad that smiled at her?

Across the crowd she saw him bow over the blond woman's hand. Maybe watching him turn his charms on yet another woman would open Dulcie's eyes.

When she glanced at Dulcie, however, she found not resignation, but determination etched onto her face. The young woman's eyes glittered with it; her lips pursed with it. "I asked George to invite him to our card party this weekend."

Hester stifled a groan. "And did he?"

"Of course. He thought it was a marvelous idea."

No surprise in that. "Does your mother approve?"

Dulcie hesitated. "Mother is a little slower to warm up to Mr. Hawke. But she no longer objects to him."

Hester did not reply to that, though it boggled her mind how swiftly the woman had changed direction on the subject of Adrian Hawke. George's selfishness did not surprise her. But Lady Ainsley was Dulcie's mother. Apparently though, that did not prevent her agreeing to sell her daughter to the highest bidder, even someone she abhorred. Just so long as she did not have to lower her own standard of living. After all, she had other daughters with whom to snare an earl for a son-in-law.

"Mama said to invite you also."

"Me? Why do you need me at a party in your own home?"

"Because she likes you. And I asked her to," she added. "You've been so good to me. To all of us." Dulcie gave her a hopeful look. "You will come, won't you?"

"Of course." The words were out before Hester could prevent them.

"Oh, thank you. Thank you. Mama will be so pleased and I—" She broke off.

Curious, Hester cocked her head. "And you what?"

The girl smiled, a hesitant, childish smile. "As much as I admire Mr. Hawke, sometimes he is . . . overwhelming. Intimidating." She blushed. "I'll be much more at ease with him knowing you're nearby."

Best you stay intimidated by the man, Hester thought. But she said nothing, for at that moment Dulcie's uncle came up grinning, his features lit by several glasses of wine too many. "Dulcie, m'dear. Come dance with your uncle on his birthday. Come along."

Giggling, Dulcie went with him, leaving Hester to stare after her. The girl had become a mass of contradictions. At times her confidence soared. She talked and laughed and even flirted as she'd never done prior to attending Hester's academy. Yet other times she seemed as young and naive as ever.

All the child needed was to marry a nice man and move somewhere far from her mother and brother. Too bad Horace didn't have deeper pockets, Hester thought. The two of them might manage rather nicely together.

But George and Mrs. Bennett would never allow it. They'd decided that Dulcie must marry money, even untitled, American money—like Adrian Hawke's.

CHAPTER 11

Adrian had been waiting for just this opportunity.

Vauxhall Gardens was well known for its shadowed paths, private bowers, and secret trysting spots. Already tonight more than one couple had slipped quietly away from the giddy center of the birthday bash. But he yet lingered.

Horace appeared to be having a splendid time, thanks to Hester Poitevant. He danced and talked and comported himself with an ease he hadn't previously exhibited. Adrian, however, found himself more ill at ease than he'd been since his Aunt Olivia had first introduced him into polite society.

The irony was that the source of Horace's newfound confidence was also the source of Adrian's agitation.

The past three days had been a resounding success on the business front. But his private life had become a living hell. He'd never wanted a woman he could not have—at least not since he'd left boyhood behind. But ever since his first confrontation with the arrogant, deceptive, delectable, frustrating Widow Poitevant, he'd become a slavering fool. The worst of it was, he couldn't muster interest in any other woman even though there were plenty to be had. But he didn't want them. He wanted her.

So tonight he'd decided to put an end to his agitation. Tonight he would start a concerted effort to seduce the woman, no matter her protests, no matter how wretchedly she dressed.

He had to have her, and finally he had his chance. Hester stood alone in the shadows, back from the partygoers, watching her students and waiting like a mother hen to prop them up should they require it.

This was one time, Adrian vowed, that they would have to perform their parts without her aid.

An energetic polka filled the air, as did laughter and breathless shouts of encouragement. To one side a firebreather raised a round of eager applause, the acrid smell of his smoke scenting the air. Elsewhere a monkey and a dog entertained with a repertoire of tricks truly astounding.

But not as astounding as Hester Poitevant's tricks, Adrian fumed. The sun had set and a cool lavender tinted the scene, with here and there a brighter gold circle of lamplight. He circled the noisy party. No, nothing here was as astounding or intriguing as the pretty deceit she practiced every day with her somber disguise.

As stealthily as a beast of prey he approached her from behind. "Enjoying yourself?"

Hester let out a little gasp at that unexpected voice from the shadows. She'd been accosted like this in the past, though not in a very long time. Yet still she jerked instinctively to the side. Then she recognized the voice and also the warm grasp that prevented her from falling.

Adrian Hawke.

Though she wanted to be angry, what she felt instead was a ridiculous spurt of gladness. He'd sought her out!

"I didn't mean to startle you," he said, his voice as

dark and sultry as the June night had become.

"Didn't you?" She faced him in the shelter of a pair of holly trees. Her heart still pounded, but no longer in fear. Well, perhaps in fear. A different sort of fear. "You may release my arm." *Your touch burns me.*

"I'd rather not."

At that the burn became a fire spreading through her entire body. She tried halfheartedly to pull away, but he did not at first release her—and the fire turned into a conflagration.

When he did finally let her go, she stumbled back, deeper into the shadows. "You . . . you are too forward, sir."

As reprimands went it was awfully weak. But at the moment it was the best she could muster.

"You think that forward?" He moved nearer and she took another backward step. "It appears the standards of what is forward vary widely." Another step nearer, another step back. "For instance," he went on. "I believe a woman with such green eyes as yours should never stare so long and hard at a man as you have stared at me tonight."

"*You* were staring at *me*."

"Yes, I was. But you stared back."

Guilty, she silently acknowledged. Guilty. She swallowed hard, vowing to hold her ground. "Perhaps it would be better for both of us if we agreed not to stare at one another."

He shook his head. "That will never work. I find you far too intriguing to ignore. And you find me . . ." He propped one hand against the trunk of an oak tree and smiled—a half-smile, really, but it had more impact than ten other men's smiles, somehow both threatening and infinitely appealing. "How *do* you find me, Hester?"

Oh, dear, she thought. *I am seriously out of practice in matters like this.*

"Come, come. I hadn't taken you for the tongue-tied sort."

Mustering her courage, she crossed her arms. "What I am is the stickler-for-propriety sort. For instance, I do not like men who grab my arm or use my given name without leave to do so. Nor men who seek to trap me in a compromising position."

"Is that what you think I'm doing?"

"Isn't it?"

He studied her as if honestly debating the answer to her question. He was a broad-shouldered silhouette against the faint light from a lantern somewhere beyond him, a dangerous, far-too-masculine predator in the handsome guise of a gentleman.

As the silence stretched out between them, Hester grew acutely aware of her own appearance. Plain gown. Strict coiffure. No adornments, not even her spectacles. With an unconscious movement she fingered the spot on her nose they usually slid down to.

He smiled at her guilty little gesture. "What I'm doing," he began, "What I'm wondering, is why you disguise yourself so. At least you've abandoned those ridiculous spectacles. But your mode of dress." He shook his head. "We both know, Hester, that the pretty dress you wore the other day is far more suitable for today's entertainments than that matron's garb you wear."

"I believe we've already had this conversation."

"We began this conversation. We haven't finished it."

"Well, I for one consider it finished. Unless it pertains to our business arrangement regarding my—" She broke off and took a sharp breath. "Regarding Mr. Vasterling," she amended. "Then we have nothing to discuss. If you'll excuse me, I believe I ought to return to the party."

"Ah, but we do have something to discuss," he said, straightening up. "Something very important."

Hester tried to swallow, but her mouth had gone dry. What was he talking about? Her already hammering heart thudded with a new fear. Could he have learned something about her true connection to Horace?

But it was not that. For while she stood there, rooted to the ground, he lifted his hand to cup the side of her face. And when she stared at him in shock, undone by the intimacy of that wholly unanticipated caress, he cupped the other side of her face as well.

He was going to kiss her.

He was going to *kiss* her!

But for a long, stretched-out moment he did not. He only held her gaze and waited.

For what?

For her to tell him to stop, she realized. But her realization came too late. By the time her muddled brain understood, he lowered his face to hers and their lips met in a whisper of a kiss.

A whisper, yes. Neither greedy nor demanding. Yet by its very restraint it unleashed a violence of emotion within her chest. She became the greedy one. She was the one with demands unmet. Ten long years of repressed emotion and repressed physical yearning caught her unawares, like a sudden storm on a placid day. Their lips met and held; his fingers slid up into her hair; and all at once what had been too much intimacy became not enough.

Not enough at all.

She leaned into him and he took it for what it was: acceptance and plea.

She'd always known the gardens of Vauxhall were dangerous. That was her last rational thought. It had never been as dangerous, however, as it was with Adrian Hawke in it. For with the subtlest pressure of his thumb at the corner of her mouth, he coaxed it open to him. Then he deepened the kiss, pulling her nearer, slanting his mouth to fit better with hers, and she rose to meet him.

And when he traced the seam of her lips with his tongue, then thrust inside to claim her and thrill her, she let him.

Claim me. Thrill me.

She might as well have shouted the words aloud, for everything in her that was female submitted to that erotic caress. She submitted and bade him continue, and he did. He heard her silent pleading and caught her around the waist. Up against him she came, breast and belly and thighs. Snug, fitting so perfectly together. And all the while he devoured her with his mouth.

But then, she wanted to be devoured. From challenging, to greedy, to the marauding Hannibal rushing her every meager defense: that was the lightning progression of his kisses. From stolen caress to carnal dominance.

She'd never let another man progress this far with her though many had tried, and she should certainly not let this one either, not if she valued her reputation. What if someone saw them?

She gasped for breath and with it came a little glimmer of sanity. She was off balance, bent backward in Adrian Hawke's powerful arms, accepting his hungry kisses, and kissing him back with equal ardor, with only the evening shadows to prevent anyone from discovering them.

"Wait." The word came out fainter than a whisper, but he heard.

"We've waited long enough."

She shivered at his dark growl, so hot against her ear. His free hand moved in her hair and she felt the twisted coil begin to collapse. "Wait—"

"I've been wanting to do this." He nuzzled her temple, her brow, then moved back to her mouth. "Your hair. Your mouth. Your lips." He nipped at her lower lip. Then, "Kiss me."

So much for her protests. He nipped at her lips, ordered her about, and she did exactly as he commanded. Open-mouthed she kissed him. Then when his tongue did not delve between her lips as she so desperately wanted it to, she thrust her tongue into his mouth.

It was like fire, like the fire-breathing man, lighting her up through and through. Her blood roared along the pathways of her veins, a furious lava flow reducing to cinders every inhibition in its way. With one hand he finished off her hair; she felt it tumble down about her waist. With his other he moved to cup her derriere and pull her against his loins.

"See what you have done?" he said, tearing his lips from hers and breathing as hard as she. He stared down at her, his eyes dark and yet on fire with desire. He thrust his hips forward so that she could not mistake the heavy swelling in his breeches. "See what you have done, Hester?"

She had no words to answer him, not words of denial nor words to accept the blame. She was too shaken, too on fire, too consumed by emotions she'd not known could exist.

No man had ever raised her to these shuddering heights of wanton desire.

These shuddering heights were what her mother had been talking about.

Her mother! Oh, God. She couldn't be foolish enough to make the same mistake as her mother!

"I . . . No . . . Let me go," she whispered through lips hot and already swollen from his kisses.

"I think not." He wrapped one long curl of her hair around his hand in the most possessive manner.

The virile threat in his voice, in his eyes, and in his physical domination should have terrified her. But it seemed only to stoke the insane conflagration in her belly. For she pressed her softness to his rigidity until he thrust convulsively against her.

Yes. She retained some power of her own, and that was somehow reassuring. If nothing else, she had the power to make him want her.

"I want you," he murmured, as if he read her mind. "And you want me too."

Oh, yes, she certainly did. She shouldn't, but she did.

Without warning he pulled away from her, so abruptly she nearly collapsed. Her legs were rubber, her mind utterly disoriented. But he kept a hand around her wrist and tugged her deeper into the leafy embrace of their bower. Somewhere beyond them a woman giggled. A man's low voice answered. Then came the muffled but unmistakable sounds of another couple's carnality.

Slowly Hester's wits began to return. She was trysting with a man like a common tart, like the woman so many men had tried to make her into during her season and a half. That he had excited her in ways she'd never known existed did not assuage her shame. Not by half.

She was stumbling into the dark of Vauxhall Gardens with a man who had one thing only on his mind. Although her mind too had just moments ago been consumed by that same "one thing," she saw now the terrible folly in it. Her hair dangled wild and loose around her shoulders. Her gown—Somehow the top two buttons of her gown had come undone.

"No." She tried to slow his determined progress through the murky shadows. "No. Wait!"

He turned back to her. "Wait for what, Hester? Are you one of those women who require seduction?" With a sudden move he swept her up into his arms. "Do you need to be pursued? Convinced 'against your will'?" He kept on through the dark, his long strides sure as he carried her farther and farther from the party. "Is it romance you want? Or perhaps drama will do."

Was that it? Romance, drama. For a moment Hester could not answer. Being swept away in the night by a tall, handsome rogue was certainly romantic and dramatic. Her dark skirts, so plain and ordinary, seemed more like a princess's sweep of frothy gown, trailing over his arm, baring her legs and the hidden lace of her petticoats and silk stockings.

The urge to surrender to his powerful embrace, to wrap her arms around his neck and nestle her face against his chest was almost overwhelming.

When he stooped beneath a curtain of willow branches, however, and they burst out into a grassy field near the carriage park, her silly bubble of a fairy tale popped. If she got into his carriage with him she would be taking an irrevocable step, one that could lead only to ruin.

Not *his* ruin, of course. Men seldom suffered for their sins. But women did. Any ruin would be hers to bear, not his. She had only to remember her mother to know that was true.

Before she could struggle down, he set her on her feet. She supposed even *he* was not so bold as to carry her across a field in full view of anyone who cared to look. He tucked her hand in his arm, keeping his own hand warm and possessive upon hers. "My carriage is close by."

"I am not that sort of woman." She tugged her hand free of his arm, but he caught her by the wrist. In the open field the rising moon limned him with a silvery glow.

"I know you're not, Hester. But you have to admit that what just happened between us has been building for days. Weeks. You're no young, giggly girl in the market for a husband. You're a widow, for several years, I understand. I doubt it's any more natural for a woman like you to deny her needs—her desires—than it is for a man like me."

Though he was wrong about her being a widow, Hester had to wonder if at least one part of his statement was true. What they'd been doing—while they'd been doing it—had felt so right. To break it off while her heart still thudded in her chest, while her blood roared in her veins, and her body burned in a fever of desire— that's what felt wrong. As he said, it didn't feel natural to stop.

Yet surely she could not continue.

"I . . . I must go." She couldn't meet his eyes but stared instead at their arms stretched out between them, linked by his hand around hers.

"Why?"

She shook her head. "You know why." Then anger supplanted her misguided regret. "You know exactly why. I have my reputation to maintain, whereas you— You will have no concern on that score. Soon enough you will depart London and never think once of the damage you leave in your wake."

"What damage? How are my attentions to you any different than those of your friend in Cheapside?"

Her friend? Was he speaking of Mrs. DeLisle? But that made no sense. What had she to do with any of this?

He went on. "Is it unrealistic of me to want you to dress up for an afternoon with me, Hester? Or an evening?"

That's when it hit her with shattering clarity. He thought she had a lover. Once before he'd asked if her friend in Cheapside was a man, though she'd thought little enough of it. But now she understood. He believed she saved her best dresses and hats and gloves to impress a lover.

He wanted her to dress like that for him.

It was so ludicrous she wanted to laugh, the giddy, flattered laugh of a young girl who has made some young buck mad with jealousy. Only she was no young girl and he was no gallant young gentleman, jealous and planning to offer for her hand so he could have her for himself. Adrian Hawke had something far less gallant on his mind.

Although a part of her—a shameful part—responded in the most basic physical way, she knew better than to trust that part of her. He'd just insulted her with his vile assertion. How dare he assume her a woman capable of such moral turpitude?

Unfortunately it seemed she was capable of such lowering behavior. For despite all her logic, she was beset by the wildest urge to just do as he wished her to do. Go with him. Lie with him. Take her pleasure of him as he surely meant to take his pleasure of her.

For a single moment she seriously considered it. Her resistance to his hold eased and when he sensed it, he tugged her forward another pace.

Then reason stepped in. Reason, logic, and blessed self-preservation. If she did this she would become her mother, succumbing to men who had only one use for her. Men who would pay the price she demanded but who neither loved nor valued her. From one lover to the next Isabelle had careened, always succumbing to the most ardent and determined of her pursuers. Men as determined as Adrian Hawke.

At least her mother had never had two lovers at one time. If Adrian thought her affections were engaged with another he might give up and leave her alone.

She turned her head away, trapped by indecision. Was that what she truly wanted, to be left alone?

A wave of longing struck her with devastating force. She'd never felt lonely before, or at least she hadn't allowed herself to feel that way. But he made her feel that way, with his kiss, with his seductive manner, with merely the heat of his hand around hers. He made her feel lonely.

He also terrified her and he had no right!

She drew herself up, facing him as she'd faced Beatrice Bennett and so many others who tried to order her about. They thought they knew her so well. But they didn't know anything about her. Nothing at all.

"Mr. Hawke. I apologize if I misled you in . . . in my behavior. I was wrong to . . . to do so. You are correct in guessing that my affections are otherwise engaged. So you will understand that I am not about to travel anywhere with you." She paused. "If you would be good enough to let loose of my hand?"

She saw his jaw tense and release. "Your affections did not seem engaged anywhere but with me."

Her heart beat a rapid tattoo high in her throat. "As I said, I'm sorry if I misled you."

Even in the dark his eyes were alive with heat. "I was not misled, Hester."

"Do not address me in that way!"

"I was not misled by either the sincerity or the enthusiasm of your kisses."

"I don't care what you call it," she retorted, growing more and more agitated. "It was a mistake and it will not happen again. Now let me—"

He released her hand and took a step backward. But instead of feeling relief, Hester felt even more threatened.

"A mistake?" he said in a slow drawl, low and mocking. "Kissing a beautiful woman in the moonlight is never a mistake. Igniting the passion within a woman like you . . ." She felt the touch of his gaze as it swept over her. "If not tonight, Hester, then perhaps tomorrow . . ."

Tomorrow. Hester had to take three breaths in quick

succession to suppress the quiver of anticipation he planted in her with just that one simple word.

From beyond the trees came the sound of music, the hum of voices, the reflected light of the busy city beyond the gardens. But right there in the grassy field with rye heads sweeping her hem and little night creatures scurrying just beyond her heels, Hester felt entirely alone with him. And utterly susceptible.

He could sweep her away with no one the wiser. She could let him do so and discover the rest of the passionate arc they'd begun to scale.

Dear Lord, but a wanton part of her wanted to do just that. But then, what would happen tomorrow? Easy to succumb to passion tonight. Dealing with the aftermath in the morning would be disastrous. And then, what about Dulcie?

"Good-bye, Mr. Hawke." That was all she could manage. She should have said, Do not speak to me again, she fumed as she hurried away. Or, Don't ever approach me or presume to ask me to dance. Or, Never, never take me in your arms. Or kiss me. Or caress me. Or let my hair down—

It took her forever to repair her hair. In the dark with most of her pins gone, she could do little more than knot it and hope it held.

Of course, the first person she ran into would be Lady Ainsley.

"Well, Mrs. Poitevant, I believe you will be most pleased with what I have to tell you."

"Indeed?" Hester blinked, giving the Viscountess Ainsley her best approximation of a bright smile.

"Abigail Fowler, Lady Hartshorn's youngest daughter." Lady Ainsley leaned nearer, releasing a whiskey-laden cloud of breath. "Plain as a mule, flat as a board, with frizzy hair and crooked teeth. But I told her mother that you could find her a husband." She tucked her chin tight against her neck, making a series of ridges in the loose flesh there. "So. What do you think of that?"

"It appears I owe you a debt of gratitude," Hester answered. Thank goodness the woman had been dipping too deeply in the punch bowl. "If you will excuse me, however, I must find the . . . the necessary," she improvised.

"It's over beyond that first arch," Lady Ainsley said, sweeping her arm in a wide gesture.

"Thank you," Hester muttered, hurrying away.

"Miss Poitroy . . . Poitevoy . . . Mrs. Poitevant." The woman giggled after she finally got it out. "Mrs. Poitevant, I think you should know that your hair is coming loose in the back."

"Is it? Why then I'd better go and fix it."

There was more to fix than her hair, however. Somehow Hester took her leave, addressing only those she could not avoid without insult. Then she found Mr. Dobbs, climbed into her carriage, and fled Vauxhall Gardens in private disgrace.

Had she known that a man followed on horseback she would have been appalled. As it was, Adrian was appalled at his own idiotic behavior. Trailing a woman who had rebuffed his advances was the behavior of a ruffian, a cad of the lowest sort.

But God help him, he could not resist. Tonight he'd kissed the sweetest, most succulent lips he'd ever tasted. He'd tangled his fingers in the silkiest, most fragrant hair he'd ever touched. And he'd filled his arms with the warmest, most enticing bit of womanhood he'd ever had the good fortune to embrace.

That she came with a starchy attitude and a mysterious other life only made him want her more. He wanted to peel back the layers of her secrets just as he would peel back the layers of her feminine garb. Dress, petticoats, corset, and chemise. With each layer removed, he would come closer to the prize he sought.

He grinned into the night. Her petticoat and drawers had been a damn sight more feminine than the dress that covered them. Yes, every layer peeled away revealed a more and more feminine creature, a woman of infinite appeal and limitless passions. He wanted to delve to the core of that hot female passion—and he wanted to make sure no other man got there first.

So he followed her, if only to make certain she did not go to Cheapside. If she went to her lover in Cheapside he would have to confront the man.

And do what? the small portion of his brain that functioned beyond the control of his straining loins asked him. Confront the man and do what? Fight for her? Bargain for her? Beg for her?

When had he become such a hopeless, horny fool?

That her conveyance made straight for Mayfair was small comfort. Adrian sat in the dark, watching as she went inside. He stayed until an upstairs window began to glow with lamplight. That must be her bedroom, he thought, which knowledge only increased his arousal. She was letting her hair down, removing her layers of clothes. Gown and stockings, corset and drawers. Down to her chemise, no doubt a gossamer-thin wisp of translucent linen and lace.

He groaned out loud. Soon she would slip into her bed.

This time he let out a low, vicious curse. Abruptly he turned his horse and kicked him forward. At least the woman slept alone, he told himself. At least tonight she was alone.

It was cold comfort though. For he would also be sleeping alone.

What an asinine waste of time for both of them.

CHAPTER 12

Hester had no time to prepare herself in the morning, for Horace arrived early for his appointment. Not three minutes later Adrian Hawke also was ushered into her parlor, Fifi and Peg close on his heels.

He'd planned it this way, Hester fumed when Mrs. Dobbs showed him in. Once Horace gained entrance, she could not very well pretend to be indisposed.

"Good morning, Mrs. P.," Adrian said, the tiniest, wickedest smile curving his lips.

His lips that had kissed her with such skill and passion and—

Stop it!

"Good morning, Mr. Hawke," she answered in her primmest tone. "I think it only right to inform you that while such familiar address might be acceptable in other circles, it is considered poor manners in town society."

He only smiled, causing the most violent trembling in her belly. That trembling swiftly expanded throughout her body, and she had to clench her hands not to reveal the awful extent of it. And all on account of his smile.

Into that silence fraught with so much tension, Horace

asked in all innocence, "What if a person gives their permission for such intimacy?"

He and Hester had been sitting at a table when Adrian arrived, starting a list for Horace—trips to the tailor and the bootmaker, social obligations, and names of acquaintances, especially unattached females. Though Adrian stood opposite Hester, after that one brief glance at him, she kept her gaze steadfast upon Horace. It was so much easier than looking at the subtly smirking Adrian Hawke.

At least Horace's question was sincere.

"If you have become friendly enough with someone that they offer that level of familiarity, and assuming you are willing to reciprocate the intimacy—" She stumbled over that last word. It conjured up so many other sorts of intimacies.

"Yes?" Horace asked, leaning forward.

"Yes, Mrs. P. Please enlighten us," Adrian added, amusement rampant in his voice. To add insult to injury, he sat down without being offered a chair, drew off his leather gloves, tucked them into his coat pocket, then crossed one ankle casually across his opposite knee.

Enlighten him? Hester wanted to strangle him. He was doing it all on purpose. Every bit of it. Even the way he'd dressed seemed calculated to upset her. For the crisp blue coat and snowy white stock sharpened his already lean features. He was all broad shoulders, carved muscles, and vivid good looks.

Meanwhile, she was frazzled, bleary-eyed, and dressed like an exhausted middle-class housewife whose maids had all just resigned their positions.

She ought to just ignore his baiting, but she couldn't. She'd lost another night's sleep due to him and she was too tired to be cautious. Added to that, Fifi had leaped up into his lap, the ungrateful little traitor.

"Very well, I'll enlighten you," she began. "If you would be considered a gentleman, Mr. Hawke, you must sit up straight, refrain from undressing in public, and never insult your hostess by seating yourself without asking, or by addressing her in a disrespectful manner."

She could see alarm in Horace's expression. But Adrian Hawke only grinned. "But why?" he asked, not even a smidgen of contrition on his face. "It's too warm for gloves, and we both know you were about to offer me a seat." He paused, his eyes alive with devilment. "Weren't you? As a good hostess it's to be expected of you."

If only Horace weren't here, Hester fumed.

But if Horace weren't here, I would be alone with Mr. Hawke.

An unforgivable little thrill ran through her, settling in some unnamable region down low in her belly. It made her want to squirm in the most unseemly way.

Unbidden, one of her mother's phrases came to her. "He makes me melt," she'd said about one of her lovers. That was exactly how Adrian Hawke made Hester feel, as if she were melting from the inside out.

It was only the fact that she might be more like her mother than she'd ever guessed that gave Hester the will to pull herself together. "The purpose of society's rules is to create some consistency in human interactions. When people find the set of rules they feel most comfortable with, they discover also the group of people they can be comfortable with. Not everyone will be content within the strict rules of British society. I believe that may be why so many people left for the colonies," she added with an edge of spite. "They were unhappy with Britain's elaborate rules of society."

"Are you implying that everyone who stayed here embraces those rules?" Adrian asked.

"No. Of course not. Even within Britain there are various strata of society. No doubt you can easily find places where bare hands, crossed legs, and people fond of overly familiar names are quite welcome."

He grinned. "But not in your parlor. Am I right?"

Their gazes clashed and held, his need to best her just as evident as her need to put him in his place. And yet, what *was* that place?

Horace coughed, jerking Hester's attention back to him. How could she have let herself become embroiled in such a heated exchange, and before an audience, no less?

To his credit, Horace did not comment on it. After all, a true gentleman or lady was never critical or rude, or made another person ill at ease. Adrian Hawke could take a lesson from him, she decided.

Then again, so could she.

Chastened by that realization, Hester folded her hands together and counted to ten. Twice. Only then did she raise her gaze to Adrian Hawke's face with its sardonic grin and predator's eyes.

"You must have come here for a reason, Mr. Hawke. Perhaps you ought to tell me what it is so that Mr. Vasterling and I might get on with our work."

"Fair enough. I came to ask Horace if he and Miss Bennett have made arrangements to go riding, and if they have, whether you and I might join them."

Why did her heart leap so? It was utterly ridiculous, yet Hester couldn't deny the truth. Her heart jumped at his casual, offhand, presumptuous invitation. Did he think by involving Horace and Dulcie that he could coerce her into agreeing to such a crude invitation?

Hadn't she turned down the very same invitation yesterday?

But that was before he'd kissed her—which ought to have strengthened her resolve but which, to her horror, did quite the opposite.

"I haven't asked her yet," Horace said, his expression thoughtful as his gaze moved from his friend to her and back to Mr. Hawke. "However, I'll do so today. But only if both of you agree to join us. *Both* of you."

Hester stared at Horace, trying to decipher the intent in his insistent words. But his expression was bland, just pleasant, well-intentioned Horace. "Please, Mrs. Poitevant. It would reinforce my confidence immensely to have you join us. Anyway, I doubt Miss Bennett's mother would allow her to ride out with me without a suitable chaperone."

Even more doubtful was the likelihood that Dulcie's mother would allow her to go riding with Horace Vasterling at all, unless the wealthy Adrian Hawke was included. That should have been sufficient reason for Hester not to go along with them.

But in spite of that logic, she found herself saying, "Very well, Horace. Make your arrangements. If it's convenient I'll try to be there."

She didn't look to see the smug expression sure to be painted across Adrian Hawke's face, and he left shortly after that, behaving perfectly, she noticed. But then, why shouldn't he? He'd accomplished just what he'd set out to do.

Hester wanted to be angry with him, only she found it too hard. Despite his blatant manipulation of her and Horace, her primary reaction to today's turn of events was anticipation. The man had in essence thrown down a challenge to her: he was pursuing her in earnest, no matter her protests, no matter the fact that he might pick from among dozens of other far more willing women.

But were there truly any that were more willing than she?

If the liquid warmth settling into her lower parts was any indication, or that breathlessness that overtook her whenever she thought of him, or that hot lava of emotions that spread through her whenever she remembered last night, then perhaps there was no one more willing.

Though her mind told him no, her body shouted a resounding yes.

To her shame and confusion, she suspected he'd received the latter message loud and clear.

Hester's only riding habit was one left over from her
days on the marriage mart. Though a sedate spruce
green, the cloth was a finely woven wool, boasting a
tiny tucked-in waist, a double march of brass buttons
down the bodice, and elaborate gold braid edging the
vee-shaped neckline and collar. Even though it still fit,
it was altogether too fetching an ensemble for a middle-
aged widow, she decided as she twisted and turned before her mirror.

"Ooh, now that's a cunning piece," Mrs. Dobbs said
as she brought up Hester's freshly polished riding boots.
She smiled and circled around Hester, fluffing the generous skirt, plucking at a bit of lint on the sleeve. "You
look perfectly lovely in that, m'dear. Perfectly lovely."

Hester scowled at her reflection. Too lovely. She
sighed, enjoying the feeling of being pretty for a change,
imagining the fun of being pretty out in public with a
man's admiring glance following her. And the truth was,
she always used to enjoy riding. But like dancing and
flirting, riding was one of the pastimes she'd given up
when she'd donned her respectable widow guise.

"Here. Put on the bonnet." Mrs. Dobbs handed her
the smart piece with its Robin Hood's brim lined in a
lighter green velvet, all tied with a wide matching ribbon.

"This will never do," Hester said, though she loved
the effect of the lighter color around her face. It gave
her eyes the dark cast of emeralds. "No." She whipped
it off. "I'll have to change the light green to black."

"But why?"

"Because this is too youthful a look for a widow like me."

"It's not as if you're an old drudge. Besides, it's been six years."

"Mrs. Dobbs." Hester turned from the mirror and thrust the hat at the woman. "If you would be so good as to have Mr. Dobbs take you to the milliners directly? I'll write down my instructions for Mr. Goswell. If he has time, tell him you can wait for it. If they can't manage that, tell them I must have it no later than Monday morning."

Though she didn't like it, the meddlesome housekeeper did as she was told, only tsk-tsking a little more than usual. Once she and her husband were off, Hester collapsed on the parlor settee.

It was a dangerous step she was taking. Like a moth, fully aware of the lantern's fatal appeal, she was fluttering nearer and nearer Adrian Hawke. The heat of their interaction last night ought to send her fleeing in the opposite direction. Hadn't she been singed enough ten years ago by men of his sort? Hadn't she seen her mother fall over and over into this same fire fueled of passion and blind hope? Did she need to be burned again, and this time to cinders?

On the other hand, her circumstances were nothing like they'd been ten years ago. Then she'd believed in love and marriage. She'd believed that she could find that one perfect man who could complete her life, something her mother had never been able to do. But she'd learned swiftly enough that when so-called gentlemen made offers to women of her background, it had nothing whatsoever to do with love.

So, what *did* she believe in now?

Certainly not in love. Staring blankly at the ceiling, she loosened the top button of her bodice and kicked off her low-heeled shoes. As for marriage, she supposed there were some that worked. But they were based on affection and compatibility. Mutual respect between married people.

Did passion have a place in those relationships?

In all the years Hester had worked to help her students make compatible matches, she'd never once considered the passionate side of marriage. In her opinion, the so-called pleasures of the marriage bed were better termed the rigors of the marriage bed. For even should the woman experience pleasure in the physical act, it was inevitably offset by the miseries the man was certain to inflict. He might not do it right away, but eventually he would.

The few times one of her students had asked through her giggles and blushes about passion, Hester had brusquely referred her to her mother. Now, however, the subject of passion confronted her. How did such powerful physical feelings fit into *her* life? What was she to do about Adrian Hawke and how he made her feel?

Without warning Fifi jerked up from her spot on the sunny window seat. Peg too perked up, and the two of them headed down the stairs, Fifi scampering in excitement, while Peg limped more slowly behind. Was Mrs. Dobbs back so quickly? More likely they'd forgotten something.

In her stocking feet Hester padded down the stairs, following the dogs to the front door. The Dobbses would not come to the front door.

A brisk knock came; she hesitated, conscious of her bare feet.

They expected the coal man today, but he should also come to the back—unless he'd seen the Dobbses leaving.

She opened the door and peered through the crack. "Could you go around through the yard—Oh!"

"Front door. Back door." Adrian Hawke stood there

smiling at her. "Whichever you prefer, Hester."

She must have fallen back in shock, for before she could turn him away, he stepped inside, closed the door, and overtook every one of her senses.

"What are you doing here?"

"I've come to call."

"But . . . But . . ." She sucked in a sharp breath. "If you're looking for Horace, he isn't here right now."

"I'm not looking for Horace."

I'm looking for you. Though unsaid, those words crackled between them, a streak of white-hot lightning. From last night's carnal tryst to this morning's more circumspect meeting, to this moment of inevitable confrontation, that lightning streak of physical awareness arced and struck with an intensity that scared Hester to death. Yet its very power drew her, heart pounding, breath forgotten, body melting from the inside out. It drew her to him when she ought to be running away.

All she could manage was, "You shouldn't be here," though she knew she didn't mean it.

He took off his hat and set it upon the demilune table beside the door. "We are two adults free to indulge ourselves as we wish."

Oh, Lord! "How like a man to couch an improper proposition in such a sensible manner."

He smiled and strolled toward her. "Yes. How like a totally besotted man who can think day and night of only one woman to tone down his words so dramatically."

Besotted? He was besotted with her? The words should not have affected Hester, but they did. They enveloped her with their seductive power, overwhelming her. Step by step she moved backward toward the parlor. But it was not a retreat. Even she, as worried about propriety as she wanted to be, knew it was not a retreat.

As he followed he left his gloves on a chair seat, and flung his coat over its back. With every item of clothing

he shed, another facet of Hester's will—of her logic—
was shed as well. She deserved a little pleasure in life,
she told herself. No one knew he was here, and no one
need ever find out. Besides, everyone knew that so long
as a widow was discreet she had more freedom than
other women of the *ton*.

Except that she was not truly a widow. Worse, she
was still a virgin.

She almost laughed out loud at the notion of regretting she was a virgin. But it wasn't funny. How would
he react if he found out that truth?

His hand came up to cup her face. "I don't understand
how you do it, Hester."

"Do what?" she whispered, undone by the burning
desire in his eyes. So blue. So hot. So endlessly enticing.

"Tempt me to such madness."

He rubbed his thumb across her lower lip, a slow
caress that made her knees turn to rubber. Reflexively
she parted her lips. One thought only consumed her. *Oh
Lord, please kiss me!*

His head lowered as if to do just that, and her chest
began to hurt from the frantic pounding of her heart. *Kiss
me as you kissed me last night.*

But he went on speaking. "I don't know if it's the
way you shield your beauty behind those spectacles and
those ugly dresses." His hand trailed down to her neck.

"Or if it's the barely restrained wealth of your hair
that torments me." His other hand slid into her careless
chignon, releasing it from its pins.

"Or maybe it's the primness you affect, that fastidious
adherence to the rules of society." One of his fingers
traced the gaping opening of her neckline. The tip was
so warm as his nail followed a dangerous path down-
ward, making her quiver.

"But now I know you're not nearly so prim. So fastidious."

His hand dipped lower and she stopped breathing. "You were made to break all the rules of society, Hester." She could feel the movement of his breath against her cheek, the heat of his body so near to her own. "You were meant to break them with me."

Then finally he kissed her. Thoroughly. Deeply. Erotically. And the erotic part was the best part of all. His lips slanted over hers and his tongue claimed the rest of her. One stroke of fiery bliss and she succumbed completely. Less than an entire day had passed since their first kiss, but it might only have been moments so far as her body was concerned. She was alive for him, waiting for him.

Dear Lord, but she'd been waiting for him since long before she'd ever laid eyes on him.

He kissed her, claiming the right as no man ever had done. When he pulled her body snug up against his she was ready, primed, damp and oozing desire. She felt him move and heard the parlor door close with a firm, final thud. They were alone in her house. Had he planned it so?

He couldn't have. She'd sent the Dobbses on their errand. Adrian had simply arrived at the perfect time. Perhaps she'd summoned him with the very strength of her longing for him. If so, this couldn't be wrong, could it?

She wound her arms around his shoulders and neck, rising on her bare toes to embrace him. As consents went, it was as blatant as they came.

At once he angled them down onto the settee, her in his lap with her bottom nestled against his rigid arousal, as he kissed her into utter submission. Her hair tumbled down around them, as did all her inhibitions. So long as he kept kissing her, sliding his tongue between her lips, drawing her tongue into his mouth, and in the process making something in her belly liquefy, she was his. She felt his hand stroke across her breast, hot even through the wool of her riding jacket, then hotter and forbidden when the jacket came open to expose her chemise.

He thumbed her already erect nipple, and against his mouth she gasped. Again he thumbed that sensitive peak, then did the same to the other. Thumbed it, rolled it between his fingers, pressed his palm in a hot circle over it. Around and around each breast, back and forth between them.

Eyes closed, Hester dropped her head back and reveled in the mindless pleasure. Then bending down, he moved his mouth to her breasts, drawing one nipple in with a powerful sucking movement.

She arched up with a cry of exquisite agony. It felt as if he had tugged something all the way down to the throbbing place between her legs. So hot, so sweet, so . . . so necessary.

"Ah, Hester. My sweet Hester. I knew you would be passionate." He did the same to her other nipple, and again she cried out. It was too powerful, too much. And yet the abandoned breast longed for what the other one had.

But he knew. He went back and forth, and each time he grew more fierce in his assault, sucking, biting, rolling the engorged tips of her nipples between his teeth.

She didn't know when he'd nudged her chemise down to bare her breasts. She didn't feel his hand push her skirts up, baring her legs all the way to her bottom.

But she felt when his hand curved into the warm vee between her legs. She gasped and stiffened, then submitted when his mouth once more captured hers. For his hand mimicked his lips, and his fingers mimicked his tongue. Circling, claiming, delving deep.

She should have been ashamed, but she wasn't. It felt too good, too hot and urgent for her to make him stop. Somehow he knew how to touch her, something she'd never quite known how to do. When she'd ached down there in the past, she'd only squirmed and suffered, not certain how to react. But he knew. He made all her previous yearnings seem like nothing.

They *were* nothing compared to this.

He set her on fire, and with his finger slipping in and out of the most private part of her, he was rousing the flames to new heights. Yet that also seemed the only way to ease the conflagration. Burn it hotter still.

Burn *her* hotter.

Then with his slippery, wet fingers he found another place, a little nub of a place buried deep within her curls, and he began to rouse it. Like a volcano it rose to him, hot, swelling, near to bursting.

But he was a man unafraid of fire, for he delved deep into the hottest part of her even as he circled the aching nub of her desire.

She couldn't bear to continue. She couldn't bear to stop. Her head thrashed back and forth as she fought the two conflicting forces.

Then he bent his mouth to her breasts once more, sucking in as he thrust deep inside her with his finger and pressed a hard circle around that nub, and she erupted.

She jerked up against his mouth, his hand, and kept on bucking. "Oh, God—Oh, God—"

He thrust up too. She barely felt it she was so caught up in the mighty upheaval that was killing her, it was so strong. He had her speared upon his finger, pressed against his rigid arousal, and spread bare-breasted across his lap, a feast displayed like some pagan offering to him, her god of fire.

She couldn't say how he slid out from under her, how he propped one of her legs on the back of the settee while the other draped to the floor. She was beyond sensible thought, beyond logic and reason when he kissed the inside of her knees, then moved a hot line of kisses up the still quivering flesh of her inner thighs, it was no more insane than what had gone before.

He raised his head to stare deeply into her eyes as his hand slid up her thighs. She stared back, utterly ensnared by this man, so unlike any man she'd ever known.

"I knew you would be passionate," he repeated, his voice thick with passion of his own.

Hester closed her eyes against the intimacy of his declaration. How could he have known when she herself had never suspected?

Then he kissed her again, only it was not her knee or her thigh, or any place a reasonable person would kiss a person—nor a place a reasonable person would want to be kissed. For he kissed her there, right on that volcano spot that he'd found before with his thumb and palm.

She jerked, but his hands soothed her, holding her open to the leisurely inquiry of his lips and tongue. Too fast she felt it begin again. Too fast. Too powerful. And when he sucked hard and made her erupt, as if at his command, she bucked again, sobbing insensibly— words, promises, pleas.

The tremors reverberated a long time inside her as Hester lay there, drowning in the aftermath. She had no strength remaining, not in any muscle of her entire body. Even her wits abandoned her, for though she was aware that Adrian still knelt between her legs, she couldn't muster the strength for embarrassment. Even when he stood over her, a man at his most powerful and virile, with every muscle straining, she could only lie there and let Adrian look at her with those burning blue eyes of his.

This was what her mother had felt and become a slave to, this terrible, delicious submission. Hester closed her eyes on that thought. She was not like her mother. She never would be. Instead she concentrated on Adrian and why, of all men, she'd finally submitted to him.

Yet even in submitting she had claimed a strange sort of power over him, for he wanted to possess her. She could see it in his eyes. She could sense it in the way he held himself so stiffly. After all he'd done to her, he still wanted more.

She blinked, slowly becoming aware of her parlor, her settee beneath her, her foot draped still over the settee back. She pushed up on her elbows, trying to rise, trying to hide her bare legs and everything else from his devouring gaze.

He watched without stopping her. But she grew more and more conscious of his eyes on her, on how she must look, a disheveled woman who'd offered not one word of resistance to him. How was she to react to him now?

Unfortunately her legs were too shaky for her to stand, so she was forced to sit there, trying vainly to recover some modicum of decency. When she pulled up her chemise and went to close her bodice, however, a panicky cry slipped out. Her chemise was wet, two damning spots where his mouth had pressed and kissed and sucked. Where he'd known her and pleasured her.

As if he heard her thoughts, he reached one finger to stroke across her left breast. She fell back against the settee and stared wide-eyed at him.

Heavens, but he made her hot all over again with just one finger upon her breast.

"Does your lover do that for you?" he asked, his words a hungry growl.

"My . . . my lover?"

"Does he bring you to your peak before taking his own pleasure? Does he make you tremble and scream and turn to honey inside?"

Her lover. He still believed she had a lover in Cheapside. And of course he thought her more experienced in the art of lovemaking than she was.

She bent back to her bodice, trying with shaking fingers to button it up. But he stopped her. "Let me."

"No—"

"Yes."

He knelt on one knee before the settee and tugged the bottom edges of her bodice together. Their heads were on the same level, their faces only inches apart as he concentrated on the buttons. It was strange, even stranger in some ways than what had proceeded before.

"Were it not that my horse is tied out front, and that your servants might return at any time, I would not be buttoning your bodice, Hester." He looked up from his work, searing her with the intensity of his eyes. "I want you naked beneath me, every pearly pink part of you open to me, to be tasted and marked. I want to eat every bit of you as I just did, your delicious mouth and your lovely, sweet-tasting bottom."

She gulped in embarrassment but could not move. He buttoned another button. "I want to bury myself inside you, Hester. In the succulent center of you. But you know that. I want to make love to you, slow and sweet. Then I want to take you again, hard and fierce. I want to exhaust myself in you. I want to possess your body in every way a man can possess a woman."

He paused and she heard the harsh rasping of his breathing. Or was it hers?

He went on. "You'd like that, wouldn't you?"

Yes. Yes! Do it now!

But Hester couldn't say a word. She only licked her dry, overly sensitive lips.

At the sight he smiled, a grim, pained sort of smile. "And maybe you'll do the same for me." He shuddered then frowned and concentrated on the next button, the one just beneath her breasts.

"When you get undressed tonight, remember whose hands dress you now. When you step naked into your bath, remember whose kisses have laved your bare flesh. Wherever the hot water caresses you, I have caressed you—and will do it again. And again."

Hester couldn't breathe when he raised his face once more. He kept his eyes on her as he tugged the bodice closed across her breasts. He didn't touch the aching, yearning nipples which strained toward him until they hurt. He only forced the round brass button into its slot, then drew his hands away and sat back on his heels.

"Think of me, Hester, with every garment you shed or don. Imagine it's my hands on you. And imagine what else my hands can do for you. You only have to ask."

She remained on the settee as he stood, then turned and left. He snatched up his coat and gloves and hat, then strode into the kitchen and out the back way. His footsteps faded away. The back door closed with its familiar thud. But nothing else was familiar, not her parlor, not this settee, not her riding habit. Most especially not herself.

How was she ever to be herself again? How was she ever to regain her old life, her old routine? Even the simple act of dressing herself or bathing—

"Oh!" She broke off that thought with a cry of anguish. At that moment she hated him even more than she desired him. For in a few brief moments Adrian Hawke had changed everything. And now she must go after him, or else find a way to pretend none of this had ever happened.

Through the years she'd become so good at pretending, at disguising her true self behind the facade she'd created. She knew, however, that she would never be good enough to pretend that this afternoon hadn't changed her forever.

CHAPTER 13

Adrian could barely walk. Donning his coat on Hester's kitchen stoop became an exercise in self-discipline. Left arm. Right arm. Pulling on his gloves was a near impossibility when his hands shook this badly. At least his hat went on easily, jammed onto his head with one frustrated motion. But he'd never be able to mount his horse.

So he stood beneath a newly budded cherry tree at the back corner of her cottage, hidden from the street and sheltered from the neighbors' view. He couldn't hide from himself, though, not from the fierce, physical pain that gripped him, nor from the madness.

He shifted his weight from one foot to the other, seeking relief but not finding it. Good God, was he insane? He should have stayed in her parlor and finished what they'd begun. Hester wouldn't have objected, and certainly he'd be feeling a damn sight better than he did right now.

What idiotic impulse had made him stop when he most needed not to stop? He'd done right by her—more than right, for he'd felt every tremor she'd experienced.

But then, he'd had a point to prove: her secret lover

had nothing on him, and now she knew it.

So why stop when she was primed, when she was melting hot for him, sweet as honey and fragrant with the intoxicating scent of aroused woman?

From another yard a woman's shout was answered by a child's call. In the street the metal-clad wheels of a cart rumbled across the cobblestones. A dog yipped, and from inside Hester's cottage her two pets answered, one a shrill excited bark, the other lower and lazier.

Life teemed around them, inside her house and out. That's why he'd stopped. He didn't want to ruin her reputation, not when she went to such extreme pains to preserve it.

So he'd stopped, when it was the last thing he'd wanted to do. But it was not over between them. She was too passionate, too perfectly responsive to his every caress not to want more, not to want to finish what they'd started.

The prudish society snob was turning out to be not so prudish and, even more surprising, not so snobbish either.

He gritted his teeth at the insistent throbbing in his breeches. In time she would come to him; he was certain of that. She would seek him out and he would be ready. More than ready.

So he willed himself to breathe and relax. He straightened his clothes and, when he felt presentable, made his way down the side alley to his waiting mount. But he didn't ride. Instead he walked the spirited gelding, taking a route that he hoped would not bring him into contact with anyone he knew.

There was no use for it. Hester had to talk to someone and Mrs. DeLisle was the only person she could trust with a subject like this. Even then it would be difficult, she knew as she perched on the edge of the ratty hack she'd hired for her hasty trip to Milton Street. But she had nowhere else to turn.

Besides, nothing shocked Verna DeLisle. Though she presented a perfect picture of propriety, she'd seen quite a bit in her long life. Certainly she could not be easily shocked if she'd been a friend to Hester's perennially shocking mother.

Hester pressed a trembling hand over her eyes. Just thinking of her mother after her own wanton behavior gave her a throbbing headache. Was this how it began? One man introduced you to the carnal pleasures of the flesh and you became a hopeless slave to them? Was she now cursed to seek out more and more of what Adrian Hawke had showed her today?

For there was no denying the awful truth: she did want more.

She'd spent the first five minutes after he left telling herself how glad she was that he was gone. How she'd never let him near her again. Not him, nor any other man.

Then she'd staggered up the stairs on legs of rubber to frantically begin shedding her riding habit. With every button released, however, she'd been forced to face the truth. She wanted him again. She wanted the final act, the one he had inexplicably denied her.

A cry of dismay slipped from her lips, and she trembled with need and fear. What was to become of her? How could she have allowed him to take such liberties with her and not have considered the disastrous consequences?

She leaped from the hack almost before it stopped, thrust the fare at the driver, and though her legs threatened with every step to collapse, she hurried up the path and into Mrs. DeLisle's house, not even waiting for her knock to be answered.

"Mrs. DeLisle? Where are you? Verna?"

Then Hester found her, just finishing her tea in the kitchen, and with a cry of relief and utter misery, she flung herself into her friend's arms and burst into tears.

Verna heard her out, every wet, hiccupping word. Her tea turned tepid as Hester wept into her lap. But in her sweet, calming manner, she only smoothed her gentle hand along Hester's hair while the sordid tale revealed itself.

"And then he left?"

Hester nodded, still huddled on the floor beside Verna's chair, her arms circling her friend's waist.

"Without even seeking his own release? Had the Dobbses returned?"

"No." Hester raised her head, wiping her eyes with the back of her hand.

"Use my handkerchief, dear. Very curious," she added in a thoughtful voice. "Very curious indeed."

"The worst part—" Hester sniffled then blew her nose. "The worst part is, should he return, I'm afraid I will let him in. I know I will."

"As well you should."

Hester straightened further and stared at Verna aghast. "How can you say that?"

Mrs. DeLisle gave her a stern look. "Hester, you are well past the age when most women have lost their innocence—whether within a marriage or without. In my opinion, virginity is highly overrated."

Hester's eyes grew round with shock at such an outrageous statement, and from such a proper person.

Mrs. DeLisle went on. "Don't misunderstand. Virginity is important enough when a girl is young and seeking to wed. But if she's older with no real prospect of marriage or no particular inclination for it—or if like me she is widowed, well." She gave an elegant shrug. "Then preserving the virgin state serves no purpose save to torment a person for experiencing the most natural of feelings. You are still a young healthy woman, Hester. You *ought* to feel good when a man makes love to you."

"But . . . But he's not my husband."

"Perhaps he wishes to be."

"No." Hester sat back on her heels. "No. He definitely does not want that. He is simply . . . well, smitten."

"I thought you said the word he used was 'besotted.' "

Hester nodded. Besotted. Him besotted with her. The very idea had thrilled her. "But he only acted that way because he assumes a widow will be amenable to his . . . you know, his attentions."

"Well, it appears he's right."

"But I'm not a widow." Hester pushed to her feet and began to pace.

"Perhaps you should tell him that."

"Oh, yes, that would be smart. Don't you see? There's just too much to explain and he's the sort that would have questions for everything. How can I be certain he's trustworthy?"

"Don't give him any answers, simply take him for your lover. From what you say, he's most attentive and considerate of your enjoyment. My dear, you cannot possibly know how rare that is." She smiled when Hester blushed. "Chances are, in the midst of passion he may not even notice your virginity." Her smile turned wry. "And if he does, you can always say that it's been a very long time for you. Six years since your so-called husband died, right?"

Hester considered. Though every logic said for her to avoid the man, something illogical, something deep and primal, urged her to do just what Verna said. "He's not going to be in London much longer."

"Well then, that's even better for you, isn't it? You may have what you want of the man and then be done with him." She laughed. "Besides, you used to say you didn't have any use for men. But you have a use for this man, don't you? So why not enjoy yourself for once and take advantage of it?"

Hester could hardly believe the conversation she was having. This was a side of Verna DeLisle she had never seen. Isabelle was the one who took lovers, something Hester had always hated. Even though she'd been far too young to understand what that meant, she'd still not liked the parade of men who'd kept her mother housed and clothed and draped with jewels.

All the years that Verna had given Hester the solid maternal comfort Isabelle couldn't offer, Hester had assumed Verna disapproved of Isabelle's men as much as Hester did. Now she was not so sure.

"You think it's all right for women to take lovers?"

Verna's face grew serious. "Some women. Not all women. Certainly not married women, or young girls who have not yet experienced life, or women who ought to set a better example to their children. Those women should *not* take lovers. But for widows, women whose husbands have mistresses, and those women who have no other obligations—" She gave a shrug. "I see no harm in it."

Hester took a moment to digest that. Then she sat down across from Verna and leaned forward, her elbows braced on the table, her hands knotted before her. "Are you saying *you* have had a lover?"

Verna straightened on her chair but her gaze did not flinch from Hester's. "Yes. More than one, actually. But then, I've been widowed twenty years."

"Oh." More for Hester to consider. "I see. But . . . Why?"

"Why?" Verna laughed and for that brief moment Hester saw her as she must have been when she was young. Pretty and feminine, charming and free. "Everyone needs to be loved, Hester. Even you, though you deny it. I have no children, no husband. No family at all. It's a terrible thing to be alone. Don't you agree?"

Hester looked away. It *was* terrible to be alone. "But a lover is so . . . so temporary."

"Perhaps. But it doesn't have to be temporary."

"But if you don't want it to be temporary, why not marry the man?"

"Oh, Hester. All these questions only convince me that this man is someone you need to—"

"No." Hester frowned down at her hands. "I am not interested in having a string of lovers. You forget that you and Mother were each married, at least for a while."

"But you've shown no interest in marriage. Certainly I would recommend marriage to the right man over simply sharing his bed. Does this mean you're reconsidering your attitude toward marriage?"

Was she? "I . . . I don't know."

"I see. Very well then." Verna sat silent a moment. "Was there anything else you wished to tell me? Or perhaps any questions about, well, about anything?"

Feeling her cheeks grow warm, Hester ducked her head. "No. But thank you. Actually, I ought to return home."

Verna chuckled. "I'll have my girl summon a hack."

When they stood Hester felt awkward in a way she'd never felt with Mrs. DeLisle before. When her dear friend enveloped her in a tight embrace, however, that awkwardness vanished. "Follow your instincts, Hester, and don't be so hard on yourself should you occasionally make a misstep. It takes experience to keep your feet on the right path in life. Of course, the best experience comes from having wandered off the path a time or two."

Hester nodded. She'd certainly gotten quite a bit of experience today.

As they walked arm in arm to the door Hester debated

asking the question that burned inside her. "Do you have
. . . I mean, right now are you . . ."

"Do I have a lover?" Verna smiled, but this time it
was sad. "No. Dear Benjamin fell ill two years ago and
his sister took him to live with her in York. I heard from
mutual friends that he passed on last fall."

The hack came; Hester hugged Verna, climbed in, and
gave directions to the driver. But she thought about her
friend's melancholy expression as the vehicle made its
way to Mayfair. Verna was lonely. She needed someone
to love, to sit with during the day, to share supper with
and gossip and pleasant strolls and card games. Someone
to ask her how she was feeling, and to squeeze her hand
in his.

Hester stared down at the buttons at the bottom of her
bodice. Verna needed not to be alone anymore, and so
did she.

Adrian walked his horse nearly an hour, all the way to
Regent's Park. Then he remounted and rode straight
back to Hester's vine-covered cottage on the east end of
Mayfair. They needed to talk about what had just happened. He didn't mean to resume what they'd been doing, though he wanted to. But now was not the time. So
he'd already resolved not to risk even touching her. But
they did need to talk, to clarify the new situation between them.

What had seemed so obvious when he'd left her parlor seemed idiotic now. What if she didn't seek him out?
What if she decided he was the worst sort of cad? What
if instead of enticing her, his passionate nature frightened her away? He had to make certain she understood
the sincerity of his interest in her, and at the same time
reassure himself of her interest in him.

When he arrived her servants were back. He braced
himself when the housekeeper opened the door. Did she

know what had happened in her absence? Had she spoken to Hester?

"Why good afternoon, Mr. Hawke."

He doffed his hat. "Good afternoon, Mrs. Dobbs. Would you be good enough to announce me to Mrs. Poitevant?"

"Ooh, but she'll be sorry she missed you, sir. She's gone off, y'see. Left me a note."

"Gone off?" Adrian stood there thunderstruck. Gone off? That was the last thing he expected. Indisposed, yes. Not receiving callers. Or even not to home, the *ton*'s little white lie, understood by all as a set-down sent via a servant. But Mrs. Dobbs's message was sincere. Hester had left the house, apparently just after he'd departed.

"Where did she go?"

Mrs. Dobbs seemed unfazed by his somewhat rude inquiry. "Gone to visit a friend, she said."

"In Cheapside?"

Mrs. Dobbs cocked her head and studied him a long moment. "She told you about her friend?"

Jealousy struck him such a sucker punch that for several seconds Adrian could not respond. He had to force the words past the constriction in his throat. "She told me."

"She must have taken a hack, as we had the coach." The woman folded her hands over her thick, aproned middle. "I don't like it when she goes off alone that way. A single woman like her. But she's a game one, our girl is. Independent-minded, you know?"

"I know," he muttered as jealousy gave way to a blind, maddened rage. He should never have left without coming to an understanding with her. He was an arrogant fool, believing he could replace her lover after just one stolen interlude that hadn't even included the full act of sex.

And now she'd fled straight to her lover!

He turned abruptly on his heel, tossing a terse thank-you over his shoulder.

But Mrs. Dobbs wasn't offended. Not in the least. Her husband came around from the yard just as Mr. Hawke rode off. "Another gentleman caller?" he said, his gray brows lowering as he squinted at the departing man.

"Not another one. The *same* one," she answered. "That Hawke fellow."

"Hunh. She ain't had a fellow to call in all these years and now there's the two of 'em."

"Oh, you hush, Fenton Dobbs. That girl is in need of another husband. Has been for years. Just like I was before you met me at the stalls in Market Street."

Even under his weather-beaten visage his face went a little red. Both widowed, they'd thought to live their lives alone until that fateful day nearly five years ago. "So," he said, his voice gruff with emotions he had a hard time revealing. "Which one d'you think she'll have?"

Mrs. Dobbs smiled at him. He was such a dear. "I'm thinking it will be the American. Indeed, I'm certain of it."

"He was born a Scotsman."

"It makes no matter where he was born. He's the right one for her. You mark my words. Now come into the kitchen and I'll make us some fresh tea."

Adrian rode to Cheapside though he knew it was the mission of a madman. Somewhere near Aldersgate Street, that's where he'd seen her that day. Close to Horace's club. And she'd been afoot, so her "friend" must not live far from there.

The streets were busy as he made his way up one and down the next, scanning the passing faces, searching for a woman of average height and average coloring but who could not in any real way be considered average.

Clouds lurked over the city, threatening rain, with a fitful wind that kept the day cool. But beneath his summer-weight wool coat Adrian was sweating.

Damn him for a fool! He had better things to do with his time this last week of his stay in England than to chase after a woman like Hester Poitevant. How had he become involved with her anyway?

Only when it began to rain did he admit defeat. She was with the man she wanted to be with and it wasn't him. Turning his horse toward Holborn Hill, he pulled his hat low and hunched his shoulders, oblivious to the cold trickle of raindrops beneath his turned-up collar.

But if he thought his day had already reached its low point, he revised his opinion when he arrived at his uncle's townhouse. As he shed his coat in the slate-floored foyer, the butler informed him, "Lord Ainsley is being entertained by Lord Hawke. They both await you in the study."

Adrian halted at the foot of the stairs. Damnation! George Bennett was the last person he needed to see. Did the man have no self-respect at all?

But Adrian's rancor swiftly gave way to a surly satisfaction. If George Bennett needed more rejection and abuse, Adrian was just the man to give it to him. Without bothering to fetch another coat, he made his way down the hall toward his uncle's private study.

"Ah, there you are."

Adrian heard the edge of relief in Neville's voice. He gave his uncle a subtle nod, then turned toward his old nemesis. "Hello, Bennett. What brings you out on such a dreary day?"

To his credit the man hardly flinched anymore at Adrian's persistent refusal to refer to him by his title. "Well, I was out for a ride, you see, and I found myself very near to here. We've been talking horses, your uncle and I. The Hawke stables are renowned, despite their distance from London."

And everyone knew the entire world revolved around hulking, stinking London. But Adrian only gave him a vague smile. "Yes. His animals are as fine as any you'll ever see. Thinking of adding to your stock?"

"Well." He rocked back on his heels. "A man has to keep an eye out. The right cattle are an investment like any other. Land. Sheep. Weaving sheds." He paused, waiting after his unsubtle hint for Adrian to turn the subject to his wool investment venture.

But Adrian had no intention of helping George Bennett out. Instead he strolled to the liquor tray, poured himself a fat glass of Scotch whisky, then held the glass up and stared through its rich amber tint. He wanted Lord Ainsley, pillar of London society, to bring up that particular subject. He wanted the desperate fool to plead for a piece of that pie, to grovel and beg and then suffer the humiliation of rejection. The same way Adrian had in essence just begged and groveled and still been rejected by that other pillar of town society.

His hand tightened around the glass tumbler. Morally dishonest, both of them. But he kept his expression even. He fixed an amused gaze on Bennett, although who he saw was Hester, and what he felt was far from amusement. "Did you know that over the past twenty years my uncle's animals have won the purses at every major racing venue in Great Britain? From Edinburgh to Doncaster to Ascot and Devon. Thoroughbreds, hunters, carriage horses. Everything but ponies—though if you need ponies for your children, I'm sure he can advise you."

"I fear my nephew is too generous with his praise," Neville said, joining in the spirit of Adrian's game. "By the way, Ainsley. Do you have children?"

"One daughter," the man muttered, his frustration

clear. "But she's too young for a pony. My sister, however, she's quite the horsewoman," he went on, forcing a smile. "Come to think of it, I was considering purchasing her a new animal—for a wedding gift, you know?"

He was making it too easy, Adrian thought. Too easy. "Don't tell me your lovely sister has accepted an offer so early in the season." He pressed one hand to his chest. "I'm devastated. Truly devastated."

"No, no," Bennett interjected, waving his hands in front of him. "No. I only meant that when she *does* wed, your uncle and I might be able to do some business together." He cleared his throat and gave one of his falsely hearty grins, first to Neville, then to Adrian. "Speaking of business, perhaps now is a good time to discuss our doing some business together."

Adrian took a long pull of whisky and let it burn through him. He already burned with lust, frustration, and anger. Why not this physical burn as well? He drank again, then turned to Bennett.

"I'm afraid it isn't a good time. I'm soaked, you see. A hot bath and a hot toddy to warm me up, that's all I can think about right now. Perhaps another time." He coughed, a loud fraudulent cough which, for good measure, he followed up with a noisy sneeze. When he spied the mottled anger staining Bennett's face and the fearful tremble of his lips, he had to cough again to cover his laughter which threatened to erupt in whoops. How bad off were the man's finances anyway?

As he strode out of the oak-paneled study, then up the stairs, he decided to make a few inquiries in that direction. And if those inquiries caused Bennett to believe he was seriously considering letting him into this deal, so much the better.

But Adrian's animosity toward Bennett did not outlast his trek to his bedchamber. By the time he closed the

door behind him and sat to remove his water-stained
boots, he was once again trapped in the quagmire of his
feelings for Hester. Even his fury at her betrayal couldn't
prevent desire from once again digging its claws into
him.

He'd given her pleasure, never thinking of his own,
and she'd then run straight to another man. He, meanwhile, seemed unable to find release with any other
woman.

What sort of madness was that?

He stripped off his waistcoat, shirt, and brecches, then
removed his stockings and small clothes as well. Though
he tried to ignore the persistent arousal that lifted angrily
between his legs, he was not successful.

Muttering a string of the foulest curses he knew, he
threw on his robe and rang for a servant. When the man
arrived Adrian did not turn from his blind perusal of the
wet street beyond the window.

"Bring me a bath." He tossed down the remnants of
his drink. "It needn't be hot."

CHAPTER 14

At the insistent knock on her front door, Hester lifted her skirts and scurried up the stairs. "I'm not receiving callers," she hissed at Mrs. Dobbs. "Not anyone." Then she fled to her room, slammed the door, and collapsed against it in a panic of pounding heart, sweating palms, and shaking knees.

She knew she was being ridiculous. What did she think, that Adrian Hawke would follow her up her own stairs and beat down her door to have her? If he'd wanted her with that sort of desperation, he wouldn't have departed so abruptly this afternoon.

But logic did little to relieve her attack of nerves. She heard the muffled voices, Mrs. Dobbs's and a man's. She was right, it *was* him.

But when the front door closed and she crept to the window to peek through the lace curtains, it was not Adrian Hawke she saw leaving, but George Bennett.

George Bennett? Why would he seek her out at her home?

She watched him climb into his gentleman's gig. Then with a snap of his whip he sent the matched pair of Cleveland Bays charging down the street.

Goodness! What had him in such a state? She let the curtain fall. Need she ask such a foolish question? It wasn't *what* had him in such a state, but rather *who*. If George Bennett had come to her house in a state of pique, it could only be owing to Adrian Hawke.

She let out a helpless, hopeless laugh. Good gracious but Mr. Hawke was certainly having a productive day. And it wasn't even suppertime. Still, she couldn't help wondering what he'd done this time to send George Bennett pounding on her door.

Poor Peg was still struggling up the stairs after her when Hester started back down. She paused to pet the loyal creature, then had to pet Fifi as well. "Come along. I'll nip a treat for each of you in the kitchen. Mrs. Dobbs?"

The woman was waiting for her with a fresh cup of tea. "I thought you'd be down. Supper's heating. Are you going out tonight?"

And chance running into Adrian Hawke? "No." Hester made a face. "The sky looks bad and it may turn even worse." She knotted her hands at her waist. "So. What did Lord Ainsley want?"

Mrs. Dobbs's plump face darkened in a frown. "What a rude man that one is. Demanded to see you even after I told him you was indisposed. Said to rouse you anyway, that he was paying you to mind his sister's needs and this was about her."

"How did you get rid of him so fast?"

A dimple crept into the woman's plump cheek. "I didn't say a thing at first. Just stared at him and shook my head. He got more and more worked up until—Now you won't like this, but it was all his doing."

"What?"

"He kept askin' me, was you sick? Was you asleep?

But I didn't say a thing. Then he said something rude about women and their maladies."

"Good lord!"

"So I just nodded and said he was precisely right, that you had your monthly malady and I was just on my way to fix you a hot pack. I tell you, that shut him up right quick. There's not a man alive who can deal with discussin' a woman's monthlies." The woman cackled with laughter. "His face got this choked look, like he couldn't get his words out, and then he turned and stormed out."

Hester couldn't help it, she laughed too. It was humiliating in the extreme, yet it was hilarious to think of ugly, blustering George Bennett intimidated by a little housekeeper and the details of a woman's monthlies. Once she started laughing, she couldn't stop. She laughed and Mrs. Dobbs laughed until their sides hurt and they had to sit down.

Considering all she'd been through today, it felt wonderful, as if something trapped inside of her had been released. Even the dogs participated, yelping and wagging their hind ends so vigorously Peg fell over. Of course, that made Hester and Mrs. Dobbs laugh all the harder.

Finally when they were sobbing for breath Mrs. Dobbs wiped her eyes with her apron. "An' here I thought you'd be angry with me."

Hester fondled Peg's ears while Fifi leaped up and down, trying to get onto her lap. "I should be annoyed, except that George Bennett deserves whatever rudeness comes his way."

Mrs. Dobbs gave her a shrewd look. "I recognized his name, of course. But why's he coming here when he's never come before? God bless that poor Miss Dulcie," she added. "The family that child is burdened with."

"Yes. It is unfortunate. As to why he came, well, I suspect he came with additional instructions for me. He wants his sister to marry money, you see. Specifically, Mr. Hawke's money."

"Oh. Now I understand. An' you disagree with that match?"

Hester didn't often discuss her clients' private business with her housekeeper. But today seemed a day for breaking all the rules of personal conduct.

"Mr. Hawke is not the marrying sort," she said by way of explanation. Hearing the words out loud had a sobering effect. He was not the marrying sort, nor was she.

But he would make a fine choice for a lover—

She shook off that unsettling thought and fought back the shiver of anticipation such an outrageous idea roused in her. "I believe I shall lie down for a while," she said, setting aside her tea.

"Are you feeling poorly?"

"No. Just a little tired."

"I'll hold supper then."

"Just leave a plate in the warming oven. No need to delay your own supper. I'll eat whenever I get up."

"Well, if you're sure. Have a good nap then."

How Hester wished she could nap. But her head was too full of wild thoughts and mad ideas. Take a lover indeed. How could Verna DeLisle have suggested such a thing?

Yet it seemed inevitable.

She sat on her bed and contemplated the shipwreck of her heretofore placid, uneventful life. She'd wished many a time for a more stimulating life than the one she led. It seemed she was getting her chance. It was now or never for her; accept Adrian Hawke's carnal interests or avoid him until he left England entirely. Then try to pretend none of this had ever happened.

And try to go back to her old, uneventful life.

Fifi barked and Hester lifted her onto her lap. "Aren't

you the demanding one," she murmured to the silky little dog. "Pretty again. And getting plumper every day."

In that moment Hester knew she could no more go back to her old dried-up life than she could send Fifi or Peg back to their neglected ones. Pretty, plump, and happy. That's how her dogs were now, and that's what she wanted her life to be like. Even if only for a very little while.

Adrian was drunk when the note arrived.

He had sat through dinner with Neville, Olivia, and Catherine, a thundercloud with no business participating in their sunny family gathering. They'd tolerated him, though, only teasing him a very little.

"Perhaps he's homesick for some special lady in Boston," Catherine had speculated to her mother.

"No. I believe it's more immediate than that," Olive responded. "An English woman, I think."

The only one taking his side was his uncle who muttered, "Perhaps it's living in a house full of nosy women that has him so out of sorts."

They'd all laughed, Adrian along with them. Then they'd gone on to other topics, not knowing how close to the truth they were. They chose not to comment when he consumed the best part of a bottle of wine. He followed dinner with two glasses of port, which he didn't even much like. Now he was on to whisky, alone in the dark of the second-floor roof terrace when the butler delivered the note.

"Shall I leave the lamp, sir?"

"Thank you."

He waited until the man left before he slit the seal. His hands shook and his vision was hampered as much by his bleary state as by the lack of bright light. Damnation! Was it from Hester?

It was.

Her signature, so refined and feminine, caught his eyes first. He squinted but the neatly slanted letters swam together and he could make out little of the brief note. What did it say?

He closed his eyes, trying to stop his head from spinning. Then a scent of lilies came to him—real or imagined he could not say, for it was faint and fleeting. Hester, he thought, lifting the single page to his nose. He kept his eyes closed as memories of their encounter flooded over him. Hester of the lily flavoring, too faint to be perfume. It must come from her soap.

He should send her a gift of fine French soaps, lily-scented. And a pot of lilies with it. White ones. No, pink ones because she was so sweetly, deliciously pink.

A surge of blood rushed to his loins, and he grew hard despite his state of inebriation. God save the queen but she was driving him mad!

He quit the terrace on unsteady feet, made unsteadier by the erection that strained painfully within his breeches, and sought the privacy of his third-level bed chamber. There with two lamps turned up high and a six-stem candelabra blazing he made out her message.

Dear Mr. Hawke,
After several hours' reflection, I have concluded that perhaps we should talk and clear the air between us. If you agree, I propose we meet at one or another of this week's galas where the security of our mutual friends will guarantee a comfortable setting.
I would have peace between us.

Respectfully,
Hester Poitevant.

Clear the air? Peace between us? Adrian fell back in his chair, his head spinning from the effort of reading and understanding her letter. From heady anticipation to crushing disappointment he plummeted. Those were not the words of a woman planning an assignation.

From beyond his window he heard the rumble of a night cart, and felt the cool caress of an easterly wind. But his besotted brain was stuck on Hester and her stiffly circumspect note.

Hester tended to be excessively circumspect in everything she did. Her dress; her dedication to her clients. Given that, it was unlikely she would send him a suggestive note. Certainly no one intercepting this missive could read anything carnal into it.

He could, though.

Yes, he wanted to clear the air between them—and be naked as they did so.

He wanted peace between them—the peace of sexual exhaustion after he'd made love to her every way he knew how. Twice over.

He stared at his bed, imagining her in it clothed in nothing but that fragrant mass of silky hair. He breathed deeply and this time when his head spun he let it, relishing the whirling spiral, the out-of-control physicality of it.

Somehow he staggered to the bed, sprawling fully clothed across it. He imagined Hester beneath him, so real he could almost feel her, and he groaned with desire. Once more he brought her letter to his nose and inhaled. Yes, lilies.

But as he spun in that cyclone of desire and need and insane longing, that sweet, sweet scent turned sweeter still. The musk of aroused female. The aroma he'd inhaled in Hester's parlor when she opened herself to him.

He thrust his hips convulsively against the thick down mattress.

By damn she wanted to meet with him. That was something. And once they met, anything was possible given her innate passion. This time they would finish what they'd begun and he would finally have her. Finally . . .

He sank down into the bed, into a deep heated slumber. Finally he would have her . . .

The next evening Hester dressed as she always had, except for the spectacles. She'd decided to abandon them once and for all. But the spruce dress buttoned to her chin; the scraped-back hair, sans curls or snood or any other conceits: these she clung to. Her disguise of respectable widowhood had never fit her so ill. Yet on this night she needed that disguise more than she ever had.

But even with her facade so firmly in place, she feared that anyone who looked closely would see she had changed. Yesterday had altered her in a way so deep and essential that she could not imagine that change invisible to others. So she took special care to appear even primmer and more unattractive than usual. Could she give her face spots and make her teeth crooked, she would have been tempted to do so.

Mrs. Dobbs noticed at once the renewed strictness of her appearance. "Oh, you've gone back to the old way of dressing your hair." She shook her head. "If you like I can help you with a softer style."

"Thank you, but I haven't the time."

The older woman watched Hester climb into her carriage, and waved as Mr. Dobbs drove her off. Then Mrs. Dobbs shooed the dogs out of the garden and back into the house.

"I don't understand that girl. Two men coming to call on her—three if you count that dreadful Bennett fellow, though I cannot think him the sort to have anything honorable on his mind."

In the kitchen the two animals looked up at her, heads cocked, tails wagging. "She could have any man she wants, you know. Any one of them. I'm just hoping she decides which one she wants before it's too late."

Hester arrived late at the Ainsleys' card party. She was a knot of nervous energy, strung as taut as the high string on a violin.

It's unlikely he'll be here. Of all places, Adrian Hawke should least like to be entertained at George Bennett's townhouse.

On the other hand, though he was always considerate of Dulcie's feelings, Adrian took a perverse pleasure in tormenting her brother.

The gathering was in full swing when the butler announced Hester. Both parlors and the drawing room had been rearranged with card tables scattered about. The dining room boasted a mammoth buffet in the French manner, and the terrace had been set as a picnic for outdoor dining. Lady Ainsley worked very hard at her social obligations, and it showed. For a family so sorely pressed by a lack of funds, she certainly displayed no sense of restraint. A hundred candles or more and all beeswax, even the ones outdoors. Flowers everywhere in huge crystal vases. More people than there were chairs to accommodate them and enough victuals for twice as many people. And of course punch, wine, and more substantial spirits for the gentlemen.

But no Adrian Hawke, Hester surmised within the first thirty seconds of her arrival.

She let out a shaky breath of relief.

No. She wasn't relieved, she was furious.

No. She was mortified.

What had possessed her to send such a blatantly worded invitation to a man whom she had no reason at all to trust? She knew what he wanted from her, and discretion wasn't necessarily a part of it.

She pressed her hands to her cheeks. How could she have been so foolish?

She turned, wanting only to escape. But Dulcie spied her and waved. At the same time her unpleasant brother George looked up from his position beside the mantel—the one with his oversized painted likeness hanging above it—and she knew she was trapped. At least Dulcie got to her first. "I'm so glad you've come. Will you play cards first, or eat?"

"Oh. Eat I think. Yes." Her pasted-on smile only stiffened when George halted before her. "Hullo, Mrs. Poitevant," he said in his typically overbearing manner.

"Lord Ainsley." She made a brief curtsy. What did he want?

"I'm glad you're here. You too, Dulls. We've got some planning to do."

Hester was already in a state of agitation, so his casual insult to his sister pushed her right over the edge. "Don't call her that." Though she kept her voice low, the tone was forged of steel.

"What?" He drew up and stared at her as if he could not believe she had the effrontery to correct him.

"I said, don't call your sister 'Dulls.' "

Poor Dulcie seemed to shrink in the face of this confrontation. Indeed, Hester didn't know why she'd chosen now to confront Lord Ainsley, and in his own front parlor. But once set on her course, she would not back down.

His face grew rigid in a frown. "Dulls is my pet name for her. Always has been."

"Only when you wish to deflate her confidence."

"Why should I wish to do that? God knows I'm breaking my back trying to get her married off."

Dulcie clutched Hester's arm. "It's all right."

"No, it's not." Hester faced down Lord Ainsley, strangely unafraid of the blustering oaf. Let him fire her;

she didn't really care. "Your treatment of her is inexplicable. First you belittle her; then you try to push her on the worst possible choice of a husband. Isn't that why you came pounding on my door yesterday, to berate me regarding your old school chum?"

His mouth twisted into an ugly sneer. "I'm well within my rights to tell you who to push her on. You needn't understand why I make the choices I do for her. All you have to do is follow my orders."

They'd begun to attract attention, but Hester didn't care. The man was a selfish clod. Dulcie would be better off eloping with a street sweeper than marrying the sort of man George Bennett would force on her.

But Lady Ainsley cared. As though she were acutely attuned to her wretched son's wretched moods, she materialized beside him. With a talon-tight grip on his arm, she forced George to look at her.

"Not now," she hissed under her breath, all the while smiling as happily as if someone had just complimented her on her son's charming manners. "And not here." Then giving Hester a sharp look that promised a later comeuppance for this disturbance, she dragged George away.

"Oh, dear," Dulcie moaned, wringing her lace handkerchief in her nervous hands. "I do so hate public scenes like that."

So did Hester. So then why, she wondered, had she leaped into just such a scene when she knew she could not possibly win?

"Are you all right?" a man asked, coming up between them. Hester's heart leaped. But the voice did not have the peculiar tones unique to a certain American. That was for the best, she told herself. The last thing she needed was Adrian Hawke thrust into the midst of all this. She turned gratefully to see her own brother there. What a dear man he was, even dearer to her when she considered that he could have turned out exactly like George Bennett. "Horace, how glad I am to see you. But you need not worry. We are just fine. Aren't we, Dulcie?"

Dulcie nodded, but it was hardly convincing. Hester sighed. "Lord Ainsley and I are not in total agreement on a particular subject. We were wrong to have discussed it here, however. Especially in Dulcie's presence."

Creased in concern, Horace's amiable face turned to Dulcie. "Not to worry, Miss Bennett. Mrs. Poitevant is the most self-possessed, competent woman I've ever known. Your brother's ill-temper should be of no concern to any of us. Especially tonight."

Dulcie looked up at him. "Especially tonight?"

He smiled. "Especially tonight, for we will need all our powers of concentration for the card games." He tucked her hand in his arm and gave it a comforting pat. "This is not like dancing where one may move through the steps automatically, all the while thinking on other matters. Oh, no. When we sit down to play cards, we must be sharp and focused. Don't you agree?"

In the face of his determined cheerfulness, Dulcie's worry seemed to ease. She gave him a little smile. "I suppose you are right."

Once more he patted her hand. "Of course I am. What do you say the three of us get up a table for a game of whist?"

Watching her brother work so hard to put Dulcie's disquiet to rest made Hester inordinately proud of him. What a kind man he was. Despite the briefness of their acquaintance, she'd come swiftly to recognize his generous nature. But never had it been so rampantly displayed as now. It filled her chest with warmth and sisterly pride. And with love, she realized.

"You two go along," she said, smiling at them. Really, but they made a very nice couple. Certainly Dulcie's face glowed tonight with admiration as she looked up at Horace.

"Very well, then," Horace said. "But before the night is done we must play a game. If not whist, then loo or quinze. Oh, and I've a surprise for you," he added to Hester as he and Dulcie turned to go.

A surprise? But Hester was too worried about her own brittle temper tonight to wonder overlong about Horace's surprise. Needing to collect herself, she circled the room, heading for the refreshment table. But all the while she berated herself.

How could she of all people have allowed herself to become embroiled in a contretemps with George Bennett? Though Lady Ainsley had interceded at a most fortuitous moment, Hester feared the subject was not done with. George Bennett had become fixated on Adrian Hawke and how he might profit from their association. He fully expected Hester to seal that association, using Dulcie as the cement.

Thank goodness Adrian Hawke hadn't come tonight.

But of course, he *had* come. Within moments of escaping George Bennett, Hester turned to see Adrian in the foyer conversing with some older man. She froze in the act of reaching for a glass of punch from the silver tray a blue-liveried manservant held before her. She should not be so affected by Adrian, yet she was.

Likewise he froze at the sight of her. He recovered first, however, when the man he was with turned to follow his companion's gaze. Adrian said something to him and the man smiled and nodded at Hester.

At once Hester's cheeks heated to crimson. Oh, dear, had he told the man about her? About what they'd done? Surely not.

Caught in the quagmire of fear and hope and fear

again, she stared as they approached. She didn't recognize the other man, though he had a vaguely familiar look to him. As they drew nearer, however, Hester's attention focused back on Adrian. What would he say to her? What would she say to him?

Then to make matters even more horrible, she realized that she was growing increasingly warm. Distressingly warm. Especially down there.

Oh, no. Her heart beat faster, her breaths came shallower, and in her nether regions she grew hot and moist.

It was the same melting sensation Adrian had roused in her before. Only this time he wasn't even touching her—except with his eyes.

In a panic she broke the hold of his too bold, too knowing gaze and focused instead on his companion. The man moved slowly as befitted his age. He had a pleasant demeanor, but he needed a haircut, she vaguely noted. His waistcoat was a little shabby, and a trifle snug across his corpulent middle.

Too shabby . . . Too snug . . . With a gasp of horror Hester stumbled backward. It couldn't be!

"Pardon me," someone said, moving out of her way. Yet still Hester continued to back up. Not him. Not her father!

But it was. He was Horace, except older. Rosy cheeked, softly plump, with that same affable expression, though grayer and with whiskers.

"No," she said, unable to look any longer at the man who'd abandoned her, who'd forgotten she even existed. It only made matters worse that he was smiling, and that he looked nothing like what she'd imagined.

She switched her horrified stare to Adrian, who frowned as they drew nearer. "Mrs. Poitevant—"

"No." She held up her hand as if warding off the devil, for indeed that's how it felt. The devil of her past had come to destroy her tenuous future. Already he'd wreaked havoc on her present.

Unable to make any explanation, she clutched her handkerchief to her mouth, shook her head at Adrian, then turned and fled.

CHAPTER 15

Adrian's anticipation turned to cinders when he saw the look on Hester's face. He had her letter in his pocket and a perverse sort of hope in his heart. But he'd been uncertain enough about greeting her that he'd decided to include a third party, a buffer of sorts. Cowardly, he supposed, and obviously not a good idea, judging from her reaction.

Like him, Horace's father stared in silence as she fled the room. "*That* is Mrs. Poitevant?" He paused. "I thought Horace said she was a proper sort of person."

"She is," Adrian muttered.

"Humph. Well, I can't say as I've ever understood the peculiarities of Londoners. Especially the women. So," he added, as if dismissing Hester's odd behavior. "I assume Horace left us together for a reason. Some business about wool. But take heed, young man. I can't say as how I'm particularly interested in linking my resources to someone who plans to leave the country as soon as he's got hold of my money."

"I don't want your money," Adrian retorted, trying to focus on the subject at hand. At the moment he didn't

give a damn whether Edgar Vasterling joined his venture
or not. Instead he wanted to go after Hester, to discover
why she'd sent that letter and then run away as soon as
she saw him.

He scanned the room, searching for a glimpse of her.
Instead he saw Horace staring at him like a hopeful
puppy.

Stifling a curse Adrian reined in his rampant emotions. What was wrong with him? Since when did he let
his fascination with some woman distract him from business? His whole purpose for returning to England was
to show these people that they needed him more than he
needed them. He would find Hester later. By damn, but
he would follow her home if he had to. But for now he
must do what he'd promised Horace he'd do: convince
old man Vasterling to throw in his lot with Adrian.

"Perhaps I haven't explained my company sufficiently, Lord Vasterling. While one aspect of the venture
requires capital investments, the bulk of it—the most
important part of it—requires a reliable source of wool.
Raw wool, carded wool, spun wool, or woven. There's
a place for every level of involvement, from the shepherd who runs a flock of twenty to the gentleman farmer
with hundreds of sheep and a cadre of spinners and
weavers."

The elder Vasterling shrugged. "If anyone can join
your group, I hardly see why you need me. England is
full of sheep."

"Yes, England is full of sheep. But I'm looking for
long-term commitment from sheep farmers I can rely on.
If a man tells me he can deliver a certain quantity of
washed, carded wool, or so many spools of a specific
grade thread, or a specific number of bolts of a perfectly
woven cloth, then I want to be sure he'll deliver when
he says he'll deliver. I'm not looking for just anyone
who runs sheep. If you want in on this—and you'd be

a fool not to—you've got to convince me you can deliver." Then with a curt bow he headed outside.

He'd been more forceful with the man than he intended, more passionate and more reckless. Some might even describe his behavior as rude. But Adrian didn't care. He was tired of the British manner of always sidestepping the main issue.

And Hester was the worst of the lot.

He snagged a glass of wine on his way outside, then pulled a cheroot from his pocket, lit it on a flickering torch, and strode into the dimly lit garden. He inhaled and blew out. Once, then again. But it didn't do much to calm him. Son of a bitch. He was acting like a madman.

But how else was he to act when one prissy prude of a woman turned him inside out the way Hester Poitevant did? Devil take her, she was leading him around by the balls and he didn't like it. But how could he make it stop?

From inside came the glow of light and laughter, sending him retreating to a darker, lonelier spot in the garden. Not that it was much of a garden. More of a service yard, bordered with rhododendron in bloom. But by the light of the half moon he spied an airy white structure. A gazebo.

He headed toward it, only to realize that it was occupied. Inside the small wood structure someone was speaking and he stopped, glad for the silencing effect of the lawn.

Then it dawned on him that it wasn't someone speaking, but rather someone weeping.

He dropped the cheroot and put it out with his heel. "Hello?"

The crying ceased at once. He heard someone fumbling around, a thud in the dark, then a soft, feminine cry.

Every nerve in his body went on alert and the hair stood up on his arms. He moved closer. "Hester?"

Another little cry, this time of alarm. Then, "Don't come in here."

The blood surged through Adrian's body like a biblical flood. "Why not?"

"Because . . . Because I'm a mess."

She couldn't have lured him more effectively if she'd extended a bare leg from the depths of the gazebo's shadows and waggled it at him. The composed Hester Poitevant a mess?

Then again, she wasn't always composed. Certainly she hadn't been composed yesterday afternoon. Nor now, it seemed. "Why are you a mess, Hester? And why are you out here crying?"

"Go away."

Like hell he would. "I received your letter."

This time his answer was utter silence. Another effective lure. With a renewed sense of purpose he placed one booted foot on the gazebo floor. He imagined her flinching at the firm sound of it.

"Please, Mr. Hawke. Allow me my privacy and just . . . just go away."

"I can't, Hester. You know that. You wrote me for a reason, so let's discuss it." He paused. "You can begin by explaining why you ran away from me just now, and why you're out here crying." Another pause. "I'm coming in."

It took a minute for his eyes to adjust; the gazebo was even darker than the yard, and Hester wore a dark dress, unrelieved except for her pale face and hands. He reached out for one of those hands, bare and damp from wiping her tears. Her skin was warm.

He drew her nearer, acutely aware of his burgeoning desire for her. Against his thumb her pulse raced. His own pounded so fiercely he feared she must hear it. The whole world must, he was that much aroused by her presence.

"I don't want you to run away from me anymore, Hester."

"I wasn't."

"Not here, to cry in a gazebo." He went on, his voice gruffer, angrier. "Nor to your 'friend' in Cheapside."

"My friend?"

"Your housekeeper let it slip." He jerked her up against him, too rough. But he didn't care, for he was enraged. Jealous. Out of control. "It's over between you and him. Do you understand? It has to be over."

Hester did not know whether to laugh, to cry, or to rail at Adrian for his thickheadedness. He was jealous of a man who didn't exist. Though she ought to correct his misconception—she should have done so yesterday— a part of her reveled in her ability to torment him so. A wicked part of her.

He deserved it, though, for he had a way of tormenting her. Like now, crushing her against him as if it were his right.

She forgot her tears, caused by her father's appearance. Instead her every thought, her every sense, centered on the power generated between them. Like lightning, it was: white hot and more violent than it logically should be.

One of his arms circled her waist, keeping her flush against him. Though it was impossible to escape him, a proper woman would have stayed rigid and disapproving in that implacable embrace. But she was not proper. Not anymore. Maybe she never had been. For she was soft and supple against him. Accepting. Encouraging.

"Don't ever run from me again," he growled against her temple, and the words sounded as warm as his breath felt.

"I won't." She slid her arms up his chest to circle his

neck. His free hand roamed up her side to her neck, and then into her hair.

"Wait—" She tried too late to stop him.

"But I must," he answered as the twisted coil of curls came free in his clever hands. Ten minutes to properly dress her hair, yet it took only ten seconds for him to release it. A half hour to perfect her proper widow's disguise, yet with one embrace he banished that as well.

Then he cupped the side of her face. "Tonight I will come to you. Tonight, Hester."

Tonight. There was no mistaking his meaning.

Slowly she nodded. It was bound to happen with some man. She did not wish to live out the whole of her life as a virgin, did she?

The problem was, she might have to explain to him how a twenty-eight-year-old widow could be so innocent about the secret goings-on between men and women. And explaining about that might naturally lead to her mother and, thereby, her father. And her brother.

Oh, Lord, she needed to think longer about this.

Only she couldn't think, not when he was holding her and touching her and kissing her . . .

"There's . . . there's just one thing, Adrian."

He hushed her with a kiss. "Rest assured, I'll be discreet." He rubbed his thumb across the remnant of tears on her cheek. "I promise, you'll have no cause to cry over me, Hester. Unless they're tears of joy." Then he kissed her again, a possessive, breath-stealing, mind-numbing kiss that melted her from the inside out.

She'd been supple in his embrace; now she went limp. She'd been accepting of his kisses; now she burned with want for more. She'd been encouraging; now she panted with urgent need.

He pressed a knee between her legs and she groaned at the rough caress. Tilted backward in his arms, she was open to his hungry kiss and the greedy roaming of

his hands. Up her side, across one breast, then back
again, thumbing the peak to agonizing pleasure until she
sobbed into the dark, enveloping night.

His knee rubbed higher between her thighs, but not
enough to appease her. She wanted his hand there. His
mouth.

Her face flamed at such a shameful thought. When
had she become so wicked? Oh, but she was most certainly her mother's daughter.

As if to confirm that terrible admission, a voice flared
from somewhere nearer the house. "Hawke. Hawke?"

It was her brother.

"I say, are you out here?"

Like ice water his words doused them, the voice of
society's conscience and of her own. Hester shoved
Adrian just as he pulled back, causing her to sit down
hard upon the gazebo's bench seat.

"I have to go," he whispered.

She nodded, her hair rippling about her shoulders.
Though still somewhat dazed, she began to gather it up
and somehow put it to rights. This was becoming a distressing habit of late.

He crossed to the entrance of the gazebo, standing
there backlit by moonlight. "When you leave the party,
I'll follow you."

She nodded again, afraid to speak. Saying the words
out loud—"Follow me to my house where we can complete the intimacies we have begun here"—somehow
that made it all too deliberate, too planned. How easy it
was to become caught up in the passion of the moment.
How much harder to arrange the secret details of so fur-
tive a tryst.

But as she later made her way home, Hester could
not hide from what she planned, nor what she'd already
done. When he left the gazebo Adrian had joined Horace, distracting him so that she could return unnoticed

to the party. She'd played one hand of loo, losing badly, before making her good-byes during the happy chaos that ensued when the elaborate desserts were brought out.

She would have left even sooner could she have managed it. After all, her father was circulating in the very same party as she, and he was the last person she wished to meet. Nor did she wish to explain why. Fortunately, in the crush Horace had not yet gotten around to introducing them, though she saw the man meet Dulcie and Lady Ainsley.

Adding to her distress, there was Adrian to avoid, which for some perverse reason she felt compelled to do. He didn't play cards, nor did George Bennett, the third man she wanted to avoid. That one only drank and glowered at everyone, especially Adrian Hawke.

Such tension and secrecy in the room, she had thought, getting almost giddy at the idea of such a ludicrous scene. Now in the fragile privacy of her little gig she rubbed her temple. Shakespeare could have created such an entertaining farce from it all. *A Midsummer's Night Fiasco. Much Ado About Something No One Must Figure Out. The Taming of the Shrewish Virgin Widow.*

She giggled, though it was more from nerves than humor. She liked that last one best. Though she might remain a shrew in some circles, and even a pretend widow, after this night she would not be a virgin.

She shivered and pressed her lips together. Was she being incredibly stupid?

Mr. Dobbs let her out at the front door, then went around to unhitch the horse and stable him. She dismissed Mrs. Dobbs before the woman could even rise from her rocker. Then alone in her bedchamber, as pristine and innocent as a girl's, she made herself ready. Off came her tight cuffs, the dark dress, and the layers of smothering, restrictive undergarments. Then came the garters and stockings, and her stylish pantalets. If ever she'd been glad to have her aqua nightgown and wrapper, it was now. Would he like it?

Something inside her vibrated with the knowledge that he would.

She tiptoed to a back window and looked out to see the light wink out in the Dobbses' room beyond the kitchen. Then she did the same at the front window, looking for her midnight caller, waiting for him on the window seat as she let her hair down and began to brush it.

A hundred strokes and he hadn't yet come. She started a hundred more. At sixty-one she saw him. On a dark horse, clad in shadows and the disguise of the night, he might have been any solitary rider. But she knew him, and in every fiber of her body she reacted to him.

The world worked that way, she told herself. There was a natural order to things. Flowers opened to the dawn, birds migrated with the seasons, crickets sang as the sun went down, and she responded to Adrian Hawke. Through the window glass, through the dark of the night. It made no difference. He was the one her entire being responded to.

Why him? she wondered as she watched him dismount and tether his animal in the shelter of the side alley. Was it purely physical? Or was it because, like her, he was an outcast of society who'd found a way in? Was it because somewhere deep inside they were more alike than different?

It was a stunning thought. But Hester had no time for contemplation. She leaped up. He was here, and she'd been so enthralled by the sight of him she'd forgotten to unlatch the door.

He was waiting on the top step. Silently she let him in and silently he entered, but there was a wealth of conversation between them. A gaze, the shifting of a stance, the pace of their breathing. The anticipation in the air.

"Are you all right?" he whispered as she led him toward the stairs.

She nodded, though she wasn't at all certain she was. Could plotting her own ruin ever be considered all right?

With one hand on her shoulder he made her turn to him. It was a possessive sort of touch, with his thumb and finger curving around the base of her neck as they stood in the dark of her little house. Despite all that had occurred between them, that warm weight of his hand on her barely clad shoulder seemed the most intimate touch of all. Hardly able to breathe, she looked up at him.

"Are we alone?" he asked.

"Yes. Sort of." She swallowed and took a much needed breath. "Mr. and Mrs. Dobbs have separate apartments in the back. Beyond the kitchen."

"Then why are we whispering?"

She didn't know.

He laughed, then planted an abrupt kiss squarely on her mouth. A different kiss than the others, friendly and easy and, again, possessive and intimate in a wholly new way.

"I said I would be discreet, Hester, and I will be. But it's good to know your servants are not under the same roof with us." Then he caught her by the hand, palm to palm, twining their fingers together. "Lead on, my beautiful, mysterious Hester. I believe I would follow you anywhere."

Propelled by his stirring words, Hester led him up the stairs to the tiny hall. At the door to her bedchamber, however, with its flickering lamplight and soft, beckoning bed, she faltered. He thought her a woman of experience. What if she did it all wrong? What if she fumbled or became afraid, or was unable to please him as he expected to be pleased?

She reached for the door latch but did not turn it. Instead she loosened her other hand from his and turned to face him. She must tell him. "Adrian," she began in a voice that quivered.

"Shh." His hand closed over hers on the latch, while the other braced against the door beside her head, trapping her between his big body and the unyielding door. But a trap was only a trap if the quarry did not wish to be caught. That was hardly the case in this situation.

"Don't talk, Hester. Let's just rely on instinct tonight. Pure animal instinct—"

She cut him off with a kiss. Her fingers knotted in his lapels and drew his face down to hers. Pure animal instinct. It was that and more. His full weight came against her, hot, full-blooded, male, ready to complete the act they'd been building to since their first confrontation at the Murchisons' ball. It made her feel more completely alive than anything she'd ever known before. Like a hot, full-blooded woman.

Against her softer, thinly clad body she felt the hard maleness of his: the buttons of his waistcoat, the seam of his breeches, and everything male that lay beneath: muscled chest, ridged belly, powerful thighs. And especially the root of his maleness, the fierce, demanding arousal that pressed into the softness of her belly.

Good Lord, the very threat of it had her melting with desire!

Then from beyond the doorway came a scratching, a snuffling, whimpering sound followed by a sharp, plaintive bark.

The dogs!

She froze, her mouth still pressed to his, her legs parted over the angle of his hip. Her eyes opened and met his, open as well. She felt his lips curve in a smile—

what a wonderfully odd sensation! "Were you planning an audience for us?"

She pulled her head back, bumping it against the door. Again Fifi barked. "I'll put them in the kitchen."

But she couldn't do that until he moved, and he didn't. In fact, he pressed his hips more heavily against hers and shifted in the most exquisitely erotic manner.

"Wait—"

"You wait," he replied, burying his lips in her hair. "I'm busy."

Busy thrusting rhythmically against her until she was panting and thrusting back. Busy exploring the shell of her ear with his lips and the tip of his tongue. His hand still gripped hers over the latch, but elsewhere he used his body, his heat, and his mouth to caress her.

She felt that helpless tide of need rise up inside her, just like yesterday, and it made her frantic. "Let me . . . Let me get rid of the dogs."

"Damn," he muttered, thrusting so hard it ought to have hurt her. Certainly she would have bruises. But it didn't hurt. What hurt was this waiting, this wanting.

Abruptly he pressed the latch down and they staggered backward into her room.

She never even saw the dogs, nor noticed when the door shut them out in the hall. If they whined or scratched, she didn't hear. Adrian was in her house, in her room, walking her backward, falling with her onto the bed. The feel of his full weight pressing down on her was a revelation even more arousing than his pressing her up against the door, and that had been incredible.

How could she, who so valued her independence, take such intense pleasure in this primitive sort of manhandling? With every kiss, every carnal liberty he took, her pleasure increased until she could hardly breathe.

"You taste delicious," he murmured, making a trail of kisses down her throat, across her shoulder, then farther down, to the upper swells of her breasts. He lifted his head and she groaned her protest. But he only shrugged out of his jacket, then returned to his task.

"Greedy little thing, aren't you?"

"Am I?" She stared at him through heavy-lidded eyes and a haze of desire. She felt like another woman, the opposite of her true self. He, however, was everything she'd imagined and everything she should fear. With one foot on the floor and the opposite knee on the bed, he shed his waistcoat. With a tug of his cravat and another swift yank, his shirt slipped over his head and he was bare-chested before her.

A half-naked man in her bedchamber. Hester had never dared to even dream such a thing. Indeed, she'd convinced herself it was the very last thing she wanted.

But staring at him, at the lamplit curves of muscle and bone, the golden skin and ebony whorls of chest hair arrowing down into his breeches . . . She now knew the truth: she'd been waiting for this for ten years and more. Ten years of repressed yearnings and repressed emotions. She squirmed on the bed, burning with desire, twitching in all the hidden places of her femininity.

As if he knew, his eyes swept slowly down her body, pausing at her breasts, almost visible through the thin aqua fabric. His gaze moved lower still, to her belly where her hot restlessness seemed to be centered. One of his hands clenched in a fist, as if he could barely restrain himself.

At once her gaze swept over him, to the thickness straining against his breeches. She let out a little moan, knowing that fire of need raging in him was all on account of her.

"I knew you would be beautiful," he said, his voice husky and low. "The fact that you hide it—" He shook his head. "I'll never understand why you hide your beauty, Hester. I only know that seeing that beauty now makes me value it even more. My beautiful, secretive Hester."

Then holding her wide-eyed gaze with his smoldering one, he removed his boots, unfastened his breeches, and peeled them off.

Hester couldn't help it. She looked her fill, seeing more muscle, more bone, more golden skin, though paler. But mainly she followed the line of hair that led to that masculine mystery, that proof of his maleness and of his desire.

She swallowed hard, then barely restrained a bubble of nervous laughter. That was to fit inside her?

He bent over her, a fierce god of all that was carnal and she felt every bit the pitiful human sacrifice. How could *she* ever please *him*?

But as his clever fingers plucked open her laced wrapper and gown, as he palmed them open and filled his eyes with the sight of her bare flesh, she saw the appreciation in his eyes. They moved over her like a hot brand, bringing her flesh to feverish life, marking her with his eyes, the first ever to see her virgin flesh.

She must tell him the truth about her.

"Adrian." She lifted a hand to him and he took it. He kissed her fingertips, her knuckles, her palm and wrist and the tender inside of her elbow. "Listen to me," she pleaded in between little gasps of pleasure.

"I'm listening," he said, coming onto the bed. He braced himself over her and she felt his heat like an aura around him, melding with her own until she was damp with perspiration.

"I . . . I'm not . . . Oh, God! I've never had a lover."

He went very still. "Then who did you go to yesterday?"

She stared up into his face, afraid to be honest but more afraid to lie. "I went to see an old friend, someone who has been like a mother to me."

She watched him absorb that, watched the emotions that were so alive in his eyes. Then he smiled and, with a slow, controlled movement, lowered his body half the way to hers. "So you were not running off to another man."

"No."

He lowered himself further and her body felt the furnace blast of his. "Have you had a lover since you became widowed?"

"No . . ." *Tell him the rest of it, the whole truth.*

And she would have. But that's when his body came all the way down upon hers. That's when his searing heat, his possessive weight, his physical desires melded with hers, and every thought burned right out of her head.

Belly to belly, chest to breast, thrusting hardness to accepting softness, they met and sank into the nest of her bed. Her breath left her in a long shivering sigh as she wrapped her arms around him.

This man, this moment . . .

He lifted her knee so that they could better fit together. He shifted lower and she felt the lethal burn of his arousal move down her belly. Then he shifted again, nudging into the open vee of her legs, probing with the male weapon she'd always feared and disdained.

She still feared it, but not enough to turn away. Not from him. Instead with every part of her quivering for some answer, some release from this terrible chaos inside her, she lifted her hips, just a faint movement, a restless plea.

But he heard it, for with a groan of his own, a harsh hitching of his breath, he thrust forward, parting her untried flesh, thrusting, thrusting, pushing in past emotional and physical barriers alike.

She sucked in a startled breath at the fleeting pain, the stretching fullness, and she shrank away. But the bed held her steady. He stopped. Hester couldn't breathe but only stared up at him.

She didn't know what she'd expected, but certainly not this. For she was impaled by him, pierced and claimed in a way too intimate to ever imagine. She closed her eyes to the intimacy of his gaze.

He knew her now, her secrets, her body. Everything. With his physical possession so real and yet unreal, he'd managed to possess so much more of her.

Tears sprang to her eyes, unwanted and wholly embarrassing. She tried to turn away but his hands bracketed her face. "I've hurt you. Damn."

He started to pull out of her until she gasped.

"Ooh . . ."

Slowly, so slowly it was a torture, he sank back into her, even deeper than before. This time her gasp was a hoarse, wondrous moan.

"Better?" He whispered the words against her lips, nipping and licking them.

She didn't answer with words, but he understood just the same. He pulled her other knee up, and this time when he pulled back it was a long, hot streak of fire.

"No!" she said, afraid he meant to withdraw entirely. But she had much to learn. For this time when he thrust inside her, it was harder, firmer. All the way in and all the way out. Then again. Hotter and faster. Impaling her on the flaming sword of erotic possession until they were racing together, mindless and yet of one mind.

His chest abraded her nipples. His tongue stabbed rhythmically inside her mouth. His hands fisted in her hair as he used her body for his pleasure.

But it was for her pleasure too and she reveled in it. It was madness, pure physical madness, that went on and on, an insane spiral that was heading somewhere . . . somewhere . . .

Then she found it, the explosion of yesterday, and she arched up against the power of it.

"That's it, that's it," she heard him say, followed by a ragged cry and spasms of his own.

He made several more violent thrusts. Then he collapsed over her, just as spent and drained as she felt.

No longer a virgin, she thought in that muddled portion of her brain still able to function. She was no longer a virgin.

What happened now?

CHAPTER 16

They slept. At least Hester thought she'd slept. When her eyes opened to the still flickering candlelight she wondered if perhaps she'd actually fainted from the violence of her emotions.

Not only violent emotions, she realized, but also violent physical reactions. Her body, her mind, and her heart—like a trio of instruments that together made a sweeter sound than they could separately do, they had come together tonight in the most magnificent concert she'd ever heard.

Why had no one ever told her about this?

She shifted in the bed, and as she felt Adrian shift to accommodate her, it occurred to her that her mother *had* told her about it. Or tried to. With Mr. Benchley, with Lord Gallatin, and the Honorable Mr. Richardson. Isabelle had tried to explain to her disapproving daughter how intense her feelings for them were, how absolute her adoration, how violent her passion.

"I am in love," she used to say, flinging her arms wide, then hugging them to her, and all the while smiling in a way that seemed to exclude Hester. *I am in love.*

Hester lay very still, conscious of the heavy thudding of her heart. She was naked in bed with a man. Not just any bed, nor just any man. But still . . .

Am I in love with Adrian Hawke?

Her heart pounded even harder. Surely she was not in love with him. How could she be?

Yet what else could account for this drastic reversal of her long-held feelings? She'd never before been so violently affected by a man. Most men she barely tolerated.

It must be love.

She closed her eyes in horror. What if she'd opened a gate she could never again close? What if she had unleashed the monstrous side of her nature? What if, like her mother, she went from one man to another, always falling in love, always seeking that pinnacle of feelings, but destined always to be disappointed?

She drew the sheets up tight to her chin. She couldn't be like her mother. She wouldn't be!

On the other hand, what if she never fell in love again? Never found another man who could rouse these terrible, wonderful, indescribable feelings in her? Inside she trembled, for she could hardly bear that bleak possibility.

Without thinking she turned to Adrian—and found him awake, his eyes open and watching. Likewise his arousal was unabated and waiting.

He draped an arm across her waist and slid her up against him. "I see you have survived."

"Yes." She could feel her heart drumming in her throat as he studied her. She studied him back. The golden light loved him, disheveled and naked, and she wished absurdly that she had a talent for art, for she would love to paint him just as he appeared now, a virile man at the peak of his masculine beauty.

She feared, however, that a painting done of herself

would not be so flattering. *The Fallen Woman and the Man She Loves.*

Life was not fair to women. It never had been.

Then he made the tiniest little movement with his hips, tiny but unimaginably erotic. He smiled. "Are you thinking what I'm thinking?"

Only if you're thinking that maybe you love me.

What Adrian was thinking was that he would never get enough of Hester Poitevant, not in the week and a half he had left in England. Maybe he could delay his sojourn to Scotland. Maybe she could be convinced to accompany him there.

He breathed in the lily-scented muskiness of her, so intensely feminine. His hand moved wonderingly in her hair, lifting a silken strand from her cheek, smoothing another curling one from her brow. Between her soft belly and his tensed one he felt his arousal thicken. Just the touch of her hair and lust turned him into a lunatic, craving her once more when he'd barely survived their last go-round.

His hand slid down her back, through the tangled masses of that lovely, lovely hair, until it rested at the top swells of her perfectly rounded derriere. "I was thinking," he murmured when she did not reply. "That we might try that again."

Her eyes, as dark as a turbulent green sea, widened as if in shock.

"You said you were all right."

She averted her eyes, sheltering her thoughts behind the sweep of her long lashes. "Yes. Yes, of course I am."

He smiled at the image she presented, so innocent and yet at her core a deliciously wanton creature. She'd been artless in her responses to him, as skittish and new as a virgin at times, which he'd loved. It only confirmed what she'd said about *not* having a lover.

"How long have you been a widow?"

"What?" Her gaze flew back to his, then away.

"Has it been a very long time since you've . . . done this with a man?"

After a moment's hesitation she nodded.

"Ah, Hester. No need to be embarrassed about that. You don't know how happy that makes me." He tilted her face up to his to kiss, and something in his chest swelled even as the demanding thing between his legs reached its full potential. He would teach her everything, this poor widow who was at once both worldly and na- ive, prudish and wanton, innocent and incredibly sen- sual.

He rolled onto his back and pulled her over him, en- joying her soft gasp of surprise and then delight. He had a week and a half left in London, and not one minute of that time did he intend to waste.

Adrian arrived at his uncle's house just before dawn. He was exhausted, barely able to dismount his horse. Yet he was also energized in a way he hadn't been in months. Years.

He paused in the stable entrance before starting for the house. He hadn't felt this way . . . ever.

Then he shook his head. It had been months since he'd bedded a woman, that's all. And this one just hap- pened to be especially good at it, the perfect combination of innocence and wild abandon. Three times they'd pushed one another to that peak, the first time wild and violent, the second slow and sensual, and the third . . .

He leaned against the door post for support. The third time had been both the most carnal and the most emo- tional joining of his body with a woman's that he'd ever known. No part of her was too insignificant not to re- quire his total attention. And she'd returned the favor, kissing him, learning him, mirroring his every action.

When he'd finally plunged into her, maddened with

lust and need, she'd been as hot and tight as the first time.

He groaned now to even remember the magnitude of his climax, as if every drop of life had been wrung out of his body. She'd taken everything he had, and everything he ever would have. If he hadn't left immediately afterward, he would have fallen into a stupor, and never left her bed at all.

The irony was, he wanted to stay. He'd wanted to sleep the day away with her in his arms, then awaken and do it all over again. If it weren't for her housekeeper and whoever else might spy his horse tied in her alley, he would have done just that.

But there was her reputation to consider, so he'd left. Damn, but he wasn't sure his legs would make it across the yard and up the stairs.

In the kitchen the cook's bleary-eyed helper was just stirring the fire in the main hearth and putting water on to heat. Adrian snagged two cold biscuits and a half bottle of last night's wine from the wide wooden table and kept going. He'd almost reached his room and escaped discovery when a door down the hall opened and his uncle came out.

With his hair mussed and his dressing gown haphazardly tied, Neville looked like Adrian felt: a man sneaking away from a romantic tryst. Except that the room Neville was leaving was his own bedroom.

Neville's brows arched in question when he spied Adrian. Adrian just shrugged and went into his room. But the image of his uncle stayed with him. Neville Hawke was obviously content with his wife, whom he loved and who just as clearly loved him.

Even when Adrian stripped off his clothes and crawled into his bed, with the cocks crowing morn in the distance, he could not stop thinking of the people he knew who were happy together. Happily married.

Certainly Neville and Olivia. Also Sarah and Marsh back in Boston. There was Catherine and her fiancé too, so giddy in love it was becoming a family joke. But there was also his own mother who by all accounts had abandoned her wild ways for the contentment of marriage to Duffy. Hard to believe, but he'd find out for himself once he reached Scotland.

Then there were those who were still looking for that sort of contentment, those who wanted to marry the right person with no cause ever to regret their choice. Horace stood at the top of that list, and perhaps a few of the young women he'd met. Like Dulcie Bennett. Those two were both naive enough to believe they could find that sort of love among the *ton*, and maybe they could.

Well, maybe Horace could. Dulcie was doomed, for her coldhearted brother fully intended to marry her to the highest bidder.

He thought of her and Horace, heads bent together, discussing horses and stables, and their favorite sort of rides in the countryside.

Of course. Horace and Dulcie.

He grinned up at the ceiling. Some pairings were so obvious they were almost overlooked. He'd have to push harder to get the two of them to recognize their eminent suitability.

Finally he could not avoid thinking about the pair of people he least wanted to think about: Hester and her deceased husband.

Had she been content with him? Or had it been a marriage arranged for practical, perhaps monetary, reasons?

Then again, perhaps she'd been in love with the man, madly, passionately in love with him.

He grimaced, hating the very idea. But he could believe it of her, now that he knew her better. That sort of deep emotional love would explain why she'd not taken a lover during the six years since he'd died.

Though the thought that she'd been celibate until she met him should have pleased Adrian, the fact that she could have loved her husband that much overshadowed it. He fell asleep frowning, pondering the mystery of Hester Poitevant, and wondering how soon he could see her again.

Horace and his father arrived at the Mayfair Academy at ten in the morning. Hester pleaded a headache, just as she had an hour earlier when Mrs. Dobbs had come to awaken her.

The Vasterling father and son were turned away as well when they called on Adrian.

"Harrumph," his father said, his mouth turned down in a frown. "These city people sleep through the best hours of the day. Carousing all night, I s'pose."

"It's not all carousing," Horace said. "People do a large portion of their business at those parties. That's where I met Mr. Hawke, and that's where I meet the young ladies on the marriage mart."

"And have you fixed on one?"

"Perhaps."

They were silent a moment as Horace guided the old-fashioned trap through the morning traffic along Gloucester Place.

"Don't go for one of those flighty ones," his father muttered.

"I won't."

"And don't be fooled by a pretty face."

"No."

"Or a bold manner. Flirts." The man shook his head in disgust. Horace didn't bother to respond. He'd been hearing this lecture for years, since before he'd even neared a marriageable age.

"You've got to know her people. They've got to be the right sort."

"We've got to be the right sort too."

"What? What do you mean? Of course we're the right sort."

Horace hunched over the reins. "We live in a cold dungeon of a place. Bad enough it's so remote, Father. But it's small and understaffed."

"It's a huge place. Too big, if you ask me."

"Yes, but we live in only four rooms."

Another silence fell until Horace said, "I want to open the south wing. For me and my bride."

"Mrs. McKeith cannot possibly manage another apartment."

"That's another thing. Mrs. McKeith is too old to run our household, especially once I have children. My wife must be free to run the household as she sees fit, and that means hiring servants. And decorating."

"We're fine the way we are."

"No. We're not." Horace turned to face his father. "Do you want grandchildren, Father? Do you want a family around you before you die? Aren't you weary of our lonely, bachelor household?"

There was no answer forthcoming from the older man. But Horace understood his father's silence as the acknowledgment it was. For five years he'd been disappointed each time Horace returned home without a bride. That was probably why he'd traveled all the way to London in his own ancient vehicle: time to ensure his son was wed.

A new worry occurred to Horace. "You're not ill, are you?"

"Me ill?" his father barked at him. "I'm never ill. I'm just irritated is all. It's damned expensive, this coming and going to town every year. It's past time that you settled on a suitable wife. Long past."

"Indeed it is. But it won't happen until I have something better to offer than a moldy old place fit only for two moldy old bachelors to reside in."

Despite the harshness of his assessment, when Horace turned his attention to the team, he had a faint smile on his face. This was the first time he'd ever broached this subject, and if not for Mrs. P opening his eyes, he never would have. It felt good. It felt right.

His father was as old-fashioned as they came: tight-fisted, set in his ways, and not particularly demonstrative in his feelings. But he loved his only child, that had always been clear to Horace.

He clucked to the horses. "It's a good thing you didn't have a daughter," he remarked. "You wouldn't be so eager for me to marry if you didn't want a woman to fuss over you in your old age."

Again there was no answer. But had Horace turned he would have seen the bleak look that came into his father's face. Bleak, but fleeting. When they arrived on Rotten Row it was long gone. And when they spied Miss Dulcie Bennett taking a turn around the park with her mother in her family's open phaeton, it was replaced by an expression of consideration.

A pleasant girl of some wealth. But the mother was quick to bid them adieu. Horace's face was wistful as he stared after them.

"How about her?" the older man asked. "Isn't she the one you said is mad for riding?"

"Yes." Horace tucked in his chin. "But her family wants a title for her. A higher title than ours," he added. "And a greater fortune as well."

"Harrumph. Better write her off then. I didn't like the manner of the mother anyway. You can tell a lot about the girl by observing the mother."

Horace nodded. "You never talk about your mother-in-law. Was my mother much like her?"

Exactly like her. Pretty. Flighty. But to his son he said, "I didn't know her well. Only met her four times before we wed, and three times after that—and one of those times was at her wake. I'm hungry," he said, changing the subject. "Didn't you tell me we were going to sample French cuisine today?"

Hester arose at half past one, sore, still in need of at least ten hours more sleep, yet energized in a way utterly foreign to her. She stretched, feeling every muscle she'd never before used. It felt wonderful.

She felt wonderful.

She vaguely recalled Adrian leaving. He'd kissed her and told her to stay put, he'd let himself out. After only one meager word of protest, she'd sunk into the deepest, most profound sleep of her life. No dreams, no restlessness. Just the sleep of the dead, or rather, the sleep of the well sated, the well satisfied, the sexually drained.

Was this what married couples had every night?

She pulled the sheets up to her neck and clutched them there. She didn't think she could survive night after night of such powerful emotional and physical exertions.

But she'd certainly like to try, she decided, giggling out loud.

From downstairs she heard Mrs. Dobbs scolding one of the dogs—probably Fifi, who had a habit of hopping up on a chair to see what delicious tidbits might be found on the kitchen table.

Her giggle died. What was she going to tell Mrs. Dobbs? Would she believe the story about the headache?

She could complain about her monthly which was due any day now. Especially if there were any bloodstains on the bed linens. Having been sorely troubled on the score herself when she was younger, Mrs. Dobbs was always solicitous of that particular female complaint.

But the truth was, dealing with Mrs. Dobbs was not

Hester's biggest problem. What to do about Adrian Hawke—that was the problem she must address. How to greet him when next they met in public. How to arrange their next meeting in private. And of course, how to deal with the crushing reality of his eventual departure from London.

Hester gazed up at her bedroom ceiling, not really seeing the whitewashed plaster or the heavy beam that ran the length of the attic room. She had taken her first lover knowing he would not be here very long.

At the time it had seemed a decided advantage. Now it seemed the worst tragedy of her life.

CHAPTER 17

Adrian called on Hester the following day only to find her already departed. Visiting a friend, her housekeeper said, giving him a curious, searching look, especially when both dogs clamored so insistently for his attention.

"D'ye wish to leave your card, Mr. Hawke?"

"Yes. Thank you." But Adrian didn't feel nearly so polite as he sounded. He'd slept through the whole previous day like a man drugged, and then had been unable to escape a family outing with his aunt and uncle. He'd prayed that Hester might be at the same event. However, it had been a small supper at a private home, and by the time it ended it had been far too late to call upon her.

It had taken all his restraint to wait until an acceptable hour this morning to call upon her. And now this. She was already gone.

He turned away from Hester's front door, so frustrated he wanted to punch someone, to kick something, to strangle anybody. He was desperate to see her, like a lunatic boy in the thralls of his first love. The difference being that he was old enough to know it wasn't love at all. But that didn't make it any less powerful an emotion.

Where in God's name was she?

In Cheapside, he realized, with her friend who was *not* her lover. With a surge of relief he headed east to Cheapside, oblivious to the noisy thrum of the city, the carriages and carts, the riders and pedestrians.

He didn't find her, of course. His luck was not running that way. Instead he ran into Horace and his father, a distraction he did not want, yet knew he needed. Chasing after will-o'-the-wisp Hester was a stupid idea in the first place. So he accepted Horace's invitation to lunch and they headed down to the Old Swan for baked oysters, potato bread, and pints of rich brown ale.

"I want real food," the elder Vasterling said. "Not that sauced-up foreign business we had yesterday."

"This place has real food," Horace replied, unfazed by his father's crankiness. "And it's cheap."

Vasterling gave a satisfied grunt and off they went, Adrian riding behind their ancient carriage. A sunny day along the Thames combined the best and worst of London in a vivid, pungent display. Watermen plied their trade, ferrying people up, down, and across the river. Ducks competed with fish for the refuse that floated along. Commercial ships, barges, skiffs, and pleasure craft jostled for their portion of the flow. Mud flats slick with debris, grassy banks shaded by willows, solid docks projecting out into the current—they were all a part of the mighty Thames, as was the fetid smell tinged with salt and the smoke from a thousand coal fires.

But on this day the wind was crisp and it cleared the air as they sat at a table alongside a set of granite steps that descended right into the river.

"This is my favorite place in London," Horace said. "You see every sort of people here. Would you like to take a water taxi after lunch?" he asked his father.

"What for?"

Someone needed to shake the old man up a little,

Adrian thought, and he was in a foul enough mood to do it. Fortunately the serving girl arrived with their food, an aproned fellow refilled their tankards, and they all dug into their meals.

" 'Twas Mrs. P who told me about this place," Horace said, wiping a dribble of oyster gravy from his lip. "Mrs. Poitevant," he clarified to his father.

Adrian paused, his fork suspended in midair. "Hester Poitevant frequents this establishment?"

Horace grinned at his surprise. "I know. Hardly what you'd expect. But then, she's full of surprises, isn't she? She knew I was being careful of my purse. She knows how to stretch a penny, that one."

Edgar Vasterling had stopped eating also. "Hester. This Mrs. Poitevant you've been going on and on about, you say her given name is Hester?"

"Yes. Did I never say so?" Spying the odd expression on his father's face, Horace frowned. "Is something wrong? Do you know her?"

The man didn't respond at first, and when he finally did, it was with a sharp shake of his head. "It's not a name you often hear these days," he muttered as he stared down into his bowl of oysters in a thick brown soup.

"No, I s'pose not," Horace agreed, digging back into his meal. "Anyway, she often comes here when she's out. P'rhaps we'll run into her. Wouldn't that be a happy coincidence?"

The rest of the meal Adrian focused less on his companions, and more on the restaurant entrance. Would she come today? A man came in with a woman just her height. A trio of women entered, none of them her.

He drank a third glass of ale and a fourth, then had to retire to the necessary, frustrated and angry but with no focus for those emotions. When he left here he was going straight back to Mayfair, he vowed, and if he had to he would camp outside her house until she arrived.

But upon his return to the table, who should Adrian spy at the base of the water steps disembarking from a boat but Hester. She was here!

He halted half the way to the table, drinking in the sight of her, struck as he was every time he saw her by how incredibly beautiful she was. Whether in her primmest guise or, as now, her most stylish, she had somehow become for him the pinnacle of womanly beauty. Maybe it was because of her guise, he speculated. For she had come to embody every sort of woman to him, moral arbiter, wanton tease, sorrowing widow, enticing lover.

She didn't see him as she turned back to her companion, an elderly woman dressed as elegantly as Hester. Was this the friend he was so jealous of?

They started up the steps arm in arm, laughing together, when Hester looked up and saw Horace. He'd risen to his feet at the sight of her and started toward them, leaving his father at the table. But Hester didn't give Horace more than a brief glance before turning a horrified gaze upon Edgar Vasterling.

Horrified? Adrian's eyes narrowed. That made no sense. But it was the only description Adrian could give to the expression on Hester's face. She reared back as if to leave, as if repulsed. But the other woman clamped a hand on Hester's arm, then murmured something that drew Hester's gaze to her.

Adrian frowned. What was going on?

He started forward, determined to draw Hester's attention to himself. But when she did see him it was clear that his presence only increased her distress. Was it pain he saw in her huge eyes, gone a tumultuous hazel shade? Was it anger? Or was it fear and confusion—and a hint of tears?

He started to reach for her, then let his arm fall when

he realized how inappropriate that was. Damnation but he wanted to take her in his arms, to comfort her and protect her and learn why she was so upset.

For Hester, Adrian's appearance in the midst of this awful run-in with her father made the disastrous situation seem almost farcical. Were it a play at the Royal Victoria Theatre she would be laughing out loud at the heroine's ludicrous plight. Father, brother, lover, all together and none of them aware of each other's relationships to her—nor in two cases, of their own true relationship with her.

She felt Verna's hand tighten on her arm and her rubbery legs somehow stiffened. Thank goodness for Verna DeLisle. If Hester got through the next few minutes at all it would be solely to Verna's credit.

Horace was beaming, a smile that required an answering smile from her.

"I say, Mrs. P—pardon me, Mrs. Poitevant. What jolly good luck to run into you today. I was hoping we might." He gave her a perfectly executed bow which would have pleased her had Edgar Vasterling and Adrian Hawke not been looking on. The best she could manage was a rather stiff nod.

At a nudge from Verna she cleared her throat. "Mrs. DeLisle, may I present the Honorable Horace Vasterling."

Between Verna and Horace the other introductions and presentations were made, all just as proper as could be and following every rule of etiquette. But even after his courtly bow, Hester could not meet her father's eyes. Nor could she look for long at Adrian. Beneath her gloves her hands grew clammy and a bead of nervous perspiration trickled down between her breasts.

It fell to Horace to bridge the awkwardness, and to his credit he gave it his best. "We'd be pleased if you would join us for luncheon," he said. "Wouldn't we, Father?"

"Indeed, we would." The senior Mr. Vasterling smiled at Mrs. DeLisle. "You must join us."

Oh, no. Hester shook her head. "I'm afraid we cannot—"

"Now, dear. I think we must," Verna countered. "It would be positively rude to turn down such a kind offer, and from three such charming gentlemen."

"But really—"

"Now, now, Hester," Verna said, patting her forearm even as she shot her a challenging look. "You were just remarking how hungry you were and what a perfectly lovely day it was for dining al fresco."

So it was that they were seated at the table, Hester between Horace and Adrian, opposite her father, while Verna sat beside the man. How had this come to be, her dining with the one man she'd hoped never to have to meet?

They ordered their meal—Hester did not recall what—and settled into idle conversation: the Thames, their boat ride, the other water traffic, the seagulls who thrived so far inland. While Mrs. DeLisle regaled the other two men with the story of a near disastrous ride she'd once made with a drunken waterman, Adrian leaned nearer to Hester.

He murmured for her ears only, "I called upon you this morning but you had already gone out."

The sound of that husky, familiar voice sent a shiver of remembered passion shooting down Hester's back. Fortunately the serving girl brought their meals and she was able to ignore him. Across the table her father's attention remained focused on Verna, who looked especially lovely today. Always one to enjoy any company, her dark eyes sparkled, and her bubbly personality, tempered so perfectly by her impeccable manners, bridged the initial awkwardness of the situation.

Then again, Hester was the only one aware of any awkwardness, and the only one affected by it. Horace was in a jovial mood and his father seemed well pleased by the inclusion of the two women in their party. Likewise Verna seemed exceedingly gay, laughing out loud as Hester hadn't heard her do in an age.

"This is the pleasantest hour I've passed since arriving in London," Edgar Vasterling said once the meal was done and the dishes cleared away.

"I second that," Adrian said.

Verna smiled at Adrian, then at Hester. They had not quite gotten around to their discussion of *that* night. Hester had been planning that conversation for the lunch table. But she could see the speculative gleam in Verna's eyes, and she sensed the approval there too.

"We'd be more than happy to deliver you ladies home in our carriage," Horace said.

"That's very kind," Hester replied. "However, it's not necessary." She wasn't certain she could survive the intimacy of a carriage ride with her so-called father. "Besides, we're probably going in different directions."

"Those clouds are looking ominous," her father said. "I'm a farmer at heart, and I know rain clouds when I see them. I'm afraid I must insist that you accept our offer," he added, smiling at Verna, who smiled right back.

Would this nightmare never end? Hester fretted as the four of them crowded into the Vasterlings' carriage. At least Adrian took his leave, departing on his horse. But her relief at his departure was offset by an irrational sort of longing for him. Would he and she ever have another chance to talk in private? Or do other things? she wondered.

Her cheeks flamed at such a wicked thought and she

pressed a handkerchief to her damp brow. She must get herself under better control. She must.

In the carriage she confined her conversation to Horace. But she could not escape a word or even a nuance of her father's conversation with Verna. That he was unfailingly pleasant, and courteous to a fault, made no impression on her; she would not let it.

"Do you agree, Mrs. Poitevant?" he asked her now.

Caught unawares, she blinked. "Agree?"

"My father thought a night at the opera might prove more entertaining than an evening at the Caldecorts' ball," Horace explained. "He's not one for dancing."

Hester sent Horace a grateful smile for covering her distraction so well. She glanced briefly at her father. "If one is an aficionado of opera, I'm certain one would much prefer that sort of activity."

Outside a rumble of thunder rolled across the sky, a perfect reflection of her mood.

"I take it you would rather dance," Mr. Vasterling said to her.

"No." In truth, Hester adored the opera. But she didn't intend to like it anymore. Not if he did. "It depends on my mood," she added. "Ah. We're here." *Thank goodness!*

To the accompaniment of even more thunder they said their good-byes, Verna's long and gracious, Hester's approaching curt.

Once inside Verna's parlor, however, Hester found little relief, for the older woman fixed her with an observant gaze. "What a rude display. Had any of your students behaved so, you would have been sorely disappointed."

Though her tone was gentle, her words nonetheless cut Hester to the quick. "What can you expect? I despise that man. Passionately," she added for emphasis.

"Yes. I know. I must say, though, he seems a rather gentle sort of man. Very like his son."

"Does he?" Hester rolled her eyes. "No doubt there are those who could find something good and gentle in even the most despicable thief or bully. Or murderer."

"A murderer? Oh, come now, Hester. You will never deal well with this situation if you persist in such histrionics."

"Histrionics? Histrionics! After that . . . that simpering display you just gave, you have the nerve to call my reaction histrionics?"

"I do not simper," the older woman stated, her voice as mild as Hester's was shrill. She laid aside her hat and reticule and removed her kidskin gloves. "Would you like tea as we continue this discussion?"

Hester huffed out an angry breath. "I don't want tea. Nor am I of a mind to discuss that . . . that man."

"I see. And what about the other one, that Mr. Hawke? Did you wish to discuss him?"

At Verna's gentle, concerned look, all the fire drained out of Hester. It was impossible to stay angry with her, and really, Verna was not the source of Hester's fury. So she told her—not the details of her night with Adrian Hawke. Just that she had done it, given her virginity to a man for no reason other than that she wanted to. No promise of marriage. No promise of love.

"At least in that part I am nothing like my mother," Hester concluded. She hugged a fringed pillow to her chest. "I expect nothing from him, least of all love."

Verna had listened to everything with an absorbed expression on her face. "I suppose that's a good thing, not to expect anything from him."

"Of course it is," Hester said. Then, "Why wouldn't it be?"

"Oh, it's only that strong emotions like love add another dimension to the physical act of making love.

Something impossible to describe. Impossible to imagine." She smiled and sighed. "Impossible to explain. You just have to experience it to know what I mean."

Hester threw her hands up in the air. "Why are you telling me this? You who have always been the sensible one. Do you want me to turn into my mother, falling in love over and over again? Getting hurt every single time? Growing more desperate with each lover?"

"Your mother rejected more men than rejected her."

Hester frowned. "That's hardly comforting to hear."

"My dear. I cannot say whether this Mr. Hawke is worthy of your love. Certainly he is a handsome, charming sort of fellow. And he's clearly besotted with you."

A sudden rattle of thunder heralded the onslaught of rain, angry pellets beating against the diamond-paned windows. Hester scowled at the blurred window glass. How well she knew that feeling of futility, the wasted time and energy of beating against that which you can never affect.

From the hall came a firm knocking. Hester and Verna both paused to listen as the housekeeper answered the door. A man's voice, followed by the slip-slip of the old housekeeper's slow approach. But Hester knew who it was, and by the smug expression on Verna's face, so did she.

"Mr. Adrian Hawke," the housekeeper said.

Verna smiled and straightened her fichu. "By all means show him in."

They both stood, but where Verna was calm and obviously pleased, what Hester felt was panic. "You have the heart of a procurer," she hissed.

That only made Verna laugh. Not a procurer, she thought as she observed Hester's reaction to the tall, rakish Mr. Hawke, and his reaction to her.

Not a procurer but, rather, a cupid.

CHAPTER 18

Adrian insisted on seeing Hester home in a hired hack.

"No one would expect me to ride outside, given this storm," he said when she protested.

"No one expects you to see me home at all."

"I expect it of me."

They stood on Verna's front stoop waiting for a lull in the downpour before dashing for the vehicle. "If you refuse to let me ride inside with you, I suppose I'll just trail behind, getting soaked to the skin."

She looked away from his darkly smiling face. Just the mention of his skin, soaked or otherwise, conjured up the wickedest curl of heat in her belly.

"But there's a more urgent reason," he went on, leaning nearer and murmuring in her ear.

Though her heart felt as if it had already stuttered to a stop, Hester tempted fate further and glanced sidelong at him. "And what is that?"

His eyes searched hers, too hot, too intimate. Then he lowered that burning gaze to her mouth—her suddenly dry-as-cotton mouth.

"I need to kiss you, Hester. If I don't kiss you very

soon, I may die of frustration." He looked back into her mesmerized eyes. "You don't want me to die of frustration, do you? Think of everything we'd miss . . ."

Hester's fevered brain tried to think. They were inside a hack with the canvas shades tied closed against the storm and the rest of the soggy city. It was just them in their own damp little world. Though they rattled through the center of town, they were utterly alone. No one would ever know if they took advantage of the situation.

Oh, but she was too bad. Yet acknowledging that fact did nothing to prevent the inevitable. From sitting beside him, to sitting on his lap, to reclining on the seat with him half covering her, it took but three blocks for him to have her melting beneath him. My, but the man certainly knew how to kiss a girl senseless. He possessed her mouth with his, heating her lips, stroking inside, claiming all in his path, and more.

But other than his intimate kisses and the tantalizing heat of his body's weight upon hers, he did not press his advantage. Her legs fell open to let his hips nestle there. She arched her aching breasts against his chest, needing that closeness, and she let her hands discover his damp hair, his wide shoulders, and the powerful muscles of his back.

He could have taken her there with the driver mere feet away and only the sounds of the storm as a buffer. She was that mad with wanting him.

But he was the circumspect one. When they passed Leicester Square he pulled them both upright and began to straighten the utter disarray of her clothing, while she sat there, still stunned by the swift violence of her emotions. He smoothed first her petticoats and then her aqua muslin skirt.

"Are you going out tonight?" he asked, as if nothing had just happened.

"I . . . um . . . Yes. To . . . To the Caldecorts' ball."

His nimble fingers moved up her bodice, fastening a loose button, then arranging her fichu along the neckline. She caught her breath when he smoothed it down, his fingers nearly grazing the overheated skin of her chest. He raised his vivid gaze from her exposed flesh to her eyes. He didn't move his hand though. "Do you have to attend that ball?"

Hester could hardly breathe, she was so aroused. But she knew her duty to her clients. "I have to be there—"

She broke off with a gasp when one of his fingertips—just the edge of his nail—slid down the slope of her breast. Lower it dipped, to the shadowed crevice the fichu was meant to cover, then up again, torturing the other breast in the same way. Her nipples hardened to aching points, needing his touch to relieve them. But she knew that touch would only be another, more exquisite form of torture.

"I need to see you again, Hester. Alone." His voice had gone husky with his own need.

She was mad with wanting him, shaking with it. Still she recognized that he too felt some portion of that same yearning. He felt it for *her*. "Maybe . . . tomorrow?"

"Tonight." He hooked his finger in the lowest part of her vee-shaped neckline, tugging, then bent forward and planted a kiss in that deep, warm crevice.

With a faint cry Hester arched toward his mouth, seeking more and moaning when he drew away.

"Damn, but I want to devour you," he growled. He pushed away from her but his ferocious gaze devoured her still. "I want you, Hester. Just as you want me. How long do you plan to make me wait?"

"I don't want to wait at all!" she burst out, then turned scarlet at so blatant an admission.

A muscle tensed in his jaw, tensed and released. "Then invite me home with you."

Oh, how Hester wanted to do just that. But there were the Dobbses to consider. Her mother's housekeeper might have been complicit in the arrangements necessary to Isabelle's romantic interludes. But Hester didn't think hers would be nearly so approving. "I can't. You know I can't."

"Then later. Send your servants out on an errand."

"I can't." Hester shook her head. "It's too difficult. Too risky."

He was silent a moment. Outside the rain still pelted down, isolating them and their urgent dilemma from the more trivial problems of the rest of the world. Only when the hack pulled up before her cottage on Portland Street did Adrian speak. He sounded almost angry, though she suspected it was more frustration than true anger.

"If you think to tease me, heed my warning: that torment can burn us both. I'll be at the Caldecort ball tonight. I wouldn't miss it for the world. But be prepared for a level of attention you have not previously received. You will not sit out any dances tonight, Hester. I'll not allow it. We'll dance and dance and dance until it is too torturous for us to dance that near each other again."

He picked up a fold of her skirt and rubbed it between his finger and thumb. "People may notice. People may talk. But I don't care. Do you?"

She jerked her skirt away. "Isn't it enough that I have—" She broke off, shaking her head. "Would you ruin me before the very people from whom I earn my livelihood? Are you that selfish? That cruel?"

"No!" He snatched up her hand. "I'm not a cruel man. But I am a desperate one." His voice grew lower. "I want to make love to you, Hester, as soon as I can, as often as I can. Do you understand?"

Though his hand manacled her wrist, Hester could not fight him. The trouble was, she did understand. Slowly she nodded. "I'll try to think of something."

Only when the driver knocked at the door did Adrian release her hand. He climbed out and assisted her down, but he let the driver deliver her to her door beneath his sagging umbrella. He didn't notice the rain as he untethered his horse from behind the hack and rode off through the sodden city. He was able even to disregard the discomfort of riding astride in his state of semi-arousal—which seemed of late to have become semi-permanent.

Tonight he would have Hester to himself. Some way, somewhere they would carve out a few hours of privacy, and they would once again climb the heights and plumb the depths of pure physical pleasure.

He smiled and lifted his face to the gray sky and slackening rain. He knew one thing about Hester that she didn't know about herself. She thrived on the danger of discovery. She looked prudish and demure, yet hid a shocking beauty and a mighty passion beneath that façade. She said no, yet melted beneath his hand. She denied the possibility of a tête-à-tête, yet followed him into shady bowers and rain-shrouded hacks.

She professed a fear of discovery, but Adrian had no doubt that she'd be as eager as ever to be enticed tonight. Who knew, maybe in a hidden niche she would succumb to him, or behind a heavy curtain, or even in the shadows beyond a well-lit terrace with the sounds of the party all around them.

He only hoped it was not the danger that aroused her so much as it was him.

From inside her own carriage in the queuing line outside the Caldecorts' brightly lit mansion, Hester knotted her fingers in her lap. Had she not had on gloves, by now all her nails would be gnawed to the quick. She was that nervous. The carriage moved forward another length.

Soon enough she'd be disembarking. Then what?

How had it happened that without her knowledge and quite against her wishes her life had spiraled so completely out of control? It was all Adrian Hawke's fault. Because of him the focus of her life had veered from seeing her three students well matched and married off, to finding time to indulge her heretofore unknown carnal appetites.

Here she was, as lost to wickedness as any woman ever had been.

Perhaps that was why she'd again dressed so severely tonight. She'd even worn her spectacles, for heaven's sake, and she hated them. But that wouldn't deter Adrian Hawke. He saw right through her disguise. Indeed, the man saw things in her, possibilities—realities—that no one had ever detected before.

She stepped down and hurried across the still damp gravel and into the brittle gaiety of the noisy ball. Waiting for her was a distraught Dulcie, being comforted by Charlotte. When Hester spied George in a corner haranguing his mother, she understood. It was to be one of *those* evenings.

Dulcie's miserable gaze fastened at once on Hester, as did her trembling grip. "Leonard Smythe, Lord Pennington's heir, has made an offer," she said without preamble. "And George says he will agree unless I come up with something better by Monday. Leonard Smythe," she wailed. "I don't even like him!"

George came up, a scowl forewarning his mood, and that fast Hester reached the limits of her patience. Without weighing her words she rounded on him. "So you plan to waste the investment you've made in Dulcie by handing her off to the first fool who waves a few pounds in your face? Have you never considered how pathetic this makes you look, George? How inept and what a poor dealmaker?"

He sputtered a full thirty seconds before getting out a word. "Mind your own business."

"Dulcie is my business."

"Then find her a husband so I don't have to!"

Around them people were beginning to stare, but Hester didn't care. Everyone knew what George Bennett was like. Viscount or no, he was an ass.

Dulcie, however, was more easily intimidated by her brother.

Fortunately Lady Ainsley could not abide this sort of public spectacle. "George. Be quiet!" she hissed, plucking at his sleeve.

He threw off her arm and lurched toward Hester as if to shove her out of his way so he could get to Dulcie.

Though George was an uncouth lout, normally Hester would not fear physical harm from him. But he reeked of liquor and that always made him meaner and more unpredictable. Still, she was not of a mind or a mood to back down.

"Don't you dare lay a finger on me," she warned, steel in her voice and in her narrowed stare.

He loomed over her, the epitome of the worst the *ton* had to offer: title without class; privilege without moral substance. But he didn't touch her. He knotted his hands into threatening fists and glared at her. "What you need," he muttered in an ugly voice, "is something up your arse besides that stick."

His mother gasped. So did Dulcie and Charlotte, though they probably didn't understand the slur any better than Hester did. That it was a coarse slur, however, was unmistakable. Without pausing to think, Hester slapped him.

Except that she missed.

Thrown off balance, she stumbled forward. But she caught herself in time to see why her palm had missed its target. Someone had spun the man around and jerked him up onto his toes.

Adrian Hawke. Where had he come from?

"You bloody ass," Adrian swore at George. Holding the man by the lapels, he shook him like a dog would shake a rat. "Still the same damned bully you always were."

Again he shook the man. "It's time someone broke you of that habit, and I'm just the man to do it."

In the foyer everyone had gone silent. From outside came the excited voices of people just arriving and pushing to enter. Beyond, in the ballroom proper music played and the buzz of voices gaily carried on.

But even those sounds dimmed as the news traveled like lightning. "Fight in the foyer. Fight in the foyer."

Hester wanted nothing more than to punch George Bennett in the nose herself. But she knew she must put an end to this fiasco before it became an out-and-out brawl. Already Lady Ainsley had switched her fury from her drunken fool of a son to Adrian. While Adrian shook the sputtering George, Lady Ainsley beat on Adrian's back with her fan.

"Let him go, you brute. You bully. You . . . You . . ." Lady Ainsley sputtered like her son. "You lowly Scottish bastard!"

Incensed, Hester snatched Lady Ainsley's fan and shoved her backward, right into Adrian's uncle, who swiftly hustled her away. Then Hester rounded on Adrian and George. "Let him go," she demanded.

At least Adrian heard her. He didn't release the man who'd begun to make a most unhealthy choking noise, but he did turn his head to look at her. "Are you all right?"

She drew herself up, excruciatingly aware of the morbid attention of the encircling crowd. She must pick her way very carefully if she were to preserve her reputation.

"Of course I am all right. But I would be even better if you had allowed me to slap him for his impertinence. His cruel remarks were, after all, aimed at me."

A muscle ticked in Adrian's jaw. An angry muscle. "I was not raised to ignore the plight of a lady."

"I appreciate that, and your mother is to be commended. Nonetheless, I believe you should let him go now. Before you strangle him," she added. George's face was very red, almost purple.

She didn't think Adrian was going to do it. If anything, his hands seemed to tighten and George let out a gagging sort of whimper. Then all at once Adrian loosened his hold and stepped back, flicking his hands as if to shake off the foulness of George Bennett's touch.

For his part, George collapsed in a boneless heap, sucking huge draughts of air into his deprived lungs. His mother rushed over, wailing her grievances, while around them the hushed silence gave way to excited chatter.

"He nearly killed the fellow."

"What was that all about?"

"Please, please. Disperse to the ballroom," Lady Caldecort pleaded, fluttering about, making ineffectual shooing motions with her hands.

"Strike up the music," Lord Caldecort ordered the butler. Then he turned to Adrian, drew himself up to his full height and glared up at him. "I say, young man, I do not allow fighting inside my house."

Adrian gave him a courteous bow. "My pardon, sir. I'd be happy to fight him outside."

The man stiffened. "My word. You Americans are worse than we heard. Gentlemen do not engage in fisticuffs except in the boxing ring."

"An excellent suggestion, my lord," said Adrian.

"No!" Hester shoved between Lord Caldecort and Adrian. "I want no one fighting because of . . . because of a silly misunderstanding." How hard it was to get out that watered-down description of events.

Adrian took her by the shoulders. "The man's a pig, Hester. He's the worst sort of bully. Besides, this fight is more about him and me than it is about you."

Hester stared up at him, and all her resolve to be angry at his interference flew right out of her head. It went against everything she'd strived to achieve to let a man rescue her from a situation she felt well able to deal with herself. But from their first run-in, it had been obvious that there was bad blood between the two men, something from their school days.

With a little nod she acknowledged Adrian's words. Only then did she become aware of the avid silence of their staring audience. Too late she realized that his hands on her shoulders and his use of her given name revealed far more about their relationship than either of them wanted revealed.

She stiffened; his hands fell away. But the damage was done. A new buzz of whispers began, and with it her face flamed with guilty color.

Adrian realized at once the mistake he'd made. But he was not about to let what he'd done reflect badly on Hester. So he turned to the real villain of this tableau, George Bennett, whom two men were helping to his feet. Again he caught the man by the front of his jacket. Everyone else fell back, expecting some new outburst of violence. Even Hester.

"So, Bennett. How many other respectable women have you insulted and terrorized? How many? Do you think because you hired Mrs. Poitevant to instruct your sister that she is subject to your vile temper and crude innuendo? You forget that there are others like myself, who respect her and who also have engaged her to polish someone for entrée into society. I, for one, do not take an attack on any of my business associates lightly." He sent a quick warning glance to Hester, then glared back at the quivering slob before him. "If you're a man, you'll meet my challenge in the ring. Just set the time and place."

In the hoopla that followed, Adrian lost sight of Hester. She disappeared in a circle of women while George Bennett slunk away with only his mother and one of the Caldecorts' footmen as escort. Meanwhile Adrian fielded all sorts of offers to arrange the boxing match. Bennett did not have many friends, it seemed. Though few would speak out too loudly against a peer, it was clear that they all relished the idea of seeing the man beat senseless.

Amid the talk of rings and Queensberry rules, and famous grudge matches of the past, however, Adrian was careful to keep Hester's innocence at the forefront.

"And her a poor widow," someone agreed with him.

"Managing as best she can, only to be insulted by one who should know better," another said.

"It's fortunate she has such staunch defenders," his Uncle Neville put in.

"Indeed." This came from Lord Caldecort himself. "She's a starchy bit of a woman. No denying that. But a widow's a widow. It behooves all decent men to see she's protected since she's got no man of her own."

In the ladies' retiring room, meanwhile, Hester was forced to sit with her feet up and a cool cloth on her head. Catherine fanned her while her mother, Olivia, fussed over her.

When Hester tried to protest, Olivia gave her a cautioning look, then a secret wink.

"Thank goodness our Adrian was there," Olivia said, loud enough to be heard by everyone in the room and in the hall outside. "I'll admit his manner may sometimes be a trifle rough. He is, after all, from America. But his good heart is what counts. That odious Lord

Ainsley should hope to someday possess the manners of my dear nephew."

One of Catherine's friends, a girl not yet betrothed, clasped her hands to her chest and sighed. "He was wonderful, don't you think? Like a knight in shining armor."

"He certainly was," Olivia said. "Even as a boy he never hesitated to defend those more vulnerable than he. His mother, other children. He has always hated bullies, and we supported that. But Neville and I used to despair that he would be seriously hurt." She smiled at her rapt audience. "Fortunately he wasn't. And fortunately he hasn't changed a bit during his sojourn in America. I only wish we could find him an English bride so that he might return permanently to us."

Hester marveled at the woman's aplomb, though that part about a bride keeping him in England seemed rather extreme. Why should he marry when he could coax any woman he wanted—even the oldest virgin in London—into his bed?

But she wasn't going to think about that. By the time they all dispersed back to the party, there wasn't a woman at the ball who wouldn't have married Adrian Hawke on the spot, would he ask her. Even the ones already wed.

It was a relief and yet it was small comfort to Hester. Olivia and Catherine had probably saved her reputation with their quick thinking. But they'd also pointed every woman of the *ton* at Adrian. As if he needed their help. With his time left in England so brief, she was unlikely ever to get him alone again.

Just as well, her sensible self scolded.

But the part of her that wore lacy undergarments and slept in a sheer, embroidered night rail, under sweetly scented sheets, was heartbroken.

She'd had one night with him. Now it was unlikely she'd ever get another.

CHAPTER 19

The next day Lady Ainsley sent a cold note, dismissing Hester from her employ and warning her to keep her distance from every member of her family.

The day after that, Dulcie sent a note stained with tears, apologizing profusely for her brother's crudeness and her mother's hatefulness. One good thing she revealed: Leonard Smythe had withdrawn his offer. It seemed he did not wish to be associated with the Ainsleys' recent shame. George, meanwhile, had fled to their country place just south of London. Apparently he had no intention of accepting Adrian's challenge to fisticuffs.

The girl ended with a particularly soggy paragraph about how wonderful Mr. Hawke had been to come to Hester's rescue, how sorely she missed Hester, and how sorry she was that she would not be able to join either Hester or Mr. Hawke on the riding excursion they'd planned.

The following day Hester received the message she'd really been waiting for, the one from Adrian. Horace delivered it, and though he was clearly curious, she waited to read it after he left.

"Dear Mrs. Poitevant," it began. Hester's heart sank at the formality.

I apologize for any inconvenience my recent, impulsive behavior may have caused you. I have been advised that it might benefit your reputation best if I not call on you again.

That was all. No pleasant closing line, no regrets. Not even an expression of sincerity. Just that curtly worded apology and his slashing signature.

Hester read it five times, perhaps more, trying in vain to interpret some emotion other than perfunctory courtesy in his words. But there was nothing. They were done, he and she.

It was no more than she expected. But the fact that their parting had come a week sooner than she'd anticipated was somehow devastating. It was ridiculous, but true. She was devastated. Crushed.

She refused to cry, however. She'd had her fling, and it was over. Now she didn't ever have to concern herself with such matters again.

Over the rest of the week Hester attended a breakfast with Charlotte, another birthday reception—this one with Anabelle, and two well-attended supper parties. None of those occasions included appearances by Adrian, which happenstance left her both relieved and despairing.

At least her reputation had not been ruined, and Hester knew whom to credit for that. Olivia and Catherine Hawke were two of the finest women she'd ever had the good fortune to meet and she would forever be grateful to them. Indeed, thanks to them she'd become a bit of a darling. Already she had two clients arranged for next season.

Even more astounding, she had an appointment next week with an ancient countess and her incredibly awkward country bumpkin of a nephew who seemed destined to be an earl despite his decided preference for farming, fishing, and bachelorhood. While the first two were acceptable, if eccentric, the latter could not possibly be allowed. An earl must marry someone.

Either Adrian or Horace must have advised the countess to consult the Mayfair Academy, and Hester ought to have been thrilled with this new aspect of her business. But she seemed unable to muster any extremes of emotion except, perhaps, for loneliness, sadness, and hopelessness.

Today she sat in her back parlor, so mired in those emotions she didn't hear the knock. So when Mrs. Dobbs announced Horace Vasterling, she gave a start. "Is he . . . alone?"

Mrs. Dobbs gave her a look, half curious, half knowing. The same look she'd been giving her all week, as if she knew what had been going on under her nose, even though she couldn't possibly know. No one but Verna knew about her dalliance with Adrian Hawke, and no one else ever would.

"Yes, miss. I'm afraid Mr. Hawke isn't with him."

"I meant his father," Hester lied, jutting out her chin. She sniffed then, regretting her ill temper, sighed and shook her head. Closing the book she held but hadn't really been reading, she said, "Show him in, will you?"

Horace had been her rock this past week, putting in an appearance at several of the same places she'd been, only once with his father in tow. He'd truly become her friend of late, so much so that she sometimes forgot the secret of their real relationship. If not for the specter of their father's presence in town, she might have put the entire business right out of her head.

When he entered, she reached a hand to him and he took it. But she sensed at once his distress. He'd forgotten his gloves, part of his hair was standing on end, and he'd overlooked fastening two of the buttons on his waistcoat.

"Horace?"

"Good afternoon, Mrs. P. It's good of you to see me."

"Are you all right?"

Releasing her hand, he paced to the window, stared a restless moment out into the blustery afternoon, then turned and paced to the fireplace. He stared at himself in the mirror and tried half-heartedly to repair his hair. Then he paced right back to the window. "I'm going home. To Cumbria," he said. "I'll probably travel with Adrian after his cousin's wedding. He's going that same route on his way to Scotland, you know."

Hester clamped her lips against their sudden trembling. She cleared her throat. "I'll miss you. Very much," she added, for it was true.

He turned to look at her, his normally amiable face downcast.

"I wanted to thank you," she went on. "For sending Lady Gorings to me. I'm to meet her nephew next week."

"That was more Adrian's doing than mine."

"Oh." She looked down at the handkerchief she'd twisted into a knot in her hands. How very good of Adrian to make sure she would have a decent income after he left for Scotland and America. Except that she didn't appreciate it at all. If he cared half as much about her feelings as he did about her livelihood, she'd be far happier.

But he didn't care about her feelings. They'd been lovers; they weren't in love. There was a huge difference between the two, even if she had a hard time remembering it.

She couldn't think about that now, though. That was for the privacy of her own chamber at night. Her lonely chamber. For now she must force herself to focus on Horace, for he clearly was upset.

"What's wrong, Horace? You don't seem at all yourself today."

He grimaced. "I shouldn't burden you with my megrims."

"I beg to differ. I believe I was engaged for precisely that purpose."

That provoked a glimmer of his old affability. "So you were. I must confess that I've come to think of you more as a friend."

"And so I am. Now tell me the cause of your glum mood. Is that why you've decided to leave London?"

"Just the opposite. I'm glum because I *am* leaving."

"Then stay."

"How can I stay?" he burst out. "When the woman I've settled my affections on can never be mine?"

He stared at her so earnestly that her face reddened. Oh dear, oh dear. She thought he'd abandoned any tendencies of that sort toward her. Had their developing friendship meant more to him than she'd realized?

"Horace," she began. "Don't leave London on account . . . on account of me."

"Don't blame yourself," he said. "All you could do was make me more presentable to her." His thick brows drew together in despair. "You can't make me into an earl or increase my fortune sufficiently to suit her family."

It took Hester a moment to digest his words. He was leaving London on account of some other woman, not her. A woman whose family did not find him acceptable.

Dulcie Bennett? She straightened at the thought.

Could it be? She searched her mind, recalling their every interaction. They'd been friendly, then warm. They'd danced at least two dances every time they'd been at the same party. And then, they'd finally had their ride yesterday morning. Instead of her and Adrian accompanying them, however, Catherine and her beau had joined them.

Hester stared at Horace. "Does the young lady in question return your affections?"

"Well, I don't know. I think so."

Hester suppressed a smile. Dear, dear Horace, and her own sweet Dulcie. "Have you expressed your feelings to her?"

He opened his mouth, then shut it. "I suppose not. Not directly."

"Perhaps you should."

"To what end? Her family will only say no to my suit."

Though she knew it was heretical to the precepts of the society whose good opinion she courted, Hester said, "Perhaps you should tell her anyway."

He was silent a long moment. "What if she sends me away? I'll end up looking like a fool."

"Well, if she turns you down because she does not return your affection, you'll probably recover from your heartbreak much faster than you think."

He looked doubtful, and indeed, who was she to give advice on affairs of the heart?

"What if she says yes?" He threw the question out like a challenge. "It still won't change her family's opinion. You of all people know how they are."

"If Dulcie Bennett says yes to your declaration of love—It is love, isn't it?"

His face reddened and he nodded. "I liked her very well already. She's very easy to talk to, you see. And she never puts on airs like some of the young ladies do.

But then yesterday when we went riding in Hyde Park ... We had such a rousing good time, Mrs. P. It was then that I realized how perfectly suited we were. Perfectly."

Hester smiled at him. Yes, they were perfect for each other. "I see. Well, if Dulcie feels the same toward you, it wouldn't surprise me one whit if she didn't consent to ..." She hesitated, then plunged on. "To running away to Winwood Manor with you. After all, it's not that much farther to Gretna Green."

Horace's eyes grew as big as saucers. "Gretna Green! You're suggesting Dulcie and I run away to Gretna Green?"

"Only as a last resort."

She could see his mind spinning. Then suddenly he frowned. "My father will have a conniption fit. What if he should deny us the succor of his home?"

"Why should he care? Why can't he be happy that you could marry for love?"

"Because *he* married for love. Only it did not turn out very happily."

Hester went very still. "Oh?"

Horace shook his head. "I know very little. Mostly from the old housekeeper. Apparently my mother was very young and very beautiful. Though much older than she, my father fell in love with her and married her against his mother's wishes. She had no dowry, you see, and no family connections. But their initial happiness didn't last. She didn't love him as he loved her and she grew very unhappy." He let out a huge sigh. "I've often wondered if her death at so young an age was more a blessing than a tragedy."

Had he not looked so forlorn, Hester would not have been able to rein in her sudden fury. Why had their father lied to him so? Horace had already been deprived of a mother and sister. She couldn't let him lose the woman he most wanted, a woman so well suited to him that it now seemed preordained for them to marry. Why should it matter if his father disapproved? Hester wouldn't allow an even greater travesty to occur than her father had done when he didn't track his daughter down.

Though she could do nothing about Horace's long-lost mother, she could restore his sister to him, and perhaps in the process, help him gain the one woman who could make him happy.

It was time to tell him the truth. Past time.

"Horace, I want you to be quiet," she began. "Just listen to what I have to say and afterward we can discuss it further."

Horace gave her a quizzical look, but like the good student he'd been since first he'd come to her, he nodded. Hester drew a breath, conscious that she was shaking. She knotted her fingers together.

"I haven't been entirely honest with you. The truth is, I am well acquainted with the history of your family. Your father and mother married when she was eighteen and he thirty-nine. They had two children, a girl first, then you."

His brow creased in consternation but she proceeded. "After you were born, your mother, Isabelle, ran away, taking only her clothes, her jewels, and her daughter. Your sister."

"Wait," he interrupted. "I have no sister. Where have you heard such a wild tale?" Then, "How do you know my mother's name?"

Hester gave him a sad smile. "Isabelle Forrester Vasterling. Her mother's maiden name was Poitevant."

She heard him suck in a sudden breath. But still he fought the truth of her words. "Poitevant. Does that make us, what . . . cousins?"

She shook her head. "No. Not cousins. I have hated

my father—our father—for so many years." Her voice
quivered with emotion. "And for most of that time I
hated you too."

"Me?" The quick tears in his eyes mirrored those in
her own. "You hated me?"

She swiped her eyes with her ragged handkerchief.
"Not after I met you. Then, against all my wishes, I grew
to love you—"

He enveloped her in a smothering hug. "You're my
sister? My sister?"

It took a good half hour for them to banish the tears
and sort out the questions and answers that were over
twenty years in the making. Only when Mrs. Dobbs
came in with tea, then drew back in surprise, did Hester
and Horace slide apart from one another.

"It's all right, Mrs. Dobbs. Come in. I think we need
that tea," Hester said, suppressing a watery giggle. Hester suspected that her busybody of a housekeeper had
been hoping for a match between Hester and Adrian.
Considering that Hester had avoided men for years, the
poor woman was obviously confounded by what must
look like an interrupted embrace.

"It's not what you think," Hester explained. "Horace
and I—" She met his gaze and they burst out laughing.
It felt so good. "I'll explain later," she said, gasping for
breath as Mrs. Dobbs's face grew only more bewildered.

After the woman left, however, Hester turned serious.
"I have told you all of this, Horace, because . . . well,
because I felt I must. And because I don't want you to
miss out on any other love due you. I'm speaking specifically about Dulcie."

"Do you think she might love me?"

"I don't know. She hasn't confided that to me. But
then, I haven't seen her in a week."

He was silent a long while, but Hester knew what
was to come. "I think I should introduce you to Father."

She squared her shoulders and pursed her lips. "No. Not yet, anyway."

"Why not?"

"This is my decision, not yours."

"I've been just as wronged as you have."

"I know. However, I told you the truth only because I didn't want you to leave London without knowing." She reached for his hand and stared into his dear, familiar face. "I couldn't have borne it."

He squeezed her hand in return. "He has much to answer for."

"In time. At the moment, however, I will be content if you stay in town, at least long enough to ascertain Dulcie's feelings toward you."

He sighed. "I shall see her at Catherine Hawke's wedding tomorrow. Will you be there?"

Hester had accepted the invitation, but this past week she'd dithered back and forth about going. If Adrian didn't want to see her she certainly would not be pathetic enough to chase after him. On the other hand, she might look even more pathetic if she stayed away. And then, Catherine and her mother had been so kind to her.

"Don't worry. I'll convince Father not to go," Horace said, misinterpreting her hesitation.

On impulse Hester lifted her chin to a pugnacious angle. "I'll be there." Whether Adrian wanted to see her again or not, she would go. She had spent too many years hiding from life. It was past time for the mousy Mrs. Poitevant to shed her widow's weeds once and for all. A wedding seemed as appropriate a place as any other.

Adrian knew his Aunt Olivia and cousin Catherine had as much to do with salvaging Hester's reputation as anything he'd done. George Bennett would be a long time showing his cowardly face in town, which only increased Adrian's reputation as the hero who'd saved the helpless widow from the dastardly Lord Ainsley.

He frowned at his image in the mirror, then jerked his cravat loose to try again. "Some hero," he muttered.

"Having trouble with that knot?" In the open doorway his Uncle Neville lounged.

Adrian scowled. "I'll get it right."

"We leave for the church in fifteen minutes," Neville said. "Don't be late or Olivia will raise holy hell—no pun intended. For some reason weddings turn perfectly pleasant ladies into madwomen, fit only for Bedlam." He ran a finger inside his own elaborately tied cravat. "I'll be relieved when this day is over. Except that you're leaving day after tomorrow, aren't you?"

Adrian nodded. "I've done everything I needed to do here. It's time I visit my mother, then get myself back to Boston. There's work to be done, right?"

"Right," Neville agreed. "Hurry up now. The carriages are coming to the front door."

Again Adrian nodded, then gave the cravat one last try. If it weren't for the near certainty that he would encounter Hester at the wedding festivities, he wouldn't care how he looked today. But unlike the past few days, he wouldn't be able to avoid her.

The pity of it was that he was desperate to see her. He hurt with his need to be with her, just to stand close enough to catch that faint whiff of the lily water she used.

His hands stilled at their task and he stared unseeingly into the silver-tinted glass.

It was insane, this obsession he had for her. If not for that pure fool Bennett, he might have enjoyed a few more nights in her arms. But suspicions had already been cast on her by the way he'd grabbed her, followed by his ill-advised use of her given name. It had looked just a little too intimate for London's incestuous society, which was always hungry for gossip.

But he refused to let Hester become their target. Not on account of him. Thank God Olivia and Catherine had leaped to her defense. On their advice he'd kept his distance from Hester, though it had nearly killed him. At the same time he'd worked to vilify Bennett, which hadn't been difficult. The man had quit London like the craven coward he was.

Everything had turned out as they'd hoped: Bennett was the villain and Hester the wronged party, while he looked like the hero. Perfect, except that he had no idea how Hester felt about him anymore.

She'd been angry at his interference, then horrified when everyone had gathered around them. What he didn't know, what he might never know, was how she felt about his week-long absence, for she hadn't responded in any way. Was she disappointed? Did she sit in her bedroom window at night yearning for him?

Or was she relieved, glad to have her reputation intact, knowing he would soon be gone, out of her life forever?

He yanked the cravat knot snug, then turned away without bothering to examine the results. He couldn't believe he would never smooth his fingertips across Hester's milky-soft skin, or taste her sweet lips again. He would never release that silken mane of hair to spill down across her shoulders, nor tangle his fingers within those warm, lily-scented curls.

He groaned at the unwelcome rise of desire, yet it felt good. Damned good. He didn't know what he would do when he saw Hester. *If* he saw Hester.

One thing he did know, however. His idea of enticing her to Scotland was far too dangerous for her to risk.

If she were even half the snob he'd once thought her, he wouldn't hesitate to do it, her reputation be damned.

But Hester was a vulnerable woman surviving as best she could in a world not inclined to do her any favors. For him to jeopardize her reputation and thereby her whole existence would be the height of selfishness. Taking her to Scotland with him was a foolish dream, a self-indulgent dream.

Yet knowing all that did nothing to banish that sweet, beckoning dream from his head.

CHAPTER 20

Catherine Hawke made a beautiful bride. Happiness fairly radiated from her. Even more moving to Hester, however, was the adoration that shone in her new husband's face. She'd watched him in the church as Catherine had come down the aisle to him, studying every expression, every glance. The small, private smiles, the huge, public ones. The intimate tilt of his head toward her, the solicitous touch of his hand to her elbow.

Every movement, every breath, seemed to prove his love for Catherine, and more than once Hester had felt the sting of silly, emotional tears.

Oh, to be loved like that!

She bowed her head once more, blinking back tears. Goodness, she hadn't even known the couple that well until the past couple of weeks. She would not make a spectacle of herself by sobbing out loud.

But she'd already made a spectacle of herself, hadn't she? Between her salmon dress, her loose cascade of curls, and the cunning little bonnet perched just over her brow, she'd made as big a spectacle of herself as a woman could and yet still remain respectable.

Except for the pale shadows beneath her eyes she knew she looked striking, certainly far better than any of these people had ever seen her look, though not as beautiful as the bride. Surface beauty could be achieved by anyone. But true beauty, formed of goodness and happiness, sprang from within.

That's what Hester saw in Catherine Hawke as she and her new husband swept down the aisle, laughing despite the solemnity of the regal St. Simone's church. No one but a bride or a new mother could ever look that beautiful.

Still, Hester was pragmatic enough to know that her new appearance would be much remarked upon today.

She cast her eyes down as Neville and Olivia Hawke followed by the rest of their family—including Adrian— trailed the happy couple. It was one thing to sit near the back of the church staring at the back of his head, noting the wave in his hair, the sheen, and remembering the texture of it beneath her fingers . . .

She shook off a traitorous little shiver. It was another thing altogether to face him, to meet that probing gaze and risk having him discover how much more he meant to her than she'd ever meant to him.

No, it was better if she waited until the onlookers on the front steps were a milling crowd before making her own exit.

"There you are," Horace whispered, pausing at her pew. "Come along. We'll miss all the fun."

Reassured by her brother's presence, Hester resolved to go to the reception, at least for a little while. It was only a short walk and Hester was calmer once they arrived. She was fully prepared to either speak with Adrian or be snubbed by him; whichever he chose was fine, she told herself. All she had to do was look nice and behave conservatively. And if her stomach fluttered with nerves, well, it was only because this day marked the beginning of her new life: no longer a virgin; no longer a mourning widow; no longer a woman hiding her true self from the rest of the world. Plus, she had a brother now, a wonderful brother.

"Where is Dulcie?" Horace whispered when they entered Sensin Gardens, which were festooned with garlands of red roses tied up with white ribbons. "I saw her in the church. Her mother was with her," he added. "I fear I shall never get her alone."

"Don't worry. Lady Ainsley will be so busy trying to shield Dulcie from me, she'll consider you a wonderful alternative. The first chance you get, ask Dulcie to dance. I'll take care of the rest."

"Very well." They both stared about at the jovial gathering until Horace said, "Ah, there's Adrian. Come on."

This was it. Hester was excruciatingly aware of every aspect of her appearance as she and Horace threaded through the crowds. She held herself as tall as she could. Shoulders down, chest forward, chin demurely tucked with a pleasant half-smile on her face. Just as Mrs. DeLisle had taught her and she now taught her students. And glide. Move smoothly and glide.

It helped having Horace with her, for he performed his role as both gentleman and brother with equal aplomb. How swiftly she'd come to love him.

Hester stumbled a little. She loved him!

Horace adjusted his hold and she recovered her balance. When he looked over at her, she smiled, so filled with emotion she could hardly bear it. "I'm so glad we found one another," she murmured.

Startled, he blushed and smiled back. He bent his head closer to hers. "So am I."

From across the lawn Adrian saw the smile Hester shared with Horace. His eyes narrowed when Horace leaned in to her and whispered something, and his already glum mood turned to utter gloom.

From the moment he'd spied Hester at the church service he'd known something was different, something not attributable entirely to the change in her public wardrobe. She looked stunning, so beautiful, so ravishing, that he couldn't keep his eyes off her. Nor could any other man there, he noticed. Especially Horace Vasterling. In his eagerness to divert Horace from Hester, Adrian had begun to believe the man interested in Dulcie Bennett.

But now he and Hester were sharing those secret looks, those secret smiles.

He'd kill the son of a bitch!

But he couldn't. After that scene with George Bennett he had to be scrupulous in his public behavior toward Hester. Besides, he told himself when Horace caught his eye and grinned, this was Horace, not George, and Hester didn't appear in the least dismayed by his close attention. Indeed, she looked at Horace in a way she'd never done before.

Had Horace finagled his way into her heart during the week since Adrian had last seen her?

Adrian realized he was clenching his jaw so hard his teeth ached. But he couldn't seem to relax it. How ironic if his original plan to force the snooty Hester to appreciate kindly Horace had worked.

He tamped down both his anger and his fear as they approached him. He had to be mistaken, he told himself, for Hester and Horace were too unlikely a couple.

Yet wasn't he just as unlikely to be paired as lover to one of them and friend to the other?

He thrust one hand through his hair. He had to get himself under better control. He was leaving London and they were both staying. The most he could do was enjoy their company, since it was likely to be the last few hours he would ever spend with them.

He addressed them first. "Well, Horace." *Too jovial. Too hearty.* "Lucky man. It seems you have arrived with the most beautiful woman of all on your arm."

Hester smiled at him with her lips, but her eyes looked troubled. "Thank you, Mr. Hawke. But no woman is ever as beautiful as a bride."

Adrian stared at her. What was she saying? That she wanted to be a bride? That since he was leaving Britain she had set her cap for Horace?

"Your cousin certainly looked beautiful," Horace said into the awkward silence that fell between them.

"My cousin? Yes. Yes, my cousin," Adrian said, belatedly understanding Hester's remark. "Yes. Catherine certainly makes a beautiful bride." As would Hester, he realized. "Can I get either of you something to drink?"

In the space of time that Hester and Horace each consumed one drink, Adrian consumed three. He needed strong spirits to steady his nerves and keep his thoughts from straying to visions of Hester on her wedding night. Hester coming to her new husband clad in filmy silks or gauzy muslins. Hester with her hair strewn across her shoulders and lily petals caught in the lush tangles. Hester revealing her bare toes, her naked ankles, her warm thighs—

He grabbed a fourth glass from a passing servant and downed it, conscious of the concerned look on Hester's face. Or was it disapproval? She'd never seen him drunk. He seldom allowed himself to get that way. But tonight it seemed appropriate.

"It's my cousin's wedding and I'm leaving soon," he muttered. "Aren't I entitled to one last night of fun?"

That fast her eyes turned fever bright, and it only took him a moment to deduce why. She was thinking of another sort of fun. One last night of fun for them to have together.

His entire body went on alert. If she was willing, and he damned well was . . .

She averted her gaze from the intensity in his, but the burn of color in her cheeks remained. "Oh, look," she said in a strained voice. "There's Dulcie."

Again she and Horace shared a secret look, and Adrian frowned. She was making him crazy. Was it Horace she wanted or him? A husband or a lover? Or had the passion he'd unleashed in her taken over so that now she wanted both?

Surely not.

Then again, other women had husbands and lovers. Why not her?

He *was* going mad! But by damn, he would not share her!

Before he could think what to do—drag her away; punch Horace in the nose; have another drink—she gave him a prim nod. Then she gave Horace a secretive wink, turned, and made straight for Dulcie and her mother.

They stood there, he and Horace, just gazing after her. Horace nudged him. "She's amazing, isn't she?"

"Yes. Amazing," Adrian responded as he watched the elegant sway of Hester's hips beneath her salmon skirts. Slender waist, proud carriage, and that effortlessly gliding gait. Yet hidden beneath all that elegance and sophistication beat the heart of a wanton. She was indeed an amazing woman.

Then jealousy reared its suspicious head and he realized that he didn't want Horace to think she was amazing. He glared down at the man, but Horace was watching Hester. "Why has she finally decided to abandon her half-mourning?"

Horace barely glanced at him. "Perhaps you ought to direct that question to her."

"I fully intend to. Meanwhile—"

"Shh!" The man waved him to silence, all the while watching as Hester halted before Dulcie Bennett and her clearly outraged mother. The happy buzz of the other wedding guests prevented them from hearing the precise gist of the three women's conversation, but their demeanors allowed Adrian a fairly good guess. Dulcie was all wide eyes and fearful expression, while Hester looked as unruffled as he'd ever seen her.

"What is she up to?"

"I'm not certain, but I've got to go." And off Horace went, straight for the three.

Not to be left out, Adrian followed.

At the sight of them Lady Ainsley's mouth closed with an audible snap. She tried to smile at Adrian, whose good favor she'd been halfheartedly courting ever since she realized that the *ton* sided more with him than with her son. But she was too flustered to do more than grimace. When Horace bowed, the perfect gentleman in every way, then offered to accompany Miss Bennett to the punch table, Lady Ainsley gave a distracted nod. "Yes, go. But come back directly to me," she added to her daughter.

Horace and Dulcie practically skipped away, which only confounded Adrian more. First he couldn't tell which man Hester wanted. Now he was confused about which woman Horace was after.

"I must insist," Hester said, obviously resuming her previous conversation with Dulcie's mother. "It was your son who caused that scene. If you wish to dismiss me on account of his behavior, then I have no choice but to engage a solicitor to make my claim for the balance of my agreed-upon fees."

"Your fees! Your fees do not come due until my Dulcie is wed, which is unlikely to happen thanks to your ineptitude!"

Adrian's head swiveled to watch Hester's response. When she smiled, however, he could swear this wasn't about money at all. There was something too smug in her expression.

She was up to something.

"Now, Mrs. Bennett. You must be careful of your temper. It mottles your complexion, you see. And since that particular shade of blue is not your best, well, we all want to look our best, don't we? Especially at such important society events as this one."

The woman sputtered a moment, glancing down at her overly ornamented dress in an off shade of purplish-blue. When she raised her face, her rage was overcast with indecision, and then frustration. She looked ready to spout something vile until she again noticed Adrian. This time she didn't even try to smile. She only muttered, "Good day, Mrs. Poitevant. Mr. Hawke."

Hester watched the woman's huffy retreat with a triumphant smile on her face. Adrian watched Hester, a curious expression on his. "What in blazes is going on here?"

She looked at him with a start, then averted her eyes. "I'm simply following through on the job you hired me for. Look at them," she added, gesturing toward Horace and Dulcie. "It started at the card party at the Ainsleys' townhouse. But it was apparently the morning that they went riding, that everything really changed between them."

It took Adrian a moment to comprehend. Horace and Dulcie. Of course!

An incredible feeling of relief washed over him, followed swiftly by a powerful wave of desire. The way was clear for him to pursue Hester—except that four glasses of liquor had turned his brain to mush and his tongue to wadded wool.

"Dance with me?"

Her brow wrinkled in a little frown. "They haven't started to play yet."

"Save me the first dance?"

She hesitated so long he shifted from one foot to the other. He needed to kiss her so badly he hurt from it. Instead he knotted his hands together behind his back.

"Very well," she finally said. "The first dance."

"And the last?"

She opened her mouth, closed it, then nodded, the whole time careful not to look at him.

"And every one in between?"

That made her look at him. "I can't do that."

"No. People would talk, wouldn't they? It's just that I hate the thought of any other man dancing with you, Hester." He shouldn't use her given name in so public a place. That's what had gotten them into such trouble before. But he couldn't help himself. He wanted her to call him Adrian. He wanted her to moan out, soft and sweet, "Adrian. Oh, Adrian."

Instead she said, with a pinched look on her face, "I didn't come here intending to dance that much."

Adrian let out a long, painful breath. "When I said you were the most beautiful woman here, Hester, I was not exaggerating. Look around. Men are staring at you, watching you, waiting for me to leave so they can hurry over before someone else does." He paused, scanning the growing throng with a baleful gaze. "Is that why you've shed your mourning garb, a signal to other men that you're available now?"

She shot him a fulminating glare but didn't deign to answer, which only fired his jealousy higher. "Damnation, Hester. Answer me."

"Very well, I will." She lifted her chin and smiled, to all outward appearances having a pleasant conversation with him. But angry emotion trembled in her low-pitched voice. "What is it to you who approaches me, who dances with me, who . . . who I should take as a lover once you are gone?"

He winced at the thought of her taking anyone to her bed besides him, ever.

She went on. "You have no more control over me than I have over you, and that is precious little."

"It's more than you know."

Her gaze darted to his and held long enough for him to see confusion replace her anger. If only he could talk to her alone, take her in his arms and show her how strongly he felt about this.

As if in answer to his silent plea the musicians began finally to play, presenting him with the next best alternative to a private tête-à-tête. Without asking her permission, he swept her onto the brick-paved area set aside for the dancing. The gods were doubly with him, for it was a waltz.

They lined up, no conversation possible at first. But once the full melody swelled to life and he held one of her hands in his while the other rested at her waist, he was free to speak. "You have more control over me than you believe, Hester."

She shook her head, refusing to look at him.

"I stayed away this whole week to protect your reputation. Olivia and Neville said it was the right thing to do. But I thought of you constantly."

His hand at the small of her back felt the slightest easing of her tension, the first hint of her unbending. But her words belied her yielding. "It doesn't matter. You're leaving anyway."

He breathed in, luxuriating in the lily-sweet fragrance of her. "You could come with me," he said, though he knew it would be dangerous for her.

"To Scotland?" Her voice was so low he had to bend nearer to hear.

"Yes. I'll hire a private coach. Or we can go by sea. Whichever you prefer."

"No." She shook her head. "I can't."

"We can leave town separately."

"No."

"Why not?"

Hester's thoughts were too fragmented for her to formulate any argument save the most basic. "I just can't."

Arguing with Adrian Hawke was useless, especially now when he held her in his arms, whirling her around the sunny dance floor, so in control it terrified her. How easy to fall in with his plans, to succumb to his every whim, even when she knew it threatened disaster to her. For the truth was, she wanted to go to Scotland with him. She wanted to throw caution to the wind, for once just abandon all her responsibilities and devil take the hindmost.

He was her first lover. Couldn't she enjoy just a little more of the heaven she'd found in his arms? Just another week or two. Or three.

But therein lay the crux of her problem. For she knew without having to be told that this intensity of feelings, both the physical ones and the emotional, could not end easily. Whether the good-bye came tonight or in three weeks as she stood on a dock watching his ship fade into the western horizon, the ending had to hurt. Did she really want to prolong that pain?

The music built to a crescendo, Mr. Strauss's specialty, and Adrian guided her in more and more extravagant circles. The dance was almost over. They would go their separate ways.

Then he pulled her close, as if he'd stumbled. Only she knew better. Her breasts grazed his chest, his thigh intruded between her legs, and every fiber in her being leaped for more of that intimate contact. Except that she wanted no clothing between them, and no wedding party around them.

"Then one last night, Hester." His hot breath upon her neck promised her everything she wanted from him and more. "Will you at least grant me one more night in your arms?"

The music ended; they stepped apart. He bowed and she curtsied. But their eyes never parted and he saw the faint nod she gave, the silent consent that formed on her lips.

Yes.

Come to me later. At least we will have that.

CHAPTER 21

Hester accepted four offers to dance; she turned down nine others. If she hadn't been so overwrought by her conversation with Adrian and what she'd just agreed to— as well as what she hadn't agreed to—she might have enjoyed the minor hoopla created by her newly freed self.

Men who'd never looked twice at her did double-takes. The single girls watched and whispered behind their fans. Their mothers stared, some with disapproving frowns creasing their brows, others with more thoughtful expressions.

Hester knew exactly what that latter group were thinking: amazing what the right color, the right style, the right curl, and the right attitude could do for a woman's looks. Though the drastic alteration in her appearance might lose her some clients, it would probably gain her others. No doubt more than one woman figured that if she could turn her old, dowdy, widow self into such a brightly plumed beauty, what might she do for someone not already so dour?

But Hester didn't care about anyone else today, for

she was drunk with anticipation. Tonight . . . Tonight . . .
She refused to think beyond tonight.

So she smiled up at her current partner. She danced
and she chatted. She toasted the newly wedded couple
and prayed as she never had that theirs might truly be a
happy and loving union. She passed the afternoon in the
world of London's town society which she knew so well
but had never quite belonged to. Today, however, she
didn't care if she belonged or not.

She was drunk and giddy and it was exhausting.
When this dance ended she vowed it would be her last.

Fortunately Horace paced anxiously in the shade of a
row of yew trees just beyond the dancing area. When
the music ended he collected her from her dance partner
who seemed loath to let her go.

"She said yes," Horace murmured, drawing her into
a sheltered area. His eyes danced with glee and he
couldn't stop smiling. "She said yes."

Hester smiled at him. "I knew that after your first
dance together; that huge grin of yours gave you away."

"But how could you have known? I just now asked
her."

"But earlier I saw the two of you staring at one another so happily I assumed you'd already revealed your
feelings to her."

"We had." He sighed. "She loves me."

Confused, Hester paused. "So what is it you asked
her just now?" Then she gasped. "Don't tell me you've
already proposed?"

"I did!" He beamed at her, looking like the happiest
man alive. "I did and she accepted."

On impulse Hester hugged him. Then she self-
consciously stepped back. "I know the two of you will
be very happy together. But how are you to manage this?
When will you ask her brother for her hand?"

"That thug?" Horace fumed. "Do you really think he

deserves that sort of consideration? Besides, he's left town."

"Now, Horace. You must consult her family. Her mother, perhaps. You'll never have a chance of recovering any portion of her dowry if you and Dulcie elope without asking at least one of them."

"It's Dulcie I want, not whatever fortune she does or does not have. We are perfectly matched," he said. "Perfectly."

"What will your father say?"

"It doesn't matter."

Hester certainly agreed with that. But she wasn't as certain about the Bennetts. She chewed her lower lip. "If you ask either of them, they will probably say no. And you're right, they don't really deserve that much consideration. However, if you're determined to wed with or without her family's approval, then it is better to have at least asked. What does Dulcie think about it?"

He sighed. "She was relieved when the Leonard Smythe pairing fell apart. But she knows her brother and mother. It's just a matter of time before they foist her off on some other equally repugnant fellow with deep pockets. She is so upset with them she says she doesn't care what they want anymore. But . . . But I suppose I do care. We should endeavor to maintain some sort of relationship with them. After all," he said, shooting her a serious look. "As we both know, it's no small thing to lose a part of your family."

His sensitivity to Dulcie's situation brought tears unbidden to Hester's eyes. She squeezed his hand in hers. How much she'd missed all these years, not knowing this brother of hers. Their whole childhood; a thousand little memories.

But George Bennett was no Horace Vasterling. Some family members were not worth having at all, as she well knew.

From beyond them came a wave of cheers. The wedding party must be preparing to depart. Hester pulled a delicate handkerchief from her sleeve and dabbed at her eyes. "If I can help the two of you, please let me know. Anything at all, Horace."

He nodded, once more smiling. "If not for you, dear sister, I would have returned home weeks ago, a failure once more on the marriage mart. But you've given me a new lease on life."

Hester laughed. "I only gave you a nudge."

"A very good nudge. By the way," he added as they approached the other guests clustered around the bride and groom. "You look exquisite today. Everyone has been commenting on it."

"Thank you," she murmured, coming down from Horace's happy dilemma to face her own more distressing one. Soon she would be returning home to await Adrian's arrival. They would have their night together. Then they would bid one another farewell. Tomorrow he would depart for Scotland and she would begin building upon the new life and reputation she'd started today.

She shivered in anticipation for tonight. But she also felt weighted down with dread for the morn.

Unwanted, the memory of her mother came to her, of men departed and mourned until a new man replaced the old one. For once she understood her mother's emotions, and she empathized with her. But unlike her mother, Hester did not hope to replace one lover with another.

There would never be another Adrian Hawke for her. Never.

The Dobbses retired to their snug back room early, for Hester had declined any sort of supper. Her nerves wouldn't allow it. The dogs she closed into the kitchen with gravy-laden scraps and two meaty bones to keep them content. Then she carried a bottle of wine, two glasses, and a small covered tray of biscuits and cheese up to her room. There she proceeded to wait.

She dressed with care, or rather, undressed with care. That had been its own form of torture, for every time she fastened or unfastened her buttons these days, she couldn't help recalling Adrian doing it. Such a mundane task, yet he'd imbued it with an eroticism that made dressing herself an exercise in controlling her more carnal impulses.

Precisely what he'd intended.

Still, even that could not compare to his actually undoing her buttons and ties and pins. So except for her corset and two of her petticoats, she left her clothing relatively intact.

Too fast her room was prepared for him, and also her person. Time began to drag. When would he come? All the lights in her house were out except in her bedroom. As she watched from the window, the lights on her street and those in the city beyond steadily winked out, window by window until all she could see was a street lamp on the corner, a faint light in an attic room across the way, and the shadow of a cat gliding silently beneath the spotty light of the moon.

That's when he appeared. Like before, Hester knew Adrian by his silhouette and by the intentness of his focus. Straight to her house he rode, a tall man on a tall horse. Not hurrying, yet had anyone else been around, they would swiftly have moved out of his way.

He's coming for me.

Hester's breath caught as she watched and waited. She couldn't breathe, yet every other part of her anatomy reacted. Racing pulse, damp palms—and damp in other places as well.

Somehow she made her way down the stairs, meeting him at the door. Silence reigned as he entered, then followed her to their private trysting place, as if they'd done this many times, not just that one earth-shattering night.

How had she come so fast to this carnal silence, this dark anticipation that managed to shut out all the logic of a lifetime? How could she of all people be doing this?

The answer was so simple it terrified her. No man but this one could have brought her here. No one but Adrian Hawke.

The very idea raised goose bumps on her arms. For it implied an exclusiveness which then implied something that simply could not be possible. She could not be in love with him. She couldn't! She'd had this mental debate before and decided these feelings could not be love. She didn't know him well enough to love him.

She paused on the landing and braced herself with one hand against the wall. This was not love.

Then she felt his hand on her shoulder, large and warm, not forceful, yet insistent all the same. At once that alien feeling that could not be love rushed in again, stronger than before. It turned her knees to pudding and her mind into a quagmire of foreign impulses, each one a trap.

"Must you leave tomorrow?" Was that her sounding so needy and plaintive, saying out loud what she least wanted to say?

"Come with me." His other hand slipped around her waist, pulling her back against him. He nuzzled her neck and slid a whisper of a kiss along the rim of her ear. "Come with me, Hester. You'll love Scotland."

Scotland. Not America. That her disappointment was so acute only proved she was going mad. Bedlam-bound, for certain.

"I cannot," she muttered. Then to forgo further discussion, she turned in his arms and kissed him. He responded with a ferocity that matched her own, which only made her fiercer. She would show him what he would be missing when he left her. She would prove herself unforgettable. More unforgettable even than he was.

They made it to the bed as if brawling their way there. She would ache tomorrow, but he would hurt more. Something popped—his waistcoat buttons. She would have to search for them before Mrs. Dobbs found them in the morning.

Something ripped—her chemise.

They never did get their clothes entirely off. He shoved her down onto the bed, pinning her there with one hand on her shoulder, his lips fastened to hers. With his other hand he unfastened his breeches. Before he could throw her skirts up, she unbalanced him and rolled on top of him. His freed erection pressed against her bare thigh as she straddled him. So hot and velvety and lethal to every modesty she'd ever held to. Lethal to her callused heart which did not want to risk love on any man.

"My God, Hester," he murmured, and even his voice aroused her. She bent over him on all fours, her hair a tangled drape around them. She was face to face with her only love, the most dangerous enemy she would ever have. For he alone could hurt her; he alone could crush her to the point of personal oblivion. To do it he need only leave her.

But he wasn't leaving yet, she told herself, refusing to relinquish any part of this night. His hands slid up her thighs beneath her knotted skirts to clutch her hips. Up he lifted her, onto the rearing source of all his danger, all his maleness. Then down, slowly piercing her womb and her heart with that simple act of intimate possession. Full possession.

She gasped as he thrust up, then gasped as he pulled away. Up and down. Thrust and withdraw. The promise of pleasure, the threat of separation. Like a battle they fought against one another, and together, side by side.

Fight, retreat. Trust, betray. Man, woman. Love, hate. Fiercer and faster.

Inside she could feel herself building to that violence she both feared and longed for. Yet she could not stop. Would not stop. Her cries filled the air and his laboring breaths. The bed trembled. The world trembled—

Something struck against the window.

Hester nearly didn't hear it. But then another one hit, harder. Almost enough to break the glass. "What's that?"

"Don't stop," Adrian groaned, using his hands to force her hips on and on.

But even he heard the third pebble—or perhaps it was the tenth. How could she be sure? This time they both froze.

"What the hell?" Adrian exclaimed. "Wait—"

But Hester pulled away as if scalded. Someone knew! Someone had seen his silent entry into her house. They'd seen the faint light through the drawn curtains and they knew exactly what it all meant.

In a panic she blew out the lamp, and for a moment she was blinded by the dark. But she heard Adrian rise and when he drew open the drape she saw his bulk against the window.

He peered through the glass. "Horace?"

He muttered the name like a curse, then followed it up with an imprecation so foul she'd never even heard it before. Still, she sensed the gist of it. Horace was outside her house?

Before she could reach the window, Adrian threw the drapes closed and whirled to face her. "Why is Horace Vasterling here?"

"I don't know." She tried to reach the window to see for herself, but he caught her by the shoulders.

"Dammit, Hester. Is something going on between you and him?"

"No. Of course not." Then hearing the suspicion in

his voice, her own panic eased. "I really don't know why he's here, Adrian. Unless . . ." Good grief, could it be? "Is he alone?"

"Yes—I don't know."

"Let me see. Let me see!" She tore from his grasp, then stared down into the darkened street. Horace, with his arm cocked to toss another pebble. And beyond him a smaller figure shrouded in a hooded cape.

Dulcie!

She sucked in a sharp breath. "They've run away!"

Adrian peered over her shoulder. "They? Who's that with him?"

"Dulcie Bennett." And the two of them couldn't have come at a worse possible moment. With a sinking feeling Hester opened the window and waved to Horace, who enthusiastically waved back. At once he turned to collect Dulcie. Hester turned with far less enthusiasm to face Adrian.

"What's this all about, Hester?"

"What do you think? They're eloping. Good Lord. You have to leave here at once!"

"Horace is eloping with Dulcie Bennett? By damn, I knew I liked the man. But this?" He peeked through the curtains again. "He's a good man, that Vasterling."

"He must not know you're here." She grabbed his waistcoat and frock coat, and cast desperately about for his hat. "You have to leave, Adrian. Now."

"I think he might have already seen me."

Hester clutched his gathered clothes to her chest. "He didn't."

"He may have. But even if he did, he might not have recognized me. You'd better get down there, Hester. They're waiting on the front stoop."

Hester's heart was racing, but whether from interrupted lovemaking, the shock of such untimely visitors, or the fear of being caught with her lover—and by her brother, of all people—she couldn't say. Nor did she care. All three were dreadful occurrences in their own right. Together they were a disaster!

But she couldn't leave Horace and Dulcie huddling on her front steps.

"Stay here," she ordered Adrian. She thrust his clothes at him, then started for the door, trying to put her own clothing in some sort of order.

"Hester. Wait."

"No." She whirled about, holding one finger up at him as she might do to a recalcitrant student. "No. *You* wait. Wait right here in absolute silence. Just wait until I return. Do you understand?"

To her dismay, he let out a chuckle. He was laughing at her while her entire life was in the worst tumult of her tumultuous twenty-eight years. He tossed his clothes onto a chair, then with too little concern and too much grace, he sat down and stretched out on her bed. To make matters even worse, he then crossed his arms under his head and crossed his ankles as well.

She glared at him, wanting to slap him. How could he be so nonchalant when she was utterly panicked? To add further insult he said, "As you wish, Hester. I'll be waiting right here when you return, ready to take up exactly where we left off."

Aghast, Hester pressed a hand to her throat. "You cannot honestly think we can—"

"Of course we can. Now, shouldn't you be heading downstairs?"

Hester had never been more bedeviled. A man in her bed and runaway lovers on her front steps. She couldn't just leave Adrian here, but it was too late to make him go. And she couldn't leave them out there.

Furious at Adrian, at herself, and at Horace's dreadful, dreadful timing, she turned in a huff. Before she closed the door, however, she heard him laugh once more. "Hurry back, love. I'll leave a light burning."

Downstairs Hester lit a candle in the foyer, then had to count to ten before she could open the door.

Hurry back, love. She wasn't sure whether to be angrier at the casual demand or the casual endearment. But she couldn't deal with that right now. She shoved her hair behind one shoulder and opened the door.

On a gust of cool night air Horace hustled Dulcie in, then shut the door with a thud. "Thank God! Can you hide Dulcie tonight? I've got to arrange transportation."

"Why didn't you do that before? Hello, Dulcie." She gave the wide-eyed girl a brief smile, then turned back to Horace. "This is not the way to go about such things, Horace."

"I know. I know. But it all happened so fast. I went to see Lady Ainsley and such an unpleasant woman I have never met. I see where her son gets his vile nature, for she behaved like a perfect ass once I revealed my purpose—pardon my French. She made Dulcie cry with all her shouting and carrying on. I didn't know what else to do. So . . . We're eloping. I'm sorry if I startled you. I must say, however, that I was considerably relieved to see a light still burning in your upstairs window." He paused and stared at her curiously. "Do you normally stay up this late?"

"Yes. Um . . . Yes, I do. All the time." Hester was glad her back was to the light, else Horace might have read the guilt in her eyes. As it was, she feared she surely must exude an aura of frustrated yearnings, incomplete lovemaking, and unrequited love.

Oh, Lord. She must stop thinking about that word "love." That foolish, maudlin emotion that had no basis in fact.

Except that when Horace put his arm around Dulcie and the girl looked up at him with such absolute trust,

Hester had to believe that love did exist, at least for some people.

"Yes. Well," she repeated. "I was reading. I had been reading and was just preparing for bed—" She broke off, feeling heat creep into her cheeks. "Come along. I'll put Dulcie in the—" *Not the spare room next to hers.* "In the parlor."

"Oh, thank you, Mrs. Poitevant." Dulcie grasped one of Hester's hands with both of her own. "Thank you. It's just for tonight."

"You're welcome as long as you need to stay. But I fear that once your mother discovers you gone, she'll come here first."

"We know," Horace said. "But I'll be back to collect her before they even know she's gone. Meanwhile, I've arrangements to make. Dulcie, go into the parlor, will you? I need a word with Hester."

Hester stiffened. He'd called her by her given name. She hoped Dulcie hadn't noticed his slip.

Out on the front steps he lowered his voice to a whisper. "I cannot thank you enough for your help. Everything you said is true. She loves me and is happy to live in the quiet countryside."

"I'm very happy for you."

"I told her about us."

"Us? You mean that you're my brother?"

"I had to. She wouldn't have come here otherwise. She didn't want to involve you, you see. But when I explained that we're family, that you would be her sister-in-law, she relented. Anyway," he finished, "she had to find out some time."

Hester supposed that was true. "Does your father know about any of this?"

"I'm going to leave him a note."

"Not about who I am, I hope."

"No. I mean, I want him to know. But I'm willing to

keep your secret, at least a little while longer."

"So must Dulcie."

"Of course." Then he glanced up toward her window. "I say, I thought you had extinguished the light in your bedroom."

Hester cast a worried glance up to the now glowing window. An incredibly arrogant, incredibly attractive man waited there to make torrid love to her. An impossible situation, yet she had a feeling Adrian Hawke would somehow manage to get his way.

"I relit it before I came down," she lied.

"That quickly?"

"Horace, please! You *must* focus on the situation at hand."

"Yes, yes. You're right." He gave her a swift, unexpected hug. "Thank you, sister. With any luck I'll find Hawke and enlist his aid. I'm off, then. But I'll be back before dawn."

He was looking for Adrian? Once more Hester pressed a hand to her throat. If he only knew.

Good Lord, he must never find out.

"We'll be waiting for you," she managed to get out as he took his leave.

Horace hurried away, grinning into the night and feeling on top of the world. Once across the street he paused and looked back at Hester's snug little abode. It now housed both his newly found sister and his newly found love who would soon be his new bride, then his wife, and hopefully the mother of his child—his children.

He fancied he could feel his heart swelling with emotion, so full of love and well-being that he wanted to share his good feelings with everyone. But especially with Hester.

She needed a husband, he decided. Someone to love her as she deserved to be loved. Once this brouhaha was settled he would have to put his mind to that task. At least she had abandoned those false widow's weeds.

Then a horse nickered from somewhere nearby and the hack animal responded. Time to go, he thought, climbing into the vehicle. With any luck he'd be back in an hour or two.

CHAPTER 22

Dulcie had only to remove her shoes and stretch out on Hester's settee and within minutes she was asleep.

Hester frowned down at her recumbent form, vaguely annoyed by the girl's ability to abandon her worries to the peace of slumber. Didn't she understand what a gigantic step she'd taken tonight, what monstrous changes she'd initiated?

Eloping was no small matter. Not only would George and Mrs. Bennett want her back for her own sake, there were the younger sisters to consider, the other Bennett girls. Their entrances into society would forever be colored by the older sister's behavior, which was certain to be considered outrageous. Yes, Dulcie's impulse would have repercussions far beyond this one evening's work.

On the other hand, Hester speculated that more good than bad would come of the girl's decision. After all, once Horace and Dulcie returned to London, happily wed and conspicuously in love, the gossip would fade away. Much was forgiven a couple if the right people considered them a love match.

So she banked her irritation and lowered the parlor

lamp to a faint glow. Then with a weary sigh, she turned for the stairs. There would be no rest for her tonight, and tomorrow Mrs. Dobbs would surely remark on her pallor.

And now she must deal with Adrian.

Sending him away before Horace returned was certain to be a struggle. Especially since she did not really want to send him away.

Beneath her door a line of light seeped out. Horace's suspicions had been roused because of that light.

"Why did you have to light that lamp?" she began as she opened the door. "Horace noticed and he asked—"

She broke off at the astounding sight that met her eyes. Adrian, naked from the top of his darkly waving hair to the tips of his long, well-shaped feet. Only one small corner of the bed linens covered the center part of him. Not his chest with its whorls of ebony-hued hair; nor his thighs with their fainter sprinkling of the same. Only a narrow strip at his hips was covered, and that so scantily as to draw her eyes straight to it.

She clapped her hands over her eyes, though it did little good. The image of him was burned into her brain. She would see it still, should she live to be a hundred or more. No woman with a pulse still beating would be able to forget how this man looked lying naked in her bed.

She turned to face the door, though that didn't help either. "You must leave, Adrian. At once."

"I don't want to leave."

She fought the urge to whirl around. "Dulcie is downstairs, and Horace will be back soon. Very soon!"

"Then we have time to—"

"No!" This time she did turn to face him, though she had to lean back against the door to support herself. Her knees had turned to water. "No," she repeated, but weakly.

He sat up and swung his legs around. Fortunately he did not rise. "We have enough time, Hester. We'd have even more time if you would change your mind and come with me to Scotland. We'd have all the time in the world."

Closing her eyes, Hester pressed her hands to her feverish cheeks. How she wanted to say yes, just throw caution to the winds and do exactly as she wanted. At that moment she could hardly recall why she'd previously said no to that same request.

"You don't understand," she began. "Horace has gone off to find you. You! He's hoping to enlist your aid in getting him and Dulcie to Gretna Green."

The seductive smile on his face faded at that. "They're running away to Scotland?"

"Yes. That's what I'm trying to tell you. You're going to Scotland; he's going to Scotland. After all, it's not so very far beyond his home." She took one steadying breath, then another. "So you see, I couldn't possibly go with you to Scotland. Nor can you stay here. It's too dangerous."

"Too dangerous?" The tiny furrow in his brow cleared. "Not too dangerous for me. Nor for you either. I'm beginning to think you thrive on danger. On deception and disguise. Have you forgotten our tryst in your parlor? Or in the Bennetts' gazebo? And what about Vauxhall Gardens? No, my sweet, passionate Hester." He stood up and the sheet fell away to reveal him in his full masculine glory. "If anything, there's never been a better time for us to make love."

Hester forgot to argue. She forgot to back away or even raise a hand to ward him off. All she could do was stare at the man advancing across her bedchamber. This would be the very last time she saw him—or kissed him or touched him.

She was not going to turn him away; she knew that

before he halted mere inches from her. She made only one more protest. "We must hurry, for Horace is looking for you—"

Then she let him undress her. Indeed, when he moved too slowly, her hands began to untie and unbutton and unfasten her garments alongside his. Their fingers brushed and tangled. Their mouths followed suit, and all at once it was a race to the finish. Her clothes fell somewhere beneath their feet as he pressed against her. His skin was fire, scorching her with its passionate demand.

But he was no more demanding than she. For she wanted him now, right here with no time even to cross to the bed. Her hands tightened in his hair, forcing him to kiss her, making him devour her mouth with his while she devoured him back. Urgent, hungry kisses. One of his hands cupped her bottom, lifting her up against his raging arousal. His whole body shifted against hers, back and forth and again, in a form of caress that left her faint.

"Adrian," she groaned against his lips.

In response he slid his hand along her thigh, angling it up until she wrapped that leg around his hip. Once more he shifted to allow his erection more freedom, and when she felt it prod the exposed opening to her femininity she moaned, ready and wanting what came next. Needing it.

He needed it too, for he came into her with one sleek, hot thrust. They both groaned. Then he hiked her other leg up and it was all she could do to hang on as he began the insane rhythm, the incredible stroking, the unimaginable thrusting that made her unable to deny him anything.

No one could have convinced her that this was possible, this fierce joining up against her own bedroom door. Impossible to perform, yet they managed. Impossible to survive, yet she felt she would die if she had to stop.

She could hardly breathe, hardly move, hardly be more aroused than this. When his thrusts came faster and faster, she knew he was at his peak, and she suddenly was too. He erupted into her and she erupted around him. On and on, laboring breaths, sweaty bodies, until they were utterly spent and could do no more than slump against the door.

"Hester." Her name was a husky struggle for breath, but she'd never heard anything so sweet. She wanted to hear it again and again. Every night. Every morning—

Oh, God! She squeezed her eyes tight against the telltale sting of tears. She *was* in love with him!

She didn't want to be, but she *was*.

"You have to go." She lifted her head from his shoulder though it felt so right resting there. She slid one leg down his damp side. He shifted and pulled out from her and she had to stifle a cry of dismay. She stood on her own two feet now, warm and damp, inside and out, all due to his lovemaking. But a chill came over her as he pulled away. He braced his arms against the door on either side of her head, just leaned over her, not touching.

"You have to leave here," she repeated, unable to meet his gaze.

With one finger beneath her chin, he lifted her face up to his. "I don't want to go, Hester." His eyes were black sapphires, burning with emotions she was unable to decipher. "I want to stay."

She clenched her teeth against a sudden trembling. "Scotland awaits you. And so does Horace."

His eyes searched hers; it was all she could do to maintain the excruciating intimacy of it. Then with a muffled curse he released her chin and backed away. "This isn't what I want."

"Nor I," she whispered to herself as he turned to collect his clothes. She wrapped herself in the bed linens and watched as bit by bit he covered his magnificent body.

Remember that strong back. Never forget those powerful thighs, that muscle-wrapped chest, those sculpted arms.

She burned every image into her brain, especially the final one, as he stood tall and handsome and respectably garbed before her. Except for the fire in his eyes and his hair still disarrayed, no one would know he had come straight from his lover's bedroom.

His lover.

She'd thought so much about him being her lover, but she'd never once considered that she was his lover. In the years to come, would he remember her as she would always remember him?

Leaving Hester's bedchamber was a torture for Adrian. He was too angry to kiss her and too forlorn to speak a decent farewell. Wild thoughts swamped his head as did murky emotions, sucking him down, spitting him back, and spinning him in a thousand directions. Any decision he made would be a bad one; each choice was filled with pitfalls.

He stood on her front steps with the door closed behind him and stared out into the equally murky night. He hated London. He could hardly wait to leave, hardly wait to stand on a fully rigged ship heading due west to Boston and the good life he'd created for himself in America.

But when he left, he would also be leaving the only woman he'd ever had difficulty saying good-bye to. Difficulty? Hah! In the end it had proven impossible. How had this happened to him?

He glanced up at her bedroom window, gone dark now. Was she peering from between the curtains, watching for him to go? Did she regret his leaving?

He thought she did. God knew she was enthusiastic enough when he was with her.

What if he asked her to travel with him to America, not just Scotland? And what if he asked her to be more than a temporary bedmate, but rather his wife?

It was a stunning idea, one foreign to his nature. His father hadn't been loyal to anyone. Nor had his mother, not until her only child was nearly grown. He'd never once thought of himself as the marrying kind. But he was thinking about it now.

Sort of.

If he made that kind of offer to Hester, would she accept? Would she leave behind the life she'd worked so hard to build for herself here?

He shook his head, but that did nothing to clarify the miasma of his conflicting thoughts. He needed to think, some time to clear his head. But if he approached her just right, maybe he could convince her.

Deep in thought, he fetched his animal from the side alley and led it into the street. He looked up at Hester's darkened window. She was watching; he could feel it. On impulse he swept off his hat and bowed to her. This passion between them was not done with. It was barely begun, he vowed, and he was renewed by his conviction.

He led his horse to the street corner, all the while lost in contemplation of his next move regarding Hester. But as he fitted one boot into the stirrup and began to mount, a carriage rattled around the corner. In the driver's box a man hunched over the reins, his worried face caught in the street lamp's steady glow.

Horace.

The man looked straight at Adrian, who swiftly ducked his head. But it was too late. For the shout of "Whoa!" came clearly and the conveyance clattered to a halt.

"Adrian? Adrian Hawke?"

It was useless to deny it. Yet what reason could he give for being here in the middle of the night? Adrian guided his animal up to the coach. "Good evening, Vasterling. Nice night if you like fog."

"By damn, but you're the very person I've been searching for. I'm in a bit of a pickle, you see, and desperately in need of your help—" He broke off with his mouth still hanging open. A peculiar look came over his face.

Adrian knew what was coming next.

"I say. What are you doing here? Where have you been?" His head swiveled to stare at Hester's house not a half block distant. When he looked back at Adrian he was frowning. "Have you been to Hester's house?"

His words hung in the air between them, and with every passing second they became less a question and more an accusation.

"Why are *you* going there?" Adrian countered, hoping to throw the man off track.

For a moment it worked. "I'm going to fetch my bride. Dulcie and I are running away together," Horace said, his chest puffing up with pride. "Hester is sheltering her while I make arrangements for us to travel north. But I need your help. Aren't you departing for Scotland tomorrow?"

"That was my plan."

"I was hoping we could travel with you. But now—" He stopped and squinted at Adrian. "I say. Why *are* you lurking so near Hester's house, and at such a late hour?"

Adrian removed his hat and raked his fingers through his hair. There was nothing to do but admit the truth. If Horace was running away with Dulcie Bennett, he was hardly in a position to condemn Hester. "I was bidding her good-bye. I had hoped for her sake to keep our . . .

the nature of our friendship private. I hope you will honor our wishes."

At first Horace did not respond. But even in the dark Adrian could see the man's ears turning red. His face puffed up with outrage and his eyes bulged from his head. "You . . . And Hester?"

Adrian's horse tossed its head and sidled away from the carriage; Adrian loosened his too taut grip on the reins. "We are two mature individuals and answerable to no one—"

"You're answerable to me, you . . . you debaucher!"

"Debaucher?" Adrian scowled at Horace's unreasoning response. "Get a grip on yourself, man. You've chosen Dulcie Bennett. You have no hold over Hester. And why in hell are you calling her by her given name anyway?"

"Because . . ." Horace was standing now, and his carriage animals were becoming almost as agitated as he. "Because she's my sister, you . . . you cad! She is my sister and not a widow at all!"

Adrian stiffened. "Your sister? Since when?" Then the rest of what Horace said struck him. "Not a widow?" Adrian eyed Horace askance, unable to believe either of those preposterous claims. "You must be drunk. Everyone in town knows Hester Poitevant is a widow."

"She just plays the role of widow. That's the only way she can protect herself from the unwanted attention of men. Men like you!" he ended on a shout.

Adrian was too stunned to be fazed by Horace's insult. Instead a sick feeling of dismay overwhelmed him. What had he done? Then anger usurped dismay. If this was true— "Why would she lie to me—to all of us? It makes no sense."

Horace glared at him. "Well, it makes sense to me, especially now. You've been toying with her affections all along, haven't you? And now . . . Now you've ruined her. She's no widow at all, and now you've ruined her!"

CHAPTER 23

Hester stood in her darkened bedroom window, strangling the drapes in both fists. She couldn't overhear Adrian and Horace's midnight conversation. But even in the weak light of the corner street lamp she could guess the crux of it. Especially when Horace stood up in the driver's box and started gesticulating with short, angry movements.

Then Horace pointed at her house, Adrian wheeled his horse around, and they both started her way. She yanked the draperies closed. Could matters become any worse?

Her first impulse was to lock herself in her attic bedroom and not answer the door. It was a stout door, with a sturdy lock.

That would not deter Adrian, however, nor Horace, by the look of him. For if they knocked hard enough the dogs would start barking, Dulcie would awaken, and Mrs. Dobbs would hobble out to investigate.

With a cry of dismay Hester ran for the stairs, reaching the front door barely before they arrived.

"Shh!" she cautioned when she spied their thunderous expressions. Especially Horace's.

"Has he compromised you?" Her irate brother hissed the words at her.

"That is none of your affair," she said, determined to brazen through as best she could. "Have you come to fetch Dulcie?"

"He says you're not really a widow," Adrian accused.

Hester reluctantly faced the man she loved and had lied to. "I . . . You see . . ." She cast about for an answer. But of course there was none, at least no truthful ones which did not include admitting that both men were right.

She tried again to change the subject. "It is not *my* situation which requires urgent attention, Horace. Dawn will soon be upon us and if you don't get on your way, George Bennett will soon be here to snatch Dulcie back. Then the two of you will never be allowed to marry."

Horace paused and cast a worried look toward the parlor where his beloved slept, unaware—thank goodness—of this latest chaos surrounding her elopement. But when he looked back at Hester and beyond, to Adrian, his good-natured features lowered in a scowl. "As your brother—"

She clapped a hand over his mouth. "Horace!"

He shook it off. "He already knows we are brother and sister. Besides, as your brother I have a right to know the truth about your relationship to him." His voice softened and he took her hands in his. "You are my family, Hester. My dearest sister. My *only* sister. I have reluctantly agreed to keep your secret. Reluctantly," he repeated. "But I cannot turn a blind eye to this situation. You, sir," he addressed Adrian who remained amazingly quiet. "You must do right by Hester, else you will have *me* to answer to."

"Horace!"

"Agreed."

Hester and Horace both stared at Adrian in shock. He too was shocked, and yet, didn't this solve his dilemma? Notwithstanding that he hadn't consciously been seeking a wife, how awful could it be?

As he stared at Hester, rumpled, distraught, exhausted—and beautiful—his primary emotion was satisfaction. Of course they should wed. It was the best solution. The only solution.

"I . . . I can't marry *you*."

He hadn't expected that. But Adrian was undeterred. "Of course you can. It makes perfect sense."

"Indeed, that would solve everything," Horace said, his anger fading at once to relief. He snatched up one of Hester's hands and held it between his. "You two will wed; Dulcie and I will wed. We could have a double wedding. But we must hurry," he added, his brow wrinkling again in worry.

When Horace's earnest plea did not erase the resistance in Hester's face, Adrian said, "You misled me about your situation, Hester. Had I known you were not a widow, I would have handled . . . matters, shall we say, far differently. But now that I know the truth—though I am intensely curious about the reason for such a disguise—I am nonetheless willing to accept my responsibilities as a gentleman."

His responsibilities as a gentleman? Hester's heart sank. Those were not the words she needed to hear. Ten years ago she might have leaped at the chance to marry a man like Adrian Hawke, even if under a cloud of suspicion. Certainly she had prayed for an honorable offer from a gentleman. But she hadn't received any honorable offers, only dishonorable ones, and over time she'd come to be glad of it. Marriage to any of those men would have been a hideous mistake.

But so would marriage to Adrian Hawke. Even more

so, she feared. For she hadn't really loved any of the men who'd pressed their attentions on her. It had been only silly, girlish infatuation fueled of her mother's lofty dreams for her and her own belief that a respectable marriage would ensure her happiness. But she did love Adrian Hawke.

She stared at him now, at the expectant look on his face, at the latent sensuality lurking in his eyes, and the temptation to just do it, just say yes and marry him and devil take the hindmost, was nearly overpowering. Why shouldn't she grab some joy for herself, some pleasure no matter how fleeting?

Because it *would* be fleeting, and she would end up just like her mother, alone with a broken heart.

How many times had her mother confused a man's lust for her with love? How many times had Hester witnessed the collapse of those one-sided relationships, and the devastation left in its wake? Long ago she'd vowed never to live her life as her mother had. This was not the time to reverse her position.

When she wed—*if* she wed—it would be because she was loved, truly loved and adored. Otherwise she'd rather remain alone.

She sucked in a shaky breath. "I . . . I appreciate your offer. But . . ." She shook her head and swallowed hard. "Thank you, but no."

In the stunned silence that followed her refusal she drew herself up. "You have done your duty as a gentleman by making the offer and I have declined. Now, Horace, we must act on the plans for your prompt departure. While you two do that I'll . . . I'll prepare a basket of victuals for you to carry with you."

"But Hester. Hester," Horace called when without a pause she turned and hurried toward the kitchen.

Adrian wanted to echo him. *But Hester*. He didn't though. He refused to. He just stood there and watched her walk away. She'd turned him down. He'd offered marriage and she'd said no.

Thank you, but no.

How many times had she put him in his place with that prissy, keep-your-distance-from-me, favorite phrase of hers? She'd lied to him about everything, misled him every step of the way, and now *she* had the nerve to turn *him* down?

"I don't understand," Horace muttered.

"*You* don't understand?" Adrian turned his fury on Horace, who'd apparently lied to him as well. "What in hell is going on here, Vasterling? She's not a widow. You're her brother. Why all these secrets? Was nobody going to tell me anything?"

Horace glowered right back at him. "If I'd known you were seducing my sister, maybe I would have! How could you behave like that with her?"

"I thought she was a widow."

"And that makes it all right?"

Into the midst of their shouting, a wide-eyed Dulcie edged into the foyer. "Horace? What's wrong?"

Horace hurried to her. "Hello, my love. My darling. Don't you worry about anything. We're just working out the details of our journey." He cast Adrian a speaking look. "Right, Adrian?"

Adrian bit back a curt reply. Could one night be any more frustrating? One thing he knew, however: leaving Hester in the lurch wouldn't help anything. He glanced at Horace, then tamed his expression for the still sleep-befuddled Dulcie. "Yes. Just a few more details to smooth out. Why don't you go on to the kitchen with Hester while Horace and I finish up?"

She did as instructed, but only after much assurance that her brother George would not find them before they left London. By that time Adrian had a better grip on his anger. Better, but not absolute.

"What in hell is going on here, Horace? Why have you and Hester kept your relationship hidden? And why has she been passing herself off as a widow?"

Horace shook his head. "I cannot fully answer the latter. You'll have to ask her that. As to her being my sister, I've only known the truth myself for a week and a half."

"A week and a half? How can that be? What, is she your father's natural-born daughter?"

Horace started to reply, then threw his hands up in agitation. "It's complicated. Deuced complicated."

"If you think the explanation will alter my desire to marry her, I assure you, it will not. My own parentage was never sanctioned within a church."

"That's not it at all. The real problem is that she turned down your offer, and I don't know why."

Adrian swore under his breath. "The woman makes no sense. She gave herself so willingly—"

"Enough!" Horace clapped his hands over his ears. "She's my sister and I don't want to hear such things about you and her. If you're set on marrying her you have my blessing and my sincere wishes for your success."

"Will your father share those sentiments?"

Horace removed his hands from his ears, averted his gaze, and began restlessly to tug at his waistcoat. "My father knows nothing about anything."

"You mean your elopement?" Adrian paused. When Horace said nothing, he frowned. "Do you mean he doesn't know she's his daughter?" This was bordering on the ludicrous. Yet it did explain a lot of things, especially Hester's noticeable discomfort every time Edgar Vasterling was nearby.

"Let me get this straight," he went on. "Your father doesn't know she's his daughter and you've only known for a week. Who is her mother?"

"Our mother ran away with her after I was born. I never knew her, either of them. Hester told me our mother died only a few years ago, although my father had always told me she died when I was a baby. It's too late for me ever to know her. But at least I have my sister. And I love her." He stared intently at Adrian. "You have to do right by her, Hawke. Or answer to me."

In the ensuing hours Adrian fumed over Horace's words. He fully intended to do right by Hester, but she wouldn't have him. What more could he do?

While the women prepared food, he and Horace hatched a plan. They would take Horace's hired carriage to Southwark and there rent a traveling coach to take them to Portsmouth. From there they would travel by packet ship to Dumfries in Scotland, then head south to Gretna Green. Any searchers would be watching the roads north, not south and east.

Adrian would travel with them as far as Portsmouth. But instead of continuing on to Scotland, he decided he would return to London. He and Hester had unfinished business together.

He'd waited twenty-eight years to propose marriage to a woman. He'd be damned if he'd be deterred by one prissy little "Thank you, but no."

Hester started to cry as soon as the front door closed. Not a stinging little dampness in her eyes. Not an emotional tear or two trembling poignantly upon her cheeks. This was a great gushing outpouring of grief.

She'd held it back as she'd found a deep basket and lined it with a tea towel. She'd buried any hint of emotion as she'd filled it with a loaf of bread, two squares of cheese, three boiled eggs, two pears, and a leftover apple tart.

Then she'd kissed Dulcie good-bye, hugged Horace,

and implored them both to write her with all the details of their romantic escape.

To Adrian she said nothing.

He waited outside during their farewells and only sent her a long, silent look as he mounted his horse, a long, silent look that seemed to her an ominous foreshadowing of the long, silent life that loomed before her.

She'd closed the door on that last glimpse of him and promptly burst into tears. Leaning against the door, she wept hard, painful sobs.

Why couldn't he have left England without coming back here, to be caught by Horace?

Why did Horace and Dulcie have to choose this particular night to elope?

Why had she fallen in love with Adrian Hawke at all, when any number of other men would have been such an easier choice?

But the biggest why, the hardest why, was why couldn't his proposal have been for any reason other than because he was doing his duty to her as a gentleman? Lust and duty, when all she really wanted was love.

Well, lust and love.

She hiccuped against her tear-soaked sleeve. This taking a lover business had not worked out at all. No wonder her mother had always become so theatrically distraught. The wonder of it was that Isabelle had continued to participate in such inevitably doomed relationships over and over again.

As for herself, Hester knew that she'd never chance it again. She was done with men, she vowed as she wiped her streaming face and searched blindly for a handkerchief. Never again. Never. When a woman engaged her heart with a man who would not engage his, there was no hope for anything but heartbreak.

From the kitchen came a plaintive yelp and a noisy

sniffling. Fifi and Peg. She mopped her face and made for the kitchen. It was a miracle Mrs. Dobbs hadn't awakened through all these comings and goings. She certainly didn't want to face the woman at a time like this.

But she could use some company right now, Hester told herself as the two grateful animals accompanied her up the stairs and made straight for her still rumpled bed. At least her pets loved her.

Hester ruffled their heads as she climbed onto the bed with them. They were the only comfort she expected to get for a very long time.

"This is very unsettling," Mrs. Dobbs muttered, bustling around Hester's bedroom. "Sleeping almost to noon, while I have to put off three callers, all of them claimin' to have very important business with you. Hunh!"

The last part of the tirade awakened Hester as no amount of startling sunshine or aromatic coffee or grumbling servant could do. She threw the counterpane back from her face and opened her swollen eyelids a crack. "Important business?"

"Very important, they said. But I've got important business with you too. The larder's bare. Someone snuck in during the night and stole the better part of our food." She stared suspiciously at the dogs. "Have they been in here with you the whole night long?"

"Yes." Hester closed her eyes, reliving last night and its myriad careening emotions. But sadness and loss had been the final emotions of the night, and they lingered still. They threatened to linger forever.

With an effort she sat up. "I'll explain about the food later. Meanwhile, who is it who has come back with such urgent business?"

Mrs. Dobbs scrutinized her with raised brows. "Child, you look like you're feeling poorly."

Yes, far worse even than I look. "I'm fine. Who were the callers?"

The old housekeeper let out a huff of exasperation. "First an old gentleman, the elder Mr. Vasterling. He was looking for his son. He seemed awful upset."

"He came himself?"

"He did. And not a half hour on his heels comes that Lord Ainsley, the one none of us likes. I thought you said he'd left London. But there he was on our front steps." She stared expectantly at Hester, waiting for an explanation.

She wasn't getting one, not just yet anyway. The fewer people who knew about Dulcie and Horace the better.

"Did he leave a message?"

"Only that you was to call on him and his mother, directly you awakened."

Hester swung her feet off the bed and stood. "He did, did he? I suppose he's forgotten that I'm no longer in his employ and therefore not subject to his orders."

Mrs. Dobbs kept her gaze sharp upon Hester. "I'm thinking his sister has run off. He was that frantic-looking, and angry too. Given what Mr. Vasterling said, well, could it be that our sweet Miss Dulcie has run off with our good Mr. Vasterling?"

Hester frowned and bent down on the pretext of donning her slippers. "That seems rather unlikely. I hope you didn't suggest that to the man."

"Lud, no. To my mind the girl would be lucky to wed such a nice young fellow as Horace Vasterling."

Indeed she would. "I believe you said there were three visitors?" Had Adrian tried to contact her again?

"There were, and that's one message I'm thinking I can figure out meself." She handed Hester an envelope. "Miss Anabelle Finch and her mother came calling together and they was both beamin'. I'm thinking she's accepted a proposal."

Hester scanned the note written in Anabelle's excessively formal script. "She has. To the Honorable Peter Martinson." She looked up. "That's wonderful news."

Wonderful. So why did Hester have to blink back a fresh onslaught of tears?

"Isn't he the one she was partial to?"

Hester nodded, afraid to speak for the conflicting emotions clogging her throat. Happy for Anabelle, depressed anew for herself. Once again the Bridemaker had achieved her aim. The season wasn't half done and two of her three clients were happily betrothed. Only Charlotte remained uncommitted.

And herself.

In the past Hester had ignored her own loneliness. Now, though, everything conspired to remind her that she was alone and always would be.

Adrian did offer to marry me.

She gritted her teeth at the reminder. Caught by her brother practically in the act, Adrian had had no other choice but to make that offer. But she was too wise to wed for such faulty reasoning and he, no doubt, was relieved as well. The insult of her rejection would not long afflict him, not once he was gone.

Indeed, he was already gone.

"I'll not be going out today," she said, donning her wrapper.

"Tsk, tsk, you are looking a little peaked. Will you be wanting your breakfast upstairs then?"

"Yes." Hester sat down at her desk, trying to think. "I'll want Mr. Dobbs to carry my reply to Anabelle once I've composed it."

"What of the other two callers?"

Hester didn't answer except with a terse shake of her head. Her father and Dulcie's brother deserved no reply from her, nor any help in locating their missing family.

Soon enough they would receive word of the union between Dulcie and Horace. Until then they could worry themselves sick for all she cared.

She was miserable; why shouldn't they be miserable too?

CHAPTER 24

Half the way to Portsmouth Adrian was already impatient to turn back.

Horace slept slumped against his shoulder, leaving Dulcie the privacy—as Horace termed it—to sleep alone on her own seat.

That made no sense to Adrian. The man was willing to elope with the girl but he wasn't willing to degrade her by sleeping fully clothed with his head upon her shoulder. Did Horace mean to keep his distance from her for the entire flight to Gretna Green?

Adrian wanted to scoff at his friend's foolishness, but something about Horace's nobility bothered him. It wasn't Horace's more than honorable behavior toward Dulcie, however, but rather his own less honorable behavior toward Hester.

With every succeeding mile the conviction became stronger. He needed to return to Hester and restate his offer of marriage in a way that she could not turn down.

A part of him, the carefree bachelor part, didn't understand any of this. She'd said she was a widow and once he'd pierced that prickly armor of hers, she'd revealed a passionate side bordering on wantonness. But even then there had remained an aura of innocence about her.

He hadn't questioned that innocence, though. He'd just considered it his very good fortune. Now he suspected—he knew—that it was more than merely an aura. She *had* been innocent.

But why the disguise? Why the secretiveness about her brother and father?

Clenching his jaw, Adrian stared out the window at the dark, amorphous night, lit only by the carriage lamps and a fitful, fading moon. He needed answers and he would not get them in Portsmouth or Scotland. He needed to know Hester's secrets; he was becoming obsessed with that need. But even then he suspected he would not be sated with the woman. As ludicrous as it seemed, as unbelievable even to himself, marriage appeared to be the logical choice for them.

Except that she did not agree with the idea.

Red as blood, the sun had just inched above the horizon when they stopped to change horses in Leatherhead. Horace mumbled something incoherent, then abruptly sat up, bleary-eyed and confused.

"I'm parting from you here," Adrian told him, climbing down before the coach swayed to a full stop.

"But . . . But I cannot possibly travel alone with Dulcie. It's not proper."

"You can and you must. Dammit, Horace, eloping has already ruined her reputation. Traveling alone with her can hardly do more damage."

Dulcie sat up yawning, and rubbed her eyes. She smiled at Horace who smiled back at her, two souls embarking on the adventure of their lives. Not just the elopement, Adrian realized, but marriage to one another. An unpredictable, lifelong adventure, one he wanted to embark upon with his unpredictable Hester.

Still smiling, Dulcie turned to him. "Are you going back for Mrs. Poitevant?"

Adrian stood in the doorway of the coach and slowly he returned her smile. "I believe I am."

"Good," she said. "Despite your difficult parting last night, I was convinced she didn't really want you to leave."

How Adrian wanted to believe that. "What makes you so certain?"

"Because she loves you, of course. Just as much as you love her."

Her simple conviction silenced everything else he thought to say. Did he love Hester? Did she love him?

He had four hours to debate those questions on his madcap gallop back to London. What did love mean, anyway? He desired her, and rejoiced in her responsiveness in the bedroom—and other rooms as well.

He was intrigued by her prim exterior and secretive manner, and despite his irritation with her disguise, he was proud of her for it. She was a woman alone, who despite the hardships of her upbringing had managed to forge a rather good life for herself.

As he drew nearer and nearer the sprawl that was London, he realized that Hester and he were not as different as he'd once thought. He'd already accepted that she wasn't really a snob, but rather a woman forced to manage on her own—much as he'd been forced to do. Now he saw that like him, she'd never known her father. They'd both been raised by women of less than sterling behavior. That alone was enough to ensure neither of them ever quite fit into proper town society.

Yet they'd both earned their way in by dint of ingenuity and hard work. Unfortunately, neither of them had yet admitted that they didn't *need* to fit into that society.

Adrian was hardly aware of his surroundings when he arrived and handed off the weary animal he'd rented to his uncle's startled groom. Like a man unmasked and finally able to see, he recognized the truth before him. He'd returned to England, still the Scottish bastard intent on proving his worth to the society that had rejected him. Hester's role as London's so-called Bridemaker, plus her association with George Bennett, had made her the focus of Adrian's ire, the prim arbiter of acceptability on the marriage mart.

But somewhere along the way he'd forgotten about his goal. In Horace he'd discovered an English lord as unacceptable as he. In Hester he'd found an orphaned soul as wary as himself.

The differences he'd initially perceived had proven all to be superficial. You had but to scratch the surface to see that they were all similar. And when he dug deeper still, down to the buried vicinity of his heart he discovered the most amazing truth of all: he loved Hester.

But was it too late?

"Prepare a fresh animal for me," he ordered the groom. "Once I wash and change I'll be down to collect it."

And then off to collect my bride, if I can find her—and convince her.

Hester left the house at half past one with no fixed destination in mind.

She knew only that hiding in her bedroom was not working. Though she looked a fright, with swollen eyes, reddened nose, and a blotchy, tear-stained complexion, she didn't care. She'd abandoned vanity years ago.

Or had it been only that she'd had no one to look nice for? She hardly noticed as Mr. Dobbs turned the team for Cheapside. She was too busy examining her unhappy existence.

It was true. For years now she'd had no one to dress

up for. Then three weeks ago, against her will, that had changed. The truth was, she'd begun to revel in the appreciative looks Adrian had given her.

She allowed herself a wistful moment of remembering the fire in his sapphire-dark eyes. Then she drew herself up. That was the past. No use to dwell on it.

How ironic that matters had come full circle. For she'd finally abandoned her disguise, only it didn't matter. She'd dressed herself in a pleasant ensemble, and even fought her hair into an elegantly casual twist with loose tendrils around her face. But the mirror did not lie. For the truth was, the light had gone out in her eyes. The spark from within that made any woman beautiful no longer burned in her.

It was the spark that Adrian had fired in her, the spark he had seen even when it had been banked beneath her spinsterish gowns and severe coiffures. She looked perfectly presentable, even fashionable. But she would never again be beautiful, for Adrian Hawke was lost to her.

She sat in the middle of the carriage seat, swaying with the vehicle's progress, looking neither left nor right as Mr. Dobbs negotiated the busy afternoon traffic. Where to?

She could visit Mrs. DeLisle and cry on her shoulder once more. She didn't think, however, that Verna would be entirely sympathetic to her plight.

She could go shopping, order a new dress for Anabelle's wedding, buy a new hat. Except that shopping seemed so unappealing.

She could search out her father.

Inside Hester went very still. Why would she want to do that?

But the perverse thought would not go away. She could search him out and tell him exactly what Horace had done without his approval. She could point out how he had driven his own wife away, how he'd abandoned his only daughter, and now had the choice to either abandon or support his son, his one living relative.

Foolish pride or precious family? she could ask him. Which do you choose?

Before she could talk herself out of such madness, Hester called directions up to Mr. Dobbs. This morning Edgar Vasterling had come looking for her. It was time he find her—and find out a lot more than he'd bargained for.

Of course, her father was not at Horace's club.

"He went out early," the doorman told her. "He came back though. Not above an hour ago. An' you never saw such a face on a man, like somethin' dreadful happened. Then he left again."

He paused in his recitation, his sparse brows upraised. Though it irked her, Hester slipped him another tuppence. Immediately he resumed. "He took a hack." He leaned past her and pointed to a hack stand across the street. "One of them blokes might know where he went."

Another tuppence and Hester had her answer, one that made her heart stop, then restart at a ferocious pace. "I delivered him to Milton Street. a skinny little house with window boxes," one of the hack drivers told her.

Verna DeLisle's house.

"Hurry. Hurry!" she exhorted Mr. Dobbs, even as he careened down the street as if he drove a sporting vehicle. When they arrived, however, Hester sat a long moment, gripping the carriage's door stile. She stared at her friend's house, knowing her father was inside, knowing she must finally confront him. But now that the inevitable moment was at hand, she was terrified.

"Miss?" Just outside the carriage door Mr. Dobbs waited. "Did you change your mind about visiting with Mrs. DeLisle?"

"No." She could do this, Hester told herself. She was

not the one at fault here. Even Horace had made it clear he could not begrudge her this moment of accusation and revenge. After all, their father's behavior had deprived them both of the family they should have had.

As did Mama's behavior.

But her mother was not here to accuse, only her father. To add to his mountain of crimes, he had no right to call upon *her* friend.

Abandoning every precept of good manners she knew, Hester barged into Verna's house without knocking. Halfway up the stairs, Verna's lifelong housekeeper halted, one gnarled hand clasped to her bony chest. When she saw Hester, however, and not some thief come to rob and kill them, she frowned. "My land, Miss Hester, but that is hardly how a proper young—"

"Where are they?"

Hester didn't wait for an answer. The parlor was empty, as was Verna's little sitting room. But a man's hat rested upon a side table, so she searched on. Not the dining room nor the flagged terrace. But Hester spied them at the back of the garden, standing beside an arch of pink roses and a bed of mingled cream and red ones.

They looked up as she burst out of the house, as if *she* were the intruder, not him, and something in Hester's chest tightened to the point of pain. They looked so . . . so comfortable together. But that was all wrong, she told herself as she clutched her skirts higher and strode down the narrow garden path.

Verna gave her a quizzical smile. "Hester?"

"What are *you* doing here?" she demanded of her father.

"Why, I was looking for you—or rather, for my son. I called at your home earlier—"

"Yes. I know." Hester broke off, unsure how to proceed. Every emotion she'd ever had swelled inside her until she hurt, until she couldn't bear it. Like poison in a wound festering far too long, it demanded release.

Verna held a rose in her hand and all around them the heavy scent of rose essence wafted. Her mother had preferred rose-based perfumes above all others. Hester had assumed that was the reason she preferred the scent of lilies. But right now, right here, the deep fragrance of the roses was a comfort. It was as if her mother were there with her, urging her to confront the man who hadn't been the man any of them needed, neither as a husband nor a father.

She lifted her chin and glared at him. "I can tell you where Horace is, so you needn't bother Mrs. DeLisle any longer."

"He's no bother," Verna began.

"You know where my son is?"

Hester gave him an arch smile. "I do. And I'll explain everything to you. But not here," she added, giving Verna an admonishing look.

She should have known, however, that she could never intimidate her old friend. For Verna met her stare for stare. "Actually, Hester, I believe now is the perfect time to explain everything to Mr. Vasterling."

"Yes. I beg you, Mrs. Poitevant. Tell me what is going on."

Hester's eyes narrowed in anger. "Very well, then. Your son has eloped."

"I gathered as much."

"He left last night for Gretna Green with Dulcie Bennett."

"Dulcie Bennett?" Verna said, looking far more shocked than Edgar Vasterling did. "I had no idea the two of them—But you knew," she said, eyeing Hester.

"I knew he was partial to her, and her to him. But not until they showed up on my doorstep last night begging my help, did I know about them eloping."

"Does her family know?" Verna asked.

"They know she's gone," Hester answered her friend, but she kept her gaze fixed on her father. "George Bennett has already been summoned from the country and was banging on my door this morning. I don't know whether or not they've guessed where she's gone—or with whom."

Edgar Vasterling turned away from them, shook his head as if bedeviled, then turned back to face the two women. "Why would he do such a shameful thing? Why didn't he approach her family as a gentleman should, with a proper offer?"

"He did. But her vainglorious mother turned him away. Her family wants a grander title for Dulcie, and a greater fortune. In short, they want someone better than Horace. The fools. They're too short-sighted to see that there is no one better."

"We agree on that," he muttered. "But surely since she was amenable to his suit, if she'd remained adamant her family would have come around."

"Her family doesn't give a fig about her feelings. They never have." She went on, in a sharp, sarcastic tone. "It's a far too common trait these days, parents who completely disregard the feelings of their children."

He squinted at her. "Are you angry at them, or at me?"

"I'm angry at anyone who can be so unfeeling about the very people they are supposed to love and protect."

He drew himself up. "If you mean to imply I am of that ilk, I assure you I am not. Yes, I want a good marriage for my son. Yes, I hoped to secure him a wife with a decent dowry. Is that so dreadful? I think not. I love my son, Mrs. Poitevant. Even though he has done his family and hers a terrible disservice, I will support him in his choice. I love him," he repeated.

"What of your daughter?" she practically shouted. "Do you love her too?"

"My daughter?" He stared at her in confusion. Around them the air seemed to tremble, turning chill and threatening, like a storm about to break.

"My daughter?" he repeated, but this time in a voice barely loud enough to hear. He blinked and she saw his eyes grow dark and wide when comprehension dawned. He shook his head as if he didn't want to believe it. But when she stood her ground, his doubt must have crumbled for he said, "Hester? You are . . . You are *that* Hester?"

It was her moment of triumph, her moment to accuse him and see him shamed and humbled by the magnitude of his failings, as a father and a man. But the triumphant expression, the arch smile that had served Hester so well would not come. Instead tears burned in her eyes, and her throat clogged with emotion. More than twenty years of anguish, of loneliness, of longing and anger too. But anger was failing her now, leaving only those other debilitating emotions.

She wrapped her arms around her waist and took a step back from him. But he took a step forward, one, then another and another until he was close enough to embrace her. Close enough, but he didn't touch her. "You are *my* Hester? My little Hester Pester-me-not?"

That's when the dam broke. Hester burst into tears and he enveloped her in his arms. She'd completely forgotten the pet name he'd given her so very long ago. But hearing it now . . .

"My little Hester," he choked out, squeezing her tight as she sobbed in his arms.

But she didn't want to sob in his arms. She didn't want this to be a sweet reunion of long-parted relatives. He never should have let her go and he never should have stopped looking for her.

She wrenched herself free and stumbled back from him. With her sleeve she rubbed off the tears that wet her cheeks. "You have no right to act the bereaved parent—" She broke off with a sob. "It's far . . . far too late for that."

"Hester." He spread his hands in supplication. "I know you don't want to believe it, but I've never stopped thinking of you. Never. Won't you let me explain what happened? I'm sure your mother has made me out to be an ogre, but can't you hear my side of the story?"

"Why should I listen to you when I know it will be nothing but lies? Lies and feeble justifications."

Verna moved nearer and placed a comforting hand on Hester's arm. "There are usually two sides to every story, Hester."

Hester shrugged off her touch. "But he lied to Horace too. He told him his mother was dead, and he never told him about me. Not once did he tell my brother about me!"

To that Verna had no reply. Nor, it became apparent, did Edgar Vasterling. Hester's chest heaved with emotion, but over the rest of her a cold sort of numbness fell. Sniffling back the last of her tears, she squared her shoulders and lifted her chin. "Horace has gone to Gretna Green and plans afterward to return to Winwood Manor. Whether or not you can expect any more warmth from him than from me, I cannot say. You deprived him of a sister just as you deprived me of a brother. But we have found each other now, and nothing you do can change that."

"I want you to know one another," he cried. "I want him to know you as I wish also to know you. You're my daughter. My Hester Pester."

"And I'll pester you no more." She started to leave but his words followed her.

" 'Twas your mother gave you that name, you know. Not I. I only took it up to entertain you."

Indeed, Hester recalled her mother using that phrase occasionally even after they'd moved to London.

Oh, Hester, don't be a pest. Stop pestering me, Hester. Must you pester me so, Hester?

She turned to him, eyes blazing, wanting to burst any niggling doubts she might have about his guilt. "My mother may not have been the most nurturing of parents. But since she was all I ever had, you'll understand why your belated declarations of dedicated fatherhood fall on deaf ears. At least *she* wanted me."

"Hester, Hester. I wanted you, too. I wanted you there with Horace and me."

"Then why didn't you come for me? Why did you forget about me and never search for me?"

"I did search. I tried." He let his arms, extended in supplication, collapse heavily to his sides. "I sent a man to find her. And you. But . . . She took a ship to Ireland and from there she disappeared. After that I didn't know where to look, how to find you."

Hester didn't want to hear any of this, and yet she needed to know. "Why did you ever let her go? Why couldn't you have made her more content?"

"Do you think I didn't try? God's bones but I loved Isabelle. I gave her everything she wanted. Only it was never enough. It broke my heart when she left." He shuddered. "Better to ask why *she* left *us,* her husband and her son." His hands knotted into fists. "Have you ever asked her that?"

He was shaking. Inside Hester was trembling, but his trembling was visible for anyone to see. She said, "Mama died six years ago."

She saw him sag, as if the starch had gone out of his bones. But he had no right to be affected by that news, Hester told herself. He'd forfeited that right twenty-four years ago.

Slowly he drew himself up. He was an old man, she

saw. She could hardly imagine her beautiful, vivacious mother with a man as old as him.

He should have married a woman his own age, someone quiet and easygoing. Like Horace had done with Dulcie.

But he had married the wrong woman, just as her mother had married the wrong man. Was one more at fault than the other?

Hester had never explored this territory before, and she didn't want to now. But she had so many questions going back over twenty years. "Why did you marry her?"

He grimaced and shook his head. "Isabelle was beautiful, so beautiful and full of life. Like you," he added with a sad smile. "She had a way of making you believe you deserved a woman like her. I was a confirmed bachelor and content in that state. But when my elder brother died without an heir, it became my duty to wed."

"Why not do like Horace has, come to London for the season and select an appropriate wife?"

"That's for young men, Hester. Dandies. Besides, I had an estate to manage. Isabelle was only a baker's daughter. But she had a lady's manner, and a lady's bearing. Good enough for the simple life I envisioned for us. We met and I—" He broke off and averted his eyes. In a lower voice he continued. "It soon became necessary for us to wed."

Necessary? Hester frowned. Had he compromised her? But that was not likely to have bothered her mother. It was more likely that Isabelle seduced him. Especially if it meant marriage and a title and big house for her to live in. A baker's daughter wed to a brand-new lord? It sounded exactly like something her ambitious mother would have plotted.

Oh, Mama, how could you?

Hester had been around long enough to know that

more than one hurried wedding was the result of a man succumbing to the charms of a willing woman who was overanxious to wed.

It didn't always work, though. Not every man fell for that trap, and not every woman who succumbed to a man had marriage on her mind. Certainly she hadn't. Indeed, Adrian's belated, businesslike proposal to her had sounded more like an insult than a marriage offer.

But Hester refused to think about that, for Adrian was out of her life. Soon enough her father would be too.

"I'm sorry your marriage was such a failure, but I don't want to argue whose fault it was. All I know is that I grew up without a father, and Horace had no mother. I've managed to build a decent life for myself without any help from you. A very good life, I might add. And while I intend to keep Horace a part of my life, you can never be anything to me but . . . but someone who was once married to my mother."

She tugged at her bodice and smoothed the ends of her fichu, fighting a wave of unwonted tears. "I'll give you credit for having raised a fine son. He is a credit to you. But as for me . . ." She shook her head. "It's too late for us ever to be anything to one another."

Struggling to maintain her composure, Hester turned her gaze on Verna, who still stood beside her father, Verna who had silently observed these most arduous minutes of Hester's life. At that moment she wasn't certain she and Verna could remain friends, not if Verna had decided to befriend Edgar Vasterling.

As if she sensed Hester's mood, Verna smiled and said, "I'll call on you tomorrow, dear. We'll talk more then."

Slowly Hester nodded. "Very well."

Neither of them spoke as she turned and made her way through the garden. Up the terrace steps she went. Into the dining room. Step by step, barely holding her fragile emotions together, and only by the strictest act of will.

She could collapse once she reached her carriage, not before. Through the parlor. Into the foyer.

Then a knock sounded on the front door, startling her to a halt. She stared at the heavy door. Was no one going to answer it? Where was the housekeeper? Or even a maid. Certainly she couldn't answer the door. She couldn't do anything right now but escape to her own carriage and her own house. But how could she do that if someone was at the door?

Then that someone knocked again, hard and demanding entrance at once. Hester fell back a step, a cry of alarm on her lips.

Not just someone. That was a man's knock. An arrogant, impatient man . . .

The door flew open, but she already knew who it was. Not just any someone, but Adrian Hawke. Adrian who'd gone to Scotland but was here instead, facing her across the tiny span of Verna DeLisle's foyer.

CHAPTER 25

He'd found her!

Adrian's first impulse was to sweep Hester into his arms and kiss her until she agreed to marry him. Just kiss her, please her, seduce her into doing what he knew she would eventually be happy she'd agreed to do. One look at her shattered expression, however, convinced him that might not be appropriate.

He closed the door behind him. "Are you all right?"

She stared at him with eyes round with shock. "I . . . No . . . What are you doing here?"

"What do you think I'm doing, Hester? Searching for you. I couldn't go to Scotland without you—"

"I won't go. I—"

"—so I *knew* I couldn't go on to America without you," he continued as if she hadn't just interrupted him.

Her face began to crumple and she shook her head back and forth. "I can't marry you. I can't."

"The thing is," he went on, determined to ignore all her protests. "The thing is, if you won't go with me, then I suppose I have to stay here with you."

"No." She started to cry. "I can't talk about this anymore. I'm too . . ."

"Why not?" Then he saw why not. For beyond her, Edgar Vasterling came through the crowded parlor, hesitating when he saw the two of them in the foyer. Adrian sensed at once that something had happened between them. "Does your father know?" he asked her in a low voice.

She stiffened and he thought she would not answer. But with a sniff she raised her head and drew a steadying breath. "I told him about Horace and Dulcie." She took the handkerchief he held out to her, and wiped her face. "Thank you. And I told him . . . I told him who I was."

"Ah. But did you tell him everything?"

"Everything?" Her eyes swam with tears but within them he saw a little flicker of alarm. Sweet, foolish girl, she thought he meant about their tryst. She raised her chin, stubborn and proud even with tears glistening in her eyelashes. "I told him everything he needs to know about me and nothing more," she stated.

It occurred to Adrian that he might never fully understand Hester Poitevant, soon to be Hester Hawke. She would be a continuing surprise to him, never reacting as women of her sort were supposed to act. A dour widow who was neither a widow nor dour. An untried maiden who gave herself to him with no ulterior motive, especially not marriage. A woman alone who knew exactly how to take care of herself. But was she happy?

More to the point, could he make her happy? All he knew was that he had to try.

He had taken a huge risk coming back here and he was about to take an even bigger one, the biggest risk of his risk-taking life. It was all or none for him, winner take all.

"You told him everything, you say." He stepped right

up to her and took hold of her, running his palms up and
down her arms. His voice grew tender. "You couldn't
have told him everything he needs to know about you,
Hester, because even you don't know everything. For
instance, did you tell him how lovable you are? How
soft-hearted? How unpredictable and brave?" He leaned
closer so that their faces were but inches apart. "And did
you tell him what you did to me?"

Beyond Hester, Adrian saw her friend Verna DeLisle
begin to smile. She knew what he was going to say. And
despite his haggard features, old Mr. Vasterling had the
beginnings of comprehension on his face. Only Hester,
his stubborn, dense, darling Hester did not know what
he was talking about. But then, who had been denser
about it than he?

"Did you tell him that you made me fall in love with
you?" He stared into her beautiful, shocked face, willing
her to believe the intensity of his feelings, the depths of
his emotions. Words were not enough to express how he
felt, but he had nothing else to use.

"I love you, Hester. I don't want to be anyplace but
where you are. Scotland. America. London. They're all
just places. A geography lesson. I love you and I need
you in my life. I want you to marry—" He broke off.
"It's beyond simply wanting. I need you to marry me.
I'm *begging* you to marry me."

He went down on one knee and looked up at her, a
half-grin on his face, but with fear thudding a terrifying
rhythm in his heart. "Will you marry me? Please?"

Hester heard what Adrian said. She simply could not
believe what she heard. He loved her?

"Marry me, Hester. Marry me because I love you and
I'll do everything I can to make you happy."

She wanted to. Oh, how she wanted to say yes, to
fling herself into his arms and run away with him
wherever he wanted to go. Scotland. America. She didn't

care where. But something in his words unsettled her. Something that mirrored too closely what her father had said.

She stared down into Adrian's handsome, earnest face. "What if . . . What if love is not enough?" She raised her gaze to look at her father. "It wasn't enough that he loved my mother. She ended up hating him."

For a long moment her gaze remained locked with her father's, and a new fear came over her. Perhaps she was not so much like her mother, but more like her father, too rigid and severe to make a happy marriage with anyone.

As if he knew her fears, her father started toward her, an old man rejected by his wife and now by his daughter. He came up to the foyer door, then stopped there, never letting go of her gaze.

He said, "I think the problem was not that I married for love, but that Isabelle did not. One person's love is not enough. The inequality of emotion becomes a torture for both parties. A trap." He tilted his head and tried to smile, but it was a weary, beaten-down expression. "Hawke here says he loves you. Tell me, child, do you love him?"

Yes!

Hester's gaze veered back to Adrian's. He hadn't moved. He still held her hands in his and peered intently up into her face. "Do you love me?" he asked, his voice less than a whisper.

"Yes." She swallowed hard and fought the return of tears. But this time the only emotion fueling them was love—and happiness. Most definitely happiness. "Yes, I love you," she whispered, her voice growing stronger. "Of course, I love you."

"Thank God." He stood and pulled her into his arms, squeezing her so close she could hardly breathe. But she didn't care. She circled his waist with her arms and squeezed him back, wanting to get as close to him as she could. Closer than was possible while they were still dressed, with onlookers so nearby.

"Then you'll marry me?" He kissed her temple, her eyes, her cheeks as he sought her mouth.

"Yes. Yes—" The rest was cut off when their lips met to seal their promise.

Someone started clapping. Someone else blew his nose.

But for Hester there was only Adrian in her arms, declaring his love which was everything she'd wanted. She was going to marry the person she loved, as her father had done. But unlike her father, she was marrying someone who loved her back. And she'd taken a lover, as her mother had. But in her case, her lover was the one true love of her life, and she would marry him.

She pulled back from Adrian at the realization: she was not entirely like either of her parents. They'd made a muddle of their marriage, and their children had paid the price. But then, they'd paid for it too.

She turned to look at her father who was smiling at them, smiling as if he were truly happy for her.

She couldn't quite bring herself to smile back. But she nodded.

It was a beginning.

EPILOGUE

Horace and Dulcie arrived at the St. Catherine Dock first. They'd brought their twin girls with them, as well as a cart to carry Hester and Adrian's baggage. Shortly thereafter Edgar and Verna Vasterling arrived. and not two minutes too soon. The American schooner eased into its berth with a minimum of fuss. Still, for those on the shore the wait for the gangway to be laid out seemed to take forever.

Hester stood on the deck with Garrett squirming in her arms. Three years away in America—three years of happiness beyond anything she could have hoped for—had done much to ease her animosity toward her father. She understood both sides of her parents' marriage now. She understood how poorly suited they had been for one another, and she no longer blamed her father for the life she'd led without him.

She had only to imagine herself growing up in the countryside, marrying some reasonably presentable fellow, never having the opportunity to meet her Adrian, to know that she would not now change anything that had happened in the past, not at the risk of losing everything she'd ultimately gained.

She nuzzled Garrett's neck, causing him to renew his efforts to get down and run. The fact was, she had more now than she'd ever imagined she could have. Certainly she had more than her father had ever had, for she was wed to the man she loved and who loved her.

She sought out her father's figure below them on the busy dock. In some ways her father had helped her know herself better. The letters they'd exchanged these past few years had allowed her to work out the worst of her animosity. But now, staring at him across the shrinking gulf of water, she worried once more that she could not do this.

"It will be all right," Adrian said, coming up behind her. He lifted Garrett out of her arms and settled the boisterous lad on his shoulders, careful to keep a grip on the two-year-old's ankles. He slipped his other arm around her shoulder. "Your father and Verna have obviously been a tonic for one another. It's not good for people to be lonely."

Hester leaned her head against his shoulder, comforted by his ability to sense her feelings, and his continuing willingness to soothe them. He couldn't erase the damage of her childhood, but he certainly had made it less important to her.

"They all look good," she said. "Horace appears quite the country lord, doesn't he?"

Adrian chuckled. "You mean plump and well pleased with himself?"

She poked him with her elbow. "Why shouldn't he be? And Dulcie too. Oh, look at the twins. What a happy trio the girls will make with their big cousin Garrett."

"Your father looks well," Adrian pointed out.

"Yes."

"Better than he used to. But then, marriage has a way

of doing that to a man. Marriage to the right woman," he added, planting a kiss upon her temple.

Hester studied her father, standing arm in arm with Verna, his wife of two years now. She'd wanted to be outraged when they'd written her about it. But she'd been too happy with the birth of Garrett to dredge up a proper head of steam over it. Slowly she'd become accustomed to the idea, and seeing them together now somehow banished the last of her resentments.

Her eyes narrowed. Her father looked different than she remembered. He stood very erect, smiling up at them. And what a smart waistcoat he wore; what a jaunty hat. She smiled to herself. It appeared her father had become somewhat vain since his move to London. Verna's doing, no doubt.

Who would ever have imagined that he could leave the family estate in Horace's care and become a *bon vivant* in his old age? But then, who would have imagined the strait-laced Bridemaker of London so willingly abandoning her business? She was far more content as a wife and mother to the pair of Scots-American men who formed the center of her life. In time, however, she might reprise the Mayfair Academy. There were plenty of American women in dire need of her help.

When the gangway went down, Hester, Adrian, and Garrett were the first across. Hugs, kisses, exclamations, and compliments. In the midst of it all Hester found her son in her father's arms. The lad looked not in the least fearful or shy as he took the watch her father dangled before him and held it ticking to his ear.

"He's a fine lad, Hester. Handsome and strong." He hesitated, searching her face. "A fine lad," he repeated.

"Yes, he is." She reached up to stop Garrett from tasting the gold case clock. "And quite a handful. He'll run you ragged if you allow him to."

"Motherhood agrees with you."

That drew her up short. "Do you think so?"

He nodded and a slow smile came over his lined face. "Motherhood and marriage too. You look happy."

"I am. Very."

And it was true. She'd been so happy the past few years. But now, seeing her beloved child in her father's arms, that happiness became surprisingly complete.

A tiny shiver sped up her spine. *Are you here with us, Mama? I feel as if you are.*

Then Adrian was guiding her toward the waiting carriages. "Well, love," he whispered as everyone climbed aboard, debating who should sit where in the pair of crowded vehicles. "I believe the worst is over."

On impulse Hester turned and kissed him, the hot, sweet kiss of lovers, right there in plain view of everyone. Someone muffled a giggle, but she didn't care. She was part of a whole, messy, healing family now: sister, daughter, mother to a beloved child, and wife to the man who was her lover and her one true love.

It had taken a while, but the Bridemaker had become a bride—and so much more.